LETHAL MINDS

A detective crosses her nemesis in this gripping crime thriller

ROBERT McCRACKEN

THE BOOK FOLKS

Published by The Book Folks

London, 2021

ISBN 978-1-913516-13-0

www.thebookfolks.com

Lethal Minds is the sixth book in the DI Tara Grogan mystery series.

PROLOGUE

The Lady Linda, a twenty-six-metre trawler out of Kilkeel on her second day at sea, was bottom trawling two miles off Copeland Island in the Irish Sea. Dessie McBratney, the owner and skipper of the boat, was hoping for a good haul of prawns on this first sweep of the morning. The sun was just rising, yielding a bright sky free of clouds in the east, although he noticed a darker gathering over land to the west. There was little swell, and while he kept an eye on the sonar display on the bridge, he stole the opportunity to cadge a ciggy from Harry, the youngest and least experienced of his crew. He'd only taken him on out of respect and sympathy. The young lad of seventeen had lost his father a year ago when his trawler went down off Port Erin. At the time it was suspected the trawler's nets were snagged by a submarine and dragged under, but nothing was ever proved. Besides, the MOD does not comment on the operational activities of its submarines, never mind the possibility that a foreign vessel was involved.

With his dad gone the kid needed a livelihood and something to keep him out of trouble on the streets, to prevent him racing cars about the town, taking drugs and burgling the big houses up the road near Belfast. So far, Harry had been a reluctant participant on deck. He hadn't taken to rough seas, was frequently throwing up over the side and needed a good kick to get to work at all. It was no surprise for Dessie to learn that the lad's father had never planned to take his son to sea. Dessie told himself it would be Harry's last trip if he didn't get his finger out and pay his way. This morning there was no excuse. The sea was calm with the prospect of a good haul.

'Away out and give Billy a hand with this catch,' Dessie said, blowing his ciggy smoke towards him. 'Nothin' for you to do in here, lad.'

Harry, dark-haired and well-developed, was already clad in his wet gear and life jacket. He didn't feel comfortable. Having been up since half five, unable to get a decent sleep anyway, he did as he was told. He realised he pissed off Dessie, but he knew also that he was not cut out for this job. The reek of diesel and dead fish made him feel sick. It would only take a slight swell, and his breakfast would be lost. Not that he cared much for the greasy fried bread, the overcooked bacon and an egg he could bounce off the wall. He waited beside Billy, an affable fifty-year-old veteran of the seas and brother-in-law to Dessie. Not a word spoken, Harry watched the cable winding in the twin-trawl, trying his best not to breathe in the sickening stench. Out in the middle of the sea, and yet he couldn't breathe fresh air. He was aware of Dessie watching him from the bridge, checking that he was working instead of getting in the way of the others as the nets were swung on board and cold water sloshed over the deck.

He hated this job. He hated boats, the sea and more than anything else he hated bloody fish.

Dessie shouted something to Billy. Harry looked at the net as it hung over the deck. Something wasn't right. For a second, Harry thought he might have done something wrong or had forgotten to do as he was bid. But all attention was focused on the net. Dessie rushed down from the bridge. Operating the winch, Billy lowered the net to the deck.

'What tae fuck is that?'

'What have you caught me this time, Billy?' said Dessie. 'Not another friggin' porpoise I hope.'

'Don't look like no porpoise to me.'

A couple of deckhands stepped forward as Billy released the catch onto the deck. Prawns, flounders, scallops, a few sole slithered across the floor leaving a long thin object motionless on the deck.

'It's just a bundle of plastic,' said Billy. 'What tae fuck?'

Harry stayed well back. He didn't want to get involved in this, whatever it was.

'Give them a hand, Harry,' Dessie shouted.

Reluctantly, he picked his way over the fish and prawns as the two deckhands pulled at the plastic sheeting. It was wrapped and tied with nylon rope, and Harry attempted to loosen one of the knots. His hands were freezing and making little impact at undoing the rope. Then Billy, impatient as ever, stepped forward with a knife and ran it down the entire length of the parcel, slicing open the polythene wrapping and cutting the nylon ropes around it. Tiny stones spilled over the deck as Billy cut through layer after layer of polythene.

There was a final wrapping of a woven material concealing something within. Billy repeated his cutting with the knife. Harry helped to pull the sheeting away, but very soon wished he hadn't.

'Holy shit,' said Dessie. 'It's a body.'

Harry managed only the briefest of glimpses. He bolted to the side and threw up.

CHAPTER 1

She couldn't run fast in heels. She'd take them off, but the ground was uneven; flagstones, tarmac, broken glass scattered, it would slow her down anyway. Leaning her back against a gable wall, she drew a lungful of cold night air, dampened with the rain of the evening. She prayed she'd lost him. Her chest ached from the pounding of her heart, and the thumping in her head fuelled her fear. She could never outrun him. She heard his call. Not angry – taunting, confident that he would find her. He was playing a game. But his shout gave away his position. He was still searching. Coming for her.

She continued down the alley between the houses, her heels clattering in double time. And she realised that he would hear them. If only she knew someone, she could knock on their door, ask them to hide her. But she knew no one around here. Not on this estate.

Except for Ryan. He'd brought her here. But he couldn't help her now. And her tears came, blurring her vision. Tears for herself and for Ryan. They'd both been so stupid. Gullible. A birthday party for his brother, Aidan; they should have realised they were being set up. And naively she had come dressed for a good time, short dress and stiletto heels. She'd even got her hair and her nails done. For what? From the moment they entered the house she felt something was wrong. It wasn't simply a place where people were enjoying themselves drinking, smoking and doing some blow. Most of the fellas looked uneasy. Only the girls were getting drunk. And then, suddenly, she was helpless and alone as Ryan was summoned. He smiled sadly as he let go of her hand for the last time. She tried to

4

follow him. She made it as far as the kitchen, but as she attempted to step outside after him three of the guys closed ranks.

They did so in a way that made it seem like they were wasted, but she realised what they were doing. With Ryan gone, one of them took his chance to cop a feel of her bum. She bounced from one to the other, each of them seizing a feel of her breasts, her bum and her crotch. She called for Ryan, but all they did was laugh at her. Suddenly her face met the floor, and when she looked up, she thought at first that Ryan was looking down on her and they were safe. But it was Craig, Ryan's best friend. He said nothing as she struggled unaided to her feet.

'Where's Ryan?'

He didn't reply. Instead, he moved right in close to her face. She backed away. He stepped closer, itching for a fight. She knew then that they were doomed. They knew about Ryan, and they knew about her. Knew exactly what they'd done.

'I want to speak to Ryan.'

Craig suddenly relaxed his stance. He smiled.

'He's just having a chat with the lads, that's all. Everything's cool.'

She pushed her way to the door.

'I want to see him.'

She was jostled from one to another, and eventually they let her go. Outside, the garden was deserted. She saw movement beyond the high wooden gate, pulled it open and stepped into the parking area at the rear of the houses. A car door slammed, headlights illuminated the empty space, an engine revved and the car sped from the cul-de-sac.

She glanced behind her. No one from the party seemed interested in her now. The back door of the house was closed, and Craig stood at the window, peering out. Only the loud music thumped into the street.

She ran, in desperation at first, hopelessly trying to follow the car. Then a boundless fear took hold, and she realised she had to get away. If only her da was here. He might get angry, but he wouldn't have allowed these guys to hurt Ryan, not when he meant so much to her. She realised too that she was in for an ear-bashing when she next saw her da. For now, though, she had to get away from this place before somebody decided it was all her fault and came looking for her.

They never should have come to Liverpool, never mind Treadwater. In Sunderland they had been safe. Once they'd made the money on the deal, they could have scarpered. It was a chance of a lifetime, one deal to make them rich and they could have disappeared for good. But somebody got to know what they were up to. She'd warned Ryan to be careful, to keep his mouth shut. Now it was too late. There would be no deal, no money, no fresh start, no new life in the sun, and they would not be going back to Sunderland. She shuddered at the thought of what they would do to Ryan. Had they plans for her, too?

She had to get away.

Pushing on from the relative sanctuary of the alleyway, trying her best to create only silent steps, she was suddenly free of the houses, into open space – playing fields. Now her heels sank into the damp earth. She wept. Stay on your toes, she thought as her speed picked up. But it was not enough. She glanced behind and saw him emerge from the alley.

Her right foot slipped from her shoe as the heel snagged in the grass. Quickly, she removed her left and ran barefoot. Now she was putting distance between them. She had more energy than she'd dared hope, and she knew how to run. She'd been running her whole life. If only she could get away now, she promised herself a fresh start of her own. She still had enough money put away to help her disappear. It wasn't the amount she and Ryan could have made on the deal, but it was enough for just her. She dared another glance over her shoulder. The figure had stopped. He stood at the edge of the green, watching her run. He was no longer giving chase. She ran all the harder. By the time she'd reached the road on the far side, she looked again and saw him talking on his phone. A car braked to a halt in front of her. She squinted into the headlights, suddenly aware that she'd stepped right into the path of the car. Holding both shoes in her hands, she moved to the driver's window.

'Please! Help me. Somebody is following me.'

The driver, middle-aged, thin-haired and smoking, had already lowered his window.

'Get in,' he said.

She stole a final glimpse of the man who'd chased her. Now he watched, as she got into the car and it drove away.

CHAPTER 2

The restaurant was noisy, not that the girls minded. Their chatter and laughter were partly to blame. Into their second bottle of chardonnay and awaiting the arrival of their main courses, Tara was ravenous. She'd been saving herself for this meal all day. She hadn't eaten since breakfast, and even then it had been nothing more than a slice of toast and a cup of tea. After a busy day spent at the station on case preparation, she'd been looking forward to meeting up with her friends, Kate and Aisling.

'Well, I fancy Cancún. It's different for us,' Kate suggested.

'Ibiza, I love Ibiza,' said Aisling.

'Do you not think we're getting a bit old for Ibiza?' said Tara.

'You're never too old, Tara love.'

'How about a cruise?' Kate chirped.

'What are you, seventy-five?'

'Plenty of people our age go on cruises nowadays. It would be great.'

'*Anywhere* would be great,' Tara admitted with a sigh. 'I just need to get away. I *really* need a holiday.'

In truth, it was more than just a holiday Tara had been considering recently. She needed a change. What shape this change should be she had no clue. Married rather than single? Possibly. Relocation? But where would she go? Change her career? Leave policing? Too much to think about. Not now, not with her mates, the noise in the restaurant and drink taken. It was best to think only of a holiday.

'How about Canada?' Tara said.

Aisling nearly spat her drink over the table.

'Sometimes, Tara, I think you say things just to wind us up. What are we supposed to do in Canada while you go chasing after one of those Mountie fellas?'

'Nothing to stop you from chasing after one of them, Aisling,' said Kate. 'Seeing as how you like men in uniform.'

The debate continued as a waitress brought their meals. The arrival of food coincided with the vibration of Tara's phone on the table. She picked it up and answered the call from her DS, Alan Murray.

'Hi, Alan, what's up?'

'Sorry to interrupt, ma'am, I know you're out for the evening, but we have an incident to attend.'

'Where?'

'Treadwater Estate.'

The very name sent a shiver down her back. She hated the place, hated more the history she had there.

'Can you pick me up, Alan? I'll meet you at the corner of Cook Street and North John Street.'

'I'll be there in ten minutes.'

Aisling and Kate didn't speak. Both faces said it all. Their evening had just been trashed. Tara knew better than to apologise but still felt the need.

'Sorry, girls. Have to go. I'm not supposed to be on call but we're short-staffed at the moment. I'll make it up to you, I promise.'

Her friends weakly smiled their understanding. Little more could be said. They were used to this.

* * *

She was hardly dressed for a crime scene, wearing a little black dress, strappy heels and a short fur-collared coat. An icy breeze cut along the street as she waited for Murray. Her cheeks tingled in the air and her breath condensed as it left her. She didn't look like a detective inspector, not at five foot one, slim figure, dressed as she was and with the face of a pretty teenager rather than a woman of thirty-one. Such things didn't bother her; she could assert herself when she needed to.

A black Vauxhall Insignia, with Murray at the wheel, braked quickly and came to a halt in front of her. Murray took a last glimpse of the cute woman with blonde hair before she climbed into the car and became his boss.

'What do we know so far?'

'A young lad's been shot.'

'Dead?'

'Afraid so. Likely that it's drugs or gang related but we'll find out when we get there.'

Treadwater was a sprawling council estate to the north of the city in Netherton. High unemployment, low-income families, anti-social behaviour, gangs and drugs: Treadwater had them all. It was not a place for a police officer to feel safe, and Tara never had. Then again, her only connection to this area had been her job. Investigating murder had brought her here, had damn well nearly killed her – twice. How could she ever look fondly upon this place?

Murray bumped the car over a series of ramps. They were intended to stop youths racing their cars around the streets; instead, they had become part of the fun. Who cared about broken suspension? The cars were stolen anyway. Several police and emergency response vehicles were parked along a street close by a row of four shop units. Only two of the units appeared to be in use: a mini-market at one end on the left, a food bank at the other. Graffiti on battered metal shutters obscured what had been a Chinese takeaway and a video store, both long since defunct.

A forensic team was coming and going from an alley to the left of the mini-market. As she got out of the car, Tara spotted DC John Wilson donning a white forensic suit. It had to be extra-large, Wilson was a tall and bulky man. Tara always felt safer when he was around.

'Evening, ma'am,' he said, looking admiringly at the stunningly dressed DI. He had one leg into the coverall, resting his hand on a wall to steady himself.

'Evening, John. What have we got?'

'One male, late teens or early twenties. Dead at the scene.'

Murray had collected two protective suits and handed one of them to Tara.

'Witnesses?' she asked.

Wilson shook his head.

'Not so far. No weapon either.'

'Who found the body?'

'A 999 call. A local resident reported hearing a commotion and shots. Patrol car responded and discovered the scene.'

When all three had dressed in the requisite suits and foot protectors, they made their way between a low wall and the gable of the mini-market. Two large metal wheelie bins obstructed their initial view of the scene, and they had to squeeze by to get a clear sight of the victim. Arc lights had been erected to illuminate the body. He lay on his left side, a dark pool of blood spread out before him on the concrete.

Tara gave a deep sigh and puffed air through her lips. No one could tell her that she would ever grow used to such a scene. He was no more than a boy, hardly a man, despite the tattoos on both arms and on his neck. His hair was shaven and there was a hefty bruise below his right eye. She thought his blood-soaked T-shirt had once been a light shade of blue, and he wore ripped jeans and black trainers.

The forensic pathologist, Dr Brian Witney, groaned as he rose stiffly from a crouch to his feet. He couldn't help but smile at Tara, regardless of the situation.

'Took a bit of a beating first, then shot twice.'

As he spoke, the victim was turned onto his back. Tara saw, immediately, exactly what a bullet can do to a body.

CHAPTER 3

Don't want to put the scud on it but I think my life is definitely on the up. My hands and feet are healing nicely after that sicko Aeron Collywell fired nails through them. I thought I was finished that night, until wee DI Tara Grogan turned up to rescue me. Who'd have thought it? The girl for whom I had already done time in prison, had saved my life. Now, I can't say that her deed wrought any kind of change in me. I haven't suddenly decided to turn over a new leaf, be a good boy, follow Jesus, or start a charity for victims of rape and murder, but things seem less turbulent. I've learned, shall we say, to be a bit more careful in what I get up to. Still off work, delivering groceries to the great and needy, I've had a bit of time on my hands. Time to go wandering, if you know what I mean?

On Friday morning I drove all the way to Aberdeen, way up in the north of Scotland. Spent a lot of time there recently, ever since I spotted a nice wee ass by the name of Megan. At least, that's the name I've given her. In recent times I've taken too many girls in and around Liverpool. It was time to spread my wings. What I do, and do very well, is that I choose a nice girl, a real looker, actually, no point otherwise. I learn as much as I can about her routine, where she goes, who she meets and so on. I make careful plans to snatch her so that I don't get caught, and once I have her in the back of my van, I drug her, do the business with her and finally put her to sleep for good. Then, I take her body out to sea and dump her.

It's brilliant, the perfect crime. No body, no witnesses and no crime scene. Been doing it for years now and only got caught once when I tried to snatch that clever wee cop, Tara Grogan. I was lucky to get away with eighteen months for aggravated sexual assault. No one knows, including the police, what I've *really* done.

Anyway, with Megan I planned everything in meticulous fashion. I'd learned where she lived, where she worked, what she did socially, where she went and who she went with. Heck, I'd even discovered her shoe size, the name of her bank, her boyfriend and her bloody dentist.

It's good when my girls have a boyfriend. It means that when the girl goes missing the suspicion falls on lover boy and never on me.

Megan's boy will forever regret having a row with her and storming off. Don't know what it was about, but it happened when the two of them came out of a pub in Belmont Street in Aberdeen on Saturday night. It wasn't late, but I'd say they both had taken a fair amount of drink. The boy headed off towards Union Street, while poor wee Megan wandered along in the opposite direction in her high heels, and bumped into yours truly, biding his time right beside his van.

I swear Megan didn't have the chance to look behind her, after the boyfriend, or to call for help. I grabbed her under the chin and marched her backwards and had her inside the van before you could say *och aye the noo*. Like all my catches, I bound Megan at her hands and feet and put a lovely strip of duct tape over her gob. Then I gave her a wee jab of China White – that's fentanyl, my date-rape drug of choice – and she drifted into a nice wee sleep.

Twenty minutes later, I'd found a lovely spot by the sea, and the rest of the night was mine to enjoy the delights of a lovely Scottish lass. Dear love her, she'd even gone to the bother of wearing a tartan skirt – not that she was wearing much by the time I'd finished.

Next morning, I drove all the way to Maryport in Cumbria where I had my boat, Mother Freedom, moored and all kitted out with the things I needed to dispose of Megan's body. When the tide was right, I motored into the Irish Sea. I packaged Megan neatly in one of those big sports holdalls, along with a couple of bags of garden stones, enough to see her to the seabed. That done, feeling refreshed and satisfied, I made for home.

* * *

Megan had been my first snatch for a while. Hadn't been feeling the same urges lately, but I reckoned I should keep my hand in. You never know when I might have to, for instance, get rid of a certain wee cop. Recently, I've been feeling a bit more settled, a bit more at ease with myself. For one thing, I have a girlfriend – a proper, no-nonsense girlfriend.

In fact, I think I might be in love. Whatever that means.

As soon as I'd got back on my feet and was walking without a bloody stick, after my near-death experience at the hands of Aeron the axe-murderer, I went down to that pub I'd been enjoying before Aeron nearly put an end to me. The Swallow's Tail is, loosely speaking, an Irish pub off Mathew Street in Liverpool. Lovely talent in there, most nights. I was minding my own business when in walked two girls I'd met a few months earlier, Kirsty and Mel. We'd shared a laugh, a few drinks and a snog, and Kirsty had given me her phone number. With all that happened, I never had the chance or the inclination to call her. She was quite tall, especially in the kind of heels she wore. She had dark brown hair, a nice smile, plenty of lipstick and eyeliner. Pretty fit-looking for a woman of thirty-five. Mel wasn't bad either, a bit smaller and plumper, giggled a lot.

'I haven't seen you in ages. You were supposed to call me,' said Kirsty, playfully taking hold of my jacket lapels and pulling me toward her.

I smiled then poured my wee heart out, telling her all about my recent experience at the hands of an axe murderer. At first, she didn't believe it, but Mel, to her credit, instead of merely giggling, confirmed my story by saying that she had read about it in the papers. Once

Kirsty was convinced, I was well in. Mel, bless her, was smart enough to see that she was a spare part and got offside. Before the night was out, I was in Kirsty's flat and doing the naughty.

A couple of weeks after that first night spent at her flat, Kirsty asked me to move in. We really seemed to hit it off, and I don't remember ever feeling this way before about a woman. What can I say? Does everything for me. The best thing and the worst thing I can say about her is that she is not the kind of girl I would ever have gone for. I would never have snatched her off the street. A bigger build than I could safely manage and although she is attractive, even pretty, she is not a stunner. As I've said before, why would I ever go to the trouble of taking a woman if she is not a total looker? Why eat a burger when you can have filet mignon?

CHAPTER 4

No murder scene ever failed to send a painful shiver running through her slight body. She'd learned in the early days of her career that the sight of a murder victim, no matter how they had met their end, was one of the most disturbing things a police officer could witness. The deliberate taking of a life could never be undone, and justice could never be fully realised. Her colleagues, those with whom she worked closely every day, had all expressed the same insight: see the victim and you won't stop looking for the killer. She couldn't help embracing the same attitude. But no philosophy or sound advice was sufficient to ease the pain of seeing a murder victim. A pain that lingered long after she'd gone home, deep into the night, into her sleep, her dreams, her waking thoughts.

With a host of such experiences now on her slate the visions came in muddled form, one victim inexplicably joined with another. Slashed bodies, blue-grey faces, bloated corpses, decapitated figures, heads on spikes, they flowed turbulently through her mind, and she had to fight hard every day not to let them win. To stay sane. To shore up her defences.

Beyond the initial scene of murder, the blood, trauma, sounds and smells, a post-mortem suite was no easier to endure. Cleaner perhaps, quiet at times, but Tara always felt strange pangs of guilt, of uselessness, when she stood over the body on the table, lying stiff beneath a sheet. The victim seemed to call out to her, to reprimand her. *I'm dead and cold lying here, and what have you done? What have you done to help me? Why aren't you out looking for the animal that did this to me?* Again, that shiver would grip at the base of her spine, sending shock waves down her legs and causing her to shuffle from one foot to the other. *We're doing all that we can*, she was inclined to think, but were they really? And then her impatience, her frustration would kick in.

Brian Witney, in his matter-of-fact tone, began his explanation to Tara and Murray.

'Two bullets, four holes,' he said. 'Both shots to the abdomen. One passed through the transverse colon and exited at the back. The second did the most damage, piercing the right side of the liver, also exiting at the back. He basically bled out. The onset of shock played its part too. He probably remained alive for an hour before succumbing.'

'The other injuries?' Tara asked.

'Severe contusions below his right eye and a broken cheekbone. Kicked or hit with a blunt weapon, I'd say. Some bruising to the lower back and the genitals. Definitely suffered a beating before being shot.'

'The beating not necessarily taking place at the same location?' Tara surmised.

'The bruises are well developed. He was probably beaten at least an hour or two before the shooting. There are rope or cord marks on his wrists, so he was restrained while being moved or interrogated perhaps? I can't say where that took place.'

'Anything else?'

'You may be interested in one of his tattoos. He had the usual fantasy images on his back and shoulders, except for this one.'

Witney lifted the left arm of the victim and pointed out the image of a snake on the forearm. It stretched from the victim's shoulder to the top of his wrist with the snake's head on the back of the hand, its mouth open and fangs protruding. Underneath the slithering depiction on the arm was a single word: 'Vipers'.

'It's a gang name,' said Murray. 'Treadwater Vipers.'

CHAPTER 5

'I love coming here to see the baboons.'

No one responded to McHugh's comment.

The silver BMW 225 rolled forward, and several young baboons nonchalantly passed by in front of the car. Suddenly, a larger male was on the bonnet and then another sat close by, resting its behind on the driver's-side wing mirror. Even the two passengers in the back of the car, who had been reluctant to come on this trip, managed a smile.

'Fucking love this,' said McHugh.

'The wee mucker's trying to pull your wiper off,' said Fitter, who sat in the front passenger seat. 'Look at that one.' A juvenile baboon sat on the rear bumper of the car ahead, trying his best to remove the number plate. 'Smart wee bastards, aren't they?'

McHugh stopped the car.

'Very intelligent,' he said, directing his comments at the rear-view mirror and staring at his passengers in the back. 'Highly organised, you know. They form groups, sometimes up to one hundred of the wee fellas, all doing what they're told. Just like a gang. They have devoted females who never leave the group. Isn't that nice? Women supporting their men.'

Both men in the back smirked their agreement, and neither failed to understand what McHugh was hinting at.

'The males defend and protect the group. The strongest take control, become the leaders. Any disrespect to the seniors has to be sorted out by the leader.' McHugh paused to look in his mirror again. 'You get my meaning, lads?'

'Answer the boss,' said Fitter, turning to face the two in the back.

Both men nodded.

'Yes, Mr McHugh,' said Fitter, prompting the appropriate reply.

'Yes, Mr McHugh,' the men chorused.

'Good.'

McHugh drove forward slowly until the car eased through the gates of the baboon compound and into the safer regions of the safari park. Both uninvited passengers on the outside of the vehicle had dropped to the ground and headed off in search of the next car. McHugh continued through the park until he pulled up again next to a hut where drinks and ice creams were on sale.

'Fitter, away and get us some ice creams while I have a wee word with our mates.'

Fitter, looking bemused and peeved at the order, got out and joined the short queue. A few minutes later, he returned to the car and handed out the ice-cream cones to his companions. McHugh, in a calm and business-like tone, continued to address his audience.

'The reason we're pals is that I want expansion in this part of the world. I like to run a slick operation. Understand me?'

Both men nodded, while licking at their ice creams. Fitter was not inclined to prompt; he too was busy enjoying his treat.

'You can't keep selling gear on that pissing awful estate. The cops will shut you down eventually. You need to start strutting your stuff, know what I mean? Stamp on the opposition. Claim some territory. Just like the baboons – the strongest become the leaders. This is the big time, lads. Clean up your shit and get to work, or I'll be looking for a new business partner. And do something about that fucking name. Vipers is a shit name.'

McHugh lowered his window and tossed out the remainder of his ice cream. He glared at Fitter beside him.

'Fucking hate cookie dough, Fitter. Why'd you get me that?'

'Sorry, boss.'

McHugh wiped his hands on a tissue and tossed that out of the window, too.

'Right, who wants to see the lions?'

CHAPTER 6

She brings me breakfast in bed every morning, before she goes to work at a clothing store in the city centre. I must confess, I've kept her late a few times. Breakfast brings out the beast in me, and I just want to pull her back into bed and do the business. She doesn't put up much resistance, even when it happens the morning after we've done it the night before. But lately, she pleads with me to let her go because she's going to get into bother with her boss for turning up late. A couple more days and it won't matter because I should be getting back to work in delivering groceries – they've kept my job open for me, seeing as how I was the victim of a crime. Can't help wondering though if being back on the road, in and out of all those MILF houses, I might get tempted again. It was certainly the best ruse I ever had for spotting and taking women, and it opened my eyes to a new type of woman I could snatch. But I owe it to Kirsty to behave myself. She seems to love having me around, and although the 'M-word' hasn't yet been mentioned I'm thinking that it won't be long. And I'm thinking that because I've already been to meet her mum and dad. What can I say? Salt-of-the-earth kind of people, and I couldn't help noticing the twinkle in Kirsty's eye when she introduced me to Mum. Jenn is a very nice lady with a big smile for her daughter and an equally big frown for her husband, Len – I noticed *that* when he started talking football.

'Let the lad sit down, for goodness' sake, before you start asking whether he's blue or red!'

You couldn't fail to see that Kirsty and Jenn are mother and daughter. Jenn has the same vocal inflection as her daughter, that 'sing it out' Scouse ending to her sentences. More Liver bird than Jamie Carragher, if you know what I mean? It's in the eyes too, dark and playful, as if everything is a bit of a laugh – except, of course, when they're scolding poor Len. But I think I hit it off with them.

'I'm red, I suppose,' I said to Len.

'You suppose?'

'I don't get to see them play very often.'

'We can soon fix that, James. I'm a season ticket holder. Never miss a home game.'

'And don't I know it?' said Jenn. 'Sometimes I think he lives at Anfield, rather than here.'

At least I'd chosen right, and that was without a heads-up from Kirsty. Len Scholes was dark-haired, but now greying and thinning in equal measure. His face was surly, a no-nonsense kind of man. The sort who'd tell you straight to your face that he didn't like you. Early seventies, I guessed, retired as a factory store man at sixty-five, smoked and drank in moderation. He and Jenn had three children, Kirsty and her two brothers, one brother older and the other younger than her. Both sons were in relationships and living away from home. Now it seemed that Kirsty, after one disastrous partnership – as I soon learned from Jenn – had at last found someone new to introduce to Mum and Dad.

Over tea that first time at her parents' house, I was asked to give them a rundown of my life to date. You can imagine I had to change things a little. But they were really astounded at my dice with death at the hands of yon crazy bitch Aeron. I had to make out, of course, that I was a complete innocent in the whole affair.

I couldn't tell them that Aeron and her brother, Jason Collywell, had been on a crusade to rid the world of sex offenders.

'And what about your family in Belfast?' Jenn, bless her, thought she should ask. Had to have something to tell her about that, too.

'Haven't seen my father since I was four years old. My mother is dead,' I lied. 'I was mostly raised by my granny. She died when I was seventeen.'

'That's a shame,' said Jenn, pouring more tea into my cup and passing me the plate of chicken sandwiches.

'I'd love to visit Belfast with you someday,' said Kirsty. 'You can show me all the places you used to hang out.'

What can I say? Bless. I smiled at her.

The Scholes family lived in a nice house, a semi-detached bungalow in Woolton. Both husband and wife were keen gardeners, and the front of the house had a drive that curved around neat flower beds and a tidy lawn. I'm not usually interested in such details, but remember, this was the first time I had ever been to a girlfriend's house without scheming in my head about how I was going to snatch her. This was a whole new realm for me.

The flat I now shared with Kirsty was in Penny Lane, not far from my old place in Wavertree. It was a two-bedroom apartment, on the first floor of a building on the corner. There was a hairdresser's underneath. Kirsty had made the flat look nice, despite it being only a rental. She'd put money into good furniture and quality electrical white goods, and it was plain to see that a woman lived there, from the pastel shades on the walls, neat curtains and candles to cheat any foul smells from cooking in the open-plan lounge-kitchen. Already we were going halfers on everything: rent, utility bills, food and drink.

This whole family thing, and me living with Kirsty, was going swimmingly – until one night, when *News at Ten* came on. We were lying together on the sofa, Kirsty resting her head on my chest and nearly asleep, when a story on the news suddenly grabbed my attention. I sat up straight, Kirsty jolted from her doze.

'What's wrong?' She saw me focused on the telly.

'Nothing. Go back to sleep.'

She flopped back down again, leaving me to concentrate on the news report. Seems that some fishing boat pulled up a body from the Irish Sea. The body was not yet identified as male or female, but police were awaiting the results of a detailed forensic examination of the remains. It was a Northern Irish boat, and the body was now being examined in Belfast. Couldn't help thinking that it had to be one of my girls.

I thought immediately of Megan, my latest conquest. Shit!

CHAPTER 7

Most of the people living on the Treadwater Estate were law-abiding. They kept their heads down and their noses out of things that didn't concern them. Tara didn't expect house-to-house enquiries to yield much in relation to the previous night's shooting. But she could almost hear the collective sigh of relief from Treadwater residents when word got out, rumours circulated and social media revealed the name of the victim as nineteen-year-old Ryan Boswell. Merseyside Police hadn't even got a positive ID on the body lying in the morgue before Facebook was hosting multiple pictures of the youth, tagged by his peers on the Treadwater Estate. So, when it came to knocking on doors in the streets around the murder scene, uniformed officers and detectives were faced with comments such as, 'good riddance,' and 'well rid,' and 'hope he rots in hell.'

* * *

On Monday morning at St Anne Street station, it didn't take long to assemble a character profile of the murder victim.

'Waste of space,' said DC John Wilson, who'd grown up on the very estate where the likes of Boswell, from an early age, had dealt drugs, bullied, stolen from and harassed ordinary people. And it seemed that no one had the power to deal with his kind. 'I remember him when he was about ten years old, putting bricks through car windscreens for laughs. He was always going to turn out that way. Pity his brother is still breathing.'

Tara stared at Wilson. She'd never heard him be quite so callously vocal about the people of his home area.

'What do you know about this gang, the Vipers?'

'Much the same as any other on Merseyside. Young lads looking for an easy way to the top, controlled by one or two guys who think they've already made it. They deal in drugs, protection, counterfeit booze. Whatever racket is going, they'll have their fingers in it.'

'You think this is simply a gang feud? That it could have been any member of the gang and Boswell was the unfortunate one caught in the firing line?'

'Seems most likely.'

Detective Superintendent Harold Tweedy entered the office to find his team of detectives deep in discussion of this, the latest killing in the city. A tall man, with a lined face and gold-rimmed glasses, his deep Christian faith helped Tweedy to cope with the rigours of police life.

'Morning, folks. What do we have so far?'

'Morning, sir,' Tara replied. 'We have an ID for the victim, yet to be confirmed, as Ryan Boswell, nineteen, from Treadwater. No witnesses yet to the incident but plenty of hearsay on the activities of the victim.'

'Does he have a record?'

'Paula is checking up on that now, sir. Seems he was a member of a local gang, the Vipers.'

'Mmm. Let's hope we're not looking at the start of another feud.'

'It's the most likely reason, if you ask me,' said Alan Murray. 'Somebody from another crew has popped him.'

Tara, and she thought Tweedy also, didn't think much of Murray's phrasing. He was prone to making frivolous quips at the most inappropriate moments of a discussion. In this case, his comment heralded an end to the meeting, and the detectives returned to their desks in the operations room.

Taking her seat, Tara prepared for the mound of tasks awaiting her. She had been busy recently on case preparation for a murder dating two years back, when one of the alleged conspirators had fled to Spain. Now, having been arrested on the Costa del Sol, Evan Blackley, former professional footballer and property developer, was back in England and awaiting trial for soliciting the murder of journalist Terry Lawler. The murder of a teenager, however, would now take precedence.

As usual, an early morning text from Aisling claimed her attention first. She knew that if she didn't deal with it immediately, she would be inundated with messages for the rest of the day.

The message read, 'My place at seven?'

Tara realised that the short missive could mean a host of things. No way was it simply a matter of calling in on Aisling for a few minutes on her way home. It meant, *we're having drinks before going to a club*, or *Kate wants to change our hair colour*, or *we need to decide on the holiday*, or most likely, *Kevin hasn't called me, and I think it's over, what should I do?* With so many possibilities it was better to confirm her attendance and ask no questions. At least she could then get on with her day's work.

As Tara relinquished her mobile, hopeful that Aisling would not be making another request, DC Paula Bleasdale approached. Tall, and the same age as Tara, she wore her long brown hair pinned up, giving her an air of confidence.

Her walk was similarly determined and reflected her athletic prowess.

'Morning, ma'am. Here's the file we have so far on Ryan Boswell. His family has been contacted. Father and brother have agreed to ID the body. There is one interesting point.'

'What's that?'

'The home address is Treadwater Estate, but it appears that he wasn't living there. His father said that he'd been staying with a girl in Sunderland.'

'Have we got a name and address for her?'

'Not yet, ma'am.'

Tara called across the office to John Wilson. He weaved his way around desks and chairs to stand beside Paula Bleasdale.

'I need both of you to find out as much as you can on this Vipers gang. Who's in charge, how many members and what they were all doing last Saturday night.'

'Yes, ma'am,' said Wilson.

'And, Paula?'

'Ma'am?'

'Keep working on the name and address for Boswell's girlfriend.'

CHAPTER 8

DCI Wallace Brown of the Police Service of Northern Ireland didn't flinch at the sight before him. He'd seen far worse in his twenty-year career. What troubled him most was the possibility that they might not be able to identify the victim. And victim was definitely the right word. A body wrapped in plastic sheeting, weighed down by two bags of stones and fished out of the Irish Sea was no accident. Somebody had made a superb job of disposing of a body. It must have been a million-to-one chance that a trawler would drag it from the seabed. Maybe, just maybe, they could catch the person responsible.

What lay before him, on the slab of the post-mortem suite, was recognisable as a human body – but so far, nothing more. Brown couldn't even tell if it was male or female. He waited for the pathologist, Dr Eugene O'Brien, to begin his explanation, and he hoped for layman's terms and not a load of scientific jargon that only another pathologist would understand. Also present was a male laboratory technician and DC Gina Marshall, one of the staff on his floor at Musgrave station, who happened to be free when he was looking for someone to accompany him.

'Right, folks,' O'Brien began, in a routine voice befitting the occasion. 'Female, approximately five foot three inches tall, but we can't be entirely accurate.'

'Why not?' asked Brown.

O'Brien, athletically built with greying hair and unshaven face, glanced over his glasses at the detective.

'The head is detached from the body.'

'You mean somebody cut off her head?'

'No. I think the body has been in the water for a very long time. It is quite common for the head, the hands and the feet to separate from the body.'

Wallace Brown, who was of a similar build to the pathologist, strong and tall, gazed along the length of the corpse. He could not discern either of the hands or feet.

'Was the body naked when it was recovered?' asked Marshall. The young constable had paled; she was not used to these circumstances, but nonetheless eager to give her input.

'Yes, completely. There were two woven polypropylene bags, like animal feed or coal sacks, one over the head and torso, the other covering the legs. The entire body was wrapped in two thick sheets of polythene. The condition when first recovered has been photographed, although the

27

fishermen had sliced open the polythene. Understandable, I suppose, given the situation.'

'Why is the body that colour?' Brown asked.

'The extensive grey patches are due to adipocere formation.' O'Brien indicated the extensive grey areas on the torso and thighs of the body. 'It's much more evident on the back and buttocks.'

'Here we go. Bloody scientific mumbo jumbo. C'mon, Eugene, spell it out for me.'

'It's affectionately known as grave wax. Basically, the fatty tissues in the body, after death and under certain conditions, may form this soapy or waxy substance, called adipocere. Usually, this can help to indicate the time elapsed since death, but there are too many variables here. The body was in seawater, it was wrapped in plastic, the depth and temperature of the water would have affected the rate of decay of tissues and the rate of adipocere formation. Although the plastic sheeting restricted access, there has been some sea life activity upon the body. Small fish have been feeding on the skin. All I can say is that it's been in the water for a considerable period.'

'What do you mean? Days? Months? Years?'

'Years... more than two, I'd guess.'

'Likely cause of death?'

'It's difficult to know for sure. She's been in the water for so long. Drowning perhaps, or suffocation in the bags and polythene prior to immersion in the sea. No clear signs of knife wounds or bullet holes. Can't say if she was strangled.'

'What about DNA?'

'Probably do some sampling of any preserved tissues or take some from the bone marrow. It'll help with identification.'

'But any chance of finding DNA belonging to the perpetrator?'

O'Brien shook his head.

CHAPTER 9

Janek Poska, a forty-year-old from Estonia, conducted his business at just two locations. For receipt and storage, he used a scrapyard in Tranmere, and for distribution he used the busy streets of Liverpool city centre. He liked to keep things simple. He kept his customers happy and his supply chain well under the police radar. Usually, he wandered around the pedestrianised areas keeping his appointments with customers. He never carried gear for more than two clients at a time. That way, if ever he was pulled by the bizzies he could claim the drugs he was carrying were for personal use only. He was not a supplier; he was a man with a habit. Aksel was his runner. He ferried the gear from the scrapyard in Tranmere and met up with Janek at various street junctions around the city. The system worked well, no problem.

Mostly he dealt in China White, fentanyl. It was very easily obtained from Estonia, his homeland. But he also supplied cocaine, tabs of ecstasy and sometimes heroin. He didn't bother with cannabis or spice, too much trouble for little profit. The hard stuff was where the money was made.

Today, it was pissing down. People rushed around, umbrella dodging. It was harder for him to look inconspicuous, creeping about in his heavy leather jacket, rain-soaked, long dirty-blonde hair, unshaven and trying to keep an eye out for bizzies. He loved that nickname for the police in this city. It had an affectionate feel about it, as if they could be your friends rather than the guys who would put you in jail.

His first meet of the day wasn't far from the railway station at Lime Street. A man he knew only as Tom, a most unlikely-looking drug user. He never bought much. It was personal use and maybe a couple of friends only. He looked like a banker; wore a business suit anyway, smart tie, expensive shoes. Not married. That's all Janek knew of this customer. He didn't need to know any more, didn't *want* to know any more. He ran a discreet business, and his customers liked it that way. He didn't ask questions, and they never offered information.

He saw Tom walking from the station and slow down, gazing around him, looking for his man. But Janek had great stealth and he always spotted his clients before they saw him. It took just seconds for Janek to step discreetly in front of the purchaser, blend into his stride and the swap could be made. Cash in his hand, the gear passed over like the offer of a fag. Tom then stopped at a pedestrian crossing, and Janek walked on.

But this morning, as the traffic came to a halt at the lights, two young men got out of a car. Janek didn't even see them. The pair, dressed similarly in jeans, long hooded anoraks and baseball caps, were suddenly on the pavement, the car moving slowly forwards when the lights changed. Suddenly, Janek had company either side of him.

His first thought was that the bizzies had finally caught up with him, but that notion vanished when they took him firmly by the arms and steered him towards the station entrance. Once inside, they stopped and turned to face him.

'Are you Janek, yeah?' said one.

He nodded once and began to relax. New customers, he reckoned, but not very discreet.

'We're Vipers. You heard of us, yeah?'

Janek shook his head and frowned.

'What you want?' he asked.

'We have a message for you and the rest of your Tallinn Crew.'

'What message?'

'You're on our patch, mate.'

'*Your patch?*' Janek scoffed. 'How *your* patch?'

'This city belongs to us, mate. Keep to the other side of the river or we'll close you down.'

'City is for everybody.' Janek glared defiantly at his rivals. He didn't think they looked so tough.

One of them stepped closer, his breath on Janek's face.

'Stay out or you'll be dead meat.'

They pushed past him, knocking his shoulder as they went, and strutted from the station. Janek took a deep breath then, unperturbed, continued with his day.

CHAPTER 10

I've been scouring the papers and the internet for news on the body they found in the sea. Don't mind saying that I'm a bit worried. I've heard they can do all kinds of things to identify bodies nowadays – DNA and the like. What if they can trace something to me? My DNA profile is on the national database after my conviction for snatching Tara Grogan. If they find my DNA on the body, then I'm in deep shit. But surely my semen and stuff would be washed away after all this time? It's been years, assuming, of course, that the body they've found is one of the girls I took in Belfast. Most of my snatches in England I've dumped off the Welsh coast, a few in the North Sea and a couple in the Channel. Then, of course, there is Megan – my latest girl. I dumped her in the Irish Sea, off Maryport. It said on the news that the body was found off the Copeland Islands. They are only a couple of miles off the coast of Northern Ireland. It has to be my first or second girl. That would make it either Millie or Gemma.

I can remember every girl I've ever had. I've given them all new names so that I don't have to think about their real ones. Maybe this is somebody else. Not one of mine. All this waiting is stressing me out and I'm starting back at work tomorrow. Kirsty is taking me out for a nice dinner for my last night. She's booked a taxi and everything, so we can have a few drinks. She's spoiling me rotten. And her da, Len, has invited me to Anfield for the West Ham match next Sunday. I reckon I've been accepted into the family already. Kirsty has started browsing holiday brochures, and she's hoping her friend, Mel, is going to stay with this new bloke of hers so that the four of us can go on holiday together.

If it wasn't for this body fished out of the sea, I'd be thinking everything was great for me at the moment.

I was just getting ready to go out, dressed in a new shirt and jacket that Kirsty had bought me especially for the occasion. I was sitting on the sofa, waiting for her to finish getting ready. I could hear the hairdryer going in the bedroom, so I flicked on the telly. Didn't think my story would be on the national news, but there – staring right out of the screen – was a picture of Millie. They had identified the body pulled from the sea. Didn't take them long. After her picture came a recap of the news coverage at the time she disappeared, nearly eight years ago. The police claimed they had never closed the case, but because Millie's body had been found they were launching a fresh inquiry into her murder.

She was my first ever girl, my first snatch. I couldn't take my eyes off the TV. Beautiful, she was. Dark hair, sparkling eyes, lovely wee body. Her picture remained on the screen as the newsreader continued with the story. I swear Millie was looking right at me, boring into my head and saying, *I'm back, you murdering fucker, and I'm coming for you.*

CHAPTER 11

Aidan Boswell, older brother of Ryan, had formally identified the body of his brother and was invited to St Anne Street to assist with enquiries.

'So, Ryan and you were both members of this gang, the Vipers?' Tara asked.

Murray sat next to her in the interview room. Boswell, twenty-six, was of mixed race, his mother having been white English and his father from Trinidad. Aidan was muscular, with a shaven head and several scars on his face, and sat opposite the police officers. He appeared understandably upset at his brother's death but seemed unwilling to talk about gang membership. He did at least manage to shrug at the question.

'Let's assume for now that you were members, since you both have that tattoo on your arms. What can you tell us of Ryan's movements in the past few days? Where was he? What was he doing?'

'Don't know, hadn't seen him.'

'Did you speak on the phone, did you text each other?'

'Some.'

'What did you talk about?'

'We just chatted.'

'Did he believe that he was in danger?' Murray asked.

'I don't know, man.'

'Do you know where he was when you were chatting?'

'Sunderland. That's where he lived.'

'How long had he been living in Sunderland?'

'Five months, six maybe.'

'Did he have a job?' Tara asked.

Boswell smirked at the question. Tara realised that the man before her wasn't about to implicate himself, or his dead brother, in any activities of the gang to which they belonged. But she needed more of a lead in this case than she was currently getting from Aidan Boswell.

'Who do you think was responsible for Ryan's death?'

Boswell looked straight into Tara's eyes; no doubt bemused by the young woman in front of him. Surely police detectives were not this hot. When she met his gaze with confidence, he dropped his eyes.

'Aidan, this is a murder we're dealing with. The murder of your brother. If you know something about how Ryan came to be in Treadwater, what he was doing there, you need to tell us.'

'I don't know nothing.'

'What was the name of the girl who was living with Ryan?'

'Don't know her.'

'Was she with Ryan at Treadwater on Saturday night?'

'Don't know.'

'What is her address in Sunderland?'

Aidan shrugged his indifference to the question.

'Who are you protecting, Aidan?' said Murray. 'Somebody else in the Vipers?'

'Don't know what you're talking about, man. The Vipers ain't got nothing to do with killing Ryan. Just back off, will ya?'

'If it wasn't the Vipers, then who do you think was responsible?'

'You're the bizzies, you figure it out. Leave me alone. I'm going home.'

* * *

DC Paula Bleasdale was keen to impart some news when Tara and Murray returned to the operations room.

'Hi, Paula. Any news on the raids this morning?'

On the Treadwater Estate the police had raided the homes of known members of the Vipers gang.

'Several arrests, ma'am. The suspects are being processed at the moment. One of them is female.'

'Good. Let me know when it's time for me to have a chat with them.'

'Will do.'

With a coffee and fruit scone, Tara sat down at her desk. She used the few moments of calm and quiet to try to make sense of the information gathered so far on the killing of Ryan Boswell. Tara hoped that the female arrested was Ryan's girlfriend. They had yet to establish the address in Sunderland that she and Boswell had been living at. But what if the girlfriend had travelled to Liverpool with Ryan Boswell? What if she was on the Treadwater Estate when he was been beaten and shot?

And what if she was involved?

Finding this woman might be the key to the whole affair.

CHAPTER 12

Bloody ironic that the girl they found in the sea was the very first one I ever had. Millie. Funny that. Not Megan, the last girl I had, not the best I ever had, but simply the first. Like I said before, I don't keep records of my girls. I don't keep anything likely to incriminate me. I'm not into souvenirs, don't keep their knickers or a lock of their hair. But everything is stored inside my head.

I can remember everything. It's my life's work, why shouldn't I? So, once I heard it confirmed that Millie, whose real name was Linda Meredith, was the body pulled out of the drink off the Copelands, my mind went right back to the time when I took her. My initial fear, that the cops would be able to trace Millie back to me, subsided when I began to consider a few of the things I'd done with her.

Firstly, I had dumped her naked. I didn't put her clothes or mine inside the bundle of stones and polythene.

This was before I'd hit on the idea of using those wheelie sports bags. Secondly, I hadn't injected her with China White, so there were no syringes to dispose of. Again, this happened before I'd even heard of China White. I'd given her a few tabs of rohypnol but in the end I still had to smother her with her coat.

I searched the internet, trying to establish whether it was possible for my DNA to be found on the body, after it had spent eight years at the bottom of the sea. My conclusion was that it seemed unlikely. Really, if they were ever going to find any of my girls then Millie was the least likely to provide any evidence that could be traced back to me. I reckoned I was in the clear. And maybe it was a wee lesson learned. In future, I should dispose of clothes and syringes away from the body. You never know when a bloody trawler might pull another corpse from the depths.

But what am I thinking? I shouldn't be concerned about what to do in the future. I'm with Kirsty now. I love her, I think. No need for me to take any more girls. But, if I'm honest, this whole episode has been a bit of a turn-on. I got a buzz from hearing about the discovery of Millie's body. I felt the adrenalin coursing through me as I listened to the news. The whole thing has got me itching again.

I could have the best of both worlds. A comfy life with Kirsty and a wee private habit of taking a nice girl, showing her a good time and nobody is any the wiser. My life is just brilliant.

Sometimes you just find yourself in the groove, if you know what I mean? Like you can do no wrong. That everything is going your way. Like, you could rob a bank and the bank manager would actually help you carry the cash to your car, or as my granny used to say, you could tread in shit, and it would turn to gold.

* * *

On my first day back at work, delivering groceries for one of the country's biggest supermarkets, the first house I called at had a beautiful young lady opening her door for me. My name for her sprang to mind right away. Daisy. Just like the girl from that old TV show, *The Dukes of Hazzard*. I used to love that. Well, this woman opened her front door and I carried in a crate of groceries. She had legs up to her oxters and was wearing denim shorts and a blue striped vest. Daisy had long brown hair, a beamer of a smile, dark eyes and stood barefoot.

I mention that she wasn't wearing shoes because she was tall. Except for her height, she was the shape and type of girl I always go for. Already, I was warming to the task of having her, but it felt strange going home that night to a flat where Kirsty was busy making my tea and nattering away about all the things that had happened to her during the day. I could hardly do the same. I had plans to make for snatching Daisy.

I was thinking of being naughty again.

CHAPTER 13

A Matrix unit, a specially trained team of officers responsible for the disruption of gang and gun crime on Merseyside, had raided two homes on the Treadwater Estate in the early morning, two days after the killing of Ryan Boswell.

Three men and a woman were arrested, and a small quantity of drugs was recovered. Those arrested were brought to St Anne Street station to assist with enquiries. Tara didn't believe that questioning any of the men arrested would yield much in relation to the murder of Boswell. All three men were known members of the Treadwater Vipers gang. They weren't likely to be co-operative. Much to Tara's frustration, the girl arrested turned out to be a girlfriend of the supposed leader of the Vipers and not of Ryan Boswell.

Tara had to go through the motions of interviewing each of them. She wasn't interested in their gang activities unless she could relate them to Boswell's murder. Ryan's brother had been less than helpful and more concerned with preserving his own reputation within this gang than assisting the police to find his brother's killer. Other members were unlikely to be more forthcoming.

Sitting opposite Tara in a ground-floor interview room, was a young man of twenty-two looking somewhat the worse for wear, thanks to whatever drug trip he was slowly coming down from. His name was Craig Lewis.

'Mr Lewis,' Tara began after the preliminaries had been completed and the recording of the interview started. 'Can you confirm that you are a member of a gang known as the Treadwater Vipers?'

She couldn't help thinking this gang's name sounded more like a sports team, but she knew the Vipers were far from sporting.

'No comment.'

'The tattoo on your left arm shows an image linked to membership of this gang. Isn't that correct?'

'No comment.'

He rubbed at his face with both hands, as if he'd just awoken from a peaceful doze. Mr Lewis didn't seem at all concerned about his current situation.

'Can you tell me of your whereabouts last Saturday evening, 15 April?'

'No comment.'

The questions continued, as did the repeated response. The interviewee was a heavily built man with shaven head. He wore a light grey hoodie and blue jeans and gazed sternly through grey eyes as she put her questions to him. His nose was crooked, improperly set after a fight when he was sixteen, and he had a tiny scar on the left side of his lower lip, this merely a footballing injury. He did not look like a man who was easily rattled.

Murray fared equally poorly with the second man to be interviewed, eighteen-year-old Adam Finlay. It seemed clear that these gang members had trained themselves in the ways of dealing with the law. Close ranks, no co-operation.

The third man arrested, Tyler Finlay, Adam's older brother, was already known to the police as the apparent leader of the Vipers, but Tara was faced with the same response, or rather, lack of response to her questions. She wasn't interested in charging him with possession of class A drugs; she wanted information on the murder of Ryan Boswell. But Tyler Finlay would not even admit to knowing the victim.

Shania Smith was seventeen years old, of mixed race, and allegedly the girlfriend of Tyler Finlay. She had been arrested at his flat and in his bed. A rather curvy girl with wide hips, a large round face and voluminous hair, she was apparently more willing than her male peers to provide information. Tara wasn't sure if the girl was dim-witted or simply frightened by finding herself in police custody.

'Please state your address, Shania,' Tara asked.

'Fifty-two Beechwood Drive, Treadwater, Netherton.' Her voice was barely more than a mumble, and Tara had to ask her to speak up and repeat her answer.

'So, you do not live at the same address as Tyler Finlay?'

'No, I just stay over some nights.' Self-consciously, the girl wrapped her arms around herself. She was wearing black satin pyjamas, pink slippers and a leather jacket.

'You're in a relationship with Tyler?'

'Yes,' she replied – rather proudly, Tara thought. The girl's eyes twinkled at the mention of the man's name.

'Did you know Ryan Boswell?'

'I knew him, like, but not really well, if you know what I mean? We didn't, like, hang out together or anything.'

'How often would you have seen him?'

'Not much. Seen him around the estate and that.'

'Did you ever see him at Tyler's flat?'

'Couple of times, I think. Sometimes he was with his brother, Aidan. I know him better, like.'

'Why did Ryan and Aidan visit Tyler's flat?'

'Don't know. Business, I suppose. Tyler wouldn't let me stay in the room. I would make tea.'

'And what about other people, say Craig Lewis and Adam Finlay?'

'Yeah, I know them. Cos Adam is, like, Tyler's brother.'

'Where were you last Saturday evening?'

The girl looked confused, as though she didn't recognise a day of the week, as if the notion of individual days was irrelevant to her life. She shook her head slowly.

'Don't know.'

'It was only two nights ago, Shania. Can't you remember what you were doing?'

'Oh, *then*. I was out with my friends.'

'Out where?'

'On the estate and that. Went to a party.'

'Whose party?'

'It was Aidan's birthday – at his house.'

'Do you know where Tyler was at that time?'

'He was at the party, too.'

'Did you see Ryan Boswell that night?'

'No.'

'What about his girlfriend, did you see her?'

'Don't know her.'

'But you do know her name?'

Shania hesitated, as if she was suddenly conscious that she might be saying too much. Tara smiled her understanding of the girl's dilemma, but she needed the information.

'If you know her name, Shania, it may help us find the person who killed Ryan. You want to see this person caught, don't you?'

'Her name is Carly McHugh.'

'Did you see her at the party on Saturday night?'

'No.'

'Do you know why Ryan was living in Sunderland and not in Treadwater?'

'He works there.'

'For Tyler?'

'Think so.'

'What type of work did he do for Tyler?'

The girl paused again and seemed doubtful about answering at all. Tara waited, knowing that she'd just placed the teenager in a difficult – and potentially dangerous – situation.

'Was it something to do with drugs, Shania?'

'I'm not sure, I mean, I don't really know. I'm not supposed to know. Tyler doesn't like me knowing things.'

'Does the work have something to do with the Vipers?'

Shania dropped her head. Clearly, she was in a quandary. Tara realised the girl knew much more than she was supposed to but was too frightened to speak of it.

'I think Ryan used to deliver things for Tyler.'

'Do you mean drugs?'

'I think so.'

CHAPTER 14

Tara was certain that it was him. Just sitting there, looking right at her. When he realised that she'd recognised him he smiled and maintained his stare. Out of breath from her running, she began to shake. Suddenly, freezing cold, she stood rooted to the spot, looking at the man who had taken her. Fear and loathing coursed through her as she tried to think rationally. She tried to think what she should do next. *Why was he here? Had he been waiting for her? Did he know where she lived?* She felt it would be a defeat to walk or run away, so she remained staring at him.

She recognised him, but still she could not recall what he had done with her on that night when he'd drugged her and driven her away. Murray and her friends, Aisling and Kate, had come to her rescue. They'd found her naked in his van in the car park at the old Leasowe Lighthouse. She'd seen him sentenced for aggravated sexual assault, but it seemed that she would never know exactly what he had done to her on that night. The last time she'd set eyes on him was when she and Murray had saved him from certain death at the hands of the brother and sister hell-bent on ridding the world of sex criminals. The few seconds that she stood, watching him smirking at her, felt like hours. Then, he calmly started the engine of his van and drove away.

It was dusk; a mild evening without a breeze and yet she was painfully cold. She gazed around her, as if she'd just been dropped from outer space onto an unfamiliar piece of earth. A few people were walking by the river towards the Albert Dock. She wanted to tell them that he'd been here, watching her, but they'd think she was crazy. A car horn sounded, long and urgent. She glared at the driver, failing at first to understand that she had just stepped onto the road in front of him. He shook his head and drove around her. Suddenly, all those occasions when she'd imagined that someone was watching her now made sense. Those times when she'd heard a car or a van roar away behind her. Times when a car had been parked on double yellows as she drove from her parking space at Wapping Dock onto the main road. A man wearing a hooded anorak who just happened to be waiting at the corner as she drove by. It all made sense.

It was him.

James Guy had been stalking her. Was stalking her. He hadn't forgotten her after his conviction for assault. Now, and despite her having saved him from certain death, he was still after her.

Going home to her flat didn't feel like the right thing to do. Instead, she ran to Aisling's and rang her buzzer. She felt ready to throw up, but Aisling was quick to answer and soon Tara was on her sofa with a glass of water.

'Have you been overdoing it, love?'

'Something like that,' she said, still out of breath.

'Are you all right, Tara? You're shaking.'

'He's been watching me, Aisling. I've just seen him.'

'Who has?'

'James Guy. I saw him just now in his van. He was waiting for me.'

'Where, Tara? What do you mean *waiting for you?*'

'I saw him. In his van, outside the Beatles Museum. He was waiting for me; I know he was.'

'What did he do?'

'He just sat there staring at me, and then he smiled and drove off.'

'Maybe it was just coincidence. He just happened to be there, that's all. At least he didn't try anything.'

'No, Aisling. It all makes sense now. I've had this feeling for ages that someone is watching me. Like in the mornings when I was going to work or coming home. And now I'm out for a run... and he just happens to be there.'

'But you saved his life, Tara. Surely he wouldn't want to hurt you after that?'

'He tried once before. Why not now?'

'I'll get you something stronger to drink and then you can lie down. You're not going home. We'll talk to Kate in the morning; she's on duty tonight.'

* * *

Aisling and Tara eventually drank two bottles of wine between them and followed those up with a couple of shots of peach schnapps. Quite drunk, Tara fell into bed in Aisling's spare room, her troubling memories of the early evening soon mingled with her dreams, and she slept soundly until six thirty.

St Anne Street station was the last place she wanted to be the next morning. Tara would much rather have started off on her holiday with Kate and Aisling, but that was still three months away.

She had no clear plan in her mind of the day's work ahead. Her stomach still trembled from the experience of seeing James Guy's grinning face and the consequent recall of her painful memories. Pictures of Guy, and of Lynsey Yeats and Callum and vigilantes and the dismembered body of Dinsdale Kirkman all swirled in her head. Then she met Alan Murray on the stairs, and her body suddenly relaxed.

Why did she always feel safer in his presence? She felt the same with John Wilson. Her protectors. Why did seeing Murray put her at ease? She cared for him, but only as a colleague, and maybe after several years working together, as a friend also. But he had a new woman in his life and didn't give any indication, nowadays, of wanting her. Even his use of innuendo had waned. He seemed happy with Trudy Mitchell, a woman who had initially been their suspect in a case of ritual murder and who was now dating Murray.

Above all this morning, Tara felt confused. Her head throbbed from the wine consumed the previous night, she'd hardly eaten, and she realised she didn't look her best – not even her workday best.

'Morning, ma'am.'

'Morning, Alan. Any news?'

They stopped on the stairs, Tara on her way up to the first floor, Murray on his way down. He was, inevitably, munching on a Twix, and it wasn't yet nine o'clock.

'Couple of people from Treadwater have come forward. Seems they remember hearing the screams of a girl on the night Boswell was shot.'

'Close to the scene?'

'One close to the shops where the shooting happened, but the other was a bit further away near the park.'

'Might be connected. Can't help thinking that it was this girlfriend of Boswell's. Any news on her whereabouts?'

Murray shook his head.

'Nothing more from Sunderland police?'

'All gone quiet. They're working on an address for her. Wilson has the forensic report on the shooting. That's it, I'm afraid.'

Wilson was already loitering close to her desk when she entered the office. He was chatting with Paula Bleasdale.

'Morning, ma'am,' he said. 'The report for the analysis of the bullets retrieved from the scene has come through. The gun that was used to kill Boswell has history.'

'Oh?'

'It was used in a shooting eighteen months ago in Belfast.'

CHAPTER 15

Iris Hamilton, a sixty-year-old woman, heavy smoker, and – from the smell of her breath at ten o'clock in the morning – a heavy drinker, spoke to Tara and Murray at her doorstep on the Treadwater Estate. Her face was heavily lined, her teeth badly stained, her shoulder-length hair turning grey and in need of brushing.

'I heard the screams first, and then I looked out the window. She was running up the middle of the road.'

'Can you give me a description, Iris?'

'Young girl, a teenager maybe. Slim, dark hair about the same length as mine.' Iris stroked two fingers through her hair.

'How was she dressed?' Tara asked.

'Short skirt, sleeveless top, high heels and bare legs. Such a cold night too. Could hardly walk, never mind run.'

'Did you see anyone else? Did it seem like the girl was running away from someone?'

'Didn't see anyone else, not right away. About five minutes later I saw a man walking along the street. Walking quickly but looking around him. Like, peering into the gardens and that.'

'Did you see the girl at any time after you saw the man?'

The woman shook her head, stepped from her hallway down onto the garden path and pointed.

'See the football pitch up there? The man went up that way. That's as far as I can see from my bedroom window. Didn't think anything of it till I heard young Boswell had been shot.'

Murray pulled a printed sheet of a photograph of Ryan Boswell from his jacket pocket and showed it to the woman.

'Do you recognise this man?'

'That's Boswell. There're not many people round here who wouldn't know him. Not with all the trouble he caused over the years.'

'Was that the man you saw walking past your house after the girl?'

'No, love.'

'You're sure, Mrs Hamilton?'

'It was dark, but the man was much bigger than Ryan. Bulky. Lighter-skinned, too.'

* * *

There was a gathering of around twenty people at the row of shops where Ryan Boswell's body had been found. The roll-down shutter of the defunct video store and the pavement below were adorned with various bouquets of flowers, cards, scribbled messages on paper and lit candles, all left in tribute to the young lad who'd grown up on the estate and had been shot in cold blood. Tara thought it ironic that there seemed to be as many people glad to see the back of the youth as there were those displaying their grief at his passing. Murray stopped the car to observe, and Tara realised that it was an opportunity to speak to some people who may not have been questioned already. She climbed from the car and stepped towards a group of four teenage girls.

'Excuse me, girls, I'm Detective Inspector Grogan, Merseyside Police. Were any of you acquainted with Ryan Boswell?'

Two of the girls in hooded tops dropped their gaze when Tara addressed them. The other two seemed prepared to answer the question.

'Knew him from school,' said a girl with bleached blonde hair and reddened eyes. 'He used to hang out with us.'

'Yeah,' another joined in. 'Was a good laugh, Ryan.'

'Do you know of anyone who would have wanted to hurt him?'

All four girls shook their heads and gave a collective answer of no.

'It's been another gang what's done this,' said one of the girls, who was wearing a black hooded sweatshirt. She had short dark hair and an array of piercings around both ears.

'Why do you think that?'

'Turf,' said the bleached blonde. 'Has to be, don't it?'

Tara gazed at the girl. She guessed her to be around nineteen or twenty, since she'd said that they'd known Ryan Boswell from schooldays.

'Why do you say that?'

'Cos some other gang wants a piece of Vipers' turf–'

Suddenly, the girl was elbowed sharply by one of her mates.

'Shut up, will ya,' said the girl wearing the hoodie. 'Don't talk about the Vipers, not to the bizzies.'

By this point, several other young people had gathered around Tara, eager to hear the conversation. She also noticed a couple of older men, perhaps in their forties or fifties, standing by the entrance to the alley where the body had been found. Both were smoking cigarettes, apparently watching people who stopped to place flowers, but Tara got the feeling that they were observing what was going on between her and the girls. She sensed an uneasy mood within this gathering. Fear or anger, she couldn't tell which. Murray had left the car and joined her, which made her feel safer. He had his eyes fixed on the two men. Clearly, they stood out from the others. But Murray's stare had induced some unease, and both men picked their way through those laying flowers and sauntered off.

'What about Ryan's girlfriend, do any of you know her? Her name is Carly McHugh.'

Most of those standing around her shook their heads, but one girl spoke up.

'She wasn't from around here,' she said.

When Tara looked at the woman, she realised she was much older than the others. She might even have been the mother of one of them. Round-shouldered, heavyset with brown hair and a square face, she looked sternly at Tara.

'Ryan was my nephew, my sister's son.'

Tara acknowledged the woman's response and spoke directly to her.

'I believe she came from Sunderland, but there is a possibility that she was here on the night Ryan was killed.'

'Not from Sunderland,' said the woman above the mutterings of the others. 'Northern Ireland.'

CHAPTER 16

I've had my first row with Kirsty. I hope she's not getting all possessive on me. Can't stand that in a woman. I mean, I don't ask her everything she gets up to when she's out with her friends. She still goes clubbing with her giggling friend, Mel, and she's out at the pub on a Friday with her workmates. I don't mind. I trust her. Why can't she trust me? The other night she started asking me a load of questions.

'Thought you'd be home before this,' she said. 'The dinner spoiled.'

'Had a delivery at Knowsley, and the traffic was a bugger.'

She was pretending to be interested in the telly, flicking through the channels, but I could tell she really wanted me to explain. Of course, I wasn't on a bloody delivery at Knowsley. I was having a wee look out for what Daisy gets up to on a Thursday.

'What did you do last night?'

Wednesday night is my night for going out without her, and she knows I don't really have any mates to hang out with, so I usually make something up. Most of the time I just go to a pub for a couple of pints. And once her da invited me to a mid-week Liverpool game. But lately, of course, I've started looking out again for Tara Grogan. Thought I might spot her jogging down by the M&S Bank Arena, and lo and behold, I'm sitting in my van, minding my own business, when suddenly she's looking right at me. Don't know who was the most surprised. I managed a smile, but she just stood there glaring at me – like I'd no business breathing the same air as her. I wondered what she was really thinking about me. How did she feel when she saved my life from that crackpot Aeron? Was she glad to have done it? Or did she not even realise at the time that it was me nailed to that bloody frame and about to have my head lopped off? But I suppose I can't expect her to have forgiven me for snatching her and trying to have my way with her. During my trial, I learned that she couldn't remember a thing about it. So, what's her problem?

And my problem at the minute is what to tell Kirsty when I'm out to all hours chasing after beautiful women.

'Sometimes, Kirsty, I just like to go for a drive,' I told her.

'But you drive all the time when you're at work. Don't you need to do something else?'

'No,' I said, pulling her close to me. 'I'm happy to be home with you.'

'You're not going off me, are you?'

'Don't be daft.'

'You're not out with other women?'

I tried to laugh this one off, but it sent her into a mood, and I realised she was deeply suspicious of what I got up to when I went out alone or came home late from work.

'Don't you trust me?' I asked.

* * *

She lay beside me, staring into my eyes, searching, I'd say, for a truth that I was never going to share. Fucking intuitive women, they do my head in.

I realised that I was growing irritable. Millie was still in the news. There were stories about how forensic analysis had solved the mystery of her identity. It even made it on to *Crimewatch* – again. They'd resurrected the story they ran on Millie's disappearance, nearly eight years ago. How she had not been seen since leaving a leisure centre in east Belfast, how her family had never given up hope of finding her and how they were devastated when she was fished from the sea. But at least now she could be laid to rest, and the PSNI had begun a fresh inquiry into her abduction and murder, although they couldn't establish the actual cause of death.

But still, I didn't like the idea of a renewed investigation. What if they had more evidence than they were making public? If they had found my DNA, for instance. They might already be looking for me.

I turned my attention to the woman lying in bed beside me.

'I love you, Kirsty,' I said.

She looked at me for what seemed a bloody age.

'Love you too,' she replied at last.

Bless.

CHAPTER 17

Aksel had parked up on William Jessop Way, an area of the city by Princes Dock that had undergone extensive redevelopment in recent years. Apartment blocks, walkways and footbridges were now the modern landscape of an area steeped in the history of the port of Liverpool. The car sat on double yellows, but he hadn't planned on being here long. He was waiting for a call. Janek was working somewhere around James Street. He would need to be picked up soon. It was not far from Princes Dock to James Street. He could have a smoke and listen to some music before the boss called. No Big Silence, a metal band from his homeland, blared from the stereo, the windows down, the sound booming across the dockland.

He reclined in the driver's seat, his right hand resting on the window which was open to let his cigarette smoke waft away. He closed his one eye to relax, his left eye he had lost as a boy, fighting with sticks in the forests surrounding Rapla, his hometown. So immersed was he in the music and thoughts of life back home, and the girl he should have married, he was oblivious to the car pulling up behind him.

Both cars were BMWs, in the same colour, black, but different models. Three men climbed out of the 5-Series and bounded to the 3-Series where Aksel lay, almost asleep, the cigarette still burning between his fingers. Two of the men held metal pipes, the third a baseball bat.

All of them laid into the car. They smashed the windows; the doors, roof and the bonnet were dented. Aksel had little time to react. He tried to start the engine. A metal pipe came through the open window, catching him on the side of the head. He slumped across the passenger seat. He thought he was about to die. With the hammering on the bodywork, the thumping music and the pain in his head, he wanted to pass out.

Suddenly, the passenger door was pulled open. A hand reached inside, fumbling for the volume control of the stereo. When eventually there was silence, Aksel dared to raise his head and look at his attackers.

'Get the fuck out of Liverpool. Next time you don't get a warning.'

Aksel looked at the brown face of the man who'd spoken. He wanted to remember him. The man laughed when he saw the contorted face and the foreigner with just one eye.

'Ugly bastard, aren't you?'

His two mates came to look and added their own laughter. Aksel lay across the seat, praying. He was covered in glass from the shattered windows, and the side of his head throbbed – although there was no blood. Silence had ensued; he hoped they'd left. A moment later, he heard a car engine revving as it sped by.

He lay still for a while longer, waiting for his heart rate to steady. Suddenly he was aware of a burning smell. He sat upright, searching for his cigarette. During the attack it had fallen into the footwell and had begun to smoulder on the carpet. Reaching down, he lifted it between two fingers and took a long drag before tossing it out of the window. His mobile rang, and he knew it was time to meet Janek.

CHAPTER 18

Early evening, and they sat around Tara's desk drinking coffee and discussing what they had learned so far about the murder of Ryan Boswell. Harold Tweedy expressed his concern that while everything pointed at a gangland killing, they had not yet identified any definite suspects.

'We need to find out more about why Boswell was living in Sunderland and what type of work he was doing there for this gang,' said Murray. Tweedy and Wilson both nodded their agreement. 'Seems obvious that it was drugs-related.'

'Chances are he was a supplier for the area,' said Wilson, 'or he may have been a delivery boy.'

'Maybe he was operating a supply route between Liverpool and Sunderland,' said Murray.

Tara didn't disagree with any of this speculation, but what niggled her most was the mystery of Boswell's girlfriend and the possibility that she was the girl who had been seen running through the Treadwater Estate on the night of the murder. So far, none of the people interviewed were even prepared to admit that Carly McHugh had been there when Boswell was murdered. She wondered too if it was mere coincidence that the gun used in the killing had been used previously in Northern Ireland and that Carly McHugh came from there.

'We definitely need to learn more about the Vipers' activities,' Tara said in agreement with her colleagues. 'And I would like to find out how and why a gun used previously in Belfast was used to shoot Boswell.'

'A paramilitary-style shooting, too,' Murray pointed out. 'Is it possible that the Vipers are somehow connected with an organisation in Ireland?'

'Could be the girl is the link between the two,' said Wilson.

'Tara, I'd like you to consult Matrix, and DCI Weir in drugs,' said Tweedy. 'They may have some knowledge of links between Merseyside gangs and those in Belfast. Alan and John, I suggest you look at the recent activities of other gangs on Merseyside. If a gang war is about to start, other gangsters will know.'

'Fine, sir.'

Tweedy's departure from the office prompted the others to return to their desks. Tara instructed Murray to liaise with the guys on the Matrix team regarding Liverpool gangs, while she would contact DCI Weir. She fired off a brief email to the detective, describing her present case and requesting a meeting as soon as possible.

Before leaving for home, she browsed the bulletins posted on the police network and looked at the BBC's news pages online. A couple of weeks back she'd heard of the body of a young woman being recovered from the Irish Sea. At the time she'd thought little of it, save for a passing thought that it might in some way be relevant to her notion that a serial killer was responsible for multiple disappearances of young women around Britain.

The murder of Terry Lawler had first brought the idea to her mind, but so far she'd found no evidence to suggest that the journalist had been right. He had been struggling to find his sister, Ruth, who had gone missing, and during his investigations gathered information on twenty-nine women, including his sister, all of whom had disappeared without trace. Their bodies had never been found, and no one had been identified as a suspect in their supposed abductions. It wasn't even a certainty that all the disappearances were connected.

Lawler was murdered before any of his thinking on the disappeared girls had been made public, or even brought to the attention of the police. Tara was convinced, however, that Terry Lawler had discovered a common thread linking the disappearance of his sister with the disappearances of other women, and that he had reason to believe that one man was responsible for all their deaths. And so, she had retained an interest in this mystery, of why so many young women had disappeared in similar circumstances.

Today, the online news pointed her again towards Lawler's – and her own – theory of the missing women. There had been further cases of women vanishing since Lawler's death.

The bulletin named the woman fished from the sea as Linda Meredith. Tara stared intently at her photograph.

'John,' she called, startling the hefty frame of the detective constable. 'Dig out those photos we recovered from Terry Lawler's flat.'

Wilson rose from his chair, doing as he was told but weary of the request. It wasn't the first time that DI Grogan had gone off on one of her notions regarding this collection of pictures. Her theorising on the missing women seemed to poke its way into every case.

A minute later, Tara had twenty-nine photographs of various shapes, sizes and quality, of the young women scattered over her desk. It took just a few seconds for her to home in on one image. The picture of a teenage girl with dark hair and a bright smile.

'That's her. That's the girl they pulled out of the Irish Sea.'

CHAPTER 19

The following morning, Alan Murray, looking chirpy, brought a report across the office for Tara to read.

'Morning, ma'am. How are you, this fine morning?'

The surprise for Tara was not so much the upbeat voice but the fact that her DS did not have a chocolate bar, doughnut or biscuit in his hand.

'You're looking pleased with yourself. Your numbers come up?'

'I wish!'

Then, Tara clicked to the reason behind Murray's good humour.

'How are things going with Trudy?'

'Brilliant. Saw her last night.'

'And?' She saw the smirk spreading over his face. 'You don't have to tell me if you don't want to.'

'And… I saw her again this morning, if you know what I mean.'

Tara nodded and made a face. In a way she was delighted for him. Divorced by the age of thirty, Murray, since that time, had stumbled through one relationship after another. Trudy Mitchell was the first woman he'd seemed sufficiently proud of to boast about. And she was an older woman too, mid-forties to his forty. Tara had thought it an unlikely pairing; Trudy a television producer and minor celebrity, and Murray a homicide detective. Mitchell had once been part of a bizarre – and highly publicised – ménage à trois with a famous actor and his wife. She'd been a suspect for a time in the Jason and Aeron Collywell case, owing to a past association with a satanic cult. A chequered history, but Tara was hardly the world's expert on romantic affairs. She'd already given Trudy Mitchell the benefit of the doubt and wished only the best for her detective sergeant.

'I do know what you mean, and I don't need you to fill in the details. I take it you didn't just come over to share stories of your sex life with me. What have you got?'

'Police in Sunderland carried out a search of the place they believe is Carly McHugh's flat. Didn't find anything untoward.'

'Any sign of the girl?' Tara asked.

'No. Neighbours say they haven't seen her for more than a week. The flat was rented in her name, rather than Boswell's. She'd been living there for over a year. Looks a fairly swanky place for such a young couple with no apparent source of income.'

He set two A4-size pictures on Tara's desk, one showing the lounge of the flat, the other the exterior of the building. She gazed briefly at the photos. It certainly was a luxury pad – expensive-looking furniture, modern fittings – and the exterior of the building was pristine.

'Unless you count drug dealing,' said Tara.

'Suppose so, but we have no evidence yet. I wonder who the brains of the operation were: McHugh or Boswell?'

'According to Aidan Boswell, Ryan had only been living there for five or six months. So, was this a staging post for Viper activity, or were he and the girl mixed up in something else? I'm going to meet DCI Weir at eleven, see if he can help on the workings of this gang.'

'Ryan's funeral is this afternoon, might be worth popping along to see who's there, paying their respects.'

'Good idea. Take Wilson with you. He's from Treadwater. He might recognise a few characters.'

'Will do.'

Tara read through the report on the search in Sunderland but couldn't help pondering the fate of Carly McHugh. Was she the girl heard screaming on the

Treadwater Estate? Had she been taken by the people who killed Boswell? Was she dead, too? Or had she simply scarpered from her flat in Sunderland? Perhaps she was back in Northern Ireland.

This last idea brought Tara to consider the history of the gun used to kill Boswell, but just as quickly she switched to thinking of Linda Meredith and the investigation begun by Terry Lawler.

* * *

Tara didn't know DCI Malcolm Weir terribly well. She'd seen him at the odd briefing, in attendance at a few murder scenes and passing by in the corridors at St Anne Street. She knew he was a Scot, and a Merseyside policeman for thirty years. He was a contemporary of Harold Tweedy but beyond that the comparison floundered. Weir was round, heavy and round, shirt strained across his belly and his trousers sported an ever-growing collection of coffee stains. He wasn't celebrated for his dress sense; his usual attire was jeans and a faded sweatshirt emblazoned with the image of a 1970s rock band, and he rarely shaved. His once thick and curly hair was now greying and thinning. Even Tara had noticed the change in Weir over the few years she'd spent at St Anne Street, but she was wise enough to know that appearances deceived. Malcolm Weir's main tag was that he did not bear fools gladly or in any other way.

Tara knocked on the windowed door. Weir, head down, gave no response, so she entered anyway. Only then did he raise a hand to stop her. He was in the middle of a phone call, conducted on speakerphone. Embarrassed already, she stepped back outside the door and waited.

Clearly, he didn't hurry himself. Ten minutes passed, and Tara stood waiting. When, finally, she was summoned inside, Weir gave no apology for the delay. Instead, he got right to the point.

'So, you're looking for a rundown on the Vipers?'

'Yes, sir,' she replied, feeling bold enough to take a seat opposite him; a seat he hadn't offered.

Weir, despite his years in Liverpool, had lost none of his Glaswegian accent. At that moment, however, Tara wished she were speaking to someone else. Someone with personality and warmth, or at least with manners.

'Small fry,' he said. 'Mostly confined to north Liverpool. They're into dealing drugs, protection and I heard recently they've attempted to set up a money-laundering operation through a couple of nightclubs. We're working on that at the moment, so I would prefer if you kept that little nugget to yourself, DI Grogan.'

'Yes, sir.' Strange, she thought, his reference to the Vipers as small fry considering Ryan Boswell had been living as far away as Sunderland, apparently working on behalf of the gang.

'Anything else I can help you with?'

Tara was astounded at the DCI's dismissive attitude. He leaned back in his chair, scratching his head vigorously with both hands and stretching. Perhaps, like others Tara knew, he didn't think she looked the part of a DI. Yes, she looked much younger than her age, but her slight frame and lack of height also made her seem weak and vulnerable, unsuited for police work. She decided to take her time, slow this copper down and, hopefully, make him less dismissive of her.

'Our murder victim, Ryan Boswell, had been living in Sunderland. Do you know if the Vipers operate that far afield?'

Weir pursed his lips. He didn't look happy.

'Not as far as I know,' he said curtly.

'What about Belfast?'

'Belfast? You're poking your finger in a lot of pies, DI Grogan.'

She didn't respond to his condescension, merely returned his gaze. He sighed and rubbed his hand across his bristled chin.

'Do you have something specific in relation to Belfast?'

'The gun used to kill Boswell had been used previously in a Belfast shooting, eighteen months ago. Boswell's girlfriend, who was living with him in Sunderland, has disappeared. She hails from Northern Ireland. I'm wondering if the connections between Belfast and Liverpool are relevant.'

'We try to keep tabs on the activities of the various gangs in this city, but it is not an exact science. You could say that Liverpool is central to a lot of the drug dealing that goes on in the North of England and for that matter in Scotland and Ireland too. Stuff comes in and stuff goes out. It's a port, for goodness' sake.'

'So, it is possible that Ryan Boswell acted as a courier, transporting drugs from Liverpool to Sunderland and perhaps he also had links to Belfast?'

'I suppose so. But as I've said, the Vipers are small players. Mostly kids. It's the big boys we need to worry about. They're the guys with the connections.'

'Thank you, sir, you've been very helpful.'

Weir didn't respond as Tara rose from the chair. Then as she opened the door, he made a request which came across as a combination of order and threat.

'DI Grogan, I want to know of your progress in this case. I want to know if you're about to go snooping into organised crime franchises. We have investigations ongoing, some of them undercover. I don't want any of our work compromised, understand? You need to OK it with me before you pull anyone in, is that clear?'

'Perfectly, sir.'

She closed the door and walked briskly back to her office. She was fuming at Weir's attitude, but she was also certain of one thing. She would clear her proposed activities with her boss, Harold Tweedy. He could decide what DCI Weir needed to know. She was investigating a case of murder. That fact was sufficient to override DCI

Weir's requests. There was no way she was involving the unpleasant man any further in her work.

CHAPTER 20

Kirsty has started acting very strange with me, and it's pissing me off. I think she is still suspicious of what I get up to when I go out. We've hardly spoken, and certainly done nothing in bed, for more than a week.

I'm getting stressed. To keep myself sane I've continued my surveillance of Daisy. She lives at Stockbridge Village, in Knowsley. It's not the kind of place that would make for an easy snatch, too many houses close together. Too great a chance of someone noticing me hanging around. So, I've had to find out what she does during the day, where she works. It took me a few days but I managed to track her one morning walking to the bus stop. I followed the bus in my delivery van, and luckily, she got off when I was still trailing it. She works in a bank in West Derby. Now I have to suss out her routine on weekdays and at weekends, so I can decide the best time and place to take her.

My real worry is that I shouldn't be doing this. Not in this city. I should be looking for a girl much further away. I've taken far too many women in and around Liverpool. A smart cop like DI Grogan might put the proverbial twos together and my name might creep into the conversation. But I can't afford for Kirsty to get any more suspicious of me and travelling to some other town would take up too much time. My job allows me to find all these beautiful girls, so I'm not going to ignore the opportunity, especially when I'm getting nothing from Kirsty.

Seeing Tara down by the Albert Dock set me thinking again. I know she likes to run, and I know where she goes running. Really, I should get my act together once and for all and have another crack at her. But if she ever went missing the entire police force in Liverpool would come looking for me. I'm the one with the previous for taking her. I'd be their number one suspect.

For now, I suppose, wee Tara is safe from me.

Last night, though, my whole world was rocked. I couldn't take much more of Kirsty's moodiness and me thinking she was growing very distrustful of me, so I tackled her about it.

'What's the matter with you?' I asked. We were out shopping for new clothes. I went with her, thinking it would help cheer her up, show her I was still interested in her and that I loved her. 'You've hardly said a word since we came out. Have I done something wrong?'

Suddenly, big tears welled in her eyes. She does have lovely eyes. She squeezed my hand and sort of smiled.

'What's wrong, Kirsty?'

'I'm pregnant,' she said.

CHAPTER 21

In the late afternoon, Murray and Wilson returned from the funeral of Ryan Boswell. Murray went to the canteen for some food, but Wilson headed over to Tara's desk.

'How did it go, John?'

'Big funeral, as you might expect, although I would say there were as many there to say good riddance as to pay respects.'

'Anything suspicious?'

'Plenty of Vipers there. Six as pallbearers. A couple of guys that I didn't recognise from around the estate, but they seemed to be well acquainted with Tyler Finlay.'

'Description?'

'Probably in their fifties. One tall, around six foot, white, short hair; the other stocky and bald. Both smoked fags, and they were casually dressed in jeans and anoraks.'

'Did you hear them speak?'

Wilson shook his head.

'Didn't get that close, ma'am. But Murray got a picture on his phone.'

A couple of minutes later, Murray strode in, a coffee in one hand, a pack of sandwiches in the other. He tossed the package to Wilson.

'Egg and cress, all they had left.'

'Gee, thanks,' said Wilson, looking disappointed.

'John said that you got a picture of two suspicious characters,' Tara said.

'Yes, ma'am. Same two guys we saw the other day at the shops.'

'Do they look familiar?'

'How do you mean?'

'I'm wondering if they're undercover cops. Part of DCI Weir's team.'

'I certainly didn't recognise them, but I suppose they could be.'

'If they're not undercover guys then perhaps they're from out of town. I'm thinking of Belfast. That's where the murder weapon came from.'

* * *

Tara had brought a change of clothes to work, which was just as well since she didn't have time to get home before meeting up with Kate and Aisling for dinner. She slipped into a pair of shiny black leggings, a flowery-patterned tunic and a pair of silver strappy heels. Before leaving the station, she brushed her hair and did her make-up. Tonight was going to be a novel night out with the girls. For the first time in years, at least since before Tara's student days at Oxford, all three of them were officially single at the same time. They had been close friends since their school days on the Wirral, staying in contact through Tara's years in Oxford and Kate's training to be a nurse.

While Tara had a trail of quite disastrous relationships behind her, Aisling had focused on the hunt for a rich and handsome partner, with less than moderate success. She had just dumped her most recent flame, a banker named Kevin. For the past seven years, Kate seemed to have been in a settled and lasting partnership with Adam. Both worked at the Royal Liverpool Hospital, Kate as a cardiac nurse and Adam as a doctor in accident and emergency. They had a baby daughter, Adele. But recently their relationship had floundered, both blaming shift work and a lack of meaningful time spent in each other's company. So, they had agreed to part ways in fairly amicable fashion, both determined to protect Adele from any real upset.

This evening was a mark of their close friendship, with Tara and Aisling eager to show their love and support for Kate. They gathered in a bar in the city centre. The bar was busy and had a lively atmosphere, the kind of place to let your hair down.

'Here's to the future, without men,' said Aisling.

The other two were well used to such sweeping statements and knew that Aisling didn't mean a word of them. All three gulped down their shots.

'I like the hair,' said Tara. Kate was prone to changing her hair style and colour at a moment's notice – or indeed without any notice whatsoever.

'I thought I would mark my separation with something other than tears,' Kate replied, touching her platinum-blonde locks. 'Another toast,' she said, raising her glass. 'To L'Oréal, Garnier and all the great hair colours of the world!'

Six more glasses were set in front of them, two for each woman, one containing Baileys, the other lime juice. The idea was to hold the Baileys in the mouth then swill it with the lime juice before swallowing. The name of this charming cocktail was quite appropriate: Woman's Revenge.

'To the three of us,' said Aisling. 'May we always be up for having a laugh together.'

Tara drank the Baileys and added the lime juice before swallowing.

'Ugh! Glad we did that one before we get *really* drunk,' she said.

As the night flashed by, the shots were ever more daring, the toasts more ridiculous and the fun more hilarious. The women exchanged ever-wilder stories, opinions and anecdotes about their dealings with men. Kate had only her recent experience with Adam to offer, while Aisling spoke of the failings of one rich boyfriend after another, and Tara exorcised the remains of her tragic encounters with Callum Armour and her first real love, Simon, the man who ended their relationship on the day they ended their student lives at Oxford.

When the night air hit them none of the girls was capable of much. Given their sudden craving for food, they decided to take a detour to the kebab shop – although Kate managed to throw up before they reached it.

Despite her drunken state, and their disarray in trying to arrange a taxi home, Tara was struck by a peculiar feeling. As they waited for their taxi to arrive, she felt on edge, unsafe. She had company, but she didn't feel secure.

She glanced around the street. A few people were making their way home or going to nightclubs, but still she was spooked. Something wasn't right in this street scene and Tara felt uneasy.

That unease rose to fear when she noticed him. Hands in anorak pockets, he leaned against a shop window on the other side of the street. And he was looking right at her.

She even glanced over her shoulder, hoping that maybe he was looking at someone else. No. When he realised that she had noticed him, he casually walked away and was soon out of sight.

CHAPTER 22

I'm going to be a good boy from now on. No more women, except maybe the odd wee peek at Tara Grogan, but I've already dropped my plans for Daisy. Such a lovely girl is going to have to do without my attention. I'm sure she will cope.

Kirsty seemed relieved when she saw that I was delighted with her news. I'm going to be a da. Me!

'Are you sure you're all right with this?' she asked me, in bed.

I kissed her on the forehead and gave her a squeeze.

'Couldn't be happier,' I said.

'I'm so happy too. I love you so much, James. You'll be a brilliant dad.'

'Why do you say that?'

'I just know you'll take good care of him – or her.'

'Have you told your parents?'

'Not yet. I've been so worried about telling you, and I thought you should be the first to know. I'll go see them in the morning.'

I nearly asked her if she was sure the kid was mine, but I realised it had to be. We'd done it so many times since I moved in with her, she wouldn't have had an opportunity to do it with anyone else. Instead, I popped the question. Sort of.

'We could get married if you like. Before it's born.'

She smiled, but tears came at the same time.

'We don't have to. I'm not trying to trap you.'

'I know that. I just thought it would be nice, that's all.'

She sprang up and sat, gazing hopefully into my eyes. I suppose she was trying to convince herself I was being serious.

'Do you really mean that?'

'Of course, I do. I love you to bits, Kirsty.'

'Oh, James, I'm so happy. I don't deserve you!'

She threw her arms around me and kissed me on the mouth. Before I knew it, we were doing the business or, I should say, she was doing the business to me.

Sweet.

So now I'm on the straight and narrow. This is a new start for me, and I'm not feeling the urge to go chasing after any other women.

I'm a settled man.

CHAPTER 23

Tara knocked on the door, but this time, without invitation, she barged straight in.

'Why have your men been following me?'

'DI Grogan, good morning. What can I do for you?'

'Last night. I was out with friends and a man followed us from a club to a kebab shop. Was he one of yours?'

Weir had a bemused smirk on his face, a look that said he was about to enjoy this confrontation. But first, he reminded Tara of something.

'DI Grogan, please remember who you are talking to.'

She didn't look the part, certainly not this morning. Hastily dressed in T-shirt and jeans, and her hair still wet from her shower, she looked dishevelled. Weir's reprimand stopped her in her tracks.

'Sir, I would like to know why you are having me followed.'

'Firstly, DI Grogan, I haven't the faintest idea what you're talking about, and secondly, I don't take kindly to officers, particularly those junior in rank, accusing me of all sorts. If you've nothing more to say I suggest you get out and do something useful.'

Tara could see that DCI Weir would not be the type to admit to anything, even if he was in the wrong. With a pounding headache and a delicate stomach, she could not think of anything more to support her accusation. She could be wrong, but she didn't think so. Without a word, she closed the door behind her and went quickly to her desk. Weir would be the type to take things further and she braced herself to expect a dressing-down from Tweedy.

When Murray entered the office, she told him about her being watched and her squabble with DCI Weir.

'You certainly don't pull your punches, Tara.'

She glared at him, fuming. 'It's ma'am to you, and no I wasn't going to let it pass. If Weir is having me followed, I want to know what he's up to.'

'Did you recognise the bloke who was watching you as a cop, ma'am?'

'Not as a police officer, no. It was the taller of the two men we saw on Treadwater, and you photographed at the funeral. It's very strange that the day I speak with Weir, that same night there he is watching me.'

'Have you told Tweedy?'

'Not yet. Not sure that I should. Besides, he may well hear it soon enough from Weir.'

'What if these men are not undercover police but are connected to the gang on Treadwater? They don't like us getting too close.'

'You think we should have another word with Tyler Finlay? If those guys we saw aren't Vipers maybe he can tell us who they are.'

'I doubt he would be willing to tell us much. The one thing these gangs hate more than bizzies is a grass.'

* * *

Finlay lived in a third-floor flat in the heart of the Treadwater Estate. On a road that skirted around the park, there were six three-storey blocks standing line astern such that the outlook for residents in one flat was to look at the rear of the building next to it. Tara always felt uneasy in this area. For one thing, it was the spot associated most with anti-social behaviour on the estate. Crowds of kids gathered in the evening, bored, with nothing else to do but get up to mischief, be it drugs, glue, throwing stones at passing cars, racing stolen cars along the road or getting drunk.

Several bangs on the door of a third-floor flat, courtesy of Murray's fist, were required before anyone answered. Eventually, it opened just enough for a face to peer out.

'Hello, Shania,' said Tara, smiling at the face peering around the crack. 'We're here to speak with Tyler, if he's around?'

The girl didn't speak, merely stepped away from the door, swinging it open for Tara and Murray to enter. Barefoot, she wore a pale pink T-shirt-style nightdress, and her hair was braided. They followed her inside to the living room, which was pungent with the smell of smoke – not that of cigarettes, but the stench of weed. Finlay was sprawled on the sofa wearing only a pair of red football shorts and watching a noisy action movie on television. He didn't seem in the least perturbed that the police had just entered his home.

'Bizzies? What can I do for you?'

Murray took up a spot between Finlay and the television, ensuring they had his full attention. Tara handed Finlay a sheet with a printed photograph. She noticed his well-toned body; he was a man obviously proud of his six-pack. So, evidently, he did do something more than lie around on his sofa all day. She couldn't fail to notice the array of tattoos, including the one of a snake on his left arm.

'Do you recognise these men?' she asked.

He glanced at the sheet then tossed it on the sofa beside him.

'Should I?'

'They've been seen on the estate in the last few days. They attended Ryan Boswell's funeral.'

'Just paying their respects, I suppose.'

'Do you know who they are?'

'Nope.'

'Are they Vipers?'

'Give us a break, will ya? Just told you, I don't know them.'

Murray began sniffing the air, his gestures exaggerated for the benefit of Finlay.

'What's that I smell?'

'All right, all right!' Finlay sat upright. 'Like I said, I don't know them. They're from Belfast. They have some connection to Ryan's girl. That's all I know.'

From the man's reaction, Tara judged that he was frightened, and not of Murray's threat to have him for possession of weed. He seemed nervous to be talking of these two men at all; it was as if they held some sway over him.

'Names?' she asked.

'I told you I don't know them, now back off, will ya?'

'Why are they here in Treadwater? Ryan's girlfriend lives in Sunderland.'

'Came to the funeral, that's all.'

'Were they here the night Ryan was shot?'

'I don't know. Go ask them yourself.'

'There's that smell again. Definitely getting stronger,' said Murray, with several more sniffs.

'Fuck sake, leave me alone, will ya? I've told you all I know.'

Tara widened her eyes, waiting for Finlay to relent. He was very agitated, and his shouting brought Shania to the door of the living room. Murray had begun to look about pretending to search for drugs.

'You won't find anything, cop. Now leave me alone.'

'Where are they staying, Tyler?' Tara asked.

The young man shook his head.

'Was Carly McHugh here in Treadwater when Ryan was shot?'

Murray dialled a number on his mobile.

'Can you get a Matrix team out here, now? Drugs bust. It's flat… what number is this flat, Tyler?'

'OK, OK. Back off, will ya?'

'Hold on a sec,' said Murray into the phone.

'Some guys *were* here the night Boswell was killed.'

'And Ryan's girl?'

'She was here too.'

'What happened to her?'

He shrugged.

'She disappeared. That's all I know.'

CHAPTER 24

Tara and Aisling spent the evening at Kate's apartment in Canning Street. Adam had now moved out and her friends wanted to be there, to support Kate and her daughter. Unlike the previous evening when the drink had flowed, they'd blown away some cobwebs and Kate had found some closure to her relationship, this evening was more relaxed. All three still felt the effects of their binge and, with the consumption of coffee and cakes, their evening took on a more sober air. The mood also resulted in an earlier than usual end to their get-together.

Tara gave Aisling a lift home to Wapping Dock, since the two women had separate flats in the same complex. As they strolled towards the main door of the building, Tara caught sight of a car parked near the entrance. It was sitting in the middle of the forecourt and not in a designated space. At first, she thought nothing of it, but suddenly, with visions of the last two days flashing through her head, she took a second glance at the vehicle. She was looking at it from the rear, a Vauxhall Corsa, dark metallic blue. It was difficult to be sure, but there seemed to be just one person sitting inside. Waiting for someone, she thought, or waiting for her?

Aisling was nattering away about a dress she was intending to buy when Tara suddenly left her side.

'Tara?'

Tara marched towards the car as Aisling stood watching.

'What's wrong, Tara love?'

An engine roared violently. Tara reached the driver's door just as the car sped off, its wheels spinning on the smooth concrete of the covered parking area. She'd caught the driver off guard, but as she was about to knock on the window he'd managed to escape. Still, she couldn't be sure who he was. One of the Vipers from the estate, one of Weir's officers or was it James Guy? She shivered as she saw the car make the exit and speed away into the quiet road of late evening. Aisling was rooted to the spot.

'What was that all about?' she asked.

Tara shook her head and took her friend's arm.

'Nothing. I was just going to tell them they couldn't park there, and they sped off.'

* * *

Tara double-checked the lock on her front door before going to her bedroom. If her exhaustion took over, then she might sleep. If not, then she would be awake half the night wondering who was keeping tabs on her life. They knew where she lived, they'd followed her on a night out with Kate and Aisling – they were taking an unhealthy interest in her activities. Surely, after her accusing DCI Weir of having her followed, he would not have continued with his prank, not now she was aware of it? So, if not Weir, then who was watching her? She'd seen James Guy a few nights ago close to the Albert Dock. Had he been waiting for her, or was it pure coincidence?

And why had she seen someone watching her in the days since Ryan Boswell had been murdered?

* * *

Harold Tweedy had left a note on her desk, asking to speak with her first thing. Her shoulders sagged in despair, knowing what was coming. Obviously, DCI Weir had bent the superintendent's ear regarding her outburst. All seemed clear when she reached Tweedy's office and saw the bulky frame of the DCI perched on a chair and chatting to her boss.

'Ah, good morning, Tara,' said Tweedy in his usual mannerly tone.

'Morning, sir.'

'DI Grogan,' said Weir, more in acknowledgement than as a greeting.

'Sir.'

'Please take a seat, Tara. Malcolm and I have just been discussing your case.'

She felt the hairs rise on her neck and couldn't bring herself to look at the DCI sitting next to her. Convinced that Tweedy already knew of her having confronted Weir, she awaited the reprimand.

'I gather you met with Tyler Finlay yesterday, DI Grogan?' said Weir.

He sounded as though he were interviewing a suspect in a case, rather than speaking with a colleague. How did he know she'd spoken to Finlay? She hadn't even told

Tweedy yet. Perhaps he'd spoken to Murray. Both men seemed to be waiting for a reply.

'Yes, sir, we did.' She looked at Tweedy, hopeful of some guidance in dealing with this unpleasant detective.

'What did you find out?'

Again, she looked at Tweedy, but he remained oblivious to her predicament. She turned back to Weir.

'May I ask why you're interested, sir?'

The fat, unshaven face seemed to baulk at the question.

'It may have a bearing, DI Grogan, on one of my operations. I did ask you to keep me informed of who you spoke to up in Treadwater, particularly members of the Vipers.'

'I was trying to identify the men seen by Wilson and Murray at Ryan Boswell's funeral. I was also trying to find out what has happened to Boswell's girlfriend.'

'And what did Finlay tell you?'

'It seems that a number of men from Belfast were in Treadwater on the night Boswell was shot. Carly McHugh was also present and, according to Finlay, she has since disappeared.'

'Is that it?'

Tara couldn't help a cold stare at Weir.

'Yes,' was all she could manage in reply.

'Is that of some use to you, Malcolm?' Tweedy asked.

'Not a lot.'

Tara was irritated by the man's derisory attitude and the increasing reek of his body odour.

'But maybe I can help you,' said Weir.

Doubt it, thought Tara, unless you're about to leave the room.

'How so?' Tweedy asked.

'If Carly McHugh has made her way back to Belfast, then I can arrange to have her lifted, and the wee lass here can go and have a chat with her.'

'What do you think, Tara?'

With a quick response in order, she had to let the 'wee lass' reference slide and answer the question.

'It would be helpful, sir. Carly McHugh must know something of what happened on the night Boswell was killed.'

'Right then, you can make arrangements to travel to Belfast. And DCI Weir can arrange with his contacts in the PSNI to have the girl arrested.'

CHAPTER 25

Kirsty is thrilled to bits, dear love her, but she's doing my friggin' head in.

As soon as the M-word was decided upon, she's off to her mother's, and now they're planning a big do. Church wedding, reception at a hotel and a bloody honeymoon in Cyprus. At first I thought, this is easy. We don't have the money for all of that, but it turns out that her parents always had money put away for this very occasion. What can I do? I have to go along with it. The church and the hotel have already been booked. Kirsty has an aunt who owns an apartment in Cyprus, and she has given it to us for two weeks, free of charge. Just have to pay for flights. I've never seen anyone look as happy as Kirsty and her ma. And then there's all this baby talk. The wedding is going to happen when Kirsty is about five months gone, but now they're discussing the right buggy to buy and the best car seat. Only time there's a break in the conversation is when she's throwing up in the toilet.

Mel is going to be her bridesmaid, plus one of Kirsty's cousins. I've seen her at Kirsty's parents' house. Lovely wee arse, dead slim and blonde hair down to her waist, she's gorgeous but needs to get rid of the acne. She could easily become one of my chosen ones if I was still thinking that way, but I'm trying my best to be a good boy. The thing that pushed me closer to the edge was the suggestion Kirsty made yesterday morning after she'd boked in the sink.

'We'll have to think about moving, honey,' she said, wiping her mouth with kitchen roll. Honey, she calls me now. That started the minute I put the ring on her finger.

'Oh, you don't have to bother with a ring,' she had said. But I reckoned I should do things right, so I bought her a solitaire diamond. She loved it.

'Thank you so much, honey.' And that's what she's tagged me with ever since. I'm her honey.

The moving house scares me though. It really ties me down. My only hope is that I will be refused a mortgage. Of course, she has said that she has enough money to get one in her name. Bloody lovely. Seems she's already got our whole life mapped out.

I'm really trying not to get tempted by other women. I've stopped following Daisy, and I haven't sought out any new totty. But the other day, in the middle of all the discussion and planning and phone calls and online booking for photographers, florists and wedding cars, I just couldn't take any more. Kirsty and Mum – I have to call Jenn Mum now I'm part of the family – were debating colours for bridesmaids' dresses and in doing so had to discuss the wedding dress, too. I was asked to leave the room because I'm not supposed to know any of this stuff. Jenn told me to go and make a list of the people I wanted to invite to the wedding. That wasn't going to take long. Just me. I've no relatives that I keep in contact with, and I don't have any friends.

I took myself out for a drive. Didn't take long to end up down by Wapping Dock and Tara's place. I managed to get my car inside her parking area, but then I nearly got caught by Tara herself. I didn't notice her coming in, and suddenly I see in my wing mirror this girl stomping toward me. Scared the shit out of me. I started the car and got the fuck out of there. Don't think she recognised me. And it was Kirsty's car, so she wouldn't have recognised that. The whole episode has started me off again. A couple of days later, I was out on early morning deliveries, and I spied Tara leaving her place in her car. OK, I admit it; I had been sitting waiting in hope of seeing her. She was probably on her way to the cop shop, but I followed her anyway. Didn't take long to realise she wasn't headed for the police station at St Anne Street. She turned onto the main road heading south. I followed. She wouldn't think anything of a delivery van sitting behind her in the traffic. We'd only gone a couple of miles when I got the feeling that she was headed to the airport.

Sure as hell, a while later, I watched her pull into one of the long stay car parks. I found a service area where I could leave my van and kept an eye out for her by the entrance to the terminal building. A few minutes later, she walked into departures. I gave her a couple of seconds and followed her inside. She was dressed in a dark skirt, jacket and black tights with mid-heel shoes, and she wheeled a small suitcase behind her. Only a small suitcase, by the look of things she wasn't travelling far. No sign either of her mates, so I didn't think she was off on a holiday. Seemed more like a business trip.

Keeping a fair distance between us, I tailed her across the concourse until she joined the queue for EasyJet. I saw she was checking in for a flight to Belfast. Why there? What business did she have in Belfast?

Then it suddenly hit me. Millie. My first girl and the one they'd fished out of the sea. What did Tara know about that? Did she know about me? Why else would she be going to Belfast?

Shit.

CHAPTER 26

Tara caught a taxi from Belfast International and twenty-five minutes later entered the city centre PSNI complex at Musgrave Street. Many of the province's police stations remained behind high walls and security gates, memorials to the troubled years; Musgrave, despite having been modernised, was a fine example of the type. Tara's contact for the visit was DS Rory Ferguson, a handsome man of thirty-five with a fair complexion.

'Pleased to meet you, DI Grogan. Is this your first time in Belfast?' He led her along a corridor and into a seminar room. There was a long pine table surrounded by a dozen metal-framed chairs. On the wall at one end, a screen was already illuminated by the light from a projector that was connected to a laptop sitting on the table.

'It is, yes,' she replied, slipping the strap of her handbag off her shoulder.

'Take a seat, ma'am. I've organised some coffee, or perhaps you'd prefer tea?'

'Coffee is fine, thank you.'

She couldn't help thinking that he was a nice guy. A pleasant manner and a firm-looking body. Before she floated off to thoughts inappropriate, she noticed the wedding ring – which quickly doused any notions forming in her head.

Ferguson sat down opposite her and typed his password into the laptop.

'DCI Weir filled me in on the background to your case, so I thought I should begin by telling you where *we* are at the moment.'

She wondered exactly what DCI Weir had told Ferguson about her. Nothing complimentary, she reckoned. Ferguson clicked the mouse several times, and the image of a man appeared on the screen.

'This is Jim Hobbs, goes by the nickname Fitter. So called because that was his trade when he worked in the shipyard, years ago.'

Tara didn't need to study the picture. A tall, muscular man with short hair. Aged about fifty, she guessed, and the man she'd first seen on the Treadwater Estate and then in the city on the night she'd been out with her friends. Fitter Hobbs was the man who'd been watching her, and, of course, it was now confirmed that he was not one of DCI Weir's undercover officers.

Another image replaced that of Fitter, filling the screen. An older male, a broad and sturdy build, dressed in a red, green and black football shirt that she didn't recognise. He had a shaven head – and a cocky smile.

'And this is Rab McHugh. Father of Carly. You'll meet her later. Do you recognise either of these men?'

'Yes, both of them.'

'The guys you came across in Liverpool?'

Tara nodded her head. DCI Weir, she noted, had passed on that piece of information.

'What do these men do?' she asked.

'Ah, that is the question. Or rather, what do they not do? These chaps are at the head of a gang, supposedly an off-shoot of a loyalist paramilitary group, although there is a suspicion that they operate well inside the main organisation under the guise of community workers. The "gang with no name" – as we call it – runs drugs, they extort money, they operate money-lending scams, betting scams, prostitutes, illegal fuel, booze and ciggies and they own a couple of "nice" drinking establishments.'

At that point a young man, smartly dressed in grey shirt and striped tie, carried a tray of coffee and scones into the room, and Ferguson paused his briefing. He poured coffee into two mugs and invited Tara to help herself to the scones. After an early morning start, she was feeling hungry.

'And how does Carly McHugh feature in this gang?' she asked.

'Daddy's little helper.'

'Any idea why she was living in Sunderland?'

'Malcolm didn't tell you?'

This felt awkward. She disliked DCI Weir intensely, but Rory Ferguson seemed well acquainted with his Liverpool counterpart. How did it look that she, the wee lass, hadn't been properly briefed before leaving St Anne Street? She managed only a single shake of her head. Ferguson smiled, and his gaze lingered on her for more than a few moments. She smiled back, and it sparked him into action once again.

'Right. Well, Fitter and McHugh's drug running activities, we believe, branch out from Belfast through Scotland, the North East of England and south as far as Manchester and Liverpool. The reason why these Belfast gangs, both loyalist and republican, are so successful in running drugs and other smuggling operations is because they've had years of experience in doing just that during the Troubles, under intense security. They've mastered all the tricks of the trade, they're very good at what they do. What we believe is that drugs, or illicit booze or cigarettes, enter the UK through any of our ports, particularly Belfast, Liverpool and then, of course, the Channel ports. Distribution is through these networks in Liverpool, Manchester, Belfast, Glasgow and Sunderland. We reckon that Carly was managing the Sunderland branch on Daddy's behalf.'

'She acted as a dealer?'

'Not so much at street level, we don't think. She was more an organiser of supplies coming through Sunderland. Like a shipping agent for moving the drugs or booze, rather than selling direct to users.'

'Which explains why police in Sunderland didn't find any drugs in Carly's flat.'

'Mmm. I would say she and her da are very careful to keep their distance from the merchandise. What we don't know is the nature of the relationship between Carly and this Boswell lad who got himself shot. Was it just business? Was he a street dealer or a courier? Were they romantically involved? I suppose that's why you're here. Remember, ma'am, this is all supposition on our part; we don't yet have the evidence to convict any of these characters. That's why we, and DCI Weir, of course, have some undercover operations in place. We must be very careful not to expose our investigations. But I can tell you for nothing that McHugh and Hobbs are nasty pieces of work. Both have impressive histories.'

'Thanks for the background, DS Ferguson.'

'No problem, ma'am. How long are you staying in Belfast?'

'Just overnight, assuming all goes well in talking with Carly.'

Ferguson grimaced.

'Don't expect too much. She's only a kid, but she has her da's genes. I reckon she'd cut your throat as quick as look at you.'

He shut down the computer and rose from his chair.

'Right,' he said, 'as far as I know Carly is already here. We can have a chat with her before her da hears about it and sends in his solicitor to stir up trouble.'

Ferguson led Tara back along the corridor and down two flights of stairs where he checked with an officer at a desk which room held Carly McHugh. Just before entering, he stopped and spoke quietly.

'I was thinking, ma'am, if you've no plans for this evening I could give you a quick tour of the city. We can have a bite to eat, and you can ask me any questions you still might have on the case?'

'That would be great, thank you. It's very kind.' She smiled, thinking how much she enjoyed hearing his Belfast accent. He returned her smile, and she noted his half-wink.

'No problem.'

They entered an interview room, where Carly McHugh sat behind a table, her arms folded defensively, her expression unhappy. She had a cute face, Tara thought, with long black hair neatly styled and brushed, dark eyes with liner and mascara, a pale but clear complexion and a small upturned nose. She was dressed in a royal blue V-necked jumper and skinny jeans with white trainers. Her demeanour, despite her good looks, was of pent-up aggression, hostility and a healthy dose of cockiness.

'Morning, Carly, how's it going?' said Ferguson, as he indicated for Tara to sit at the table.

'All right, Fergie?' the girl replied in a bellicose voice. 'You're in for it when my da hears you've pulled me in.'

'Calm your flaps, Carly. Nobody said you've done anything wrong. We just want to have a wee chat. This is Detective Inspector Grogan of the Merseyside Police. She wants to ask you a few questions.'

Carly smirked like a school kid, seemingly amused by the sight of the young woman before her.

'Nice to meet you, Carly.'

'How's it going?'

Ferguson started a voice and video recorder before Tara put her first question to the girl.

'Carly, can you tell me what you were doing on the Treadwater Estate in Liverpool on Saturday, 15 April?'

The girl remained with arms folded, her legs outstretched, and her feet crossed beneath the table. She glared at Tara.

'Wasn't there. Never heard of the place.'

'Ryan Boswell was a friend of yours, isn't that correct?'

The girl shrugged.

'You shared a flat together in Sunderland?'

'Don't know what you're talking about.'

'Was he your boyfriend?'

Another shrug and she re-crossed her feet.

'On Saturday, 15 April, Ryan was shot and killed on the Treadwater Estate. What do you know about that?'

There was no response; the girl remained steely calm.

'The gun used to kill Ryan had been used before, to shoot someone in Belfast. What can you tell me about this gun?'

This prompted a snigger, and Tara realised that this young woman, despite her age, was well versed in handling police interrogation.

She continued. 'I have a witness who claims that you were in Treadwater on 15 April and another who saw you running through the streets late that night, apparently being chased by someone. Have you anything to say about that?'

'Nope.' She looked at DS Ferguson. 'Can I go now, Fergie?'

Ferguson glanced at Tara, no doubt wondering if the Liverpool detective had anything to say that might prise something from this irascible girl. Tara decided to have one last attempt. She'd hoped for more co-operation from Carly McHugh, particularly if she had cared for Ryan Boswell.

'Do you know, Carly, your boyfriend bled to death that night? He might have survived if someone had called an ambulance and tried to help him.'

Carly's eyes widened; they glanced at Tara then quickly retreated to the floor. But Tara had noted the reaction. She hoped that she had stirred something.

'He was only nineteen. His whole life ahead of him. Needlessly killed, don't you think?'

Carly's gaze remained fixed upon the floor.

'Did you love him, Carly?'

She jumped to her feet, startling both officers.

'Can I go now? I've answered all your questions. Done nothing wrong. I've stuff to do.'

'Are you going back to Sunderland, Carly? To the flat you shared with Ryan?'

'What are you? A bloody social worker? You're wasting your time, love, trying to get something out of me. Piss off home to Liverpool and leave me alone.'

CHAPTER 27

Suddenly, I'm as horny as fuck. Could hardly get my day in, driving around dumping groceries in houses. I looked forward to getting home, to Kirsty, to going to bed early and doing the business with her. But, wouldn't you know, as soon as I walked in the door there she was, puking in the bathroom, and when she came out, she went straight back to writing wedding invitations. Just great.

'I'm away out,' I said.

'Where are you going? I need to talk to you about the menu for the reception.'

I slammed the door behind me. What the hell am I getting into? Can't take much more of this.

By the time I'd driven around for a while, I'd started to cool down. I knew it wasn't Kirsty's fault. She's pregnant, and she's excited about the wedding. That's not what is bothering me. I'm worried about what Tara Grogan is up to in Belfast. It was clear she wasn't going for a nice wee city break. She was dressed in her work clothes, and her mates weren't with her. I can't help thinking that she has an interest in Millie, and if so, has she connected her to me?

Don't know if it was deliberate, or if I did it automatically, but I found myself driving out by Stockbridge. When I realised the significance of where I'd ended up, I parked the car and went for a walk. It was a pissing awful night, the wind howling and rain coming down in sheets, and I'd only a light jacket on me, but I soon ended up in the street where Daisy lives. Couldn't help myself. I strolled by her window several times hoping for a glimpse of her, but although a light was on in the living room, the blinds were closed. That was enough. I was back on a mission. Until I could relax over what Tara was up to, I had to have something to occupy my time. To take my mind off it. And while Kirsty and her ma were so busy planning the rest of my life, I decided to do some planning of my own.

I would have a go at Daisy.

CHAPTER 28

In the late afternoon, DS Ferguson drove Tara around the city centre, pointing out places of interest, explaining the history, both ancient and modern, of Belfast. Tara was impressed by his knowledge and was struck also by his lack of prejudice, his disinclination to favour one side or the other, even though the political divide was clearly still in existence. Tara had only a cursory knowledge of such topics, which were mentioned at times by her mother, whose family came from Dublin originally.

An hour later, after returning his car to Musgrave station, they went on foot to a restaurant close to the City Hall.

'What did you make of Carly?' he asked as they ate their starters. Tara had chosen seared scallops and Ferguson spicy prawns.

'She's definitely angry about something. I've no doubt that she was the girl seen running through Treadwater on the night Boswell was killed. Whether she had witnessed the shooting or had anything to do with it is another matter. I do think that she cared for him. Her reaction, when I told her that he might have survived if he'd received treatment, was a giveaway.'

'Do you know what they were doing in Liverpool that night?'

'Not yet, but I'm assuming for now that they were attending a birthday party for Ryan's brother, Aidan. That's been denied by the girlfriend of Tyler Finlay, but it seems to me that it was the reason for Boswell to be in Treadwater on 15 April. Whether it was the only reason, remains to be seen.'

'Maybe Boswell had stepped out of line with those who run things in his gang. The birthday party was a ruse to bring him to Liverpool.'

'Perhaps, but who was his boss? Someone in the Vipers, or your Mr McHugh? And there remains the possibility that the killing is part of a gang feud confined to Liverpool or even Sunderland, and is not connected to Belfast at all.'

'What does Malcolm Weir make of it?'

'Hasn't said much, but his view is that the Vipers are a small-time gang. Truth is, he doesn't seem bothered by the killing. He is more concerned that I don't compromise any of his investigations.'

'Do I take it that you and Weir don't get along?'

Tara blushed. She hated the idea of admitting that she did not have respect for a colleague. When it came down to it, they were all trying to do a job in whatever way they could.

'I haven't had many dealings with him,' she replied, hopefully laying the subject to rest.

'He's been over here a few times. Seemed decent enough.'

She had to change the subject. Even though the man was on the other side of the Irish Sea, Weir was spoiling her appetite.

'I was wondering if you could help me on another matter, unofficially that is.'

'What's that?'

'The body of the girl retrieved from the Irish Sea recently, it's been on the national news.'

'Linda Meredith?'

'Yes. Would it be possible to speak with the officer in charge of the case?'

'Wallace Brown. I'm sure I can arrange it.' He pulled his mobile from his jacket pocket and began texting. 'What's your interest?'

Tara explained the background: she told him of the murdered journalist Terry Lawler, how he had been searching for his sister and apparently had connected a host of similar disappearances.

'I have a collection of photographs of missing women, photographs taken from Lawler's flat. We've identified most of them, one is Linda Meredith. It might be nothing at all, or simply that Lawler had been comparing each of the disappearances, but I was thinking there may be a chance that one individual is responsible for all of them.'

'Jeepers, how many women are we talking about?'

'We have names for twenty-four of the twenty-nine pictures found at Lawler's flat.'

Ferguson puffed air through his cheeks.

'I think Wallace will be very keen to talk to you.'

At that point his mobile beeped, and he checked his message.

'There we are. Ten o'clock tomorrow morning. I'll take you down to meet him. He's on the floor below ours.'

'That's great, thank you.'

After dinner they collected her case from Musgrave Street, and Ferguson drove to her hotel next to the Waterfront Hall where a crowd of people were gathering for a concert within. He climbed out of the car to fetch her case from the boot.

'There you are, ma'am. I hope today has been of some help.'

'Absolutely, thank you, Rory.'

She reached out her hand to shake his. They held the handshake long enough for her to gaze into his eyes. Reality quickly settled matters; she drew back and smiled warmly. He seemed to hesitate.

'Thanks again, Rory.'

'See you in the morning, ma'am. Sleep well.'

She watched him get back in his car and drive away. She got the impression that DS Ferguson would not have needed much coaxing.

She walked into the hotel foyer, her mind and tummy battling the sensation of what had nearly happened.

CHAPTER 29

The next morning, she was surprised to see DS Ferguson seated in the hotel reception. He got to his feet when he saw Tara approach.

'Morning, ma'am. I thought I would give you a lift to the station.'

'That's very kind, but it's only round the corner. I could have walked.'

He took her bag, while she checked out. She was aware of him staring at her, but her night's sleep had cooled any rising passion, and he was still a married man. Just as well that she was going home this evening. It was back to business.

'Sleep well?' he asked as they walked out to the car.

'Perfectly.'

Nothing more was said, on the brief drive to Musgrave Street. Ferguson showed her into the office of DCI Wallace Brown, who stood up when she entered the room.

'DI Grogan, very nice to meet you,' he said, offering his hand.

'And you, sir.'

'Please have a seat.'

She sat down and noticed that Ferguson was about to join them.

'Rory, you've no need to stay. I'm sure DI Grogan can manage.'

'Yes, sir.' Smiling rather sheepishly at Tara, he left the room. Tara, for some reason, felt slightly more relaxed now that he had done so.

'So, how can I help you?' said Brown.

He was a man of about forty, Tara guessed. Striped shirt and dark tie of his golf club. She couldn't make out the detail. He looked quite serious, intense, despite the pleasant manner when he spoke. She thought he could improve by offering the odd smile. His eyes were small, quite sunken, and he seemed to squint as he listened to her theories concerning the disappeared women, Terry Lawler and his sister, Ruth. From her bag, Tara produced her collection of photographs and set them in front of Wallace Brown.

'These pictures were all found on a wall in Terry Lawler's flat. We managed to identify most of them from the missing persons list. All these women apparently disappeared without trace. None of their bodies had ever been found, until you recovered Linda Meredith from the sea. I believe that Lawler must have stumbled upon some reason to connect all of them.'

'Is it not simply that they, as you say, all disappeared without trace?'

'Possibly, but I wonder if he had some evidence to suggest that a single individual is responsible.'

'Was that why Lawler was murdered?'

'No, sir. He was killed for an entirely separate motive.'

'And his sister went missing?'

'Yes, she was a nurse at the Royal Liverpool Hospital.' That fact suddenly jarred in her head. She couldn't think why.

In silence, Brown sifted through each of the pictures. He certainly was not instantly dismissive of her theory.

'And where is your investigation at the moment?'

She flushed and shifted in her seat. How could she explain that it wasn't actually a case – and certainly not one of her cases? Since the investigation into Terry Lawler's murder had closed, it was purely a matter of personal interest.

'Well, sir, it was part of our investigation into Lawler's killing. At first, we thought that he may have been responsible for taking these women, until we discovered that his sister was one of the disappeared.'

'And now?'

'No further progress. The individual disappearances around the country are a matter for the relevant local constabularies.'

'So, you're not actively investigating this?'

She detected a change in his tone, of frustration or impatience.

'No, sir, not as such. I've kept an eye on any developments, but there have been none – until Linda Meredith.'

'I see.'

'The picture you're holding, sir. That woman also comes from Northern Ireland.'

Brown examined the laser-copied photograph of a beautiful young woman with long fair hair.

'Her name is Diane McCartney.'

He jumped from his chair and went to a filing cabinet in the corner, opened the bottom drawer and began searching through folders.

'I should have at least one file here relating to Diane McCartney. I actually worked on her disappearance at the time.'

A minute later, he removed a thin folder from the drawer and returned to his desk. He pulled out a couple of photographs of the missing woman and passed them to Tara.

'She was a student at Queen's University. Last seen leaving the university library one evening. She didn't make it back to her room in the halls of residence. And that's all we have, despite numerous appeals and reconstructions. Nothing. Not even a mobile phone, a text, not a thing. Do you not think this Lawler bloke did little more than gather together a bunch of missing persons cases?'

'It is possible he knew nothing more, but why specifically this group of women? They all disappeared without trace, no bodies, no messages; all were of very similar – slight – build and when we look at the disappearances in chronological order, they are all well spaced out. There's another two that occurred on the same day, in London, after Lawler had been killed, and there have been more since. But all these pictures are related to what Lawler had been working on. I haven't included the cases occurring since his death.'

'So, we could be talking about more than twenty-nine?'

Tara nodded.

Brown looked rather sympathetically at her and smiled, albeit thinly, for the first time.

'I'm not saying it isn't possible, Tara, that one person is responsible for all of these disappearances, but do you have any other leads?'

She had to admit the answer was no, but this morning she felt that something had registered with her and yet she couldn't grasp what it was. Something had registered in her mind; a spark had ignited. She needed time to think.

'Have there been any similar cases in Northern Ireland since Diane McCartney?' she asked.

'No case that is exactly the same. Not that I know of. Plenty of disappearances that have been solved, some unfortunately became murder investigations when a body was found.'

'If you follow the timeline of the cases I've shown you, they begin with Linda Meredith then Diane McCartney and then move across to England. Firstly to Merseyside, then further afield. There is, however, a concentration around the North West, particularly Merseyside.'

'What you're suggesting is that the killer began in Belfast and then moved to England?'

'Yes, I believe so.'

She felt herself flush, not from her conversation with DCI Brown but from a sudden realisation. James Guy, originally from Belfast, had moved to Liverpool. He had snatched her. Had driven her away to a lonely place in his van. Had he done so to rape her or had he intended to kill?

And just as quickly the thought from earlier hit her like a blow to the solar plexus, taking the breath from her lungs. Ruth Lawler had worked at the Royal Hospital.

So had James Guy.

CHAPTER 30

I couldn't settle myself until I was sure that Tara Grogan was back from Belfast. On top of that I was worried sick about what she was finding out and how it might involve me. Had she gone there to meet with the cops and to tell them about me, or were they giving her all the details on Millie? Then again, maybe I was panicking over nothing. Maybe it was a different case, or maybe she had gone for personal reasons.

This stuff was bouncing round my head, while Kirsty was telling me all about the house she'd seen. It was close to her parents, close to a primary school and a park. I was hardly listening, and she knew it. It was enough to dent her enthusiasm, and I was the one to lose out because she was sitting astride me, not a stitch on, ready to do the business. With me not paying attention, she climbed off me and without a word rolled over and went to sleep.

I couldn't be arsed thinking about a wedding and a baby and a new house when I was worried that I might not be around for any of it. Not if Tara was finding out about me. I could be banged up for life.

In the middle of the night, I was struggling to sleep. I got up, poured myself a whiskey and switched on Kirsty's laptop. I checked the airport website for arrivals from Belfast for the forthcoming day. I was hoping that she was only staying a couple of days. Maybe she was already home. Anyway, I noted all arrivals from Belfast. I would have to take time off work because I had to be at the airport for most of the day checking to see when – if – she came home.

* * *

There are four flights from Belfast to Liverpool every day, and I got to the airport half an hour before the first arrival at 11.20 a.m. I stood well back from the door; didn't want her to see me. Needn't have worried. The same happened at 4.20 p.m., 6.00 p.m. and 8.35 p.m. She was still in Belfast.

Before going home, I drove to her flat and hung around for a while. Her car wasn't there, so either it was still parked at the airport or else she was out working or enjoying herself with her mates. That pissed me off. The thought that she might know all about me, be planning to arrest me – and yet she could be out drinking and having a great time with her friends.

Freezing cold, hungry and frustrated, I finally drove home around midnight. Kirsty was sound asleep, and I crawled into bed beside her. She nestled into me, and for a few brief minutes I felt safe and warm. Tomorrow I'd go back to the airport. I could only afford one more day off work.

If Tara didn't show up, I wasn't sure what I was going to do. I really needed to know what she was up to.

CHAPTER 31

More out of courtesy than anything else, Tara thought, Wallace Brown went through all the known facts concerning the Linda Meredith case. She examined the photographs taken at the post-mortem; a body unrecognisable as the pretty teenager whose image she'd found among the collection of pictures retrieved from Terry Lawler's flat.

'How was she identified?' Tara asked.

'Some of the inner body had been preserved to a certain degree, by this adipocere stuff.' He pointed out the extensive areas where the waxy substance had formed. 'They managed to retrieve DNA and it was a match for Linda Meredith.'

'Anything on the perpetrator?'

Brown shook his head.

'Nothing conclusive. She'd been in the water for almost eight years and besides, the killer knew what he was doing. No clothing, jewellery, weapon, not a thing.'

'And you never had any suspects at the time when she went missing?'

'Nothing. We checked out the family first. She had a younger brother, but nothing pointed to him or the father. A close loving family, by all accounts.'

'Would it be possible for me to meet them?'

Brown hesitated. He didn't look keen on the idea. Then he glanced at his watch.

'Give me a few minutes and I'll see what I can do.'

'Thank you.'

While Brown was out of the office, Tara made a brief call to Harold Tweedy.

'I would like to spend another day here, if that's all right, sir?'

'Are you making progress?'

'I've spoken with Carly McHugh, and I'm fairly sure she is holding something back. But another matter has arisen.'

'And what's that?'

'Sir, if you recall the list of disappeared women we came across in connection with the Lawler case?'

'Yes, I remember. It included Lawler's sister.'

'That's correct, sir. I've been speaking with the officer involved in the recent finding of the young woman's body in the Irish Sea. Her name is Linda Meredith, and her photo was among those found in Lawler's flat.'

'Do you have a lead?'

'Not as such, but I may have something by the end of the day if it is all right to stay another night.'

'That's fine, Tara, we'll speak further when you return.'

'Thank you, sir.'

Wallace re-entered his office carrying several folders.

'I've arranged for you to meet with the Merediths and the McCartneys. We are at a loss in both cases, so anything you uncover will be of help.'

'Thank you, sir.'

'DC Marshall will accompany you. She's been involved in the investigation since the recovery of Linda's body.'

* * *

Gina Marshall was of a similar age to Tara, with close-cropped black hair and lively dark eyes. She wore a light grey pinstripe jacket and skirt, and a pair of flat brown brogues.

Marshall seemed happy to be going along with Tara. They drove in a marked police car across the Queen Elizabeth Bridge and into the east of the city.

'So how are you enjoying Belfast, ma'am?'

'It's been fine so far. DS Ferguson showed me around last night.'

The girl glanced to her left with a wry smile.

'Did he take you for dinner?'

'He did, actually.'

Marshall grinned.

'Smooth operator, is our Fergie.'

'Has a reputation, does he?'

'Oh yes.'

Tara thought it best to change the subject. She wasn't about to gossip and feed this girl with details of her encounter with Ferguson, not that she had anything of significance to divulge.

'And how do you find DCI Brown?' Tara asked her new companion.

'One of the best. Likes to think he takes care of us younger ones.'

Tara couldn't help thinking of how Tweedy was the same.

She gave Marshall her reasons for meeting the families of two women who had disappeared years ago, and within minutes they pulled into a street off the Holywood Road. They stopped outside a terraced house that had square bay windows on the ground floor. A woman in her fifties, with short brown hair flecked with grey and wearing a grey lounge suit, answered the door.

'Come in, Inspector. Mr Brown phoned to say you'd be coming.'

'Thank you, Mrs Meredith.'

The slight, almost frail woman, slow on her feet and breathing heavily, led them to a front sitting room snugly furnished with a sofa and two armchairs. There were photographs of family on the walls and several set into a mahogany wall unit. Nearly all of them featured her daughter, Linda.

'Are you OK, Mrs Meredith?' asked Marshall.

'Asthma is playing up today, love.' She had noticed Tara looking at the pictures. 'That's our Linda.'

'She was a beautiful girl,' Tara said. 'I'm so sorry for your loss.'

'At least we got her home in the end. Gave her a decent resting place.'

'That must have been very difficult after all this time.'

The woman nodded and Tara continued. 'If you don't mind, I wanted to ask you some questions about the time Linda disappeared.'

Karen Meredith dropped into an armchair and took a puff on her blue asthma inhaler.

'Go ahead, love, although I don't know if I can tell you anything new.'

Tara sat on the sofa, Gina Marshall taking the other armchair, where she could gaze sympathetically at Karen Meredith. Tara began.

'At the time when Linda disappeared, did she have a boyfriend, or did she mention any male admirers?'

'She had plenty of admirers, but she had no one on the go at the time. She'd finished with her boyfriend a few months earlier.'

'And what was his name?'

'Tim Bradshaw. They'd been friends since primary school.'

'Ma'am,' said Marshall. 'We checked him out at the time. Nothing to suggest any involvement in Linda's disappearance.'

Tara nodded her acknowledgement.

'Were you ever contacted by a journalist from Liverpool?' she asked. 'His name was Terry Lawler.'

'Yes, about two years ago, I think, maybe three. He telephoned me, asking about Linda, and a couple of days later he showed up at the door.'

'Did he tell you anything of what he was doing, what he was investigating?'

'Didn't really tell me much. His sister had disappeared in Liverpool, and he was trying to find her. He told me that the circumstances of her disappearance were similar to Linda's.'

'Did he mention anyone he thought may have been responsible?'

'No, love. He had an idea that one man may have taken a whole lot of women, but he said that he didn't know who he was.'

'Did Linda ever mention a man named James Guy?'

Karen Meredith was silent for a moment, and Tara noticed the surprise on Marshall's face at hearing a name she probably had not encountered before in this case. Eventually, the woman shook her head.

'No, love, never heard her talk about such a man. Do you think it was him?'

'I'm afraid I can't say, for now.'

'Who is he? Why did you mention him, then?'

'I'm sorry, Mrs Meredith, it's part of another investigation. It may not have any connection with Linda's murder.'

Tara asked several more questions relating to Linda's interests, her activities and her job at the time of her disappearance. Karen willingly described her daughter's happy life at home and with her friends. There wasn't anything said that gave Tara hope of a lead, or a connection to James Guy. Karen Meredith insisted on making tea, and Tara was soon quizzed about life as a police detective in Liverpool. She left the woman with the promise that she would contact her if ever she made progress in finding Linda's killer.

Gina Marshall, however, didn't wait long before tackling Tara over the reference to James Guy. Karen Meredith had just bid them goodbye and closed the door behind them when Marshall spoke.

'If you don't mind me asking, ma'am, what do you know about the man you mentioned to Karen?'

Despite having known the detective constable for little more than an hour, Tara felt she could be trusted. She'd liked her instantly, and she hoped that the officer could be of some help. As they set off for the family home of Diane McCartney, she told Gina Marshall all that she knew of James Guy, and of how Terry Lawler had been searching for his missing sister.

'He served eighteen months for abducting me, and two months after his release I saved his life when he was about to be killed at the hands of two vigilante-style murderers.'

'Wow! That's a story and a half, ma'am.'

'I don't think it ends there. I suspect, but can't be certain, that he has continued to stalk me.'

'My God. And you think he is the man who killed Linda Meredith and Diane McCartney?'

'Believe it or not, Gina, it really only hit me this morning, while I was speaking with DCI Brown. And for now, it is merely a thought. I would appreciate it if you kept the information to yourself, for the time being. I could be completely wrong about James Guy. I will share whatever I find out with DCI Brown, but for now it is just me thinking aloud. I don't want Guy tracked down by any police force unless I can find real proof that he is a serial killer.'

'I understand, ma'am, but how did you realise only this morning?'

'Two things. Firstly, I was explaining to DCI Brown how, if there is a single killer of all these girls, his killing began in Belfast with Linda Meredith and Diane

McCartney before he moved across to England. Most of his killings since then have been centred around the North West although there have been others elsewhere. That fits with the timing of James Guy having moved from Belfast to Liverpool.'

'And the second?'

'Again, this only occurred to me this morning. I don't know why I hadn't realised this before now. Terry Lawler's sister was a nurse at the Royal Liverpool Hospital at the time of her disappearance. James Guy was working there at the time I first met him, and right up until he was convicted for abducting me.'

Gina stopped the car on a side road close to the village of Hillsborough, thirteen miles from Belfast. She appeared completely enthralled by Tara's story.

'Unless it is a weird coincidence, ma'am, I reckon you may be on the track of your serial killer.'

CHAPTER 32

The McCartney home was a large and attractive detached bungalow with a huge expanse of lawn, and bordered with Castlewellan Gold leylandii trees. Eleanor McCartney was a bright-faced and shapely woman in her fifties, with shoulder-length strawberry blonde hair and a splash of freckles on her cheeks. Wearing slim jeans and a Beatles T-shirt, she sat opposite Tara in a spacious lounge, its huge picture window framing a vista of the County Down drumlins. Instantly, the well-spoken Eleanor McCartney seemed to Tara a woman who had fought to remain positive about life despite the tragedy that had befallen her family.

'Are you sure I can't get you a coffee or tea?'

'No, thank you, Mrs McCartney,' Tara replied. 'We don't want to take up too much of your time.'

'Please, call me Eleanor.'

Tara explained the purpose of her visit. Eleanor nodded her understanding and reported on her meeting with Terry Lawler.

'He came to see us about two years ago. Very chatty sort, very friendly – but also determined that he was going to find out what had happened to his sister.'

Tara was a little surprised to hear that Lawler had seemed friendly. Most of the people she'd spoken to who had been interviewed by the journalist had not found him to be pleasant.

'I told him all that I knew about Diane's disappearance. I suppose at first, I'd thought that Mr Lawler was bringing me some hope, hope that she might still be alive, but he was quite candid and convinced that Diane and his own sister were dead. He was frustrated that the police had made no progress in finding out what had happened to all of those women.'

'Did he give you any explanation or theory as to what may have happened?'

'Oh yes. He was convinced that Diane's disappearance was similar to his sister's and to other cases. He told me that he'd visited the parents of Linda Meredith, who disappeared in Belfast a while before Diane. And there were other disappearances he mentioned, that had taken place in England.'

'What did he think had happened to these women?'

'He thought that one man was responsible. He said that the disappearances were so similar, that one person had to be the killer. I wanted to go to the police with what he'd told me, but he said that he was the only person taking an interest and he still needed proof that he was right. He said that he would keep me informed. I never heard from him after that visit.'

Tara explained that Terry Lawler had been murdered shortly after his return home and that his death was not linked to the disappearances, but to another case.

'I'm so sorry to hear that. He was the only person to give us hope that we would ever find out what happened to Diane.'

'Did he mention any names of people he suspected?'

'He refused to give me the name of the man he was investigating, whom he suspected of killing his sister and my daughter. But he told me that there was a man who'd been behaving strangely around his sister. She worked at a hospital in Liverpool, isn't that correct?'

'Yes, the Royal.'

'His sister had told him about a man who also worked there, who she thought may have been stalking her.'

'He hadn't passed this information on to the police?'

Eleanor shook her head.

'He wanted to look into it himself before going to the authorities.'

Just one name screamed in her head. James Guy. Had Terry Lawler really found a serial killer but then was murdered before he could pass on what he knew?

'Inspector, do you think that if one man is responsible for all these women disappearing and given that Linda Meredith's body was found in the sea, that others, including Diane, are also down there?'

'I'm sorry to say that it is a possibility, Eleanor.'

Tara noticed Gina's eyes widen at the thought. The scale of what they were considering was almost too horrific to take in. More than twenty young women may have been dumped in the Irish Sea. Would it ever be possible to find them?

Gina could hardly contain herself as they left the McCartney home.

'Ma'am, the man Eleanor referred to, would that be the same man you're thinking of?'

'I'm fairly sure, yes.'

'But it has to be. You said that Guy worked at the hospital, and now you know that this journalist Lawler was thinking the same way.'

'That doesn't mean that he was right, or that I am right.'

As they drove back to the city Tara asked a favour of Gina Marshall.

'I'll have to get back to Liverpool tomorrow. Do you think you could try to find some information on James Guy, about his life during the time he lived in Northern Ireland?'

'I will try my best, ma'am.'

'Thank you. Now, I really should get back to the reason I came here, Carly McHugh.'

'Are you going to speak with her again?'

'Yes. It might be worth having another chat. But I'll have a word with DS Ferguson, see what he thinks about it.'

* * *

It was late in the afternoon before DS Ferguson was free to speak with her. She'd hung around the station, filling her time by checking back into her hotel, arranging her flight home for the following morning then looking over the shoulder of Gina Marshall while she searched for local information on James Guy.

'Nine James Guys with current Northern Ireland addresses.'

'I don't think any of them will be our man,' said Tara. 'As far as I know, the James Guy in question is still resident in Liverpool.'

'Maybe one of these addresses could point to a relative?'

'I'll leave you to check that out, Gina. Anything you find on this man will be very useful. I really appreciate your help, thank you.'

'No problem, ma'am.'

When eventually she met up with Ferguson, he led her to a vacant meeting room and closed the door behind them. But Ferguson seemed uncomfortable. He cleared his throat, and nervously pulled out a chair from the table. Tara sensed an awkward situation was arising.

'Have a seat please, ma'am.' She sat down at the table and waited for Ferguson to do the same.

'Do you have some news for me?' she asked.

'Not something you're going to find useful, unfortunately.'

'What do you mean?'

'You know, ma'am, in this part of the world sometimes it's still hard to divorce crime from politics. Some people have connections to those in positions of power, and when that power is exercised certain things happen and others don't happen.'

'I'm really not following you, Rory.'

Ferguson smiled and winced at the same time. He wrung his hands.

'We've been told to leave off Carly McHugh.'

'But she is central to a murder enquiry!'

'I know, but what is meant by leaving off Carly is that we're not to go poking our noses into the current activities of her da, Rab McHugh.'

'Why the hell not?'

'I can't tell you. What I mean is, I don't know.'

Tara glared at Ferguson demanding more, simply by waiting. It didn't take long for him to capitulate. 'It may be that the order has come from on high. Rab McHugh does have connections to politicians and councillors in this city. Or it may be that an operation is ongoing, and we would be interfering and risking its collapse.'

'So, which is it, Rory?'

'Can't tell you that, ma'am. I'm sorry.'

'But you heard Carly. She's up to her eyes in this Boswell case, and you're saying she can't be arrested. This is ridiculous.'

'I can only apologise, ma'am. All I can tell you is that there are bigger fish to fry.'

'For now, that is no help to me.'

And she couldn't help thinking that the frying fish metaphor had DCI Weir stamped all over it.

* * *

She left the station in the early evening, having first caught up again with Gina Marshall. The detective constable was diligently working through names, addresses and files, making calls to those she thought might have a connection to James Guy.

'I was going to ask if you would like to join me for dinner,' she said to Marshall.

'Thanks, ma'am, but I really would like to get on with this. Maybe I can find something for you before you go back to Liverpool.'

'Thank you. I really appreciate your help. I'll see you in the morning before I go to the airport.'

* * *

She'd acted on a recommendation from Rory Ferguson and went alone to a restaurant beside St Anne's Cathedral. She started with a caesar salad and followed it with baked salmon, accompanied by a light Australian chardonnay. After dinner, she walked slowly through the Cathedral Quarter, as it had become known in recent years, which was primarily an area for socialising, with many bars, restaurants and clubs tucked away down narrow alleys.

Her mind battled the horrors of her experiences of James Guy. Life was strange... her main reason for coming to Belfast had been to gather information, to help in solving the murder of Ryan Boswell, but the thought of catching the man who had killed so many young women blotted out everything else.

It was a mild evening, and as she reached the junction of one narrow street with another, she noticed a group of people standing around outside a pub. The street was little more than an alleyway but was lit by fairy lights and had some benches to sit on, a jolly scene with laughter and chat from those enjoying their drinks. She couldn't resist the cosy setting and, with nothing else but thoughts of a serial killer to occupy her time, she stepped into The Duke of York and stood at the bar.

At least all thoughts of serial killers had been dispelled for a while.

Darkness had descended on the narrow alleys, but she remained cheerful as people strolled by on their way to bars, restaurants and gigs. Within a few minutes, she emerged from the Cathedral Quarter into wider streets and crossed the road into Victoria Street beside the Albert Clock, a structure not unlike Big Ben, she thought, and with a gentle tilt less severe than Pisa's. As she walked by yet another restaurant, a car drew up at the pavement. It was a large silver Audi, and a youth was climbing out in something of a hurry. She thought nothing of it as she passed them by.

Then, suddenly, she was aware of a horrifically searing pain in her right arm. Someone had a tight grip and was wrenching it behind her. She called out for help, but it was lost in the noise of traffic. She no longer had control of her feet, and before she could react further the youth thrust her into the back seat of the car.

It roared off and beat the lights near the Albert Clock, passing just as they changed to red.

CHAPTER 33

Another day spent loitering about the airport and still no sign of her. I hung around by the police station on St Anne Street for a couple of hours, but nothing there either. Before going home, I checked out her flat at Wapping Dock. I even rang her doorbell. Nothing. I finally convinced myself that whatever she was doing in Belfast had nothing to do with me and drove home to Kirsty.

For a while over dinner, I listened to her go on and on about our wedding, and I tried my best to look interested. Like I give a fuck. It felt like Tara was standing in the room with us, listening to Kirsty prattling on about table settings, flowers and menus and the whole time Tara's glaring at me with a face on her like thunder. *I know what you've done*, she was saying in my ear. *I'm coming for you.* I shivered at the thought.

'Are you all right, honey?'

'What?' I said, distracted.

'You've hardly touched your lasagne. You're not coming down with something?'

'I'm fine. Just a headache.'

She smiled sympathetically and rubbed my arm with her hand. I really don't deserve her.

'I have to go for my first scan next Tuesday. Do you want to come with me?'

I knew I should say yes. I mean, I wanted to go – but right at that minute I had Tara whispering in my ear, and it wasn't anything nice. Kirsty bore the brunt of my frustration.

'I'm working, Kirsty. I can't just take the day off.'

'But it's a morning appointment. You could go into work late. It's not a whole day.'

'I can't, I'm busy.'

I could tell she was hurt, but I had more important things to worry about. She didn't speak for a while, and then she came up with another date for me to refuse.

'Dad wants to know if you're free this weekend. He got you a ticket for the match.'

'I'm working on Saturday. He should have asked me first.'

'He was thinking you could get the afternoon off.'

I threw down my knife and fork. They clattered over my plate and fell on the floor.

'I just told you I have to work. Are you stupid or something?'

As I sprawled on the sofa and flicked through the TV channels with the remote, I could hear her banging about the kitchen as she cleared up the dishes. Then the front door slammed. She'd stormed off to her mother's or to Mel's. Give it ten minutes and my ears would be burning.

And still Tara was getting to my head. *I know it's you, James. I fucking know. I will get you.*

What the hell am I going to do about her?

CHAPTER 34

Shania couldn't move her left arm. Not without great pain that made her call out for help. But the sounds from her mouth were muted. Her face seemed paralysed; she couldn't move her lower jaw and if she tried, a sharp pain shot upwards into her head. She had the metallic taste of blood on her tongue and felt the trickle of warm liquid leaving her open mouth. Why didn't somebody come?

She was cold. Cold and wet, her hair soaked in a puddle. She couldn't get up. Not on her own. She thought she might die here, squinting through blood and tears at the night sky with its hue of yellow light reflected from the damp streets. How long had she been like this? How long had she been lying here? How long since they had dragged her to this spot, kicking her, pulling her hair, ripping her dress. And the sticks and baseball bats cracking at her body, her arms and her face. She must have passed out. They were gone now. Not a sound. What was the time? Had she been lying here for hours or just minutes? Why didn't somebody come? Where was Tyler? What was he doing to help her?

She'd worn her new dress just for him. Her hair and nails were done especially for the party at Craig's place. Why had Tyler left her on her own? She wanted her mum. Her mum could help her, take care of her, get her to a hospital. But she loved Tyler, yet he'd beaten then abandoned her. He'd left the party without her. And not long afterwards, as she walked home alone, they'd grabbed her by the hair and pushed her down the steps. And Tyler just stood there, watching. No one came to help her. Even then the pain in her arm made her cry out. Some of them were laughing. People she knew. People from the party. Some she'd called her friends. Girls as well as fellas. And the more she'd screamed, the more they'd jeered. What had she ever done to them?

Her cries for help were little more than whimpers now. Her only thought as she drifted to unconsciousness once again was that somebody should come to help her.

CHAPTER 35

'Who are you? Where are you taking me?'

'Shut the fuck up.'

'I'm a police officer.'

'Know who you are, love. But you don't get to say anything.' This was a different voice from the first, and it came from the figure sitting in the front passenger seat. He didn't turn around but spoke directly at the windscreen. It was dark; she couldn't make out his face but thought immediately of the men she'd spied on the Treadwater Estate and of the man she'd noticed watching her on the night she'd been out with Kate and Aisling.

The man sitting beside her in the back seat of the car was younger. Late teens maybe, his head shaven, a tattoo on the side of his head of a soldier bearing arms.

'But you have no right to do this.'

'Give her a smack, will ya? She doesn't understand the Queen's English.'

The youth grabbed her by the hair with one hand and with the other gripped her chin and squeezed. As he let go, he slapped her across the mouth and laughed.

'Any more cheek and you'll lose that pretty face of yours,' said the man in front. 'Whatever you think you're doing here, leave it. Forget about it. Keep your nose out of what doesn't concern you. Go back to Liverpool and forget you were ever here, understand? You don't know who you're dealing with. And like I said, be a shame to lose those good looks by doing something daft.'

Suddenly, the car slowed and turned left. When she glanced out, she saw the entrance to her hotel and felt some relief. The car braked abruptly at the drop-off space, and the youth leaned across her and opened the door.

'We'll not charge you for the taxi fare,' the man in front said. 'Safe home.'

She stumbled out of the car, and it sped off before the door was closed behind her. Too shaken to even attempt to note the number plate, her hand went to her mouth, still stinging from the slap by the youth. Her shoulder ached as she walked unsteadily into the foyer, unsure for a moment of where she was or what she was supposed to do. Should she call for the police, for Rory Ferguson? She took the lift to the fourth floor, then followed the corridor to her room. Somehow, she'd managed to keep hold of her handbag and rummaged inside to retrieve her keycard. It took several swipes for the door to unlock, but at last she felt sanctuary as she closed and locked it behind her. All her actions from that point seemed instinctive, as if her body knew how to repair itself after the frightening encounter. She stripped off and went to the bathroom. In a few seconds, her stomach parted company with her evening's food and drink when she dropped to her knees at the toilet. Her eyes watered and stung; her mouth was rancid.

When she could yield no more she got to her feet and turned on the shower. She couldn't help glancing in the mirror. Her face looked ghastly – reddened and drawn. She had hardly realised she was crying. Her slight body, now trembling, didn't seem cut out for this sort of life, certainly not for such terrifying activity. She felt so alone, so helpless. Hot water was insufficient balm for her pain.

Now clean and wearing the hotel-issued bathrobe, she managed to find a couple of paracetamol capsules that had been languishing in the bottom of her handbag. She swallowed them down with a glass of water from the tap and felt her stomach lurch on ingesting the cold liquid. She hoped the tablets would stay down.

Her final act of obedience to instinct that evening was to flop onto the bed and fall asleep.

* * *

She awoke just after six, to find the lights still on. It took her a few moments to get her bearings and to recall what had befallen her the night before. Another ten minutes passed before she rose gingerly from the bed and shuffled to the bathroom. Glancing in the mirror, she thought she looked even worse than the last time. Hair awry, bags below her watery eyes. But how could she expect any better?

Back in the room, she checked her mobile for missed calls but found only a couple of WhatsApp texts from Aisling. One asked how she was getting on, the other reported Aisling's latest deliberations over the purchase of a pair of shoes and came with photograph attached. Tara tossed the phone on the bed without replying and went for a shower.

When eventually she made it to Musgrave station at nine o'clock, Gina Marshall was waiting eagerly to see her.

'Morning, ma'am. Are you OK?'

Tara wondered exactly how obvious her state of distress was to others.

'I'm fine, Gina. I'll catch up with you later. Have to speak with DS Ferguson first.'

'OK, ma'am. I have quite a lot to tell you.'

'Good. I'll come straight back to you.'

She left the detective constable and went in search of Ferguson, one floor above. He was at his desk, browsing a newspaper.

'Ah, good morning, ma'am. How was your night? What did you think of the restaurant?'

'The restaurant was fine, but unfortunately the rest of the evening proved unpleasant.'

'How so?'

She rested her bottom against the edge of his desk, nursing her right arm across her stomach, and related the story of her encounter with the men in the Audi.

'Are you all right? Were you hurt?'

'I'm fine, just a bit stiff and shaken.'

She had already mused on how her abductors had either been following her all evening or had been tipped off to her whereabouts. The only person who could have tipped them off was Ferguson. Only he had known which restaurant she was going to.

'Further to our conversation yesterday,' she continued, 'I suppose my little adventure is related to the order from on high, as you put it, to step away from investigating the McHughs.'

She couldn't come right out and accuse the DS of passing information to a criminal gang, but she wanted to judge his reaction to her words.

'Did you recognise any of them?'

'No. I'm quite sure they knew what they were doing. No point in providing me with evidence to go after them.'

'I suppose not. Probably just sabre-rattling. Making sure you stay away from the case.'

'If I had enough evidence to charge her, I would be ordering Carly McHugh's arrest this morning, regardless of what you said yesterday afternoon.'

Ferguson grimaced but did not offer any argument. The PSNI had jurisdiction here and not Merseyside Police. He was probably comforted by that fact, she thought. But she didn't think much of his reaction. A police officer had been bundled into a car on a city street, hit and threatened, and this DS was writing it off as sabre-rattling. For now, she would let it pass. The investigation into Ryan Boswell's murder would continue in Liverpool, but, if necessary, she would come back to Belfast and have this gang for murder. And DS Ferguson, involved or not in the conspiracy, would not stop her.

Bidding him a curt goodbye, she left Ferguson and returned to Gina Marshall, who was brimming with excitement. She pulled a chair close to her desk for Tara to use.

'I did some checking first on the name James Guy. There are only nine people listed on the electoral register in Northern Ireland with that name. Four of those we can eliminate because the men are over sixty.'

'Hold on, one of those could be his father.'

'I understand that, ma'am, but the next piece of information will explain all.'

Marshall opened another window on her screen. 'I ran a check for James Guy's birth records. The father named on the birth certificate did not have the surname of Guy. The mother's name, however, was given as Rachel Guy.'

'So, it's possible that James Guy did not know his father, or at least his mother and father didn't marry. Have you tried to trace Rachel Guy?'

'That's where it gets interesting, ma'am. I checked the address given on the birth registration; there are members of the Guy family still living there.'

'The mother, Rachel?'

Marshall shook her head.

'No, ma'am. Rachel Guy disappeared twenty-eight years ago. She has never been found.'

CHAPTER 36

Mikk Klavan had answered the mobile phone that he found lying on Janek's desk. Janek had left it behind before going to the city to do some business. Aksel had taken a few days off. His head was still hurting after the attack on his car. That left only Mikk and Sepp to work in the breakers' yard today. During the phone call, the man on the other end had all the right passwords to place an order. The only problem was, there was no one here to be the contact and make the sale. Mikk didn't do the sales. It was usually Janek or Aksel.

Mikk was new here, new to Liverpool, new to England. Janek, his cousin, had put him to work in the scrapyard, operating the crush machine. Mikk realised that Janek was being protective, taking care of him, aware that Mikk had a seriously ill mother and teenage sister to provide for, back in Tallinn. Under no circumstances was he to venture into the city on drug business. So, during the call, Mikk had written down the details of the deal to be done and taken them to Sepp. He'd expected Sepp, in his grumpy manner, to scoff and tell him to leave the message for Janek to deal with when he returned. Or perhaps Sepp might go on the errand himself.

Instead, Sepp – sheltering from the rain and lounging in the front seat of a car ready for scrap, reading a porn magazine and already drinking vodka although it wasn't yet lunchtime – tossed a set of keys at him.

'You go. Don't take all fucking day.'

Mikk gathered the drugs that he needed, coke and China White, from the locked cabinet in Janek's office and jumped into the old Renault van that Sepp used for work. It didn't have satnav, but Mikk had a good sense of direction, and he could read the road signs.

From the yard in Tranmere, he used the Kingsway crossing then followed signs for Bootle and then Bootle Golf Course. It was a foul day, with rain bouncing on the road and spray engulfing his windscreen. Once he reached the Dunnings Bridge Road, Mikk turned left into a retail park just beyond a McDonald's. He parked in a space well away from other cars and looked around for his customer. Only then did he realise that he had no idea how they would arrive, or what they looked like.

Forty minutes later, he still had not seen anyone who might be wanting drugs. He watched cars come and go from the park. At times vehicles parked closer to his van than he would have liked. He knew that Janek was a cautious man, didn't take too many risks, and he tried to be the same.

After an hour of waiting, a black BMW pulled into a space several yards away. There were two other vehicles between Mikk and this car. He watched as a young man got out from the passenger side of the BMW, but he couldn't see the driver's side. The young man wore a dark puffa jacket and baggy jeans. He had a red baseball cap pulled down over his face and was headed right for him. This was it. This was his customer.

Mikk lowered his window to be ready to do the deal. He nodded once at the man when he reached his car.

'You got it?'

Mikk leaned across to the passenger seat and lifted the small package of drugs. As he turned to face his customer, he saw the gun in his hand. The gunman fired two shots, hitting Mikk in the face each time.

As Mikk slumped in his seat the youth reached for the package, tucked it into his pocket and coolly strolled back to the waiting BMW.

CHAPTER 37

At long last. She's home. I wandered through the car park at her apartment building and saw her car in its usual space. Thank God for that. Three days I spent hanging around the airport, in between deliveries, waiting for her to step off a flight. I was getting seriously spooked and hacked off, wondering what the hell she was getting up to in Belfast. Could only have been about me. Why else would she have scooted off like that? She wanted to find out about the body they dragged out of the sea. Millie, I'd called her, but now the whole country knew her real name – Linda Meredith. Eight years she was safe at the bottom of the Irish Sea, and now this.

The worst thought, and it's been keeping me awake at night, is what if Tara already knows it was me who put Linda in the sea? What if she has already connected me with Terry Lawler's sister and all the others?

Things have settled down a bit at home with Kirsty. She's got most of the wedding planned, and now she's reading up on all things childbirth. Been talking about a birthing pool and breastfeeding and prenatal classes. The other night, she asked me if I would be at the birth.

'Of course I will.' Just so long as I'm still free, I thought. She gave me a big hug.

'I love you so much, James. You've made me very happy.'

'I love you too, Kirsty,' I replied, and I did really mean it. I'd never been in this situation before, someone loving me and me loving them. It's just that I was worried sick that my past was coming back to haunt me. For the first time since taking any of my girls I began to regret ever having started. Why would I ever have taken a girl like Millie, if I'd had someone like Kirsty to love me?

I never thought anything like this would ever happen to me. No one was ever supposed to love me. My granny had cared for me, but she never told me that she loved me. My mother, from what I could remember, never said that she loved me. For a few minutes, lying awake with Kirsty breathing lightly beside me, the desire, the longing to take another girl deserted me once more. I was going to have a family of my own. If we were to have a daughter, I wouldn't like to think that in a few years there would be some madman out there watching her, wanting her and finally taking her in the way I'd taken Millie and all the others. I rolled onto my side and slipped my arm around Kirsty. We snuggled together, and finally I must have dozed off.

Soon I was awake and breathing hard. I felt the sweat on my forehead. I jerked away from Kirsty. Only then was I sure that it was a nightmare.

I was at Anfield with Kirsty's da. And he was telling me over and over that I was part of his family now. That if I ever did anything to hurt Kirsty, he would kill me. And the crowd and the players on the pitch, every one of them, had the faces of all my girls, and the noise was deafening, yet I could still make out the words of her da saying he would kill me.

For hours, it seemed, I lay awake thinking. What did Tara know? Maybe if I didn't do any more girls, it would all go away quietly. I had something to protect now. It was about more than just self-preservation. I was going to have a family and the feeling was growing inside me that I would do anything to protect them.

So, if Tara was really coming after me, I realised that I would have to get her first – before she got me.

CHAPTER 38

Tara made an appointment for the following day, to see her physio. Her arm still ached from the sudden twisting of it, inflicted by the men who'd pulled her off the street in Belfast. Grateful to be home safely, she lay on her bed staring at the ceiling, trying hard to force the horrible feelings of anxiety and fear from her mind. How many times would she have to endure a confrontation with ruthless men before she succumbed or decided that enough was enough? Would she know when it was time to get out?

Aisling was always nagging her to leave policing. To come and work with her in promotions, use her good looks and charm, to enjoy what she was doing. But bizarre as it probably seemed, she did enjoy her work. Not as Aisling did, not in the way that you ran around smiling, feeling bubbly inside and pondering what shoes you were going to buy with this month's salary. Tara found great satisfaction in solving a case, in knowing that she had pulled someone bad, someone evil, from the streets – and that somewhere there was a person who would live, who would sleep comfortably in their bed, thanks to what she had worked so hard to achieve. And she relished the challenges involved. Although Tara knew, if she was honest, that there was a need to feel threatened, to experience fear and doubt. What better feelings could there be to drive her on?

So, now, she needed to focus on what to do about the threat from the men in Belfast. There was little doubt in her mind that the effects of Ryan Boswell's murder reached further than the Treadwater Estate, and Liverpool, and were firmly connected to matters across the Irish Sea. They extended so far that a senior police officer, yet unknown, had ordered that the investigation of Carly McHugh be halted. Was that done to protect Carly, or her father? Were the police in Belfast actively protecting criminal gangs? Or were they merely trying to preserve their own operations? Specifically, an operation that she was stamping all over with her need to question Carly McHugh. If DCI Weir's assessment of the Treadwater Vipers was accurate, and this gang *was* small fry, then what had the small fry got themselves into? Drugs appeared to be at the centre of the issue, but how were they connected to the gang in Belfast? What had Ryan Boswell done to get himself murdered? And why had men from Belfast shown up on the Treadwater Estate?

Tara's recent experience of that well-known occupational hazard, insomnia – or at least, of getting no sleep before three in the morning – set her thinking of all she had learned about James Guy in Belfast. She had delayed her flight home so that she and Gina Marshall could call at the house in Bangor, twelve miles along the coast from Belfast, where members of the Guy family still lived.

A sister of Rachel Guy's, Margaret, lived there with a son, daughter and grandson. She was a slim, petite woman in her mid-sixties, with tidy blonde hair in a bob, a small, wrinkled face, with fine glasses on a tiny nose and a small mouth. She wore a fawn-coloured jumper and black jeans. For a second, Tara thought she knew the woman – or at least had seen her before. They were not invited inside the 1960s semi-detached, red-brick house and remained on the doorstep. Gina Marshall took the lead.

'Can you confirm that a man named James Guy used to live here?'

'He did, but it was years ago. James is my nephew, but I haven't heard from him for a long time.'

'Do you know where we could find him?'

'Why, what's he done?'

'We would like to speak with him as part of an enquiry.'

Margaret Guy seemed perturbed by Marshall's reply.

'As I've said, it's been a long time since I've seen him. He grew up in this house. Mostly raised by my mother, after Rachel took off.'

'Took off?' said Marshall.

'Yes, upped sticks, walked out, disappeared. Call it what you like, but Rachel left my poor mother to bring up her son.'

'Are you in contact with Rachel?'

'Never heard a word from her since the day she left. Poor wee James was devastated at the time. Cried his wee heart out for days.'

'Do you know anything of her whereabouts?'

The woman scoffed. Clearly, she had finished talking about her sister.

'And James?' Tara added. She knew the answer she wanted to hear.

'Went to England.'

'Whereabouts in England?'

'Liverpool. Don't know where he is now, though.'

* * *

Before attending her physio appointment, Tara went to her office at St Anne Street. She had to update Tweedy on what she had learned in Belfast, but she was also eager to speak with Murray. In recent months she had begun to feel a deeper, more personal, working relationship with her DS. She could speak freely with him, trusted him and was glad of his advice. She understood he'd been resentful when she first joined Tweedy's squad. Murray believed, given his longer experience, that he should have become DI, rather than her. It had taken a while for mutual respect to emerge but gradually, the chip on his shoulder had eroded, and now she valued him as a close friend as well as a colleague.

Over coffee in the canteen, where Murray tucked into a cooked breakfast of bacon, eggs and sausages, Tara him told about the events surrounding the Boswell case.

'I'm certain that Carly McHugh was the girl seen wandering through Treadwater on the night Ryan was shot. What I haven't decided yet, is whether or not she killed him.'

'But you reckon that all fingers point to Belfast? That the Vipers were not responsible?'

Tara winced. It was difficult to claim categorically that the Vipers had not been involved. After all, Ryan Boswell and his brother, Aidan, were both members.

'All I know is that Carly McHugh is up to her eyes in it, and now we can't touch her, because it is somehow sensitive to the PSNI, DCI Weir, or both.'

'Why can't we just issue a warrant for her arrest and have the PSNI ship her here?'

'I've suggested that to Tweedy. He's going to speak with DCI Weir, in case it would have a bearing on work he is doing with the police in Belfast.'

'These guys who picked you up, are they definitely connected to Carly McHugh?'

'It would seem so. DS Ferguson wasn't inclined to chase it up. Given what he told me just before it happened, he wasn't at all surprised that I had been pulled into a car and threatened. Sabre-rattling, he called it.'

CHAPTER 39

Tara was about to leave for her physio appointment when Murray suddenly realised that he'd forgotten to tell her something.

'Ma'am, when you get back, I think we should go have a word with Shania Smith.'

'Why is that?'

'She was badly beaten a couple of nights ago. Found lying on some waste ground in Treadwater.'

'How is she?'

'Broken cheekbone, broken arm, two cracked ribs, lost a couple of teeth and was suffering from exposure when she was found. No word on who did the deed, but worth checking in case it has a bearing on Boswell.'

* * *

After Tara's physio session, her arm felt worse. With all the manipulation, her shoulder ached, and her neck was stiff. The pain in her arm seemed trivial compared with the injuries inflicted on the young girl. Shania Smith lay in a ward at Aintree Hospital. Despite her discomfort, she instinctively reeled back when she saw her visitors approach but being confined to bed she had nowhere to go. It would prove a difficult meeting, for Shania was unable to speak clearly.

'If you can manage to nod your head, Shania, that will do fine. And maybe you can write some things down for us,' said Tara, looking sympathetically at the young woman.

'Do you know who did this to you, Shania?' asked Murray.

The young woman made no attempt to nod or shake her head. Tara placed her own hand lightly on Shania's right hand, the one that was not encased in plaster.

'We want to help you. You're not in any trouble, but the person who did this to you needs to be caught.' She watched tears emerge from the corners of the girl's eyes. 'Do you really think you deserve to be in this state?' Slowly, Shania moved her head once to the side. 'Was it Tyler? Are you trying to protect him, Shania?'

Whimpers turned to sobs and she shifted on the bed. The mention of her boyfriend's name had struck home but served only to increase her pain. She tried to shake her head to say no.

'Can you tell me who it was, if not Tyler?'

She gestured with her hand, and Murray handed her a pen and set a notepad in front of her. Writing awkwardly, she managed to complete a couple of lines, which Tara read back to her.

'Not Tyler. Don't know nothing. Leave me alone.'

* * *

As they drove away from the hospital, neither felt surprised by the reactions of Shania Smith. From their first meeting, Tara had thought her a shy and frightened young woman. Shania had become involved with a criminal gang simply because she was besotted with its leader. She didn't have the nous to stand up for herself, or the sense to realise that she was mixing with dangerous people. Her beating surely had been a warning as well as a punishment. Tara was in no doubt that Tyler Finlay was behind the attack. Shania Smith had, in some way, stepped out of line.

'Where to now, ma'am?'

'Back to the station. I think it's time we brought Mr Finlay in to see us, don't you?'

* * *

By late afternoon, uniformed officers had arrested Tyler Finlay at his flat on the Treadwater Estate. After being processed and cautioned he was placed in a room where, within a few minutes, Tara and Murray arrived to interview him.

'I want my brief!'

'Calm down, Tyler. You'll get one,' said Murray.

At that point there was a knock, and the door was opened by a duty solicitor, a man well known to both Tara and Murray from previous cases. Martin Grimshaw, a fifty-year-old with a red-blotched face sporting dark-framed glasses, wheezy breath and a blue shirt straining at his belly, stepped into the room. His striped tie rested on his bulging tummy as he sat. He was neither a friend to his proposed client, nor to the police officers.

'A few minutes with Mr Finlay if you don't mind,' he said.

Tara and Murray duly obliged and waited in the corridor while Grimshaw got a handle on his client's situation. When they were called back inside, Grimshaw was the first to speak.

'Mr Finlay, I believe, has already been questioned regarding the death of Ryan Boswell. He can offer nothing further, and if you have nothing new to put to him, he should be allowed to go home.'

Tara smiled at the solicitor, a smile with a sprinkling of contempt. She didn't like the man and didn't care for the way his eyes travelled around her body. But she had to respect his professional status.

'Mr Finlay knows fine well the reason why he is here. It may well have a bearing on the Ryan Boswell investigation, but for now we will discuss the attack on his girlfriend, Shania Smith.'

'Don't know nothing about that,' snapped Finlay.

Grimshaw widened his eyes as if to say there you have it, but Tara ignored him and began to record the interview.

'Tyler, can you confirm that you are in a relationship with Shania Smith?'

Tyler remained silent, leering at Tara, a sly grin developing on his mouth.

'Used to be. Broke up.'

'When was that, exactly?'

'Day after you last came to see me.' He fired a smirk at Murray, who adeptly fired one back.

'When did you last see her?'

'Day we broke up.'

'Did you see her last Thursday night?'

'No.'

'Shania was attacked and badly beaten on Thursday night, at some point after nine o'clock. Where were you at that time?'

'At a party.'

'Can anyone vouch for that?'

'Yeah, loads.'

'Some names please, Tyler.'

The interview dragged on for another twenty minutes, with Tyler giving nothing away. Tara realised that she should have known better. Since Shania had refused to name her attacker, it was always going to be difficult to get anything from her boyfriend.

Frustrated, she concluded the interview with a speculative shot at the young gang leader.

'I was in Belfast this week. Fitter Hobbs was asking after you.'

She watched the change in his expression. It looked as though a shock wave had just passed through him. He made no reply, but his smugness disappeared, and was replaced by a look of unease.

'You do know Mr Hobbs, don't you?'

'Never heard of him.'

CHAPTER 40

When Tara got back to her desk, intending to collect her coat and bag and be off home, she found a Post-it stuck to her screen.

See me. DCI Weir.

She didn't think it wise to put off the irascible cop until the next day. Whatever he wanted, it was best to deal with it now instead of letting it play on her mind all night. She had more than enough to think about.

She knocked on Weir's door and waited to be summoned. The knock was answered immediately by his shout. 'Come in!'

'You wanted to see me, sir?'

'DI Grogan, yes. Have a seat. You can start by telling me how you got on in Belfast.'

Weir looked rough, unshaven and probably unwashed, and sounded as though he had a heavy cold. Tara hoped the meeting wouldn't last long.

'Well, sir, I spoke with Carly McHugh. She was not forthcoming.'

'Doesn't surprise me. Her father's a tight-arse as well. Did she tell you anything?'

'Not really, but I believe she and Ryan Boswell were romantically involved.'

'You mean they were shaggin' each other? Doesn't tell us much, does it? So, you got nothing on their drug running activities?'

'No, sir, but I'm certain Carly knows who was responsible for killing Boswell.'

'And who do you think was responsible?'

'Someone from Belfast. I didn't get to investigate any further. Seems there was a sudden moratorium on asking questions about the McHugh family. Indeed, I experienced at first hand the implications of pursuing the inquiry.'

'How so?'

'A couple of heavies warned me to stay out of it. Suggested I left Belfast.'

Weir raised his eyebrows but wasn't about to come over all sympathetic.

'I think you'll find, DI Grogan, that whoever killed the Boswell lad probably has connections to this area. One of the other drug gangs on Merseyside, I suspect. Best to leave this Belfast crowd out of it. Safer, too.'

Tara thought that a strange response to what she had just reported. Surely, to anyone with an ounce of sense, her experience suggested that whoever killed Boswell was to be found among this gang in Belfast? Why had Fitter Hobbs and Rab McHugh been hanging around on Treadwater if they didn't have some involvement with the Vipers? And McHugh's daughter was certainly wrapped up in the events of 15 April.

'Sorry, I can't agree with your analysis, sir. I shall be after Carly McHugh when next I have the opportunity.'

'Time will tell who is right, DI Grogan, but remember you'd be well advised to stay out of operations that do not concern you. That'll be all.'

'Sir.'

She left the room quickly before drawing a deep, longed-for breath. That man was so infuriating. What did he know that made him think that another Liverpool gang was responsible for the death of Ryan Boswell? And what had stopped him from sharing that information with her?

Continuing to seethe, she recounted the conversation she'd had with DCI Weir to Alan Murray.

'Sounds like a right can of worms. I think Weir is just trying to keep you out of whatever operations he has going on, that might relate to this crowd in Belfast.'

'I hope that's all it is, Alan. The whole thing is beginning to smell. Meanwhile, our best lead on the murder is safely under the shelter of her father and, it seems, the Belfast police and DCI Weir.'

'Welcome to the wonderful world of drug dealing. Do you fancy a pint and a bite to eat?'

She was surprised by his offer.

'Not seeing Trudy this evening?'

'She's working tonight. I might call on her later.'

Tara knew she could really do with getting home to a hot bath and an early night, but at the same time she relished the company.

'In that case, let's go. I'm starving.'

* * *

Over savoury mince pie and chips in a tired pub on the London Road, Tara related her findings to Murray connected with Terry Lawler's list of missing women. She couldn't help her enthusiasm from bubbling over.

'Lawler was definitely onto something, Alan. He had someone in mind, someone he suspected of taking all those women, including his sister. He said as much to the mother of Diane McCartney.'

'Did he mention any names?'

'No.'

'Then you're no further on.'

'But I can name a suspect that fits.'

Murray took a long drink of lager from his glass.

'Go ahead,' he said. 'I'm all ears.'

'I know you're going to find this hard to swallow, but just hear me out.' He smiled and sat with arms folded, ready for her story. 'Terry Lawler's sister, Ruth, disappeared, and he came across similar disappearances of women, while he was searching for her.'

'Yes, hence the collection of pictures we found at his flat.'

'That's right. Taking those cases chronologically, the first and second disappearances occurred in Northern Ireland about eight years ago. Nothing more for close to a year, and then similar cases arose on Merseyside, in Greater Manchester and eventually London, Glasgow, Leeds and another spate around Liverpool. So, the killer begins his work in Belfast, then moves to Liverpool and continues from there.'

'There's nothing to say that he stayed in Liverpool. He could have been operating from anywhere, and that's assuming that it is just one perpetrator.'

'Fair enough, but now consider this. Ruth Lawler was a nurse at the Royal when she disappeared. Eleanor McCartney told me that Terry Lawler mentioned his sister being worried about a man who may have been stalking her. Someone she knew at work.'

'Your friend Kate works there, doesn't she?'

'Yes, but who do *we* know of who comes from Belfast and moved to Liverpool about eight years ago? This person also worked at the Royal at the time Ruth Lawler disappeared. I don't know why I didn't connect the two things before.'

'James Guy. But that's a big leap, Tara. It's purely circumstantial.'

'I looked into him when I was in Belfast, Alan. It has to be him.'

'Hold on, what did you find out?'

'Well, I confirmed that he moved from Northern Ireland to England eight years ago. His aunt told me that when James was a young boy, his mother disappeared. Was never heard of again.'

Murray puffed air through his cheeks but didn't seem convinced.

'It could fit his psychological profile,' said Tara.

'What are you going to do about it, bring him in?'

'Not yet. I have someone in Belfast working on a history of the young James Guy. She's trying to contact childhood friends, teachers and so on.'

'We're up to our necks in this Boswell case, Tara.'

'I know, I know. But I can at least speak with people at the hospital who knew Ruth Lawler and maybe some who worked with Guy. And…'

'And what?'

'I was thinking that we could speak with Jason Collywell. Find out what he knew of James Guy, before he and his sister decided to kill him.'

'You're going to ask one serial killer to spill the beans on another? I say that's brilliant, Holmes.'

'Don't be sarcastic, Alan. It doesn't suit you.'

CHAPTER 41

I wandered around by the M&S Bank Arena, hoping to spy her jogging along. It's not like I could do anything, even if I suddenly spotted her right in front of me, but it would be comforting just to be close to her. With all my anxiety over what Tara may be finding out about me, and how she could ruin my new life of love, I hadn't registered the fact I still fancy her. Of all the girls I've taken – and there have been some absolute stunners – Tara is the prettiest girl I've ever clapped eyes on. What can I say? She floats my boat. What such a beautiful woman is doing working as a police officer, when she could adorn the cover of any fashion magazine, is a mystery to me. But I suppose she's too friggin' clever to consider selling her body.

Tonight, there was no sign of her. I dandered through the car parks and around the Albert Dock. Both my feet were giving me gyp. The wounds, where yon bitch Aeron fired big nails through below my ankle bones, caused me some discomfort. The pain was in my Achilles, and it slowed me down. With no sign of Tara, after an hour or so, I limped back to my car.

But the worry over what the hell she had been doing in Belfast sat on me, like a big dinner I'd eaten in a rush. I had to believe it related to the finding of Linda Meredith's body, but what else did she find out? Who did she speak to? What did she learn about me? I haven't been home to Belfast in eight years, but I was really itching to discover what Tara knew about me. Then I had an idea. I phoned my Aunt Margaret.

'Who is this?'

'It's James, Aunt Margaret. How are you doing?'

'My goodness, James. I've heard nothing from you in years and now it's twice in one week.'

'What do you mean?'

'The police were here the other day wanting to speak to you. I told them I hadn't heard from you in a long time.'

'What sort of police, what did they want to know?'

'Two policewomen. One of them was local, and the other sounded English. Wanted to know where you were living.'

'Did they give their names?'

'Oh, they did, love, but I can't remember now. I hope you're not in any kind of trouble?'

'No, Aunt Margaret. Can't think of any reason why the police want to speak with me.'

'Are we ever going to see you again, James love? When are you coming home to visit us?'

'Maybe sometime. I'm getting married this summer. You and the kids are welcome to come to the wedding. I'll send you an invitation.'

'That's lovely! Congratulations. I'll look forward to it.'

'And I'm going to be a da.'

'Ach, that's great, son. Your granny would be so proud.'

'Have to go now, Aunt Margaret, you take care.'

'Nice talking to you, love, bye-bye.'

Shit! My worst fear confirmed. Tara had discovered where I used to live. I'll bet that was just to satisfy her curiosity. She knows where I am in Liverpool. She saved my life, knows all about my recent history. But now she must be linking me with Linda Meredith. Why else would she be asking my Aunt Margaret about me?

She has to go. She has to go – before she puts the whole thing together and discovers exactly what I've done. I must find a way of getting her without every cop in the country chasing after me.

CHAPTER 42

Tyler Finlay didn't want to do this but they'd ordered him, and he couldn't say no to these kinds of people. He saw what they'd done to Ryan. No mercy shown. One wrong move and you were wasted. They didn't give a shit.

And all his mates, his brave fucking mates. Not one of them volunteered to accompany him. He regretted ever hooking up with another outfit. But if he hadn't done it, they would have found another crew in Liverpool and the Vipers would be going nowhere. He wanted the big time, the big money – and so did the others. But where were they when he needed them? Fucking cowards, all of them.

Even Craig pretended he was keen. He said he would hand the gear over to them. Big fucking deal. He wasn't the one who had to drive all the way to Sunderland, find the place and hope the bizzies weren't waiting for him. No one else, including those hard nuts from Belfast, fancied it.

'You fucked up,' Fitter had said to him. His rough Belfast voice always sounded threatening, and he didn't think the man had a kind bone in his body. 'Your man, Boswell, tried to pull a fast one, so if you want to keep doing business with us you can clear up his mess.'

A million quid's worth of gear, Ryan and his girl had creamed off. Stupid bastard. He should have known that these guys would catch on. His girl might have been the one who squealed to her old man. He didn't trust her. And now they were all in the shit. The Vipers had to do as they were told, or else they'd all get the same as Ryan.

A grey, overcast day, a wind funnelled down the street – if you could even describe it as a street. An old red brick wall bordered one side, the remains of an old factory. The other side had several more recent buildings, a car body repair shop, a steel fabricator and a warehouse for plastics for the catering trade. Tyler stayed in his car, observing the sparse activity. A couple of cars came and went from the garage, a white van was parked at the warehouse. Now and again a van or a lorry would drive by.

He didn't know Sunderland; he had never been here before. Close to the docks were the only directions Fitter had given him. He assumed this was the right place. He realised that Fitter had extracted the address from Ryan, just before he was shot. Ryan had hoped they would spare him if he told them where he and Carly had been hiding the gear. Stupid wanker. Fitter and McHugh beat him senseless to get what they needed.

There were no signs of any bizzies around. He'd been watching for more than an hour. It looked like a disused business unit. A faded blue sign with white lettering hung above the doorway. *Trade Paint Supplies*. Sooner or later, he would have to open the shutter and look inside. He jangled the keys in his hand, in time with the rap anthem thumping from the radio.

His stomach felt empty, and his body shivered as he ventured from the car and walked the few steps across the road to the lock-up. He looked around, watching for signs of trouble, expecting a shit-load of bizzies to appear at any minute and slam him to the ground. But, other than the wind whistling by and causing the shutter to rattle, the street stayed quiet.

There were two heavy padlocks securing either side of the shutter to the wall. With the keys, he released them and pulled on the bottom of the shutter. It rolled up easily, squeaking its way into the housing above. He peered inside to the gloom, searching for a light switch. He found one to his left and flicked it downwards. A single fluorescent strip flickered to life in the centre of the room.

The place stank of rat's piss, and he was sure he heard something scurry away behind a stack of empty pallets. It seemed that the place had only been used for storage. In addition to the pallets, there was a set of metal shelves against the right-hand wall but nothing else. No side rooms, no office, toilet, sink, workbench – nothing.

Several cardboard boxes sat on the lowest shelf, and he went straight to them, hoping he'd find the merchandise. He lifted the flaps on one of the boxes and found four paint tins. He checked the other boxes and found the same in each. The tins were unlabelled. He pulled one out, set it on the floor and using one of his keys, he levered the lid open. The tin was three-quarters full of a white powder. He assumed it to be cocaine, but he'd never come as close to so much gear in his life. Replacing the lid, he returned the tin to its box and selected one from another box next. This was the same as the first. There were six boxes, and he inspected a tin in each. The final box, however, held just two tins, but also contained a woman's leather handbag. It probably belonged to Carly. Inside, he found loose banknotes, tens and twenties mainly, but also fivers and fifties. He didn't bother to count it – he wasn't great at counting anyway – but he guessed that around ten grand was stuffed into the bag. He was wrong, underestimating by a margin of fifteen thousand. But it was the finding of the cash, more than the discovery of the drugs, that spurred him to action. One by one, he carried the boxes to his car and loaded them into the boot. The bag containing the cash, he kept beside him on the front passenger seat.

Now, in a hurry to be well away from the street and out of Sunderland, he lowered the shutter on the store without bothering to replace the locks. Then he roared away, headed for Treadwater and home.

It was dark by the time he pulled into a parking space just below his flat. Before going in and settling down for the night, Tyler made a quick call.

'Yo, it's me. Got it.'

'We get the stuff to them, and we're in the clear,' said Craig. 'What about Shania?'

'She won't say nothing. I've fixed her.'

'You sure?'

'Yeah, I'm sure, man,' said Tyler. 'Bizzies pulled me in a couple of days back, but they got nothing. Don't think they'll bother us again. We have to keep these dudes sweet, Craig. Do what we're told. Could be a lot of earning for us. I'll get the gear over to your place, but not tonight. I'm going to crash out, man. I'm whacked. Been on the road all day. Need to get my head down.'

'Tomorrow?' said Craig.

'Yeah, tomorrow. Cool yeah.'

Tyler smiled to himself. He hadn't told Craig about the cash. It could be his alone for having taken the risk of going to Sunderland. No one else needed to know.

There was a knock on his window. In the evening gloom, a dark figure peered in at him.

CHAPTER 43

The last person Tara wanted to see taking charge of a crime scene was DCI Weir. At least, the last person she wanted to see taking charge of *this* crime scene. Tara had no doubts that he was an efficient and experienced officer; she simply did not wish to be involved in any investigation of which he was a part.

She had arrived on the estate with Alan Murray and Superintendent Tweedy. Rain pattered on the car roof and Murray managed to stop where water had gathered in a dip in the tarmac of the road. Fortunately, she'd slipped on a pair of knee-high boots before rushing from her flat, remembering also to grab an umbrella. Opening the car door, she stepped over the puddle with one foot but wasn't so lucky with the other. Quickly, she raised the umbrella and joined her colleagues as they approached the scene.

The street below a block of flats had been sealed off with incident tape, and SOCOs were already scouring the road and pavement for evidence. DCI Weir was in conversation with a uniformed constable when Tara, Murray and Tweedy reached him.

'Morning, Harold,' he said jovially. He didn't acknowledge the presence of Tara or Murray, nor had he afforded Tweedy the appropriate greeting for his rank. That was no surprise to Tara. The man lacked manners.

'Good morning, Malcolm. Not a pleasant day, unfortunately. What do we have?'

'One male, dead. Shot multiple times. The MO is still looking him over.'

'Any ID?'

'We reckon it's Tyler Finlay. Car is crammed with drugs. Paint tins full of cocaine. It's worth a fortune.'

Tara wandered towards the car, a black BMW, not the most recent model, complete with spoiler, lowered suspension, tinted windows and twin exhausts. A symbol of dubious prosperity in these parts – locals would know it to be a drug dealer's car. She watched the photographer taking pictures under the direction of Dr Brian Witney, the medical officer in charge of examining the victim.

'Hello, Brian,' she called from a few yards away. 'Anything peculiar?'

'Ah, morning, Tara. Miserable day for this caper.'

He beckoned her forward. Witney, a man in his fifties, always seemed delighted to meet her and never made her feel uncomfortable. He was a gentleman, with good manners.

'The victim has been shot several times in the head and face, also one or two places in the upper body. We found a wad of cash when we sat him upright.' He indicated the passenger seat of the car.

Tara was never particularly strong at a crime scene, not hardened like some to the sights of violent death. She had to peer over the victim's body to see what lay on the passenger seat. It was a leather handbag, smeared with blood, open and brimming with banknotes.

'Seems to rule out robbery as a motive, I would guess,' said Witney. 'The driver's window had been lowered. He wasn't shot through the glass. Forensics already have his mobile phone.'

'Indeed. Maybe he knew his killer. Thanks, Brian.'

Tara stepped away from the car and looked around her. She was standing in a parking bay below the block of flats where, she knew, Tyler Finlay had lived. A group of approximately thirty people, mostly teenagers, had gathered beyond the incident tape at the far end of the parking area. From forty yards away she didn't recognise anyone, particularly anyone she might know who was associated with Tyler Finlay or the Treadwater Vipers. If they've any sense they'll stay well away, she thought. Catching Murray's eye, she indicated for him to go with her, towards the flats.

'I want to get a look inside Finlay's place before DCI Weir realises that this is where he lived.'

They climbed the interior stairs to the third floor and stood by the door of the flat they had visited only a few days earlier. As expected, there was no reply to Murray's knock. He thrust his shoulder against the door, but there was no give. Tara sniggered.

'Not every door will just cave in, you know.'

'I know. I'm sorry.'

He lifted his right foot and kicked out at the lock. Several attempts splintered the wood around it, and one final kick forced the door backwards. It hit the wall with a bang.

'Well done,' she said. 'You're so strong.'

'What were you saying last night about sarcasm?'

Suppressing her smirk, she stepped into the hallway with Murray following. The place still had the all-pervading smell of smoked weed and was in a very untidy state.

Tara couldn't decide, at first, whether it had been ransacked or had fallen into disarray following the departure of Shania Smith. The bedroom had male clothes strewn on the floor and across the unmade bed. Drawers and a wardrobe door had been left open. Used cans of lager sat on the coffee table in the living room, an ashtray overflowed with fag butts and the remains of reefers. A remote control for a video game lay on the sofa, beside a small spiral-bound notebook. She leafed through its mostly blank pages. On a couple were scribbled various addresses. No names, just addresses, one of which was in Sunderland.

Tara heard a shout of discovery coming from another room, and Murray appeared at the door, holding aloft a small self-seal bag.

'No surprise there then,' he said.

Inside the bag was a small quantity of what Tara assumed to be cannabis. Then they heard voices in the hallway, and in marched DCI Weir with one of his detective constables, a smooth-faced young man whom Tara knew only as DC Roley.

'Ah, might have known you'd be first up here, DI Grogan. Find anything interesting?'

Murray was still holding the bag of cannabis in the air.

'That's right, son, it's drugs.'

Murray fumed at Tara.

'Well?' said Weir.

'Nothing so far, sir,' Tara replied. She'd managed to slip the notebook into her anorak pocket, although she thought DC Roley may have seen her do it. She beamed a smile at him, but he didn't respond.

'I think you'll find that my assessment of the situation regarding the Vipers was correct. There's a gang feud in play round here,' Weir continued.

'You don't think Belfast has anything to do with this murder?'

'No, I wouldn't think so, DI Grogan. Much closer to home, I'd say.'

'It's all a bit one-sided though. Two members of the Vipers dead, but no retaliations.'

'That's where you would be wrong, lass.'

Not for the first time, she let the DCI's condescension pass. She was keen to hear his assessment of the situation.

'How so?'

'I take it you heard of the shooting the other day in Bootle.'

'The lad shot in the car park off the Dunnings Bridge Road?'

'That's the one.'

'You think it's connected with the shootings in Treadwater?'

'The victim was Mikk Klavan. Estonian. I believe he is connected to a group known as the Tallinn Crew. I think a turf war is going on between the Vipers and these Estonians.'

'Right then. We'll leave you to it, sir. But I would be interested to hear how things turn out with respect to the Boswell shooting.'

'I'll keep you informed, DI Grogan. If you wouldn't mind leaving that evidence here, son,' he said to Murray.

Murray tossed the bag at DC Roley and followed Tara from the flat.

'Arrogant sod,' said Murray.

'I agree,' said Tara taking to the stairs. 'But I don't believe this is a gang feud confined to Liverpool. I think there is a link to Belfast. What is Weir playing at?'

CHAPTER 44

At St Anne Street, Tara had asked DC Wilson to trace some former colleagues of Ruth Lawler at the Royal Hospital. She hoped that they might be able to confirm her theory, that someone at the hospital had been stalking Ruth before she vanished. People who had known Ruth might be able to tell her something about the events leading up to her disappearance.

She left Murray to follow up on points relating to Boswell, one of which was establishing the whereabouts of other gang members when Ryan had been shot, and to also establish the whereabouts of those same people when Tyler Finlay had been killed. It would be helpful also to get the results of the examination of Tyler's mobile, but she realised that would be for DCI Weir to consider, before her.

Wilson had traced one former colleague and friend of Ruth Lawler's. He also located the former supervisor of James Guy at the hospital.

Tara drove to the Royal Hospital on Prescot Street and met firstly with a former nursing colleague of Ruth Lawler. They talked over coffee in the restaurant on the lower ground floor of the main building. Staff Nurse Mary Bautista was a thirty-nine-year-old woman, originally from the Philippines, with dark hair tied back and a small, round face. She recalled Ruth Lawler with great affection.

'She was very good to me when I first came to Liverpool. She showed me around the city, helped me find a flat and brought me to dinner at her home. Ruth was a lovely girl.'

'Did you work together on a ward?'

'Oh yes. When I first came to the hospital, I worked the same shift as Ruth.'

'At the time she disappeared, did she mention anything that was troubling her? Any problems?'

'She had broken up from her boyfriend, Gary. I know she was upset about that.'

'Did she mention anyone who may have been causing her problems? Was she frightened, or did she talk about anyone following her?'

Mary looked thoughtful and paused briefly.

'No, I don't remember any problems like that.'

'Do you recall a man named James Guy paying her attention?'

'James? I remember him. Nice man. He would joke with the nurses all the time.'

'And Ruth? Did she say that he was bothering her?'

'No. Ruth flirted with all those boys. Nothing serious.'

At least now Tara had confirmation that Ruth had known James Guy; the first connection she'd made between Guy and one of the disappeared women. She thanked Mary and went off to meet the man who had been James Guy's manager when he'd worked at the hospital.

Dennis Cranley, a man already into retirement age, silver-haired with a sagging stomach, almost collided with her as she entered his office. His face surly, he stepped back abruptly as if he thought he could be prosecuted for accidentally touching a woman.

'Mr Cranley?'

'Yes, what can I do for you?'

'I'm Detective Inspector Tara Grogan, my colleague DC Wilson arranged for me to see you.'

'Oh yes. You wanted to know about that loser, James Guy. Take a seat.'

Tara sat on the only spare chair in the office, to the right of Cranley's untidy desk. He made a display of shuffling some papers, replacing a pen in a desk-tidy and clicking the mouse on his computer. Only then did he sit down.

'Right, what do you want to know?'

'How well did you know him?'

'Well enough.'

It was no answer, but it was clear that James Guy did not feature highly on Cranley's list of best friends.

'You were his supervisor, I believe? Was he a good worker?'

Cranley snorted.

'He was lazy and a poor timekeeper. I came close to sacking him on several occasions. Took liberties if you ask me.'

'How well did he get on with other staff?'

'I didn't take much notice of who he talked to, but he didn't seem to be particularly friendly with any of the lads.'

'What about the nurses and other females?'

'He thought he was God's gift. I didn't like him much. Too cocky, too cheeky.'

'Did he ever cause trouble with any of the nurses?'

'Not that I got to hear about. But you never know with the likes of him. After all, he got put away for raping a young girl, you know?'

Tara blushed, and suddenly she had a flashback of herself with James Guy. She could see herself lying naked in the dark. There was a body beside her; a hand was stroking her leg. Somebody was calling out. She heard the screams of a woman. She felt cold. Momentarily, she closed her eyes trying desperately to flush away the vision.

'Are you all right, Inspector?'

'Er, yes, I'm fine thanks.'

* * *

She left the hospital, feeling rattled. Nothing that she had learned about James Guy or Ruth Lawler pointed to Guy having killed her. More disturbing was the vision that now rested within her mind, a sickening image of a man's hand exploring her naked body and of herself lying helpless.

She ought to make one more call, but she decided to go home. She could no longer function, not with disturbing pictures flicking through her mind. A cold sweat enveloped her, and her hands were shaking; she tried her best to steady herself by gripping tightly on the steering wheel. She never thought that regaining her memory of the incident could affect her so badly. Indeed, she had convinced herself that the memory of what happened to her on that night would never come back. Now the images were popping up in swift sequence. She was reliving the harrowing experience, her tears flowing, her breathing unsteady. His hands were all over her, stroking and probing.

She drove as fast as she could to reach home. She was fighting the need to vomit before she'd even made it to the door. Once inside, it took only seconds for her to succumb. She cried out in desperation and couldn't dispel the feeling that his hands were on her right now.

Jason Collywell would have to wait until tomorrow.

CHAPTER 45

Janek Poska had only just set foot in Duke Street. Aksel, feeling better following his encounter with thugs unknown, had left him by the junction with Campbell Street. Janek watched as his companion drove away. He felt nervous pangs rise in his stomach. This was his first day of conducting business since his young cousin, Mikk, was murdered. His first day of crossing the river and walking the streets of the city. But no one was going to stop him. He had as much right to peddle drugs on these streets as anyone. There was room for everyone. No need for war.

The bizzies had already spoken with him, as Mikk's next of kin in England. They'd come to the scrapyard in Tranmere and told him what had happened. He was devastated. He blamed himself. He was supposed to have been looking after his cousin; Mikk was only a kid. That's why he didn't let him do any of the drug deals. But that lazy moron Sepp had sent him out in the van, had sent him to his death. Janek felt like cutting Sepp's throat for what he'd done.

And Janek was the one who had to phone Mikk's ailing mother in Tallinn to break the news. Her beloved son, who'd come all the way to England for the chance of a better life, had met with a violent death. Of course, through her grief, she had berated Janek for not taking better care of Mikk. To be honest, he could not disagree with the woman.

He'd only managed a few steps along the street when a car drew to a halt beside him. His thumping heart nearly choked him. He knew they'd come for him. He was about to die as Mikk had died.

Two men were suddenly on the pavement, the car moving slowly forwards as Janek turned to face them. He wanted to run but fear somehow held him firmly to the spot.

'Good morning, sir,' said one of the two detective constables.

Within seconds, Janek was sat in the back of the car on his way to a police station and an interview with a detective interested in what he referred to as *the* Tallinn Crew.

* * *

'I'm very sorry for your loss, Mr Poska,' said DCI Weir, leaning both elbows on the table so that his burly face came closer to Janek's. 'Never easy, losing a loved one at such a young age and in violent circumstances. He was only eighteen, I believe?'

Janek nodded, once. He felt relieved at still being alive, but as his fears of death had subsided, his anxiety that the bizzies were about to nail him for dealing in drugs, began to grow. He'd been carrying some coke for a client – not much, not enough to prove he was dealing. They'd held him in this sparse interview room for most of the day. He sat on a plastic chair, wearing jeans and his elderly leather jacket. He'd drunk two cups of piss-weak coffee, waiting for this big policeman to reappear and ask him questions in his very peculiar accent.

But Janek had already learnt the drill required to deal with police questioning. He'd experienced several interrogations from the police in Tallinn and had heard that questioning by English police was an altogether more pleasant activity. All he had to do was reply 'no comment' to every question, and unless they had evidence to nail him, they would have to let him go. This scruffy-looking policeman with the unusual accent, certainly not one he'd heard in Liverpool before, would have to settle for his non-cooperation.

'Was Mikk involved in drug dealing?' DCI Weir asked.

Janek looked directly into the watery eyes of the detective then replied with a 'no comment'.

'Are you associated with drug dealing, Mr Poska?'

'No comment.'

At that point, Janek could see that DCI Weir realised he would get nothing. Weir smiled thinly.

'Are you a member of a gang called the Tallinn Crew?'

It was Janek's turn to smile.

'No comment.'

'Have you been in contact recently with a gang known as the Treadwater Vipers?'

'No comment.'

Now he knew that the police were aware of this gang, the Vipers. Maybe they could do something; maybe they would arrest them for the murder of his cousin. If they didn't, then he would fight back. He would avenge the death of Mikk, and he would fight to keep his right to sell drugs in this city. The Vipers would be sorry for starting this war.

'Tell me what you know about the death of Tyler Finlay?'

'No comment.'

'Tell me what you know about the death of Ryan Boswell?'

'No comment.'

CHAPTER 46

Despite its modern architecture and layout, there was nothing cheerful about Altcourse Prison in Fazakerley. It was designed to hold category B prisoners and was built to be operated by a private company. Nobody knew why its blocks had been named after Grand National fences, but regardless, the debate continued in public and political circles as to whether the establishment had been a success.

Tara had a ten o'clock appointment, rescheduled from the day before, to see Jason Collywell. Jason was a serial killer of sorts, a man who, with his sister, Aeron, had come very close to ending the life of James Guy. Had Tara and Murray not discovered the location where the planned execution was to take place, she would not now be investigating Guy for the murders of so many young women.

She was shown to a booth within the visitors' centre and afforded the same treatment as a solicitor who had come to speak with their client. Collywell was serving a full life sentence for the murders of five people, including his natural father. He would never be freed. In partnership with his sister, he had administered summary justice; initially to the people he believed were responsible for the death of his mother twenty-five years earlier. Inspired by the Bible, particularly the Book of Proverbs, he had later extended his version of justice to others he believed deserving of it, specifically convicted sex offenders. As a probation officer in Liverpool, he'd had access to the records of many of them, including James Guy. Tara wondered just how much Collywell had known of Guy's activities before abducting him.

Jason Collywell, a man of slight build with fair hair and smooth face, entered the room and sat opposite Tara. He was dressed in blue jeans and a plain, olive-green shirt. He set a leather-bound Bible between them on the table. She couldn't help thinking of Harold Tweedy, who kept a Bible sitting at the top left-hand corner of his desk.

Collywell smiled wistfully at the young woman responsible for putting him in prison. He had no qualms over admitting what he had done. His only regret, revealed at his trial, was that he had caused great distress to his adoptive parents, Alec and Daphne Collywell.

'Inspector Grogan, to what do I owe the pleasure? You haven't uncovered another body, by any chance?'

He smiled at his own little joke and watched carefully for Tara's reaction. She made no response.

'Mr Collywell, I was hoping you might be able to help me with something.'

'Always keen to serve the needs of justice, Inspector. I'm sure you know that.'

'What did you know about James Guy before you tried to kill him?'

Collywell's simmering grin persisted, but Tara continued to ignore it. She wanted information from this man; there was no relationship to cultivate. She would get what she needed from the cold-blooded killer and be out of there. She owed him nothing.

Collywell paused and seemed to examine Tara as if he were putting a story together, one that had involved her, intimately.

'He is a very lucky man, to have you fight his corner for him.'

'I am not fighting his corner.'

'You saved his life.'

'I saved the life of whomever you were about to butcher on that night.'

'Do you mean to say that if you'd known it was Guy, you would have let my sister finish the job?'

This was exactly what she'd hoped to avoid, this descent to a debate over whether James Guy had deserved to die or not. She hadn't come here to argue the merits of the criminal justice system with the likes of Collywell. So, she waited. Soon, Collywell would feel the need to plug the gap.

'All right,' he said. 'I take it you mean, what do I know of James Guy apart from his conviction for assaulting you?'

She gave no reply, merely waited for him to continue.

'I realised on first meeting him that he was a serial offender. It struck me that he was bound to have committed other offences long before he was apprehended for abducting you.'

'Do you know of anything specific?'

'Aeron and I had our suspicions. We kept him under surveillance for a while. As his probation officer I was able to recommend certain activities to help him slip back into normal society after his spell in here. Ironic, isn't it, that he should now be free while I'm in prison? I suggested places he could go to meet people, certain pubs for instance. Then Aeron would keep an eye on what he got up to. She was quite certain that he abducted at least one woman during that period. Of course, he was extremely careful. If we'd been police, we could never have proven anything.'

'Do you recall the name of this woman, the one he abducted?'

'I'm sorry, I don't, Inspector. If you care to look back through news reports, you might find something. I think she was abducted about two weeks before we tried to rid the world of Mr Guy. Tell me, Inspector, why exactly are you investigating him now?'

'I can't answer that, Mr Collywell.'

'My actions were justified then, in trying to eliminate a beast?'

Tara could only wonder at the unshakeable confidence of the man before her. He was a multiple murderer yet saw no parallels between what he'd done and the acts allegedly committed by James Guy. Collywell's was a strange kind of justice.

But what if he was right? What if the only effective means of dealing with sex fiends and murderers was to remove them from society and put an end to their existence by the cruellest means? If there were people willing to carry out such work, should society allow them to do it?

'Thank you for your time, Mr Collywell.'

'My pleasure, Inspector. If you don't mind, I should like to end our meeting with a few words of scripture.'

He lifted the Bible and found his place. 'From the Book of Proverbs, chapter fourteen, verse twelve. "There is a way that seemeth right unto a man, but the end thereof are the ways of death."'

* * *

She left Altcourse prison feeling short-changed. Collywell had provided some information, had perhaps given the impression that he wanted to help her, but no detail for her to pursue. The impression grew inside her as she drove away, that Collywell would never want to help the woman who had effectively taken his life from him. And with that thought she wondered if he had given her anything useful at all. His final words to her had been draped in warped justification for his actions. But they *did* unsettle her.

'Let's hope that Guy has not claimed any more victims since the time you rescued him, Inspector,' Collywell had said. 'It would be a sad thing, the death of another innocent woman, when there had been an opportunity to remove him from this world.'

CHAPTER 47

Tara asked Wilson to check on disappearances that had occurred around the time James Guy so nearly met his end at the hands of Jason and Aeron Collywell. She also thought they should investigate whether any similar disappearances of young women had occurred during the time Guy was serving his sentence for assaulting her. If there had been something of a hiatus during that period, it would strengthen her theory that Guy was their serial killer.

By late afternoon, John Wilson had unearthed some data on missing persons covering a two-week period leading up to Guy's near-execution. Yet this information didn't clarify anything for Tara.

Each year in the United Kingdom, more than 250,000 people are reported missing. Most are found within 48 hours and their vanishings usually have reasonable explanations: domestic crises, mental illness and people simply choosing to drop out of contact for short periods. There are, however, approximately 20,000 people each year who go missing for prolonged periods, some of whom are never found. The data in front of Tara related to just two weeks prior to James Guy's abduction by Aeron and Jason Collywell. It made for difficult reading. Wilson had extracted from the missing persons list those females from the Merseyside area who had disappeared. Two cases stood out. The first was eighteen-year-old Carrie-Ann Steed from Wallasey, last seen leaving a nightclub in Liverpool city centre in the early hours of Saturday, 12 November. That was just five days before Guy was taken by the Collywells. The second missing person was

Stephanie Weeks, forty-three, married with two teenage daughters. She came from Woolton but was last seen leaving work at a faculty office at Liverpool John Moores University. She disappeared three days before Carrie-Ann Steed.

Tara's problems remained. She had no firm proof that Guy was a serial killer of women. She had no bodies and no forensic evidence. She persisted only because of her suspicions, and her own chilling experience of the man.

On her way home she stopped off at a Tesco store and bought some wine and nibbles for the evening ahead. She and Kate had been invited to Aisling's for a catch-up night, their first since Tara's return from Belfast and the last before Kate went on a fortnight's holiday with her mother and Adele – a sort of pick-me-up following Kate's split from Adam. Tara had been looking forward to it all day. It was just what she needed to purge some horrendous impressions from her mind. In the absence of a lover, there was no one better than Kate and Aisling to help her unwind.

'Hiya, Tara love,' sang Aisling, handing her a hefty glass of chardonnay. 'You'll be needing this.'

Aisling always looked immaculate – unless you caught her first thing in the morning or as she was getting ready to go out. Copious black curls tumbled over her shoulders, her make-up and eyes illuminating her pale face, giving the appearance of a porcelain doll. She seemed happy.

The girls always had fun together and talk soon turned to their planned trip to the sun.

'Just because you're jetting off to Lanzarote with your mum doesn't mean we can't finalise our holiday together.'

'Let's get it over with,' said Kate in reply to Aisling. 'And remember what I said last time, I'm not bloody going to Tenerife. I want to go on a cruise.'

'OK, OK, we hear you, Kate love. Tara has a new idea for us, don't you, Tara?'

Tara stared in confusion at Aisling. She hadn't the faintest idea what her friend was talking about.

'Come on, Tara, let's hear it,' said Kate, throwing herself onto a sofa then reaching for her wine glass.

For Aisling's sake, Tara knew she had to come up with something.

'Well,' she began, 'I was thinking of Thailand.'

Kate looked sternly at her.

'No, you bloody weren't. You've just said the first thing that came into your head.'

Aisling roared, clapping her hands in delight, and Tara couldn't keep her face straight.

Much debating, bickering and several glasses of wine later the three of them tentatively agreed that their summer holiday would be a cruise to the eastern Mediterranean.

Tara laughed herself hoarse. She and Aisling were drunk, and Kate had fallen asleep an hour earlier. Aisling tipped the last of a bottle of chardonnay into her glass, while Tara nursed a glass of Baileys.

'What would we do without each other?' said Aisling. She set down her glass, and went to her bedroom, returning in a few seconds with a blanket. She placed it over Kate and gently stroked her friend's blonde hair.

'Seems like we've been friends forever,' said Tara.

'Do you think it will always be like this? Will we ever get married and have kids and husbands to train?'

'Who knows, Aisling?' smiled Tara. 'Look how things have turned out for Kate. Who'd have thought she and Adam would break up?'

Aisling smiled.

'You know, sometimes I think as long as we three have each other I don't much care about a husband.'

'But you'd miss…'

'I don't mean for us to go without sex, for goodness' sake! I just mean that it might not be so important, to have a man to live with forever.'

Tara couldn't bring herself to agree, but so long as they were drunk, she was happy to talk the type of rubbish that Aisling currently was spouting. Tara would hold on to the belief that one day all three of them would be happily married, settled with a couple of kids each and hopefully still the best of friends. Not everything had to change.

Aisling was now fading, sinking back in her armchair, her half-full glass resting precariously in her hand. Tara studied both of her friends, her confidantes. Tonight, was the first in years that she had sailed through without thought or mention of her job. For this moment they could be teenagers again, sleeping over at Aisling's house, discussing boys and sex and music and clothes without a care for tomorrow or what it might bring. Maybe Aisling was right, maybe their lives should remain free of further change. Maybe there was more safety to be had in keeping everything unchanged, keeping three friends loving, and watching out for each other.

CHAPTER 48

I saw it on the news. What the fuck is going on? The bizzies arrested Janek, my dealer. Do they already know that Janek supplies me with China White? Does Tara know that's what I use to put my girls to sleep? Of course, she does. She was tested the night I snatched her. It was mentioned in court when I got done for aggravated sexual assault. The wee bitch is putting it all together. First, she goes to Belfast to find out all she can about Linda Meredith, then she's talking to my Aunt Margaret about me, and now she's arrested Janek and no doubt is firing all sorts of questions at him. And you can be sure it's all about me.

If I don't act soon, I'm fucked. Tara could be ready to arrest me any day now. I keep telling myself that she has no real evidence. How could she? I don't leave any traces. Unless the cops in Belfast have managed to find my DNA on the body they pulled from the sea. But I don't believe they have. That leaves only Tara's suspicions about me. Maybe she has remembered what I did to her, and her wee imagination is running riot in that pretty head of hers. But she must be thinking of me. Why else would she speak with my Aunt Margaret?

Janek's arrest really scares me. What is he likely to tell them? He doesn't have any loyalty to me. I'm just one of his customers. But it was all over the local news. They're saying that a gang feud has erupted in Liverpool, and it's linked to drugs. Next thing I saw was Janek walking from St Anne Street nick, wearing his stinking leather coat. Released on bail apparently. But why St Anne Street, unless it has something to do with Tara's investigation? And I know she doesn't work with the drug squad. She works on murder investigations.

The big question for me now, is how much do her colleagues know about me? How much of her flying to Belfast, her talking to my Aunt Margaret, and questioning Janek has she shared with her mates? If she's keeping most of it to herself, I still might have a chance. I could snatch her, do what I should have done ages ago and dump her in the Irish Sea.

Kirsty went out with her mates this evening, to plan her hen party. That left me time to plan a party of my own. A stag party with a difference, you might say. No other blokes involved. Just me, one of Tara's mates and, hopefully, Tara – to end the party of a lifetime.

With all the thinking I'm doing, planning and stuff, I realised I now have another wee problem. It may not be such a clever idea to go bothering Janek for a supply of China White. I'm quite certain the bizzies are keeping a close eye on what he gets up to. Besides, Janek is not going to set himself up by traipsing around the city carrying a stash of drugs. He's not that stupid. I'm sure he'll be lying low for a while. That means I will have to suss out another supplier before I go after one of Tara's friends.

This is getting so messy.

CHAPTER 49

It didn't take long to dispel Tara's memory of a fun evening. Facing her on her screen was a comprehensive dossier on James Guy. Gina Marshall had been thorough and successful in researching the early life of her suspect. She scrolled through the file hoping, somewhat ridiculously, that the key to this mystery man, the vital evidence that proved him to be the serial killer she believed him to be, would leap from the screen. With no such clue immediately apparent, she began reading the file from the beginning.

Several documents were embedded within the report. A birth certificate confirmed Guy's age as nearly thirty-six. His mother was named as Rachel Guy; the father's name was Trevor Mount.

The only home address provided for the young James was the house Tara had visited with Gina Marshall – the family home in Bangor and occupied by Rachel Guy's sister, Margaret.

The next item in the file had Tara calling out across the office for Wilson. He rushed to her desk.

'Yes, ma'am?'

'John, I need the photos again from Lawler's flat.'

'Yes, ma'am.'

It seemed like the hundredth time she had made the same request, on each occasion for a different reason.

When Wilson retrieved the folder, Tara spread the photos across her desk. Wilson couldn't help looking on. So many times, they had discussed the significance of this collection, speculating on why Terry Lawler had compiled it.

Quickly, she selected one photograph. Twenty-four of the twenty-nine photos, thanks to Wilson's hard work, had names attached. The one that Tara lifted from the desk did not. It was a faded colour snap of a woman, roughly in her early twenties, with a hairdo reminiscent of the 1980s, blonde highlights swept back and high, long dangling earrings and shoulder pads. Tara compared the photograph with the image on her screen, a picture of Rachel Guy, at an age given as twenty-one. According to Marshall's report, Rachel was only twenty-four when she left home. James was eight years old then. That meant she had been sixteen when she gave birth to her son.

The woman on the screen had a more natural look than the young woman in the snap, with less make-up and longer fair hair. But there was no doubt it was the same woman in both pictures. Rachel Guy. Tara wondered if Terry Lawler had figured out who she was.

What had caused a mother to leave home for good, to abandon her young son? The implication by her sister, Margaret, was that Rachel had deliberately taken off, not that she had been abducted. It was difficult to imagine how a young mother could leave home and, quite deliberately, never contact her family again.

She wondered how James had dealt with such loss, and what he thought of his mother.

Tara kept reading, and Wilson returned to his desk. There was nothing exciting in the remaining text. James was abandoned by Rachel when he was eight years old, and she hadn't been heard of since. James then lived with his grandmother, Agnes Guy, who died when he seventeen. He attended the local primary school and moved to grammar school when he passed the transfer examinations at age eleven. He got two A levels, in English and History, but did not go to university. Instead, he held a series of jobs in the Greater Belfast area: working at McDonald's, then at a service station and finally as a delivery driver. The document contained other information that Tara already knew about Guy's life since he moved to Liverpool. It was sketchy, to say the least. Nothing about friends or relationships, and nothing to suggest that James Guy had ever done anything untoward to young women in Northern Ireland or England. His school reports marked him as a student with potential for academic achievement, but quiet and lacking friends. That was not enough to prove he subsequently snatched women, murdered them and dumped their bodies in the sea. All she had in terms of evidence was his conviction for what he had done to her.

Her phone rang, and when she picked it up the voice was that of a female with a Belfast accent.

'Good morning, ma'am, it's DC Marshall.'

'Ah good morning, Gina. Thank you for the report on James Guy. I was just reading through it.'

'No problem, ma'am. I'm calling, though, about the murder of Ryan Boswell. Thought you might be interested to know that Carly McHugh is missing from home.'

'Oh. Do you think something has happened to her?'

'No, I don't believe so. Officers at Belfast Port clocked her boarding the ferry for Cairnryan four days ago. It has just registered on our system.'

'Do you know of any reason for her going there?'

'No. It could be entirely innocent, or she may be on a job for her father.'

'Do you think it's possible she's travelled to Liverpool?'

'Hard to say, ma'am, although I would guess she's returned to her flat in Sunderland. It is more likely she'd take the Liverpool ferry, if she was coming your way.'

'True. Many thanks for that, Gina. I'll be in touch if anything happens over here.'

'Bye, ma'am.'

Tara put down the phone and leaned back from her computer. James Guy was once again relegated to the lower leagues of her thinking. Perhaps Carly McHugh had returned to her flat in Sunderland to pick up her life again. Perhaps she was going there to clear things up on her father's behalf, before starting again elsewhere.

Or perhaps she had entirely different intentions.

CHAPTER 50

Much to the chagrin of DCI Weir, the investigation into the murder of Ryan Boswell remained the responsibility of Harold Tweedy's team, while he took charge of investigations into the killing of Tyler Finlay. Since both victims had been members of the same gang and their deaths seemed to be connected to the drug trade, it would usually have made sense for the investigations to be brought under one senior investigating officer. But Tara knew well that operations and police staffing arrangements didn't always follow the most logical route. Having left the briefest of meetings with Tweedy and Weir, she felt stifled in her pursuit of Ryan Boswell's killer.

It transpired that the gun used to shoot Tyler Finlay was not the same weapon used in the killing of Boswell, nor did it have a history of use in Belfast. For Weir, this pointed to gang activity on Merseyside, while for Tara it didn't necessarily rule out a link to the McHugh and Hobbs gang in Belfast. She had even dared to ask Weir what he had gained from the arrest of another supposed drug dealer, Janek Poska. He had answered with his increasingly familiar condescension.

'You're assuming, DI Grogan, that my interest in Poska is connected solely to the murders of Finlay and Boswell. I haven't said so.'

'Well, is Poska linked to the murders?' she asked brusquely.

Tweedy was a pensive-looking bystander, but Tara guessed he had sensed some of Weir's petulance. Weir, rather than respond to Tara, addressed Tweedy directly.

'I am not prepared to disclose my interest in Janek Poska, Harold. You're forgetting that I have several ongoing operations relating to gangland activities in this city. I am not going to compromise my investigations. In my opinion, these murders are down to a feud. Don't forget, Poska's cousin, Mikk Klavan, is another victim, and it adds weight to my theory that a gang war is in full swing.'

Tara was tempted to throw in her news that Carly McHugh had left Belfast and, in her opinion, was quite possibly now in Liverpool. She didn't think Weir deserved to hear it. Besides, she wouldn't want such details to interfere with one of his ongoing operations. She bit her lip and thankfully, Tweedy put an end to her discomfort.

'OK, Malcolm, we'll continue to liaise with you over anything we turn up in relation to Boswell. If you would do likewise regarding Finlay, I would appreciate it.'

'That's fine,' Weir replied, rising from his seat and squeezing his frame through the door ahead of Tara.

She caught a whiff of his delightful fragrance as she followed him from the office. When she reached her desk, she called out, in irritated tones, for Alan Murray.

'What's up, Tara?'

Murray had chosen the wrong time to be familiar, and Tara glared at him.

'Really, Alan, do I need to remind you?'

'Sorry, ma'am.'

She let it rest. She'd vented enough anger.

'We need to search for Carly McHugh. I think she may have returned to Liverpool.'

'To do what?'

'Well, it could be she is on her father's business, but I can't help thinking that she's here to find whoever killed Boswell – that's if she doesn't already know.'

'Do you think she killed Finlay?'

Tara closed her eyes and drew a deep breath. She feared getting this wrong. She dreaded another confrontation with DCI Weir. But she had met Carly McHugh, she'd witnessed her bravado and saw it crumble when it was suggested that she had been romantically involved with Boswell. And she'd caught a glimpse of the girl's anger.

'I really don't know, Alan. What I can't get out of my head is the idea that Boswell's murder is linked with Belfast. The gun used to kill him had been used there previously. Those men who showed up on Treadwater were from Belfast. I was warned, in Belfast, to keep my nose out. Yet Weir has told me repeatedly that it's got nothing to do with Belfast. So why do I keep returning to Carly McHugh?'

'What do we do next?'

'I know it sounds implausible, but we have to search for her. Maybe she has gone to Sunderland, but if she has come back to Liverpool then surely, she will turn up in Treadwater. Firstly, check with police in Sunderland whether Carly's flat is now occupied and have them check out the address we found in Finlay's notebook.'

* * *

Murray didn't think they would achieve much, and he told her so. Sitting in a car by a row of shops on the Treadwater Estate, they were doing little but hope someone interesting was going to pass by. Weak sunshine entered from her side of the car, making it difficult to see anything when she looked in that direction. Tara tried to convince herself that they were doing the right thing.

The outcome of Murray's communication with Sunderland Police added to her tentative beliefs. There was no sign of activity at McHugh's apartment in Sunderland. The address found in Finlay's notebook turned out to be a disused industrial unit near the docks.

'If she's out to avenge Ryan's murder, she has to come to Treadwater.'

'But you said Boswell's killer probably came from Belfast. Why would she come here?'

'No, I didn't, Alan. The gun used to kill Boswell had been used previously in Belfast.'

'It amounts to the same thing. And then there were those two heavies hanging around at Boswell's funeral.'

Tara fell silent and watched as a woman wheeled a child's buggy past the car. Why else would Carly McHugh have returned to Liverpool, if not to seek revenge for the death of her boyfriend? Had she begun by shooting Tyler Finlay? He was the supposed leader of the Treadwater Vipers, so who had taken over from him? Her thoughts drifted and she was only dimly aware of the tones of Ken Bruce on Radio 2, asking phone-in listeners questions about pop music from before she was born. Murray answered a few and wasn't bad on music from the eighties and nineties.

'What do you think Carly was running from, the night Boswell was shot?'

'Isn't it obvious?' said Murray. Then, 'Red Hot Chilli Peppers,' he blurted in answer to a question on the radio.

Tara sighed in exasperation.

'The shooter, yes, but what happened after Boswell was killed? We know she ran through the estate, but was she being chased or was she merely running in fear or running from the crime scene?'

'I thought one of the door-to-door witnesses said that they saw a man searching the streets shortly after the girl had run by.'

'So, who was it?'

Murray looked incredulously at his boss.

'Um, that would be the killer.'

'You're being sarcastic again, Alan, and I can do without it, thank you. What I'm trying to figure out is how she got away. If the killer was chasing her and caught her, why wasn't she killed?'

'Well, obviously he didn't catch her, and she scarpered back to Northern Ireland.'

Tara closed her eyes in frustration. Either Murray was being obtuse, or she wasn't explaining herself very well.

'What if the killer was one of Rab McHugh's men, under orders to shoot Boswell and bring Carly home to Belfast?'

'That fits since the gun used had a history in Belfast. But if that's true, then why would Carly be back in Liverpool seeking revenge? She would already know who killed her boyfriend. If you ask me, Carly could be anywhere in England.'

They were getting nowhere with the discussion, and nothing of interest seemed likely to appear before their eyes. Now feeling rather foolish for wasting their time, Tara ordered them back to the station. Murray was happy, not least, for the opportunity to have an early lunch.

From Tweedy, Tara managed to get a copy of the crime scene report for the murder of Tyler Finlay. She hoped the report might have some relevance to the murder of Ryan Boswell. She did not, however, want DCI Weir to find out that she had been reading details of his case. After a morning spent in discussion with Murray, she was no closer to believing Weir's interpretation of the events unfolding on the Treadwater Estate. She didn't like him, and she was certain he didn't like her.

Tyler Finlay had been shot five times; two bullets to the upper body and three in the head and face. All from close range and through the driver's-side window of the BMW. Finlay died instantly. Twenty-five thousand pounds, in used and mixed notes, were found on the passenger seat of the car. The boot was full of drugs. These had been sent for analysis but seemed likely to be cocaine. So, the motive, even if gang-related, had not been theft.

The gun used had no prior history, therefore nothing to indicate it had originated in Belfast with McHugh's organisation. There were no significant prints lifted from the car, but a mobile phone belonging to Finlay showed recent calls to several numbers. Two of them were traced to other members of the Vipers, namely Craig Lewis and Aidan Boswell. Tara wondered if DCI Weir had interviewed either man. House-to-house inquiries had yielded little significant information. There were apparently no witnesses to the killing of Finlay, despite the shooting having taken place in the evening at around nine thirty. The only scrap of information was that several people who had heard the shots said that they'd heard a motorcycle roaring by their homes shortly afterwards. Of course, alibis were easy to come by for the other members of the Vipers. They had all been at home with their girlfriends, or working late, although this latter excuse Tara found hard to believe, since most of the Vipers didn't have regular jobs. Apparently, no gang members were nearby when the killings of Ryan Boswell and Tyler Finlay occurred.

Before leaving for home, Tara made a mental note to ask Gina Marshall if she knew how Carly McHugh had boarded the ferry from Belfast. Then, her phone beeped. She had a message from Aisling.

CHAPTER 51

It was all air kisses and loose hugs – some kind of VIP do at a club in Harrington Street. I could have stood at the corner and watched the totty come and go all night. Four honeys, all dressed the same in tight black trousers, waistcoats and white bowties, with bare arms and spike heels, greeted the guests as they arrived. I recognised several of them. A couple of Premiership footballers, a locally bred actress who'd made it big and got herself on TV chat shows and even an Oscar nomination. But I wasn't interested in her. Not for now, anyway. She was pleasing enough, in the shortest dress I've ever seen, with blonde hair extensions and dripping with jewellery. One of the four hostesses handed her a glass of champagne as she stepped from the car under a canopy and onto the red carpet.

It was a bizarre scene in such a narrow, unappealing street, little wider than a back alley. A small group of press and photographers was hanging about, shouting questions and asking for pictures. A dozen or so fans and autograph hunters looked on eagerly alongside the paparazzi. The actress posed with her man, holding his arm as the photographers snapped. Then the guy was told to step aside, and they got a few solo shots of the girl. I could see she was loving it.

Other guests were snapped too, as they entered the club with their complimentary glass of bubbly. It was fun to watch. But I wasn't there to have fun. I had a job to do.

I was observing one person in particular. Her long black hair dangled down her back. She looked fantastic in her skimpy waistcoat, smiling and embracing the guests, giving the standard-issue air kiss on both cheeks. Aisling was good at this job. She was made for it. Stunning, vivacious and thus given access to the type of social gathering that let her mix with the rich and famous.

I wondered what time she finished work, and whether her work then became her leisure. But I needed answers to other questions. Did she go home alone? By car? By taxi? Would she be drunk or sober? And how did her days begin? I knew I didn't have time to spend on this target in the way I generally liked to with my girls. Usually, I worked on every detail of a girl's routine, to the point that sometimes I even knew their time of the month. I worked out the time they got up, when they got home, the people they were sleeping with, the places they went for lunch or dinner. Every detail was noted so that when the time came to snatch them, there would be no mistakes, no miscalculations.

But Aisling had to be taken before her mate, DI Grogan, found out anything more about me. In other words, as soon as possible. I had considered her other friend, Kate, the nurse, but I hadn't seen her about, either at her house or at the hospital where she works. So, it had to be the leggy Aisling. A bit of a novelty for me, taking a tall bird — although I'd recently had Daisy under consideration.

Of course, Kirsty has been wondering what the hell I'm getting up to, staying out late and leaving early in the morning. I've told her I have to work a new shift pattern, but I've hardly been to work since setting my sights on Aisling. I don't have the time. I phoned in sick, told my supervisor that I have recurring PTSD after my experience with that nutter Collywell and his crazy sister. The very mention of PTSD is enough for the boss to leave it be. They don't want to poke their noses in too far. I can always shout harassment.

So that leaves me free to do my recon on the girl who will lead me to Tara Grogan.

I went down to Runcorn and managed to buy a nice van at an auction. Quite big. The usual sliding door, handy for pushing my girl inside. Big enough to take two girls and me, comfortably.

I had to find somewhere secure to leave it until I needed it. I can't let Kirsty see it. She's been looking at family cars and child seats for the baby. She wants everything sorted before the wedding. This Saturday I'm supposed to go with her da to get fitted for a wedding suit. And she's still hassling me over a best man. I don't have a friggin' best man. I have plenty of best girls, but that's none of her business.

Besides, by the time the wedding comes around I could be well gone, serving a lifer for taking wee Tara or, if I'm lucky, on the run. Somehow, I can no longer visualise Kirsty and me settling into a life of happy families.

I was frozen hanging about the street, but I wouldn't get a better chance of watching Aisling without drawing suspicion. Looked as though I was one of those saddos who hangs around VIP functions just waiting for a chance to see a celebrity. Maybe I should get a selfie with one of them.

Other people came and went, while I leaned my back against a wall, stuffed my hands in my pockets and kept an eye on the gorgeous Aisling. A woman worth watching, especially if she leads me to Tara.

CHAPTER 52

There were no buttons remaining on Janek's leather jacket, but he pulled it close around him as he waited for his partner to show up. A wind was strengthening, lowering the temperature; he couldn't recall feeling this cold since he'd come to Liverpool six years ago. It felt more like January in Tallinn.

The shower of rain had caught him unawares as he walked the length of Hanover Street, then Ranelagh Street and finally Brownlow Hill, where he stood close to a bus shelter alongside the Adelphi. His jeans were soaked through, and his left shoe must have a hole because he felt his foot, wet and cold. He'd made his last deal of the day, there were a couple more to do later in the evening but for now he could return to the scrapyard in Tranmere and maybe get some fish and chips on the way.

Janek liked this English tradition, fish with chips, plenty of salt and vinegar. All his life spent running wild in Tallinn had set him up for his move to Britain. Liverpool suited him; he liked the people and business was good. Now, of course, he had to be extra careful. He had bizzies watching out for him and there was the threat of those animals, the Vipers. He now realised they were serious about chasing him from the city, but until he could find and establish a new patch, he had to do his business in the centre of Liverpool. He had clients to supply. The Vipers might want him out, but they would never take his customers away.

Fifteen minutes in the cold was about all he could take, and he told Aksel in his own language exactly what he thought when he arrived in the car, forty minutes later. His mood was foul, and he knew it as he reprimanded his younger friend. Aksel was nearly half his age, black greased hair and short-clipped beard. He really should not be driving these streets having sight in only his right eye, but Janek needed him to do it. He didn't trust his other associates. Too fucking lazy. They were happier to run the legitimate car breakers business, but the first to complain if they didn't get their cut of the drug money. His waiting in the cold and his soaking had really set him on a downward spiral. Tonight, he thought he might get high. It was not something he usually did, but he felt so fucking wretched.

Aksel bought the fish and chips from a shop in Birkenhead and drove to the scrapyard in Tranmere. The corrugated-iron gates were still open. Someone was working late or, more likely, the lazy bastards were playing cards. Janek was too cold and too hungry to care. He was already tucking into his chips as he stepped into the darkened office.

No one here after all. Had they simply forgotten to close the gates? Useless cretins. He switched on an old CD player and instantly it blasted the familiar rock music of his homeland. Without waiting for Aksel to join him, he sat down at his desk and ate his battered cod. It wasn't yet dark outside, but the small and filthy window did not provide much light. His mind was swirling. He felt strange. Still cold, but also on edge as if things weren't quite right or he had forgotten to do something. He had some gear to put together for tonight's deals. Some China White for that prick Mr Guy. A meeting at seven o'clock outside Liverpool One. Easy money. Where the fuck was Aksel? Why wasn't he coming to eat his dinner? He called out his compatriot's name.

'Fuck him,' he grumbled, and tore into a piece of fish.

When he'd had enough food he rose from the cluttered desk, wiping both greasy hands on his jeans, and opened a drawer of an old wooden cabinet. He lifted out a half-empty bottle of Smirnoff, twisted off the cap, placed the bottle to his mouth and took a swig.

Then he heard a noise behind him and turned around.

The bottle shattered with the first shot, the second bullet settled in his brain, and Janek Poska slumped to the floor.

Outside, a car engine idled. The interior of the BMW was splattered in blood. Aksel's head rested on the steering wheel.

CHAPTER 53

The past four days have been hectic. I know I don't have much time, but still the perfectionist in me wants to get it right. On Tuesday I ventured down to Mother Freedom, moored at Porth Penrhyn. Kitted her out with a fresh mattress, food, some drink, got her fuelled up, loaded six bags of loose gravel, all ready and waiting for Tara and her mate. When I got back to the city I bought a couple of mobile phones, pay-as-you-go, of course, so they can't be traced to me. I devised the routes I want to take from Liverpool to Mother Freedom. You see, I must be sure that when I use Aisling to draw out Tara, no one else is tagging along. By that I mean other cops. If anyone gets to hear what's going on, I'm fucked. If things go to plan, Tara and Aisling will disappear like the rest of them, not a trace left, and I can get on with the rest of my life.

Honestly, I'm so stressed out over this that I doubt I will ever take another girl. I'll marry Kirsty, be a dad to my kid, maybe have a couple more and life should be too sweet for my eye to go roving again.

Last night, I left Kirsty shopping in Liverpool One and sneaked off to buy the gear I will need to see off two girls. I was supposed to meet Janek outside, in Paradise Place, close to the John Lewis store. He didn't show. I know he's a cautious bastard, wouldn't attempt a meet if he thought something was up, the cops watching or something, but usually he finds a way to communicate that he can't make the deal. I'm sure he must be uneasy after getting pulled into the cop shop, but when I took the chance and contacted him, he said it would be no problem. I waited for nearly an hour. He's never late. Has this uncanny way of finding you when you least expect it, no matter how good you think you are at spotting him, he always sees you first.

Kirsty was on the phone, asking where I'd got to. I told her I was browsing in Waterstones, and lost track of the time. At that point I wasn't too bothered that Janek hadn't turned up. A couple of phone calls and we could arrange another meet.

Kirsty was laden with shopping bags when I met up with her at Starbucks.

'Didn't you buy any books?'

'Nah, didn't see anything I liked.'

We chatted over coffee, like an old married couple. She went through everything she'd bought, mostly stuff for our new house. That project seems to have forged ahead without much input from me. But I can't be arsed. I know I'll feel more interested when I lay the Tara Grogan problem to rest. So, I let Kirsty prattle on, nodding, throwing in the odd supporting comment, smiling in delight at a set of towels she pulled from a bag. You see, I knew that if I kept her sweet then when we got home, she would be all sweet to me in bed.

From habit, I checked the news on TV when we got back to the flat. Kirsty was changing into her new maternity dress to let me see it. All of this was piss poor timing. I'd just finished reading a bulletin on the shooting of two men in Tranmere, earlier in the evening, and was worried that it was Janek – drug dealing was mentioned in the report. Then, in twirls Kirsty in her new dress and I hardly looked at her.

I couldn't sleep. Couldn't think about sex with Kirsty, not that she was up for it anyway after my failure to enthuse about her dress. My head was buzzing. What if Janek had been arrested again? What if he was involved in the murders of the guys in Tranmere? Or what if it was Janek who'd been killed? Then where would I get my gear from? I know I could eventually find a new dealer, but I don't have the time right now. I needed some China White to see off Tara and Aisling.

Next morning, I patched things up with Kirsty before she left for work. I really do love her, don't want her upset, not with the wedding, the new house and the baby coming.

Before I went out, I couldn't help checking the news. My worst fears were confirmed. Janek, my supplier, was dead. What the fuck is going on? Did this murder have anything to do with Tara investigating me? Bloody strange if it was just coincidence.

But I had no time to worry about an Estonian drug dealer. It's not like he was a mate or anything. I needed to get an alternative supply. If Tara was really coming after me, I knew what I had to do.

CHAPTER 54

Tara had also listened to the breakfast news with interest. And like James Guy, she had not slept well. Her arm still ached from the rough handling she'd suffered in Belfast and from the manipulation by her physio. She was never one for taking painkillers. Instead, she curled up on the sofa in her dressing gown and nursed a cappuccino. It was Friday morning, and she could hardly wait for tomorrow, Saturday, a chance to rest, to unwind, to catch up on laundry and tidy her bedroom, which was currently a bomb site of discarded clothes and shoes.

Her phone lay on the arm of the sofa, happily pinging texts from Aisling, WhatsApp messages from Kate on holiday and emails from all the usual spam merchants. She ignored it all and listened intently to the breakfast news on BBC One, which regaled her with the continuing political debate, the effects of climate change, the failure of the

NHS to meet targets and the sacking of a Premiership football manager.

All this became irrelevant when the local bulletin reported the murders of two men at a scrapyard in Tranmere. The opinion of a senior Merseyside Police detective, whose name was not familiar to her, was that a gang war had erupted between rivals in the Liverpool drugs trade. That statement could have been written by DCI Weir, she thought. She would take some convincing before she could believe that these killings were linked to the murder of Ryan Boswell. Yet she knew that DCI Weir would currently be wallowing in a bath of vindication – if he ever took a bath.

* * *

Arriving at work later that morning, Tara heard the story going around the station at St Anne Street – that the Vipers had taken revenge on the Tallinn Crew for the shooting of their leader, Tyler Finlay. Matrix had acted quickly, and several prominent members of the Vipers had been arrested in the early morning. Homes had been searched, mobile phones seized, and house-to-house enquiries instigated. Tara imagined that DCI Weir was having a busy day. Maybe he was right, she thought. She couldn't imagine how the two men in Tranmere fitted into the story of Carly McHugh, her father and Ryan Boswell. A feud had begun, a turf war between rival gangs in the city, and maybe Belfast was involved only because Carly had had a relationship with Boswell. Or maybe they had interests in the Vipers and were now feeling threatened by the killings and by the police investigations. But none of that answered Tara's questions. Why had Carly McHugh left her home in Northern Ireland, where had she gone and what was she doing now?

Tara called DC Gina Marshall in Belfast.

'Hi, Gina, it's me again, come to ask another favour.'

'Hello, ma'am. No problem, what can I do for you?'

'You told me that Carly McHugh had travelled to Scotland on the ferry. Was she a foot passenger or did she have a vehicle?'

'I don't know, ma'am, but I can soon find out.'

'That would be great, Gina.'

'How are you getting on with your serial killer?'

Tara sighed.

'All quiet again, I'm afraid. I spoke with his former probation officer, Jason Collywell, the man who tried to kill him. Collywell is convinced that James Guy is a sex fiend, but he had nothing concrete to give me. I would love to find out what happened to Guy's mother, Rachel, to see if it has a bearing on how James turned out. Unfortunately, I don't have the time to begin a search.'

'If you don't mind me saying, ma'am, the circumstantial evidence you have from the pictures and the timeline of Guy's life, it all fits. Why not pull him in for a chat?'

'Mm, maybe you're right, Gina. Nothing to lose, I suppose. Right now, though, I'm up to my neck in this Boswell thing.'

As Tara put down the phone, her mobile beeped with another text from Aisling. So far this morning she'd managed to ignore her friend's pleas to go shopping with her on Saturday. Aisling liked to make an early start on purchasing clothes for her holiday. Kate did too, but as she was currently away with her mum that meant Tara, who usually left that kind of shopping to the last minute, would have to go with Aisling. Feeling sorry for her friend, she was about to forgo her planned day of housework, when her desk phone sounded.

'Ma'am, it's Gina. I have that info you wanted.'

'That was quick!'

'Carly boarded the Cairnryan ferry on a motorbike. A green Kawasaki Ninja 300. I have the registration for you.'

Suddenly, Tara felt her heart rate increase. She ordered Wilson to issue an alert for the motorbike. If Carly

McHugh was in Liverpool, she hoped they would soon find her. She called out for Murray.

'Alan, let's pay another visit to Treadwater.'

CHAPTER 55

I didn't have time to hang about; I would have to take whatever I could get. No chance of getting my hands on China White, not with Janek out of the frame. I contacted some waster by the name of Cheez who hangs out near my old flat in Toxteth. He was a creepy wee shite. Looked the type of dealer who usually sold to schoolkids – lowest of the low. Tried to fleece me and then thought he could offload a bag of ecstasy pills. No bloody use to me. Then he tried to sell me spice, legal highs. A walking supermarket, this guy. Spice is too risky, there's no telling what reaction I'd get from the girls, and besides, I would have to get them to smoke the stuff. No good for me. In the end he sold me some roofies. I'd no idea how much I was going to need. Didn't think there would be enough to see off my lovelies. But I was hoping that I had enough to keep them quiet when I needed them to be.

I picked up the van from the street where I'd left it, a mile away from our flat. It was already kitted out with a mattress, blankets, cable ties and gaffer tape, the usual tools of my trade. Then I set off for Wapping Dock, to wait for the sultry Aisling.

It was gone half ten in the morning; I didn't think she would be out of her bed yet. I settled in on the road by the exit to her car park and prepared myself for a bit of a wait. But my luck was in already – I'd only just finished an egg sandwich when I saw her pull up to the barrier in her wee sporty hatchback. She was leaving, but Aisling was so easy to follow, and besides, I already had a good idea of where she was headed.

Just past the Liver Building, she turned right into Chapel Street and then left into an alley and the entrance to a small private parking area. I drove on by, to a spot I knew where I could park the van and pretend to be unloading. Hurrying back to the alley on foot, I caught a glimpse of her going in by a side door to the offices of the promotions company she worked for.

I had already sussed out the likely progress of Aisling's day. She would either be inside the office until lunchtime, when she would wander around the shops, maybe have a coffee and a snack, or she would leave the office soon and be on her way to a job somewhere in the city. Easy.

I paced the alley and Chapel Street, keeping an eye on the front and side entrances to her office. It was quite a cool day, with a breeze blowing, an inconvenient time to be without a jacket, but I wore a baseball cap to hide my face from any CCTV. It wasn't long before she emerged from the side door, carrying a cardboard box. Another honey appeared beside her, also struggling with a large box.

These girls really knew how to dress. Aisling wore a short pink leather skirt and black suede boots, a woolly jumper and scarf, while her mate had enormous heels, black leggings and a yellow leather jacket. I watched the pair of them wiggle to Aisling's car and jogged by to get to my van. I caught sight of the wee red car as it left the alley and turned into Chapel Street. Both girls were on board.

I followed them all the way to a shopping mall in Bootle. It seemed obvious to me, when I saw them unload their boxes and carry them inside, that they would be working here for a while, so I took myself to Costa for a coffee and a muffin. When I'd finished, I strolled through the shopping centre, and it didn't take long to spot the pair of them working at a small promotional stand. Feeling bold, I walked past slowly; close enough to reach out and grope Aisling's bum if I'd wanted to, as she chatted with two young girls about the benefits of using the moisturiser she was holding. She didn't see me, but the other girl spoke.

'Hiya,' she sang, holding a bottle of the cream. 'Would you like to try our moisturiser?'

'No thanks,' I replied.

The girl had a narrow face and small mouth, but lovely red hair and green eyes. At that point, I saw Aisling look at me while continuing to chat with her two customers. I was not sure if she recognised me, but she had that slightly confused expression that suggested an alarm had just rung in her head.

It was then that I realised I was going to have to get her away from her colleague. I couldn't afford to wait until the evening when she would be headed home. I had far too much to do. This would have to be a snatch unlike any I had done before.

I tried to find a place nearby from which to keep a close eye on her. She had plenty of potential customers strolling by, and that kept her busy. When she wasn't pushing her face cream she was on her mobile, talking, texting, browsing. The mall was filling up as lunchtime approached and I hoped this would provide my opportunity. Usually, I wouldn't dare take a girl in this kind of place, too many witnesses and the scourge of CCTV, but I would just have to try my best to make everything look quite innocent.

I went back to Costa, bought another coffee and sat down in a quiet corner. I pulled out one of the new mobiles I'd bought on which I'd made a note of the office number for the promotions agency where Aisling worked.

A cheerful female voice answered.

'Hello, this is DC Wilson, Merseyside Police,' I said in my best Scouse accent. It was handy that I recalled the name Wilson from the time he interviewed me in hospital after my experience at the hands of that crazy bitch Aeron.

'Danielle speaking. How may I help you?' said the girl.

'I was hoping to speak with Aisling Doherty.'

'She's not in the office right now. Would you like to leave a message?'

'I really need to speak with her right away. Can you give me her mobile number?'

'Sorry, I'm not supposed to give out personal information on the telephone.'

'I understand, Danielle, but this is urgent. Aisling's friend, DI Grogan, has been injured, and she's asking to speak to her.'

'Tara?'

'That's right. Do you know her?'

'Not well, but she comes to our events sometimes. Hold on, I'll get Aisling's number for you.'

Sweet.

I finished my coffee, then casually strolled by the wee promotion stand where Aisling and her mate were still chatting with all the passers-by they could catch. In the adjoining multi-storey car park, I moved my van to a space as close as possible to Aisling's car. It was still about twenty yards away, but it would have to do. Then, I dialled in the number that Danielle had given me. At first, I thought it was going to cut to voicemail; then Aisling answered.

'Hello, who's this?'

'Hi, Aisling, DC Wilson from St Anne Street station. Tara asked me to call you.'

'Why, what's wrong?'

'She's been injured in an incident. She's fine, but she's in A&E at the Royal.'

'Oh my God, what's happened to her?' Aisling sounded panicky.

'She'll be fine, Aisling. She asked me to call; she can't get to her phone at the minute.'

'OK, I'm on my way. The Royal?'

'That's right. I'll see you there.'

I cut the call.

Sweet.

Two minutes later, I watched her rush into the car park as fast as she could in her high-heeled boots. And before she knew what was happening, I was walking beside her. At first, she gave me no more than a sideways glance, but I got her full attention when I pricked her side with my knife. Then I got my left hand around her head and over her mouth. I imagine that her screams would have been bloody loud, had I not muffled them. Abruptly, I changed our direction and marched her to the van. I slid open the side door and bundled her inside. I didn't mean to but as she tried to wrestle from my grasp the knife went into her side. The cut was not deep, but there was blood.

'Shut the fuck up, Aisling, or you'll get worse.'

She looked a sight, no longer the cracking bird I'd been watching for the past few days. Her mascara was smudged, and tears were streaked on her face. She looked more like Alice Cooper than a glamorous promotions girl. I had to act quickly, before she gave me away with all her struggling and attempts at squealing.

Holding the knife to her throat, I warned her again.

'Not a fucking word, Aisling. Do as I say, and we won't have a problem. Understand?'

I shook her, once. Her eyes looked ready to pop from their sockets.

'Understand? You wouldn't want anything to happen to your wee friend, Tara.'

She shrieked in horror.

At last, she seemed to catch on. I ripped a piece of gaffer tape from the bulkhead of the van, another preparation of mine, and stuck it over her mouth. Then I bound her hands with a cable tie and, removing her boots, did the same to her feet. There were no syringes filled with China White this time. I pulled back the tape from her mouth and forced a pill inside, replacing the tape. Even if she didn't swallow, it would dissolve in her gob. That done, I left her in the back and went to pay for my parking at the pay station.

As I walked back to the van, I could hear the wee cow kicking up a racket, thumping the wall of the van with her feet. I thought, if she would only use her head to do the thumping, she might pass out a lot quicker. I jumped into the driver's seat. Starting the engine, I eased from the space, drove by her car, slipped my ticket into the machine, waited for the barrier to lift and drove onto the road. I realised that much of what I'd just done would be picked up by the CCTV in the car park, but I'd had no choice. I would have to burn the van this time and perhaps get rid of Mother Freedom too. There could be no traces left for the bizzies to connect me with Aisling and Tara.

With Aisling drifting into oblivion, I was already past the point of no return.

CHAPTER 56

Tara was wary of treading on DCI Weir's toes, of interfering in whatever investigation he had going. But she hoped that speaking with Shania Smith once more would not encroach upon the DCI's operations.

They were shown into the lounge of the Smith household in Treadwater by a large lady in her late thirties. She hadn't said much when greeted by police officers; her drawn face and tired blue eyes seemed weary of it all. Wearing a grey dressing gown and well-worn furry slippers, she called out to her daughter.

'Shania! Bizzies here to see you.' With that, she pointed to the lounge door and proceeded upstairs.

Shania was lying on a sofa, a duvet pulled up to her waist despite the warmth of the room. Her face was heavily bruised, a mess of purples and yellows, her left arm still in plaster and strapped up to her shoulder. She didn't look happy to see them.

'How are you feeling, Shania?' Tara asked.

Shania didn't reply, merely watched Murray as he browsed the living room. It was not a large space, not with two over-sized sofas, a TV with a fifty-inch screen and a heavy-looking coffee table plonked in the middle of the floor. Murray flicked through a couple of women's magazines he'd lifted from the table, as Shania continued to watch him.

'I'm sure you know by now that Tyler was killed?' said Tara.

Immediately, tears began to flow, and Tara quickly rifled through her bag and produced a fresh tissue for the girl.

'You have nothing to fear from speaking to us, Shania. We just want to find out who attacked you and who killed Ryan and Tyler. Anything, no matter how small you think it is, could help.'

'It was Tyler.' She dabbed the tissue at her eyes. Her speech was still constrained by the wiring of her jaw, but she managed to form the words.

'Tyler what? It was Tyler who beat you?'

The girl nodded. Tara hoped that she had more to say, but silence ensued, and Murray moved on to examine various family pictures in frames on the wall. Still Shania watched him.

'Why did Tyler beat you?' asked Tara.

'Had a row, that's all.'

'What were you rowing about?'

Shania lowered her head and sobbed into her chest. Tara could wait. The girl's mother, however, had other ideas. She stood at the threshold of the room with her arms folded.

'Tell them, Shania. Tell them everything and be done with it. If you don't, then I will.'

Tara was surprised by the woman's tone. On first meeting, she hadn't thought the mother was the least concerned by her daughter's woes. Now it seemed that Shania had shared what she knew, what she had been through, with her mother. But still the teenager could not bring herself to explain.

'Tyler said that you knew too much, didn't he, Shania? Saw too much, as well. Go on, tell them, Shania.'

'OK, Mum,' she said irritated. She blotted the last tear from her right eye. 'It happened at a party,' she began. 'Tyler had taken something – coke, I think. He wasn't himself. Started shouting at me in front of his mates. Had everyone laughing at me. He pushed me down the stairs. I ran outside, but they came after me. I asked him to take me home, but he kicked me in the backside then punched me in the face. His mates joined in, and I don't remember anything after that.'

Tara brushed her hand gently across Shania's bare arm and smiled sympathetically. It wasn't difficult to recognise an innocent young girl who'd been caught up in the wrong company.

'Why was he angry with you?'

'He thought I'd told you too much, that time at the station.'

'What do you know that made him concerned over what you'd told us?'

'Drugs and stuff.'

'Do you know what happened to Ryan Boswell?'

'A little bit.'

Shania looked at her mother, whose demeanour had softened. Now she was shedding tears for her daughter, wiping them away with the back of her hand.

'Can you tell me about it?'

A frightened look came over her face, the expression they'd seen when they last saw her at the hospital. For a moment Tara feared they'd taken another backward step.

'Tyler can't hurt you anymore, Shania. But we need to clear up this mess before other people get hurt.'

'I know.' She wiped her eyes again with the tissue. 'It was Ryan's brother Aidan's birthday party. Ryan and his girl came over from Sunderland.'

'Who else was at this party?'

'Tyler and the rest of the Vipers, but there were men that came from Belfast. It caused a lot of arguments between Tyler and Craig. They weren't very happy with Ryan, but I'd say they were more frightened by the men from Belfast.'

'Do you know who they were?'

'No. I never saw them until after Ryan was killed. But they seemed happier then, Tyler and Craig, I mean.'

'What about Carly McHugh?'

'Don't know much about her. She came along with Ryan. She smiled at me once, that's all.'

'Was she definitely Ryan's girlfriend?'

'Think so. They were holding hands when they arrived at the party.'

'What happened that night? Why was Ryan shot?'

'I think it was because he had been stealing some of the drugs and some of the money.'

'Were the Vipers working along with these men from Belfast?'

'I think the men from Belfast were in charge. That's why Tyler was scared of them.'

'Who killed Ryan?'

Tara looked hard at Shania and the girl took a deep breath before continuing.

'I don't know. They took him away during the party.'

'And Tyler?'

'I don't know!'

Shania burst into tears once again, and Tara placed a consoling hand on the girl's arm.

'It's all right, Shania. You've been really helpful. We'll leave you in peace. I'm sure your mum is taking good care of you.' Tara looked at the mother, who managed to summon a weak smile of agreement. 'If you think of anything else that might help us, please call me.' She placed her card on the coffee table.

As they walked towards the car there was a loud revving of a motorcycle engine. Tara swung around in hope that she would spy Carly McHugh, but just as quickly realised that things were seldom so simple.

'What do you think, ma'am?' Murray asked as he drove away from the house.

'Exactly what I've been thinking since I first heard of Carly McHugh. That she is the key to it all. We just have to find her.'

CHAPTER 57

While eating her lunch in the station canteen, Tara sent a text to Aisling confirming their shopping trip on Saturday morning. She realised that she should spend more time with her friends whenever she could – far too often, a night out or plans for a day away together were trashed by her job. Intending to catch up on housework was no excuse at all; both Kate and Aisling often said that life is too short. So, she expected an immediate reply to her text of 'Yay!' or 'Great!', but nothing came.

She'd passed on the registration for Carly McHugh's motorbike, upon which she had boarded the ferry in Belfast, to Traffic branch. If she was right about Carly's intentions, it would soon be spotted somewhere around Liverpool.

Tara couldn't dismiss the subject of James Guy from her thoughts. Wilson had been asked to compile a timeline of the disappeared women and to obtain details of Guy's attendance record when he worked at the Royal. This investigation wasn't an official case, certainly not one assigned to her, but she couldn't leave it alone. Even if just one of the disappeared women had been a victim of James Guy, that was enough for her to want to prove his involvement. She was cooking up an idea that if she could collate the dates of his absences from work and establish that these coincided with the dates on which some of the women had disappeared, it would add to the evidence against him.

Having asked Wilson to also check if there had been a lull in women reported missing during the spell that Guy spent in prison, she understood from his brief report that it was impossible to be certain. There had been, of course, cases of women having disappeared during the time Guy was in jail. Such disappearances happened every day. Whether or not they were similar in circumstance to the vanishing of Ruth Lawler or Linda Meredith would require more detailed investigation, and Tara could not afford the time needed for such an enquiry. Soon though, she hoped, she would have enough information to pull Guy into the station for a chat.

Since her meeting with Guy's aunt in Belfast, Tara had been pondering the case of his mother, Rachel. What had happened to her? Surely, if hers was not a mysterious disappearance and merely a case of a mother having left home to start a new life elsewhere, it should not be too difficult to trace her. Perhaps James already had done so. And to what end? A wonderful and tearful reunion? Would he have held a grudge against his mother that might that have led him to killing her? Tara looked at the picture of Rachel, removed from the flat of Terry Lawler. She realised that Lawler must have suspected Guy of being a serial killer. What reason could there be for him having a photo of Rachel Guy among the other pictures of women on his wall unless he believed that Guy had killed her, too?

Had Lawler been aware that the sweet-faced women was the mother of a serial killer? What might be gained from searching for this woman? Tara couldn't really answer that question.

Later in the afternoon, with thoughts of James Guy overshadowing her work on the Boswell case, Tara decided to call it a day and make for home. On her way out of the station she checked her mobile. There was still no reply from Aisling.

A misty rain was falling as her car crawled along in heavy traffic, seldom in top gear, towards Wapping Dock. It was an evening for curling up with a good book or a film on the telly, but she'd decided that since she was spending her Saturday shopping with Aisling, then she should at least devote her Friday evening to some housework. She parked her car in her usual place and strolled towards the lift. On the way, still holding her keys, she went to her postbox and opened it. There were a couple of letters inside, one obviously junk mail promoting a new credit card and the other, she guessed, from the company frank on the envelope, an invoice from her physio. In the lift she checked her phone again, still no response from Aisling. She quickly tapped in another message. Maybe Aisling was huffing because she hadn't got an immediate reply to her suggestion. But that wasn't like Aisling; she didn't take offence easily. She would be more likely to have bombarded Tara with messages until she had agreed to go shopping.

Stepping from the lift, Tara sensed immediately that something wasn't quite right. The door to her apartment was the second along the hallway. She quickened her step. A package had been fixed to her door with gaffer tape. Her first instincts were that it was a device of some kind, and she readied herself to phone for help. Reaching the door, she saw that the package was a mobile phone, held within a plastic self-seal bag. A piece of paper was also inside. The bag had been taped to the door, just below the lock. Tara's heart thumped. It might be quite innocent, but as a police officer she was conditioned to think the worst. She didn't dismiss the idea that it was a bomb, but curiosity overcame her fear and sensible thinking, and she peeled the package from the wood of the door and removed the mobile from the bag.

It was a basic model, a call and text device but not a smartphone, and it was already switched on. The piece of paper was folded in two – she pulled it from the bag, opened it up and read. One brief sentence had been written in pencil. Upon reading it, she fought to catch a breath.

If you want to see your friend Aisling again call this number.

Beneath that line was a phone number.

Her first instinct was to dial the number into the phone. That was a mistake. She should have called for help, or at least used her own mobile. When the call went through, a hauntingly familiar voice answered.

'Hello, Tara. You got my message. I'm sure you remember me.'

In less than a second all her thinking, her theorising on missing women, Terry Lawler's collection of pictures, the bright smile of Linda Meredith, the grinning face of James Guy, his hands on her naked body, all swept before her. And she realised that there was no joy in being right. Only fear of what was to come.

'What have you done with Aisling? I'll find you; I know who you are.'

'I know that, Tara. You're very good at your job. Too bloody good. Now you have to listen to me.'

'I'll have every police force in the country after you.'

'Now, now, calm down, Tara. You won't be doing anything of the sort. Not if you want to see the beautiful Aisling alive. Here's what you're going to do. Throw away any other phone you have. You'll be using only this one to contact me. You call me on another phone and Aisling dies. If you attempt to bring your mates at the station into this, Aisling dies. I get a sniff of any cops and Aisling dies. You'll go where I tell you to go. Alone. If I think anybody is helping you, Aisling dies, understand?'

Tara couldn't speak.

'Do you understand, Tara?'

'How do I know you haven't harmed her already?'

'You'll have to take my word for it.'

'I want to speak to her.'

'Not right now, she's having a wee doze.'

'You hurt her in any way and I'll…'

'You'll what, Tara? What are you going to do, eh?'

Tara was blinded with tears. She couldn't think straight. Couldn't think as a police officer, only as Aisling's friend.

'Please don't hurt her, James.'

'Just do as you're told, Tara. Be at the car park at Brunswick station on Sefton Street as soon as you can. Any tricks, and your mate is finished.'

He cut the call, and Tara stood helpless on the landing. Her body trembled as her sobs grew. She managed to unlock her door and stumble inside the flat, making it to the kitchen sink before throwing up. Her cries were loud and desperate. She had no clue what to do next. She knew that she should not act alone, so she must tell someone. Her training told her that much. But she had no doubt that James Guy would carry out his threat to kill Aisling. He'd killed dozens of women already.

Murray. At least call him. He would know what to do. The face, the pretty, laughing and loving face of her friend flashed before her. Aisling would die if Tara got things wrong. Guy must be watching her, had been watching her. But her only objective for now was to free Aisling.

It was ten minutes past four in the afternoon. Meeting him at Brunswick station meant braving the Friday rush hour. Guy would be watching her while remaining hidden amongst the public.

Then, her own mobile phone burst into life. Dashing from the sink to the door where she'd dropped it, she lifted her handbag and pulled out the phone. It was Murray. Thank God. She swiped the screen to answer.

'Ma'am?'

'Yes, Alan,' she managed, breathing deeply, hoping she sounded calm, normal.

'Traffic have arrested Carly McHugh; they're bringing her to St Anne Street.'

'That's good.'

'I'm still here, if you have time to call in, we can have a chat with her?'

'I can't at the minute, Alan,' she said, in a voice she knew was shaking. Should she tell him about Aisling?

'OK,' he replied doubtfully. 'Do you want me to go ahead and question her, or do we leave it until tomorrow?'

'You go ahead. I can't make it in the morning either. Let me know how you get on and I'll see you on Monday.'

'Right, ma'am. I'll keep you posted.'

She ended the call, unable to tell Murray because she was too frightened of what would happen. She tried calling Aisling's phone but there was no reply. Quickly, she tried to clean away her tears and smudged make-up. In the bathroom, she threw some cold water on her face and wiped it away with a towel. But she still hadn't stopped herself crying. In a blur, she picked up the mobile Guy had left her. She couldn't help picturing an image, conjured from her own experience, of Aisling lying in the back of a van, naked and at the mercy of a madman. Paying no further attention to her own appearance or what she might need to bring with her, she dashed from the bathroom. The vision of her friend, alone and helpless, overwhelmed her thinking. Her keys were still hanging from the door; she pulled them out, slammed the door behind her and hurried to her car.

CHAPTER 58

It took a wee while of driving about the city before Aisling finally settled down and fell asleep. I pulled into a lay-by to catch my breath. My next trip was to Tara's flat. I left the van in the car park by the M&S Bank Arena and hurried to her block. I had with me one of the mobile phones that I'd bought. When I got to her door I switched on the phone and slipped it into a plastic bag along with a wee note and taped it to the door. Hopefully, no other plonker would come along and nick it before Tara got home. That done, I hurried back to my van and the slumbering Aisling. Bless. I must admit I was tempted right then and there, but I knew that Aisling was only a means to an end. Tara Grogan was my target and my prize. Still, there was hardly a better sight than a gorgeous girl like Aisling, sprawled out in the back of my van.

Just after four, the mobile rang. It was Tara. I gave her instructions and warned her against any nonsense like squealing to her colleagues. Before driving to Brunswick station, I sent a text to Kirsty, told her I had to work a late shift and then I would be going fishing for the weekend. It would be enough to stop her from worrying about me for now. Hopefully, it would all be over soon, and I could get back to my new life. Tara would be long gone and with her all suspicion that I had anything to do with the disappearances of so many lovely girls.

I found a parking place a street away from Brunswick station. Aisling was purring away nicely, still bound and gagged. I pulled on a grey hoodie and went for a gander. The station wasn't that far from Wapping Dock, so I knew it wouldn't take Tara long to show up. I stood on the station footbridge. It was covered, and from there I could see the entrance to the car park. Fifteen minutes since our phone call, and in drives her blue Ford Focus. I'd been looking all around me for any signs of police, uniformed or otherwise. If I smelt anything fishy, I would be out of there and on my way with Aisling. I had no intention of meeting Tara at this spot, nor had I any intention of snatching her – yet. I had to see how things went. I had to be sure that she was not trailing half the cops in the country behind her. If it turned out she was trying to set me up I would have no qualms about killing her mate.

I watched Tara getting out of her car. Dear love her, I could see she wasn't looking her best. A bit stressed, I'd say. She stood in the middle of the car park looking every which way, holding tightly to the phone I'd given her.

Keeping an eye on her, I keyed in a brief text on my phone and pressed send. Couldn't help a wee grin as I watched her read it. Her arms dropped to her sides, and she gazed around with a pained look on her cute face. Finally, she walked back to her car and climbed inside.

I got a bit worried when she didn't drive off immediately. Thought she might be checking in with one of her police buddies. I was still feeling very nervous, scared that secretly she had a whole bunch of cops just waiting to pounce. Eventually, she drove away, and I strolled back to the van, all the while looking out for anything suspicious. Uniforms, cops in plain clothes, I felt they could be everywhere, ready to grab me. I had to keep telling myself that I had something valuable. I had her friend, Aisling. Surely, she wouldn't gamble with her friend's life?

CHAPTER 59

Instead of heading home and making a start on his weekend, Murray decided to have a chat with the individual recently brought into St Anne Street.

When he entered the interview room he was faced with an attractive young woman, looking slightly tough in black motorcycle leathers and boots. Her jacket was open to reveal a white T-shirt underneath and her arms were folded in defence, or defiance, waiting for him to speak. Murray swiftly conducted the preliminaries – introductions, an explanation of the procedure for recording the interview – then posed his first question.

'What are you doing in Liverpool, Carly?'

She tightened her pose, visibly fumed but didn't reply.

'Where have you been staying in Liverpool?'

At that she kicked the leg of the table like a petulant schoolkid. Still no reply.

Murray did not have the same patience as his boss, Tara, and found it hard to wait for the woman to melt and give up some answers. He cut to the chase.

'Tyler Finlay was shot and killed a week ago on the Treadwater Estate. What can you tell me about that?'

Her shoulders jerked upwards in a shrug of indifference.

'We know you were in Liverpool at that time, Carly. It wouldn't hurt for you to tell us what you have been doing.'

She met his gaze with a hard stare. Such a cute face, yet such ice-cold emotion. Murray continued in the same vein. 'We know you were on the Treadwater Estate on the night of 15 April. That was the night your boyfriend, Ryan Boswell, was killed. Have you anything to say about that?'

'Are you mates with that snotty-nosed cow who asked me this stuff in Belfast?'

'If you're referring to DI Grogan then yes, she is a colleague.'

The girl laughed heartily.

'You're dying to give her one, aren't you? I can tell.'

Murray ignored that remark and ploughed on with his questions. Carly now had a smirk on her face. Still, her arms remained folded. Then, without a preliminary knock, the door opened and in strode DCI Weir. It wasn't difficult to see that he was peeved. He looked at the woman and then sternly at Murray.

'You can go, lass. Pick up your things at the desk on the way out.'

'See ya.'

Carly McHugh wasted no time in leaving the room but not without sniggering at the man who had tried and failed to get information from her.

Murray looked puzzled by Weir's actions, but it was the DCI who spoke first.

'DS Murray, who gave you authority to question that woman?'

Murray got to his feet. At least he could look down upon the smouldering bulk of Malcolm Weir.

'We've been waiting to question her in connection with the murder of Ryan Boswell, sir.'

'I didn't ask you that, son. DI Grogan has already spoken to the girl in Belfast. Did she instruct you to carry out another interview?'

'Not directly, sir.'

'Not directly? Mmm. I warned her about encroaching upon my investigations without consulting me first.'

'But, sir, we think Carly McHugh is involved in these gang murders. She knows something about it.'

Weir's face reddened, his watery eyes bulged.

'I don't give a shit what you and DI Grogan think! You're interfering in my operation, son. Keep out. I'll be having a word with Superintendent Tweedy. He needs to rein in the pair of you.'

Weir slammed the door behind him as he left. Murray scratched his head, drew a deep breath, forced it out through pursed lips, gathered his files and retreated to the operations room. Before leaving for home, he sent a text to Tara warning her of Weir's anger and urging her to prepare herself for trouble come Monday morning.

CHAPTER 60

Naively, she'd hoped that driving into the station car park she would see Aisling seated on a bench, waiting for her. Tara felt sick to her stomach although she hadn't eaten since lunchtime and even that had been swiftly despatched down her kitchen sink. Now, her head pounded, her temples were pulsing, her throat dry and her eyes seeped tears. Nothing. She saw nothing in the car park at Brunswick station. There was no sign of Aisling and no sign of Guy.

Tara could hardly think what it would mean for her when she finally caught up with Guy. Would Aisling be freed? More to the point, would she be freed unharmed? What was Guy likely to do after that? With her?

She should have told Murray when he called. He could have done something. But it was too risky, she'd already decided that. If James Guy was the serial killer she believed him to be, he wouldn't baulk at killing Aisling. She had to get her friend away from him. She'd tried calling Aisling again, but her mobile went to voicemail. If Guy really had her, then he also had her mobile phone.

Suddenly, as Tara stood forlornly in the car park, the phone in her hand beeped. She looked at the screen and saw a text. From Guy.

Well done Tara. Good so far. Stop calling her.
Car park on Holloway, Runcorn station.

Frantically, she ran to the station entrance, searching for him. A train arrived; people got off and a few got on board. Weaving through the moving figures of men, women, students, kids, she convinced herself that Guy was among them. He must be. How else could he have known when to text her in the car park? She ran back outside, examining each of the parked cars, trying to catch a glimpse of the animal who had taken her friend. She hoped too for a sighting of Aisling. But she realised that he was in control, he was calling all the shots. She would have to do as he commanded her.

Frustrated and angry, she returned to her car and for a few moments just sat, trying to ease her breathing and think of what to do next. Against Guy's instructions, she'd brought her own mobile phone and now considered calling Murray. But no. She felt beyond help and it was all down to her now. Guy had taken Aisling to get at her. If anything happened to her friend then she, Tara, was to blame. She'd brought all this trouble to her friend's door. She, the policewoman, the detective, had caused it all. Why hadn't she become a lawyer like so many of her colleagues at Oxford? She was to blame if Aisling was to die.

Ignoring Murray's incoming text, she switched off her mobile and drove away without calling him.

Runcorn station, why there? She wondered if Guy was travelling by train and choosing these landmarks for her to suit his intended destination. Then, she recalled the van in which he had imprisoned her two years ago. When he had drugged and assaulted her. She pictured the same for Aisling, and more tears slid down her cheeks. Her friend lying bound and gagged having been injected with drugs, naked, frightened. Was she already too late to save her? He may not have killed her yet, but had he raped her?

Tara did her best to drive quickly in the evening traffic spilling from the city, while wondering if Guy could make it to Runcorn any faster than she would. After what seemed an eternity, she pressed the button on the station car park barrier for a ticket, and when it lifted, she swept into an almost deserted car park, most commuters having already collected their vehicles and driven home. Without bothering to park within a marked space, she jumped out of the car and looked around her for signs of Guy or Aisling. She didn't have long to wait before the mobile in her hand beeped with another text.

Tryfan car park, Llyn Ogwen, 2 hrs.

The contents of the message hardly mattered, she realised that he had to be here watching her. She looked at the other vehicles around her. There were a dozen or so, but nothing remarkable. She stamped her feet in desperation, then noticed the covered walkway over the rail tracks. She ran. A train had just left the platform and people were departing the station, some taking to the steps of the footbridge. It added to her anxiety trying to catch a glimpse of him. He had to be here. He must have seen her arrive. How else would he have known when to send the text?

She took the steps two at a time then ran across the bridge and down the other side. There was a figure ahead of her, a man wearing a baseball cap, his hands in his pockets, walking nonchalantly into the street beyond the station. She caught up with him, and just before she drew level, he spun round to see who was running towards him.

A guy of eighteen perhaps, thin-faced, bony, not at all like the man she sought. He looked her up and down and smiled quizzically. She stopped running and turned back.

She saw nothing more on her way back to the car. If Guy had been watching from the bridge, then he'd made a swift escape. She made another search of the parked cars and ran into the adjoining street. Through her tears, she saw nothing of interest. A few cars drove by, but there was no one walking, no one watching. She returned to her car. Now she needed her own mobile, to find out exactly where she had to go next. Somewhere in Wales, obviously – beyond that, she had no idea. She realised that James Guy was waiting, carefully choosing his moment. He wanted her completely alone, without people around, and with no police. Then he would have her.

Google Maps showed her the way to Llyn Ogwen. It would be dark by the time she got there. Something else to add to her fears. She tossed her own phone onto the seat beside her and drove away.

CHAPTER 61

Murray checked his phone as he entered Tweedy's office. Tara had not replied to his text about Carly McHugh having been released on the orders of DCI Weir. It was twenty past seven and Tweedy was still working, seated at his pristine desk, some paperwork in front of him and his Bible sitting as usual at the top left-hand corner of his desk.

'Evening, sir, working late?'

'Evening, Alan, nearly finished. Lorraine and I are off to the lakes in the morning, for a couple of days. I wanted to get this finished before I go. A clear desk makes for a clear conscience. What can I do for you?'

'Well, sir, I just stopped by to tell you that Carly McHugh was brought in earlier today for questioning.

Unfortunately, she was released shortly afterwards on the orders of DCI Weir.'

'Ah, that is awkward. I can understand your frustration, and Tara's, but I'm quite certain DCI Weir knows what he is doing.'

'But, sir, Carly McHugh is central to our enquiry into the murder of Ryan Boswell.'

'DCI Weir is aware of that, Alan. I don't believe he is being awkward for the sake of it. His investigations run deep into the gangland activities in Liverpool. We do not want to be responsible for compromising his operations. For now, we will have to tread lightly regarding those people we suspect of involvement in the Boswell killing.'

'Fine, sir, understood.'

'Please make Tara aware of this.'

'I will do, sir, although she isn't replying to my texts.'

'It is the weekend, Alan. She is quite possibly trying her best to enjoy it.'

'Yes, sir. Enjoy your break.'

'Thanks, Alan, goodnight.'

Murray left Tweedy's office, picked up his coat from the back of his chair and strode from the room. He too had a weekend ahead to enjoy.

CHAPTER 62

Aidan Boswell was beside Craig in the car, so he felt a little safer. Several vehicles were dotted about the place, and he wondered if they were hiding in one of them.

It was dark, a place without cameras but bleak and sinister at this time of night. The old fort was floodlit, beyond that lay the void of the Irish Sea. These guys had chosen the meeting place well. A wide-open space, a car park with just one entrance. If anything was to kick off, there'd be no chance of escape. And now he regretted that only two of them had come here. What if they showed up with an army? They'd be dead meat.

Treadwater lay across the Mersey. They may just as well have been in a jungle in Africa as Perch Rock in New Brighton. He was out of his territory, out of his comfort zone, but this had to be done. McHugh and Fitter demanded it. They told him that they would be here, too. To show the Vipers how it was done.

He watched a car drive onto the esplanade. Well over the speed limit, it suddenly swerved and braked, the rear sliding outwards as wheels spun and tyres squealed. Then another car did the same, speeding after the first, racing towards the road. Kids having a laugh. He drew a breath, and Aidan laughed but it was more in relief than in humour.

'What if they don't show?'

'Then no change, man,' Craig replied.

'What if they didn't kill Tyler?'

'What's with all the fucking questions?'

'What's McHugh going to say if they don't show?'

'Shut it, will ya?'

Craig examined his phone, hoping for a message, something to say that the meet wasn't on, that everything was cool, but as he scrolled aimlessly through texts a dark-coloured Audi rolled into the car park.

Aidan rose in his seat. Craig glanced from his phone and felt the instant strike of his heart in his chest. He watched as the Audi came to a halt forty yards away. Three men emerged, leaving the driver behind the wheel. Twice the number they'd agreed. He nudged Aidan, and they climbed from their car and watched as their three adversaries approached. Two were slim, lanky, and looked as though they needed some nourishment. As they drew nearer, Craig saw that they wore dark bomber jackets, no doubt with guns concealed. If it weren't for that, he reckoned that he and Aidan could take them if they had to.

The third man, without a jacket, stood between his minders. He was not tall but stocky and completely bald, with a tattoo of a naked girl astride an anchor on the left side of his neck. He wore a tight-fitting polo shirt that only served to highlight his physique. He looked dispassionately at the men standing before him.

Now, the Treadwater Vipers were face to face with the Tallinn Crew.

Before anyone spoke there came the sound of another vehicle entering the car park. Craig saw the silver BMW 225 roaring toward them, and he drew a breath of relief. The car braked to a halt a few feet behind them, and the sturdy frame of Fitter Hobbs emerged from the passenger side followed, a moment later, by the bulk of Rab McHugh stepping down from the driver's seat. Craig saw concern in the faces of the Estonians. The bald man with the tattoo was first to speak.

'I'm Sepp, you want speak with me?'

Craig was much taller than the man he faced; beyond that he had little confidence he and Aidan would get away alive if things went badly. Craig was about to reply when Fitter cut in.

'You're finished doing business in Liverpool, mate.'

Sepp had so far maintained his gaze on Craig, but now looked towards Fitter. Following the death of Janek, Sepp had seized control of the Tallinn Crew.

'You think we killed your guys? Is that what you think?'

'Don't give a fuck if you did, mate. You were warned to stay out of the city. It belongs to these lads now.' Fitter nodded towards Craig and Aiden.

'Who are you, fighting their battles? You're not from Liverpool.'

'Fucking choice that is, coming from a Pole.'

'Not Pole, Estonian.'

'All the fucking same to me.'

Rab McHugh had been silent to this point, but impatience was kicking in.

'Don't cross the river again or try to stop my partners from doing their business. Understand?'

Sepp, silent, stared coldly at the competition. He was not Janek. He was not brave enough to continue this war. For now, he was happy to run the scrapyard in Tranmere. But he didn't want it to look as though he were backing down.

He stepped forward and looked up at the face of Craig Lewis.

'I ever see you again, my friend.' Then he drew his right index finger across his neck. His companions laughed aloud, and finally Sepp joined them.

Seconds later Fitter and McHugh were laughing too. Craig and Aidan, not impressed by the humour, backed away, slowly at first, until they were beside their car. Fitter and McHugh returned to their BMW. The four of them watched as the Estonians drove away in the Audi.

'Time to get the ferry home,' said McHugh. He turned to face Craig Lewis, the new leader of the Vipers. 'You're on your own now, big lad. No more fuck-ups, understand?'

'Yes, Rab,' Craig replied.

'It's Mr McHugh to you.'

'Yes, Mr McHugh.'

Rab McHugh slapped Lewis playfully on the cheek.

'Good lad. When the time's right we can start up again in Sunderland. You'll have to get one of your lads to work with our Carly. This time, make sure he keeps his dick in his trousers when he comes anywhere near my daughter. Understand?'

'Yes, Mr McHugh.'

'Good lad. Any more competition and I expect you to take care of it on your own, understand?'

'Yes, Mr McHugh.'

The two men from Belfast climbed into their car. Craig Lewis could hear them laughing.

'Mr McHugh! You're a fuckin' geg, Rab,' said Fitter.

Lewis and Boswell watched them drive away.

CHAPTER 63

The car park at Llyn Ogwen was little more than a lay-by at the side of the road overlooking the lake. It was deserted. Darkness was closing in and there were mountains to every side. Occasionally, a vehicle passed by on the road, and each time her nerves were strained, Tara thinking it had to be him. She couldn't see any buildings or houses around her; he had chosen a lonely place.

Both mobiles lay on the passenger seat. When she'd last checked them there was little signal on either and low battery on her own. Below her, a breeze cast ripples on the lake's surface, and she wondered if this was a place where he disposed of his victims.

With the engine off, she soon grew cold. She hadn't come prepared and was still in her work clothes. How long was she going to have to wait? Was he already here, watching her from the slopes of whatever mountain rose beside her? Her nerves forced her to concentrate on Aisling. She prayed she was safe, still alive. She couldn't take Guy's word that she would be traded for Aisling. Crying was doing Tara no good, but she couldn't help it. A police officer shouldn't be sat crying in self-pity, but she was also a woman worried sick about her friend.

Headlights appeared in the distance as a vehicle wound its way along the mountain pass. She tried to steady her breathing. She wanted the car or van to be his but feared what would happen when he did arrive. Then the vehicle raced by, and her body slackened. She drew a breath, then picked up his phone. Nothing. Seconds later a lorry thundered by, the silence shattered once more. A sudden thought crossed her mind; perhaps she had the wrong place. So, she started the engine and rolled slowly forwards, approaching the junction with the road. Decision made, she pulled onto the road and continued along the shore of Llyn Ogwen.

In a few hundred yards, she came upon another car park on her left, the road running between that and the lake's shore. She slowed the car and pulled in. It was deserted.

Back on the road, the same again a quarter of a mile further on. This car park, too, was empty. She passed some buildings, all unlit, and then a junction in the road. Following the shoreline, she very soon came to the end of the lake and within a few yards, met utter darkness. Nothing to be seen but the tarmac of the road ahead. She didn't go much further before deciding to return to her original waiting place. Never had she felt so alone and so far from comfort.

Sitting in the gloom, the only light came from the radio display. She had locked her car doors. Sleep was trying to claim her, but she fended it off. She had to be awake when he finally showed up. Her mind travelled back through time, recalling the laughing face of Aisling, always to the fore, fussing and scheming, bubbling over with ideas – things to do and places to go. How she was going to find the fella of her dreams, the shoes she would be wearing when she met him. Tara struggled to blink the vision away. In seconds, another vision would take its place, but always it was Aisling.

A softly spoken DJ announced the time as midnight, and she listened to the news headlines. Nothing, of course, was said of a woman having been abducted in Liverpool, while her best friend sat uselessly in her car by a lake in the middle of nowhere.

CHAPTER 64

I had no intention of going anywhere near Llyn Ogwen. At least, not straight away. I just wanted to be sure that Tara was doing as she was bid. Do her no harm to sit quietly for a while and I could be sure that her mates in the police weren't keeping tabs on her.

Meanwhile, I could concentrate on the lovely Aisling. All evening she'd been dozing peacefully in the back of the van, the roofie having done its job. Once I'd seen Tara on her way to the backside of beyond, I drove to Penrhyn harbour where I had moored Mother Freedom. She was already kitted out with everything I would need to despatch two girls to the bottom of the sea.

I sat patiently in the van by the quayside, waiting for Aisling to revive. I wasn't about to drag her from the van to the boat. I'd do my back in! She was a bigger girl than I was used to. Instead, I would gently lead her on board.

There was no one about the place. Friday night, weather not the best, dry but windy and cold, there was no one to notice me taking my girl by the arm and helping her down the stone steps and onto Mother Freedom.

About midnight, I heard her stirring in the back of the van. Her legs had bumped against the side. I slid open the door and peered inside. Her eyes were open and reacted to the light, but she didn't seem agitated or alarmed. Perfect. Groggy, I'd say. I climbed inside and immediately cut the cable ties around her ankles. Her legs parted slightly, but she wasn't putting up any resistance and she didn't start kicking out.

I replaced her boots. A quick look around the harbour, then I helped her out of the van, holding tightly to her arm in case she keeled over. She didn't struggle as I guided her along the quayside, although she was a little unsteady on her feet. I'd kept her hands bound and the gag over her mouth. I steered her the thirty yards to the steps that led down to the boat. It was dark, the steps were wet with one or two slippery with moss, it would be quite easy for someone to lose their footing and topple into the drink. So, I gripped her tightly, my arm around her waist, and when we were level with the gunwale of the boat I lifted her in my arms and stepped on board.

When I placed her back on her feet she flopped in a heap on the deck. She let out a whimper, and for the first time, her eyes seemed to focus on me. I bundled her below into the forward cabin and laid her on the mattress. Quickly, I returned to the van, gathered my spare clothes and my stash of drugs, locked up and went back on board. Aisling lay with her eyes open, watching my every move. She didn't look particularly frightened, which could only be good news for me. I removed the tape from her mouth, raised her head and put a bottle of water to her lips. She managed a few sips, but I saw her eyes roll in her head. She was still groggy. I laid her on her back, reached for a blanket and spread it over her.

There was nothing to do now but wait, wait until I felt like meeting up with Tara. I had switched on a small light in the cabin, and for the first time since I'd snatched her, I got a proper look at this beautiful girl. Aisling had wonderfully pure skin and the most luxurious soft and dark hair. It took a lot of effort to prise myself from the bed and to leave her be.

I slid the door closed and made some tea. It was a bloody cold night. I boiled the kettle on the gas stove and poured some water into a mug containing a teabag. It felt great, a strong brew and a handful of chocolate biscuits. There wasn't a sound from the cabin, only the lapping of seawater against the hull and the odd thud as the boat knocked against the bumper of the harbour wall. I couldn't help congratulating myself on how well things had gone, so far. I was so looking forward to hooking up with Tara again and chuckled to myself that I had the most delicious of prizes already on-board Mother Freedom. Hell, I had time to kill.

I finished my tea and slid open the cabin door to check on Aisling. Her eyes open, she lay motionless. I couldn't help myself. I pulled the blanket away and swooned at the vision before me. Slowly, I removed every piece of her clothing and, finally, did what I like doing most.

Not once did she put up a fight. Such a cosy moment.

CHAPTER 65

Craig dropped Aidan home, but before going to his own place he fancied some time with his girl. He needed release. He needed soothing. And Tanya knew what he liked most.

His nerves still jangled. He was as much disturbed by his dressing-down from Rab McHugh as he was by the confrontation with the Tallinn Crew. Fitter and McHugh had made them look like amateurs. Already, he'd convinced himself that there would be no more trouble, nor any competition from those Estonians.

He couldn't help smiling that he was now the appointed leader of the Vipers. Appointed, not by the other lads in the crew, but by their masters from Belfast. If they did as they were told, got things right, then they could be earning big time.

Ryan Boswell had been a daft prick. Firstly, for getting involved with the daughter of their boss and then by trying to rip him off, creaming off the profits and setting up other deals. Now he realised that Ryan had got what he deserved. It was the price to pay if you tried to live by the big boys' rules.

Craig left his car by his block of flats and walked the two hundred yards to Tanya's house. If her folks were home, they could always go to her room. He was feeling better already. It was a miracle that the Estonians had let them both go free without a scratch. Thinking about it now, it was a mad thing to have done.

But he still worried over who had shot Tyler. He hoped that was an end to it. As he turned a corner onto the path leading to Tanya's house, he glimpsed a figure a few yards behind him. He hadn't heard the footsteps. Craig turned to face the stranger but, in the darkness, he couldn't make out who it was. As he was about to turn away, he saw two hands rise and take aim with a gun.

He couldn't believe what he was seeing. Before he could bolt for cover, two shots were fired and he tumbled over a low wall, into a garden. For the second time in one night his heart thumped, but this time it was outdone by the burning sensation in his neck. Sprawled on his back, he peered into the night sky, aware of the blood seeping from his mouth. The darkened figure stood over him and Craig's eyes met those of his killer. Now he had all the answers to his questions.

He knew nothing of the next two bullets breaking into his chest.

CHAPTER 66

Tara jerked awake. Startled for a second, she quickly took in her surroundings. It was still dark, nothing to see beyond her misted windscreen. She rubbed the back of her neck. Stiff and cold, thirsty and hungry, in need of a pee, but above all Tara was worried sick about Aisling.

Why hadn't he come? Why no contact? She checked her watch. Nearly four in the morning. She lifted the mobile that he'd given her. Nothing, no recent messages and precious little signal. Her tears resumed, her head throbbed, and she couldn't help visualising her friend lying helpless, bound, gagged and drugged in the back of his van.

Then, she noticed spots of light appearing on her windscreen. They moved across the glass. She switched on the engine and got the heater and wipers to clear the mist. She tried to focus beyond the screen into the distance. A car perhaps, rounding the bends in the road, its light momentarily vanishing then reappearing with increased intensity. It was a car, or maybe a van. She hoped that it was Guy at last. Surely, at this hour, it must be him. The driver had his full beam on, and she squinted from the glare as the vehicle approached. She heard the wheels on the road and watched, forlornly, as the car sped by.

A silly notion surfaced again, the idea of driving around the countryside to look for a van. Or a car? Or what? She had no idea.

Pushing her door open, she felt a rush of cold air that helped to revive her. She climbed out, leaving the engine idling, and at first remained by the door, gazing into the blackness. Soon, feeling a tad braver, she paced forwards, leaving the door open and the interior light on to provide some comfort. The only sounds were of the car's engine and her boots on the tarmac, taking tentative steps into a blanket of darkness. She couldn't even be sure that to her right the lake was still there, or that the road lay to her left.

She had to pee.

Why didn't he call? Surely, he was convinced by now that she had brought no one with her, that she had told no one where she was going or what she was doing.

Another set of lights swept across a bend in the road, near the end of the lake where she had driven a few hours earlier. Strange that people were still up and around at this hour, going about their business. She watched the lights snake around the bends, fast approaching the lay-by where she lingered. Suddenly, she felt vulnerable, being no longer in the relative safety of her car. Glancing behind her, she saw the dim interior light. It was forty yards away from her now, and she could hear a vehicle approaching. Even if it wasn't Guy, the driver would see her car, maybe notice that it was empty. Then bright lights caught her full in the face and she raised a hand to protect her eyes. The driver had surely seen her, the proverbial rabbit in the headlights.

She heard the car slow. It must be him. Suddenly, it slipped from the road into the lay-by and braked to a halt beside her. She wanted to run, but this was what she had been waiting for. James Guy. A monster come to claim his next prey.

So, she remained motionless, powerless to run, to react, to scream. It was a large silver car, a Mercedes or a BMW, she didn't know. The window on the passenger side lowered and a voice spoke.

'You all right, love? Have you broken down?'

A man, around fifty she guessed, leaned across from the driver's side as she bent to gaze inside the car. Relief and fear collided in her head. Tears filled her eyes. He seemed normal, bald with glasses, neatly dressed in shirt and tie. But what was normal? Could there be more than one madman on the prowl, in this place, at this hour?

'No, I'm fine,' she stuttered. 'Long drive, taking a break.'

Now she wanted him to go, to leave her alone. And suddenly there was the new fear, that somehow Guy could be watching her. Right now. What would he think if he saw her beside this car? What would he do to Aisling if he thought Tara was talking to a copper? If he thought she had brought help with her?

'OK, love. Just thought I would check. Take care.'

'Thank you.'

She cried as he drove off. The rear lights vanished as the car rounded a bend. Her Good Samaritan had disappeared into the gloom. She ran back to her car, climbed inside and locked the doors. In despair, she fell over the steering wheel, praying for an end to this anguish.

CHAPTER 67

I lay beside her in the bunk, rocking gently as the hull bobbed on the swell. Soothing, it was. Such a lovely thing, lying beside me, I couldn't help my hands roaming her soft skin. Couldn't help having another go with her, too. I'd be knackered when this weekend was over.

For a while I lay there, trying to think of a way to keep Aisling – a sex slave sort of thing. I'd never had such a glamorous woman, a real girlie girl. I'd read stories of these blokes in America, where some fella had managed to keep a girl prisoner for fifteen years. She'd even had a couple of children to him. Can't say I would be into that, but I wouldn't mind giving it a go for a year or two.

I'd really love it to be Tara, but as I've said before, once the cops in Liverpool realise that Tara is missing, they're going to tear the place apart looking for her, and they'll certainly come after me. So, I have to get rid of her before the weekend is out, get back to my normal life and show that I had nothing to do with it. I suppose, for the time being, I could keep Aisling on Mother Freedom, but then I would have to keep her drugged and tied up all the time.

No, I reckoned I needed a wee cottage somewhere, like in the mountains, where I could call with her when I'm feeling horny or when Kirsty is pissed at me, or she has her time of the month. A bolthole, eh?

When I'd had another taste of Aisling, I climbed off the bunk and got dressed in the dark. It was time to fetch Tara.

Before leaving, I made sure that Aisling was securely bound at the hands and feet, and I tied her hands to the bunk. Didn't want her to go wandering about the place. She was conscious and looking around her, although I'm not sure if she was really with it. I left her naked but covered with a couple of blankets. I didn't want her to die of cold while I was out. Rather than replace the gaffer tape on her mouth, I thought it wiser to slip her another roofie, to help keep her quiet. I didn't have many left, though. Certainly, wouldn't have enough to kill both Aisling and Tara. Fucking curse that Janek got himself shot. I really needed a supply of China White for this weekend.

It was three o'clock in the morning when I set out for Llyn Ogwen. Still pitch dark on the mountain road, but I was confident that my wee cop would be there, waiting patiently. I was less sure whether she would have the fucking cavalry with her as back-up. I was going to have to be careful in my approach to the car park. The A5 was mostly deserted on the run up to the lake. I knew I could take my time, although I wanted Tara on Mother Freedom safe and sound before it was daylight. That also meant I could get away from Penrhyn and out to sea in the early morning.

The car park came upon me quicker than I was expecting once I'd reached the lake's shore. And then I spotted the car all alone in the lay-by.

Dear love her. I didn't even slow the van. Didn't want to raise her suspicion that I was about to join her. Instead, I sped past and continued along the road a few miles, until I reached a junction. All the while I kept an eye out for other vehicles just in case her mates were hiding behind every hedge along the way. Crafty fuckers, these Liverpool cops. No telling what they would do if Tara had tipped them off.

I couldn't see far beyond either side of the road in the darkness, but I was reasonably confident that there were no surprises waiting for me. Just to be sure, I drove past the lay-by one more time, turned around again at the next opportunity and drove back to meet her. I pulled up so that the front of my van was right against the bonnet of her car. In my headlights, I could see her squinting out at me.

Shit, before I could do much more, except switch off the engine, she was out of her car and banging on my window with her wee hands.

'Where's Aisling? What have you done with her?'

I could hear her shouts through the glass. She jumped backwards as I thrust open my door, and it caught her on the chest. Nearly went on her hoop. I stepped down from the van. A barrage of punches rained down on me. Then she tried to open the side door, yelling all the while.

'Aisling? Are you in there?'

I let her pull at the door, it saved her from punching me. She slid it open and looked inside. Little did she know she was doing half my job for me. I grabbed her, one hand at her neck, the other at her ass, and shoved her inside. She could yell the place down for all I cared, there was not a sinner about to hear her. Finally, though, I had to slap her. Well, she was fighting me to get out of the van again. She dropped to the mattress, and I flipped her on her back and sat astride her at the hips. She writhed and screamed and spat at me. Feisty wee thing, but I'd always known that. As she thumped at my chest, I gripped both her wrists, leaned forwards and forced her arms above her head. I pinned her with one hand and pulled a cable tie from my pocket. It was bloody difficult trying to secure her hands while the wee bitch was yelling in my ear.

'Tara, shut the fuck up, love. You're doing my head in.'

'Tell me what you've done with Aisling!'

'Oh, you don't want to hear what Aisling and I have been doing.'

She screamed in my face.

'You bastard!'

I ignored the insult and finished securing her wrists with the cable tie. Fighting off her kicks and her struggling, I got her ankles nice and tight with another tie and pulled off her boots. Then, as I'd done with her mate, I popped a roofie in her gob. Wee bitch spat it out, and in the dark I couldn't find it. This time I squeezed her jaw with one hand and forced another pill through her pursed but open lips. I pulled a piece of gaffer tape from the roof and stuck it over her mouth, but I knew with her hands tied in front of her she would soon rip it off. I had to sit with her until the roofie began to do its work.

As she relaxed, I undid her hands, rolled her over and secured them again behind her back. Ten minutes later she was almost asleep. I was tempted to have a go then and there, but to be truthful by then she was a bit of a sight. Her hair was a mess, and her make-up was smudged. I would prefer to have her when she was looking more her usual ravishing self. Besides, having enjoyed double helpings of her mate, and with all the excitement of the day and night, I was feeling a bit punctured.

I climbed out of the van and went to Tara's car. Two mobile phones were lying on the passenger seat. I lifted them out and threw them as far into the lake as I could manage. Slipping the keys from the ignition, I closed the door, locked it and threw the keys into the drink as well.

Job done; we were off to the seaside.

CHAPTER 68

Murray awoke beside his girlfriend. Trudy Mitchell slept quietly, her left arm lying across his chest. His first thought, however, was for Tara. He lifted his phone from the bedside table and scrolled through his messages. Why hadn't she responded to his texts? It wasn't urgent, but it wasn't like her not to reply.

He slid from the bed, went to the bathroom and a few minutes later was getting dressed. When Trudy awoke, her blonde hair splayed over the pillows, her nakedness revealed from the waist up, she watched him dress with a wistful smile on her face.

'Where are you going? Come back to bed.'

'Sorry, have to call at the station this morning.'

'But I thought you had the weekend off?'

He finished tying his laces then leaned over and kissed her. She responded by slipping her tongue inside his mouth and her arms around his neck. This made it difficult for him to leave her. She moaned and tried to pull him down upon her, but he gently yet firmly drew himself away.

'I do. I just have one thing to sort out and then I'll be back. We can go for lunch if you like.'

He was out of the bedroom before she had the chance to reply.

* * *

At St Anne Street he wanted to check for any news of Carly McHugh, although since DCI Weir had demanded she be released, he didn't quite know what he expected to hear. Instead, he learned of the death of Craig Lewis, a

214

leading member of the Treadwater Vipers. The twenty-four-year-old had survived the shooting until reaching hospital but had succumbed soon after. It seemed now that Weir had been correct that a gang war had erupted on Merseyside. Their investigation into the murder of Ryan Boswell was enmeshed in these latest killings. First Tyler Finlay, then three members of an Estonian outfit in Tranmere and now Craig Lewis. It would be difficult to separate the Boswell investigation from the others, and yet they had been told to keep their noses out by DCI Weir. The one fly in the ointment for the Scot was that Tweedy's team was still officially in charge of the Ryan Boswell investigation.

Murray sat at his desk drinking vending-machine coffee and munching his breakfast of two chocolate bars. When he'd seen enough on his computer screen, he sent another text to Tara. Whether she was having a relaxing weekend or not, he knew that Tara would want to be informed about the latest developments. He realised also that she firmly believed a local gang feud was not why Ryan Boswell had been killed. Tara insisted that Carly McHugh held the key to that mystery. Anything that had occurred since Boswell's death would, in time, prove either Tara or DCI Weir right. It wouldn't look good for the acerbic DCI if, having released her from custody, Carly McHugh was found to be in any way responsible for the murder of Craig Lewis.

Murray switched off his screen, checked his phone for a reply from Tara then hurried back to his flat where – hopefully – Trudy had kept the bed warm.

CHAPTER 69

From the end of the road, Aidan Boswell looked upon the scene of his best mate's murder. Police and forensics staff were performing a detailed search of every garden, and the pavement around the home of Craig's girlfriend, Tanya. He'd been only a few paces from her house when the killer struck. It all happened just two minutes after he'd dropped off Aidan, when Craig had parked his car by his own flat then walked towards Tanya's house.

Another group of bizzies, in plain clothes, were going from one house to another, asking questions, taking notes. So fucking what? Then something nipped at Aidan's thinking. Everyone else around him, his fellow Vipers – what was left of them – girls, neighbours, their chat and conclusion was that a gang war was in full swing. Speculation over which gang had put an end to Craig, Tyler and Ryan dominated whispered conversations. Another Liverpool outfit? From Toxteth, maybe? Or Bootle, or Speke? Some, better informed, guessed at Birkenhead or Wallasey and Aidan, of course, had his mind on the meeting the previous night between the Vipers and the Tallinn Crew. It would be easy to believe that Sepp had raised two fingers in defiance of Rab McHugh, that he'd blamed the Vipers for the killing of his men at the scrapyard and wanted revenge. Maybe they'd followed Craig back to Treadwater and done him. It was only luck that they hadn't come after him.

But still he had this nagging doubt. And he knew exactly why. Yeah, it could be a gang war, could have been the Tallinn Crew that killed Tyler and now Craig, the senior members of the Vipers. But he knew it was no

Tallinn Crew and it was no other outfit that killed Ryan. It wasn't even their newly acquired masters from Belfast. When it came to Ryan, the Vipers had killed their own.

The big men from Belfast had sanctioned it, of course. Ryan and his girl had stepped out of line. They tried to set up their own operation in Sunderland, skimming off profits that should have come to the Vipers and then to Belfast. Fitter and McHugh weren't happy, and neither was Tyler or Craig, but they had simply been doing what they were told by the men from Belfast. So, Ryan had been summoned to Liverpool, along with his girl. Tyler assured his masters that he would sort it, but it wasn't enough. McHugh and Fitter wanted blood.

But they weren't going to do it. No way. The Vipers would have to clean up their own shit. McHugh and Fitter had been in Liverpool that night, but not at the birthday party. Those guys didn't want to get themselves implicated. Smart they were. When Ryan turned up with Carly, only Vipers were waiting for them.

Nearly all the Vipers, seventeen in all, were squeezed into his living room. Ryan was separated from his girl and driven to a place where Fitter and McHugh were waiting. They had asked the questions and delivered the beating. Ryan would have to pay for ripping off his own, but what Aidan despised the most was the fact that Carly would be allowed to go home. No one would lay a finger on her. Fitter, with a fucking huge grin on his face, handed a gun to Tyler and whispered something in his ear. That was all. Sentence had been passed.

After his brother was dead, Aidan went after Carly. Why should she be allowed to go home without a word, just because Rab McHugh was her father? She'd stolen from him, same as Ryan. He chased her all through Treadwater, but the bitch had flagged down a car and escaped.

Aidan listened to them, one after another, blaming this gang and that, while he stood watching the bizzies piece together evidence for Craig's shooting. He shivered. The more he thought on the night his brother, Ryan, died, the more he was convinced that a gang war had not put an end to Tyler Finlay and Craig Lewis. They could gather all the evidence they wanted, but the bizzies were pissing in the wind.

CHAPTER 70

He couldn't relax. A whole day spent in the company of Trudy, a woman he hoped would be the one for him, and all he could think about was Tara. None of his texts had been answered and his calls went immediately to voicemail. He had already abandoned Trudy once today, when he went to the station, and now he was thinking that he should call at Tara's place. Just to check that she was all right.

Most of their day had been spent in bed, making love, dozing, reading and watching movies, so seldom did he have an entire weekend free. Now, after they had showered together, he came up with an excuse to leave Trudy for a short time.

'I'll cook dinner,' he said.

'We can go out or get Chinese takeaway.'

'No, it's no problem. I'll nip out and get a couple of steaks and a good bottle of wine.'

'I'll come with you.'

'No, it's OK.' He stumbled over the words. 'You stay here. I won't be long.'

He was out of the door again before she could say anything further.

* * *

There was no reply when he rang Tara's buzzer, so he managed to get up to her landing by swiftly following another tenant as they entered the building. There was no answer to his knock on her door, either. Maybe she had gone away for the weekend. He understood at times she could be quite secretive, private about things, particularly when she had a new man. But nil reply to any of his texts was concerning.

He was about to leave her block when he remembered that her friend Aisling lived close by. Perhaps she knew what Tara was up to this weekend. He checked his phone; thought he might have her number. Heck, he didn't even remember the girl's surname. He scrolled through his contacts. He couldn't see a number for Aisling but found one for Tara's other close friend, Kate. He dialled it and waited for what seemed like an age for the phone to ring. Eventually, a cheery female voice sang out a hello.

'Kate? This is Alan Murray here, Tara's colleague.'

'Oh yes, Alan, hi, what can I do for you?'

'I'm just wondering if Tara is with you this weekend. I'm having trouble getting hold of her.'

'No, Alan. I'm in Lanzarote with my Mum. Have you tried Aisling?'

'I don't have her number; can you give me her address? I'm in Tara's block now, and I know Aisling lives close by.'

Kate gave him the address, but her cheerful tone was now one of deep concern.

'Is there anything wrong?'

'Just something urgent at work. Tara probably has her phone switched off. Nothing to worry about.'

'It's not like her. She always has her phone on in case they're trying to get her at the station.'

'I'm sure it's nothing. Sorry to interrupt your holiday. Thanks for the address.'

He rang off, not wanting to raise Kate's fears any higher. He was aware the girls were very close, and, from previous experience, he knew how much Kate and Aisling worried about Tara.

Murray received a text from Trudy, who was wondering why he was taking so long. He replied saying he would be back soon. There was no answer at Aisling's flat. The only other possibility that he could think of was that Tara had gone to her parents' house for the weekend. Still, that did not explain her failure to reply to any of his calls. They didn't live so far away, in Caldy, on the Wirral. He called the operations room at the station. Paula Bleasdale was on duty.

'Hi, Alan, what can I do for you?'

'Can you look up the telephone number for Tara's parents?'

'Yes, sure. What's up?'

'Just having trouble getting in contact with Tara. It's not like her.'

'Maybe she wants a break from hearing your smooth voice.'

'Funny. Just get the number, please.'

Paula called him back a few minutes later with the telephone number of the Grogan household. But before calling Tara's parents, he had to think of how best to ask after their daughter without causing alarm. Bleasdale, despite her quip, might well be correct that Tara was simply taking a complete rest from policing for a mere two days.

He dialled the number. A female voice answered, Murray assumed it was Tara's mother.

'May I speak to Tara Grogan, please?'

'I'm sorry, but Tara is not at home this weekend. May I ask who's calling?'

'Merseyside Police, St Anne Street.'

'You might try her mobile.'

'OK, thanks, will do. Sorry to bother you.'

'It's no trouble.'

Murray ended the call. He couldn't help being worried. He knew that Tara had continued to pursue her theory on missing women, a theory she had evolved since their discovery of the photographs at the flat of the murdered journalist Terry Lawler. She tended to dwell on such things in her spare time, then come to him with her latest thoughts on how to further the investigation. Relaxing weekend? Tara never relaxed. Had she gone off in pursuit of one of her notions?

As he made his way from Wapping Dock to the supermarket, he worried that Tara, rather than having gone off somewhere, had been taken against her will. If so, the number one suspect was the man who had done it once before – James Guy. Then, he recalled her telling him what had happened to her in Belfast. Had someone connected to the Boswell murder found reason to snatch her? Maybe those same men who had forced her into a car in Belfast and warned her to stay out of their affairs had decided that she needed to be silenced. Someone connected to Carly McHugh, perhaps? Or even Carly herself?

CHAPTER 71

She was floating. Weightless, in the arms of – someone. A man. Warm and cosy, her head was swooning. She felt safe, cosseted. She could feel his heart beating, or was it her own? Something wet on her face, cold, refreshing. Rain. She was outside in wind and rain and in the arms of a strong man. Still, she was flying, his warm breath on her face, and the sky above him steely grey like the dawn. She wanted to sleep again. It was fine. She was safe in his arms.

When she opened her eyes again, either minutes or hours later, she took in her surroundings but failed to understand them. A kettle sat on a small stove, a tiny window behind it and a green-grey nothingness beyond. A jar of coffee and a packet of biscuits sat to the right of the stove, and now she heard a knocking and thumping above her. She felt cold, her head ached, and her throat was dry. What was this place? Her hands were gone, no, they were stuck fast behind her. She was bound. Her feet wouldn't move apart, and she couldn't open her mouth. Her voice came as a whimper and a groan. Moving on the narrow bed was difficult, but her eyes caught sight of another space, a darkened room with a low ceiling. There were noises from within.

She felt her stomach rise and fall. Realisation at last began to creep in, but her memory had still to gain pace. She was inside a boat, a cabin. She sensed the rise and fall, the floating and swaying on water. Her eyes settled on the dark space where the sounds of sobbing, grunting and thrashing grew louder. She tried to sit up, her muscles tightening with the effort. There was an open hatch at the other end of the cabin. She could feel the wind and the occasional spots of rain blowing inside and she smelt the complex odour of sea air. She tried to call for him. The man in whose arms she had slept and felt so comfortable. She couldn't think of his name. Why was she here?

The cries from the darkened room rose again. Aisling? Her friend. Recent images surged back. For a second, she closed her eyes wishing she was wrong, but when she opened them, he was standing above her. She glanced from his grinning face to the dark room where Aisling lay. He had been in there with her. He had done something to her friend. Tears filled her eyes as she fought to be strong in front of him. She wanted to run, to get away, but she wanted also to comfort Aisling.

'Don't fret yourself, Tara. She enjoyed it.' He pulled up the zipper on his jeans.

She tried to speak, to yell at him, but the tape held everything back.

'Glad to see you're awake. I have to say, I've seen you looking better.'

She kicked out with both feet, but he dodged them easily. She tried to stand, but with one hand he pushed her back onto the bunk, and her head jerked then thumped against the wall. She groaned and collapsed on the bed. She was helpless. She could only watch as James Guy grasped her feet and swung them onto the bunk.

'Aren't you the lucky girl, Tara? Getting to spend time with me and your wee mate. Maybe later you might fancy a threesome. How does that grab you? Can't do much else for a while. The weather's closed in; there's a bit of a swell out there. We'll have to wait for a calmer sea. Can't have you and Aisling throwing up everywhere.'

She watched him through tear-filled eyes as he stepped towards the open hatch and slid the small door closed. Then he turned and smiled at her.

'Now, we're all nice and cosy.'

He unlocked a drawer beside the stove and produced a medium-sized bread knife. Sitting down beside her, he gripped her blouse and bra at her cleavage and pulled her up to a sitting position. Suddenly, he jabbed the knife point at her neck. She cried out and tried to pull away.

'Here's the deal,' he said in a harsh whisper. 'I remove the tape and you promise not to yell or scream, understand?' He pushed with the knife; the point broke her skin and blood trickled along the blade. 'Understand?'

Through tears she gazed into his eyes and saw only evil peering back. She nodded her head once, and it brought a wide smile to his face.

'Good.'

He gripped the edge of the tape and pulled it roughly from her mouth. Suddenly, she could take a deep breath.

'Remember, any noise and this goes back on, and I draw some more blood.'

'I want to see Aisling.'

'She's sleeping, maybe later.' He reached her an open bottle of water, holding it up to her mouth.

'Let her go. You wanted me; she's done you no harm.'

He smiled menacingly but didn't reply.

'Please, James. Do what you want with me, but I'm begging you. Let Aisling go.'

'Drink up and shut up, or I'll put the tape back on.'

She watched her blood dripping onto her white blouse. She could do nothing about it, her hands were still bound. She drank some water as he held the bottle to her mouth. When she tried to take more, he took it away. Her heart raced as she wondered how she could tackle him. Her eyes traversed the cabin, searching for a weapon, anything she might use to bring him down, and she watched as he replaced the knife in the drawer and locked it. If she couldn't overcome him then she and Aisling were lost.

Whatever this man did with his victims after raping them, it involved taking them out to sea. Now she regretted her decision to do what he'd ordered in not alerting her colleagues. Now she was on her own, and her macabre thought was that his raping her was not the worst thing that could happen. If anything happened to Aisling, she would never forgive herself. She must find a way off this boat.

CHAPTER 72

Murray got a call from St Anne Street. It was eight o'clock, Sunday morning, Trudy asleep beside him. They'd planned a walk at Crosby and a pub lunch before she had to head back to Salford. But the news wasn't good. Another shooting at Treadwater. What was worse, however, was that there was still no word from Tara.

Trudy continued to sleep as he eased himself from the bed, dressed hastily in jogging trousers and T-shirt and went to his lounge. There, he scribbled a brief note of where he was going and an apology for scuppering their Sunday morning. Pulling on a pair of trainers, he grabbed his keys and hurried out.

On the way to the car, he composed another text to Tara, informing her of yet another shooting. He had quickly become used to not expecting a reply. He stopped the car on what was now a familiar road on the Treadwater Estate, close to the shops and by the entrance to the park. Twenty yards beyond, a piece of incident tape stretched across the road and effectively blocked access. An ambulance was just moving off as he walked to the scene of the incident, passing a cluster of uniformed officers and a dozen or so residents. His heart sank when he saw DCI Weir dishing out instructions to a couple of SOCOs dressed in hooded white overalls. Now, he regretted coming. But it wasn't long before Weir clocked his approach and turned to greet him.

'DS Murray, sorry to spoil your lie-in, but we're a bit light on detectives this weekend.'

'Morning, sir. What have we got?'

'Another shooting, not fatal. One male, hit in the leg.'

'Is he a Viper?'

'Oh yes. Seems the gang war goes on.'

Murray, looking around him, taking in the blood spattered on the pavement, posed another question.

'The leg wounds, were they punishment style?'

Weir glared at him, looking irritated by the question.

'No, Murray, they were not. Someone, unseen, took a potshot at the lad.' After a pause, he added, 'You know, Murray, I wouldn't advise that you throw your lot in with DI Grogan.'

'Why's that, sir?'

'Not a smart career move, that's all. You could do better than to traipse around with her.'

Rather than indulge this petulant copper, Murray decided to mention his present concerns.

'I'm having trouble making contact with DI Grogan at the moment. She's not responding to my calls.'

'Probably out on the rip with some lad.'

'It's not like her not to respond. She's always clued into her work. I'm worried that she may have been taken by someone.'

Weir scoffed. Murray expected an offensive reply from the DCI but was surprised by his quite sober question.

'You're not thinking that she's got herself caught up in this gang fight?'

'I'm not sure. She *was* pulled off the street by some guys in Belfast.'

'I warned her to keep her nose out of this affair. She has no idea who she is dealing with. How certain are you that she's disappeared?'

'It's just not like her to drop off the radar. I'm worried about her.'

Suddenly, Weir seemed fired up.

'Well, you'd better get your arse to the station and get to work. Let's hope she's not caught up in this mess, or we'll be looking for another body.' He bounded off as Murray's thoughts immediately turned to the other possibility – that James Guy had snatched Tara.

At St Anne Street, it took a while to contact Tweedy – who was enjoying a family weekend in the Lake District – to give him the news that Tara had apparently disappeared. He explained that DCI Weir was considering the possibility that she'd become embroiled in the gang war. But Tweedy, like Murray, thought it more likely that Tara had gone off investigating the cases of the missing women. So, when he'd finished speaking with Tweedy, Murray managed to dig out a current address for James Guy. He was still on probation after his conviction for abducting Tara a couple of years ago. The current home of Mr Guy had to be the obvious place to start looking for Tara.

Before leaving the station, Murray organised an officer to search for Tara's car using automatic number plate recognition, usually referred to as ANPR. Hopefully, if she had driven somewhere this weekend her registration had been picked up by a road camera and logged. He rushed from the station, thinking that if he eliminated the possibility of James Guy having snatched Tara, the likelihood was that she had been taken by the drugs boys who had threatened her in Belfast. Neither possibility filled him with much hope for her safety.

CHAPTER 73

Of all the bloody days for a storm, it had to be a day when I had two women to dispose of. The wind was cutting up the water, even in the harbour at Penrhyn, and Mother Freedom was constantly thumping against the wall of the quay. My biggest concern, though, was that the cops would now be wise to the fact that Tara had disappeared and that they were already searching for her. Their first place to call, I was sure, would be my flat. Dear help my wee Kirsty. She would get one hell of a shock, and her pregnant. I would have some explaining to do when I got home.

It was strange that I still felt confident of getting home and resuming my new life, even after I'd disposed of Tara and her mate. If I supplied the police with a good alibi for my weekend away from home, they wouldn't have anything on me. Like I said before, I'm careful, I'm meticulous; I don't make mistakes. Tara must go before she discovers anything further about my life. She went to Belfast and started digging. That's the only reason I'm doing this. I wouldn't have gone near her otherwise. I have a new life now; I'm going to be a husband and a father; I don't need to be taking women.

It is fun though. And it's all gone smoothly so far. If I've done things right, Tara and Aisling will disappear without trace, and no one will ever hear from them again. That's if a bloody trawler doesn't fish them up in a year's time. One thing I can't be certain of is whether Tara has or has not discussed what she's found out about me with any of her police buddies. I won't know for sure until after she's gone.

I had only a few pills left. Didn't have many to start with. That wee creep in Toxteth didn't have much to sell me, and I swear it was sub-standard gear anyway. Hardly enough in one pill to keep Aisling sleeping for more than a couple of hours at a time. Now I won't have enough to see off either woman. I'll just have to drop them into the water alive. Sleeping maybe, but still alive. I couldn't bear to kill with my hands, it's not my style. I don't get a buzz from the kill. My joy is in what I do with my girls before they snuff it.

Killing's just a necessity.

I got sick listening to Tara whingeing on and on, begging to see Aisling. You know, you can really go off people, when they turn out to be someone you don't much like at all. Tara is gorgeous, but let's face it, my experiences with her have been far from pleasant. First, I got caught for snatching her and spent eighteen months in jail. Next time she's saving me from the hands of that mad axe murderer Aeron and her brother. Now, I'm having to take her again – simply to stop her finding out exactly what I've done. It's not the way I wanted it to be. Love is a sweet, pure thing and her nagging me to let Aisling go free is just spoiling the mood.

I stuck some tape back on her mouth.

She lay on the bunk, but all the while her eyes never left me. I was quite sure she understood that I had been with Aisling more than once since taking her, and that would be more than enough for her to hate me. Her eyes were red from crying, but she maintained an icy stare, as if she was trying to curse me or paralyse me telepathically. I made some tea, opened a pack of chocolate biscuits and sat down opposite her.

'You know, Tara, this is all your fault.'

I sipped from the mug and munched on a biscuit, letting my words sink in. 'You couldn't keep from poking your nose into my life, could you? What do you think you were doing, going to see my Aunt Margaret and asking all about me? I suppose you're thinking I'm this way because my mother left me when I was kid?'

She tried to speak, her eyes begging me to remove the tape. Shit. My curiosity got the better of me, so I ripped it off with some aplomb. She cried out, but I warned her to settle herself.

'If you don't quieten down, I'll do more than put the tape back.'

She fumed. I reckon she was considering yelling the place down, in the hope that somebody was nearby. But it was an awful day, a day when no one in their right mind would be anywhere near a boat.

'Do you want some tea?'

'Tell me about your mother,' she asked, ignoring my offer.

I fucking glared at her. Felt like giving her a slap. I knew what she was doing. Trying to get under my skin, trying to gain my trust and explain away all my sins. Fuck her. She was dead anyway. In a few hours she wouldn't be saying much, and I would have given her a good send off.

From my wallet, I slipped out a small photograph, passport size, and held it up to her. She looked closely.

'I've seen that picture before.'

'Oh aye, where'd you see it?'

'I found it on the wall in Terry Lawler's flat. Along with two dozen others. She disappeared on you, James, isn't that correct?'

'So what? She was beautiful, wasn't she?'

'Did she even say goodbye to you?'

For a moment I debated with myself whether to answer the bitch.

'Told me she was going to Dublin for the weekend.'

'And she never came back?'

I shook my head but couldn't summon any words. The clever wee bitch was going for it.

'Did you ever try to find her? She might still be alive, unless…'

'Unless what? Unless I killed her? Is that what you think? I was only eight years old, for fuck's sake! What was I going to do, eh? And no, I never tried to find her. She wouldn't be interested in me.'

Then Tara had the bloody nerve to ask the obvious question.

'Is that why you killed all those women? Because you're angry that your mum walked out on you?'

'You think you're so fucking clever, don't you, Tara? You think you have all the answers.'

'I know you've killed young women, innocent women who did you no harm. How many, James?'

I changed the subject. No *way* was she going to rile me.

'I'm going to be a da, you know. And I'm getting married.'

'Who's the lucky girl?'

'Her name is Kirsty. Everything was all rosy in the garden until I saw you sneaking off to Belfast. When I'm finished with you, I'm going home to Kirsty and getting on with my life. You aren't going to cause me any more trouble.'

'You think I went to Belfast because I was investigating you?'

'Why else?'

'I do have other cases, James. I didn't go to Belfast because of you.'

'Sure you did. You went to find out about Linda's body being dragged from the sea. And then you went to visit my aunt.'

She smiled at her little victory.

'Was Linda your first?'

'Shut your face, Tara.' I grabbed the tape and stuck it back on her gob. 'First light in the morning, we're out of here. By then you won't give a shit how many women I've taken.'

CHAPTER 74

Murray was greeted at the door of the Penny Lane flat by an attractive brunette, Guy's fiancée Kirsty. Wearing a pale blue T-shirt and denim skirt, her hand went instinctively to her small pregnancy bump as Murray introduced himself.

'James has gone away for the weekend,' she replied cheerfully to Murray's enquiry.

'Do you know where he's gone?'

'Not exactly, he's fishing but I don't know where. Is there something wrong?'

'I need to speak with him. Do you have a number for him?'

Kirsty was growing less comfortable with the situation.

'Why do you need to speak with him? What's happened?'

'Hopefully, it's nothing, Miss Scholes, I just need to eliminate him from our enquiries.'

'What sort of enquiry? What do you think he's done?'

'If you could get me his number, I won't trouble you any further.'

Kirsty, now visibly nervous, went inside to her lounge and a few seconds later returned, holding her mobile. She dictated a number that Murray tapped into his phone. He walked away from the door of the flat, but Kirsty came after him, her fears rising that something was amiss with her fiancé. Murray listened to the phone ring and then switch to a voicemail message.

'Mr Guy, it's Detective Sergeant Murray, Merseyside Police, please give me a call back as soon as you can. Thank you.'

As he began to walk away, Kirsty followed.

'Aren't you going to tell me what this is about? I'm his fiancée.'

'I can't do that, miss.' He handed her his card. 'If he gets in touch with you, please call me on that number.'

James Guy's absence from home and his failure to answer his phone did nothing to soothe Murray's unease, specifically his growing fear that he had taken Tara. If she had been abducted, it seemed more likely that someone connected to this Belfast drug gang was involved, but still James Guy had previous. If Guy had been gone all weekend, he may have already carried out his intentions concerning Tara.

Time may have already run out for his DI.

* * *

He drove quickly back to St Anne Street. John Wilson had come in, having received a message from Murray that Tara was missing. He had taken charge of co-ordinating the survey of traffic activity recorded by roadside cameras.

'Any joy?' Murray asked as he barged into the operations room.

'Some,' replied Wilson, flitting from his desk to another where the computer was running the camera check. 'Tara's car passed a camera in Speke on Friday evening, 17:46. Then Runcorn station car park at 18.21, again at 18.33. Another trigger near Chester on the M56, then another in Wales on the A494 at 19.28. Nothing after that.'

'Where the hell was she going? Is there anything for Saturday?'

'Not a squeak.'

'Does that mean she is stationary, or is she some place with no cameras around?' Murray looked for a phone number on his desk then tapped it into his mobile.

'Miss Scholes, what vehicle is James using this weekend?' There was silence at the other end. 'Miss Scholes?'

'I'm sorry, Sergeant. I don't know what James is driving. Our car is here.'

'Does he have another car, or a van or something he drives for work?'

'He drives a delivery van, but he doesn't get to bring it home.'

'Are you telling me that James has gone fishing, you don't know where, and you don't know how he's travelling? Has he gone alone?'

'I think so.'

Murray cut the call. He'd learned nothing. Tara, it seemed, had driven into North Wales on Friday evening. James Guy had gone fishing on Friday. And Murray had no clue as to what became of either person after that.

CHAPTER 75

Tara felt exhausted, but no way could she sleep. Her arms ached at her shoulders; her hands still bound behind her. She had managed to stretch her legs, but it resulted in more discomfort at her neck and shoulders as she lay without a pillow on the bunk.

Guy, before drifting off to sleep, had risen from his seat and draped a blanket over her. So at least she was warm. Strong winds continued to sweep the coast, and heavy rain spattered the roof of the cabin. She prayed that someone would come, but who was likely to be around, in this weather and at this hour? And she didn't know where she was, except that it was a place where a boat could be moored. No one was searching for them, because she had failed to follow police procedure and inform her colleagues of what had occurred and where she'd be going. A mistake, a deliberate decision she'd made to keep her friend alive. Now she realised it had been a catastrophic error. She and Aisling were both dead if she couldn't overcome James Guy. They were no different from any of the women he'd taken before, and who had died at his hands. No one would be coming to help them. She must find a way off this boat.

Every sound, from a wave slapping the hull to the thud of the boat against the harbour wall, set her thinking that something was happening, something was changing that could aid her escape. If she could get away, she could raise the alarm and come back for Aisling. Or maybe she could disable Guy in some way. In the darkness, she couldn't see his face clearly, but she was sure he was sleeping on the bench seat to the left of the cooker. His breathing was steady, his body quite still.

In the bow cabin, the sliding door had been left open, and she sensed that Aisling was beginning to regain consciousness. Tara's immediate thought was to get to her, to comfort and reassure her friend that all would be well. She was surprised that Guy hadn't secured her to the bunk because that meant that, in theory, she could rise and attempt an escape. Maybe he was confident that she wouldn't get far, convinced that she wouldn't take off without Aisling. Hopefully, she could make him pay for his complacency.

But her first attempts to move weren't promising. She struggled to raise herself to a seated position without fuss and noise. Eventually, she sat with her legs over the side of the bunk, waiting and watching to see if she had disturbed Guy's slumber. With no sign of him waking, she pushed herself to her feet but remained on the spot, fighting to maintain her balance and control her breathing, worried that Guy might hear even the pounding of her heart. With her feet strapped tightly together, she was capable only of tiny shuffling steps as she edged towards the bow cabin.

Aisling was thrashing in her sleep, moaning and sighing periodically. When Tara reached the doorway, she had to descend slowly to the floor and sit on her bottom to lift her feet over the lip of the door frame. Once her feet were inside, she wedged her back against the frame and tried to raise herself once more. In seconds she was upright. A few more shuffled steps and her legs met the edge of the double bunk. She sat on the mattress and tried to focus on the form of her friend, who lay naked and still asleep. She cried for her. If they survived, would Aisling remember anything of what Guy had done to her? She prayed not, but it didn't halt the tears sliding down her cheeks. What could drive a man to do such things to a woman? Why did he need to do this? How many lives had been shattered by James Guy?

Then she heard him. Awake. Stomping on the floor of the galley. Suddenly, the cabin filled with light, and Guy stood over her.

'Found your wee mate then?'

She couldn't reply, her mouth still covered with tape.

'What am I going to do with you, Tara Grogan?'

CHAPTER 76

James Guy had not responded to his message, so Murray was now convinced that he had taken Tara and possibly her friend, Aisling. He ordered a data check on Tara's phone and on that of James Guy. Even a signal registered on an identifiable phone mast might help to pinpoint her location.

Patrols, all over the northwest and into Wales, were now on the lookout for Tara's blue Ford Focus. Everything suggested Guy was responsible for whatever had happened. Murray had to bring himself up to date with what Tara had discovered about the man. He felt at a loss, powerless to act as he thought of what Guy did to his victims. He recalled Tara's interest in the pictures of disappeared women found on the wall in Terry Lawler's flat and how she had theorised that one man was responsible for all the murders. He found it easier to believe that James Guy could be the killer. But where did he go, what did he do with his victims? The story given to him by Kirsty Scholes, that her boyfriend had gone fishing, sent waves of sickening dread through him. He thought of the recent find in the Irish Sea, the woman's body hauled out by a trawler, and his conversation with Tara when she'd returned from Belfast, convinced that at last she was onto something regarding the missing women. Where did Guy go fishing? Presumably, if he dumped his victims at sea he owned or had access to a boat. But where? Which port?

He was startled by Wilson calling from across the office.

'Sir, we've found her car!'

Murray rushed to his colleague's desk and read the screen as Wilson narrated.

'Llyn Ogwen? Where in hell is that?'

Wilson typed the name into a map search and a red flag appeared on the screen. Both men tried to make sense of the location.

'Middle of bloody nowhere,' said Wilson.

Murray was pulling on his jacket and gathering his keys.

'Let's get out there,' he said.

At least it felt like he was doing something at last. But how did finding Tara's car in the middle of the Welsh countryside stack up with James Guy dumping his victims at sea? Llyn Ogwen was a lake; perhaps Guy used any convenient stretch of water. If that were so, and Tara's car had been found abandoned by the lake, then they were already too late. His heart sank.

* * *

A patrol car containing two officers from North Wales Police drew up beside them at the lay-by where Tara's car had been found. Two in the morning, and the wind and rain beat at their faces as they first broke into and then inspected the Ford Focus.

Murray hoped to find some clue as to where Tara had gone. He dared to believe that she may still be free and on the trail of the serial killer, but his doubts held sway when he realised that she would not have ceased all contact unless she'd got into difficulty. In the violence of the storm, he sensed rather than saw the stretch of the lake alongside them. Wilson was searching the car's interior, but there was no sign of any written message, Tara's bag, her phone or any clue to suggest where they should look for her next.

Murray thanked the two constables, and then from the shelter of his own car attempted to call St Anne Street station. There was little signal. What else could be achieved out here? Did they wait for daybreak to conduct a search around the lake's shore? All manner of scenarios played out in his head, the worst being Tara already lying at the bottom of Llyn Ogwen. He decided he could take better control of the situation back in Liverpool. He was eager to see the mobile phone data; that, surely, would provide the best chance of finding Tara.

As he drove away from the lake and the signal strength improved, Wilson managed to contact St Anne Street. But rather than hearing an update on the search for Tara, both detectives were told that all hell had broken loose on the Treadwater Estate.

CHAPTER 77

I must have dozed off. The thud of the boat against the harbour wall woke me with a jolt. My first thought was, what the fuck am I doing here? My second was to wonder why Tara wasn't in her bunk.

I flicked on the lights and instantly saw her through the open door of the bow cabin, sitting next to Aisling. Sweet. I saw the fear in her eyes too, as I came to join them. Couldn't help smiling. Aisling was now awake and crying, and I realised that after the last time I'd been with her I hadn't re-bound her hands or feet. That was careless. Tara, though, was securely bound. Just ripe for me.

'I know you want the same as Aisling, don't you, Tara?' She tried to roll away from me, but where could she go? I fetched another roofie from the little bag I had in the galley. I didn't have many left now, but hopefully sufficient to have my girls comatose when I had my final fling, and maybe they would still be out of it when I tipped their bodies into the drink.

I sat astride Tara as she tried to wriggle free. It was comical to watch. I pulled the gaffer tape partially free from her mouth, squeezed the roofie pill through her lips and replaced the tape. For a while, I sat watching her, feeling her slight body struggling beneath me. A bit of a turn on, I have to say. Aisling wasn't doing anything. Just lying still. I don't really think she was with us at all, her head in a daze. The roofies were messing with their heads. She didn't make any attempt to help her friend.

I was quite happy sitting there, Tara between my legs, watching her slowly fade, losing the will to resist. I was about to have the time of my life.

When her eyes began to lose focus, I climbed off her and went to the galley for a knife.

'Don't worry, Aisling, it's not what you think.'

The poor girl seemed to think I was about to stab them both. She backed away on the bed as far as she could, into the bow. Aware of danger it seemed, so not that far gone. I cut the plastic cable ties at Tara's hands and feet and placed her in a comfortable position. I slid her skirt down her legs and dropped it on the floor. Next, I took hold of her tights and began to pull them down.

Suddenly, I felt as though my head had just separated from my body. I couldn't hear; I couldn't see clearly, and I collapsed on top of the unconscious Tara. I felt close to passing out. Aisling clambered over us both as I regained my bearings. She'd swung her foot and caught me on the side of the head. Now she'd pulled the tape from her mouth and was yelling the place down. She was grappling to get by, to get out of the cabin and off the boat.

'Come here, you wee bitch!'

She tripped over the step and fell into the galley, me diving on top of her. She screamed in pain as my knee thumped into her lower back. Scrambling to my feet, I tried to keep hold of her, but it was difficult, with her being naked. Digging my nails into her arms, I managed a firmer grip and dragged her back into the cabin. She collapsed on Tara, who didn't budge. But Aisling wasn't finished. She scrambled onto her knees and rained punches down on me, squealing like a banshee for help. She'd lost it completely, off her head, and she was bloody strong.

Then I saw the knife I'd used to cut Tara's binds. I dropped to the floor as Aisling kicked at me with her bare feet. Honestly, I only meant to use it to scare her off, to calm her down, but the wee bitch wouldn't give in. She

239

was leaning over me, slapping and punching at my head and scratching my face. I thrust upwards with the knife, and it sank into her belly, her warm blood splattering down my arm. That shut her up. I pulled the knife out again. She clasped both hands over the wound. Her blood dripped all over me. I got to my feet, went to the galley and cut another piece of gaffer tape. I stuck it over her mouth to stop her crying and pushed her over Tara so that she lay on her back still clutching her belly.

Fuck! This was not how things were supposed to happen.

Immediately, I went to the wheelhouse and started the engine. The wind was still howling, and rain was bouncing off the harbour wall. It was still dark, but I couldn't wait any longer. I had to get out to sea. I would have my day with Tara, to hell with the weather. I cast off and aimed the bow of Mother Freedom at the open sea. I had one hell of a headache.

CHAPTER 78

An entire street, Elmwood Crescent, had been cordoned off on the Treadwater Estate. A line of police vehicles, cars, vans, swirling blue lights, plastic tape, and uniforms engulfed the street. Clearly, a major incident was unfolding, residents were being guided away from the cordoned off area, and armed police officers were developing a plan of action.

Murray and Wilson arrived when the area was still in darkness, still in pouring rain, to find DCI Weir heading up the incident. They slipped by the cordon and bounded up to the big Scot.

'What's happening, sir?' Murray asked.

For once, DCI Weir looked pleased, or at least relieved, to see members of Harold Tweedy's team standing before him. Strange, that in heavy rain one tended to shout to be heard. Weir, in a waterproof anorak, his fat head encased in the hood, was his usual caustic self.

'Bloody gang wars for you, sonny. Didn't I tell you it was all about drugs in this city?'

Murray didn't rise to Weir's condescension. His allegiance lay still with his DI, even though she could not be found, and he was worried sick. For the briefest of moments, he wondered if Tara was caught up in the drama on this estate. Had she managed to nail the people responsible for the shootings in Treadwater? But just as quickly he dismissed the notion, since he and Wilson had just left Llyn Ogwen, where her car lay abandoned. Surely, there was no logical connection between the two situations. Now this incident was preventing him from continuing his search. For a moment, as he only half-listened to Weir's account of the present circumstances, he tried to think of where to go next in looking for Tara.

'As far we know,' Weir explained, 'the house we've sealed off belongs to Aidan Boswell. Number thirty-six. There are two people left inside. Aidan Boswell and Carly McHugh.'

'Are they armed?' Wilson asked.

Members of the firearms unit were moving into position around the perimeter of the house and in the gardens of houses opposite.

'According to a Kimberley Lloyd, Aidan's girlfriend, McHugh is armed with an automatic pistol.'

'Carly McHugh?'

Murray knew then that Tara had been right. The Belfast woman was at the centre of these murders. And on Friday evening, DCI Weir had set her free.

'Yes,' replied Weir. 'Seems she came to the front door, asking for Aidan. When Kimberley told her that he wasn't home she forced her way in and decided to wait. When

Boswell returned, Kimberley tried to warn him off, but before he could escape Carly shot him in the leg. In the confusion, Kimberley got away and raised the alarm.'

'Is Boswell still alive?'

'I think so. McHugh is threatening to kill him if she doesn't get safe passage out of there. The wee lass isn't going to get that now, is she?'

'Who's handling the negotiations?'

'I am at the moment.'

Murray met Weir's glare full on, but he was shocked by what the DCI said next.

'Therein lies the problem, DS Murray. The lass says she will only speak with DI Grogan. So, tell me, where the hell is she?'

Murray felt like punching Weir, not that the man would feel much, with such a fat head. His insouciance had helped create the present situation, and now he was trying to lay blame at Tara's door. This trouble would never have happened if she had been allowed to do her job. Carly McHugh should have been in custody, had been in custody.

'We think she has been abducted, sir.'

Weir scoffed and turned his hefty frame back towards the besieged house.

'Then you'd best be off looking for her, sonny.'

CHAPTER 79

She leaned over the edge of the bunk and vomited. Only then did she realise that she was not bound hand and foot, for she was able to peel the tape from her mouth just before she threw up. In the half-light, she turned to see Aisling beside her, crumpled to a foetal position, her hands tucked into her tummy. She reached out and stroked her friend's hair. Aisling didn't flinch. Tara's hand went to Aisling's face. It felt cold. She sat up, aware now of the loud drone of an engine and the violent swaying to and fro. They were at sea. She shook Aisling's arm to wake her, but there was no response. Her fears rose instantly, her body trembling, her mind racing to an answer she didn't want to believe. She placed two fingers at Aisling's neck and felt for a pulse. Nothing, but she couldn't be sure, not with the rise and fall of the boat, the noise and vibrations from the engine and her fingers shaking against her friend's ice-cold flesh. Then she felt the mattress wet beneath her. She saw a dark stain on the pale mattress cover. She vomited again as a scream rose in her throat. She didn't want to believe. It couldn't be. Surely, he was going to let Aisling go. He wouldn't have killed her. Not like this.

In panic, she pushed herself away from Aisling. As she tried to stand, she realised that her tights had been pulled down below her knees and her skirt was missing. In the dim cabin, she couldn't see her clothes or any of Aisling's. Quietly, yet with tears streaming down her face, she pulled her tights up then stood by the closed door of the cabin, listening. If they were at sea, then surely, he was in the wheelhouse above? Slowly, she pushed on the door until it began to slide open, revealing the galley. Deserted, as she'd thought. If Aisling was dead, then Tara had no further hope of survival other than to resist this monster at every opportunity.

She stepped into the galley, and for the first time she saw the magnitude of her dire situation. From the starboard window, in the grey dawn light, she looked upon a distant horizon, a thunderous sea separating her from nothing. When she glanced to the portside, she saw land, dark cliffs and rocks – a few hundred yards away, she guessed. That was all she had, standing in the galley shivering from cold and fear and desperation. She had no plan and could only pray that her death would come quickly. Aisling, it seemed, had died in agony, Tara lying uselessly beside her friend as she'd bled to death. Shame and guilt now swam alongside her fears. It was not a helpful combination. Her mind drifted to visions of the many times she'd felt fear in her job, times when her life had been in danger. Yet she had always acted. Always, the instinct to survive had kicked in. She wasn't sure if she even wanted to survive now. Why should she live when her beautiful friend had perished? She had failed Aisling. Why should she live?

Heart thumping, rooted to the spot, her mind unable to spark the need for self-protection, Tara gazed about the cabin. She knew he was at the wheel, powering the boat to who knows where. To a spot where he could rid himself of two more victims. How many times had he done this? How many women had sunk to the bottom of the sea because of him? She had to know. She must win justice for every single one of them. She had to overcome him. He mustn't win again.

Now, her fighting spirit erupted inside her.

She searched the cabin for something, anything she could use to defend herself. She found little but her skirt lying on the bench where, a day earlier, he had sat for hours watching her. At the small stove and cabinet, she couldn't even find a knife, a fork, or a spoon. He was well practised in keeping weapons from his victims. All that sat before her was a kettle, half-full of water. She managed to strike the lighter on the two-ring gas stove and set the kettle over the flame. She prayed that he would stay outside. She urged the water to boil. Time froze as she waited. The boat cut awkwardly through the waves, and she struggled to keep on her feet.

Then a whistle. She'd forgotten about the sing from the kettle. Quickly, she snatched it from the stove, leaving the flame to burn. Then two conflicting thoughts. One, that Guy had heard the whistle and would come down to see.

Two, that he hadn't heard, and she could lie in wait for him. Clutching the kettle by its handle, she squeezed into a small gap between the bunk and the hatch to the wheelhouse above. She had to stand on one foot. It was the only spot where she could have complete surprise if he entered the cabin. Then panic gripped her once again as she realised that she'd left the sliding door open to the forward cabin. Still holding the kettle, she scurried forwards and slid the door closed, her dead friend banished from sight. As she was about to retake her hiding place she felt the boat's engine slow, and suddenly the hatch opened, and he stepped inside.

'What the fuck?'

She swung the kettle.

CHAPTER 80

Aidan Boswell writhed in agony and couldn't stop himself from looking to his leg. His right kneecap was gone, only a bloodied pulp of cartilage remained. He lay sprawled across the sofa of his living room, groaning from the searing pain, on the verge of throwing up or passing out. Maybe both. There was blood everywhere. His clothes, the sofa, and a deep red trail on the carpet leading all the way from the door. Carly, girlfriend to his now dead brother, Ryan, sat on the arm of a chair pointing a gun in his direction. She'd fired it once, and he didn't doubt that she would do so again.

'Tell me again what happened to Ryan that night?'

Her voice was hard, the type of hard that comes with a tough upbringing in a tough neighbourhood of a city well-used to sorting its problems with a gun. The tragedy was that she was such a pretty woman, beautiful in the right circumstances, a face easy on the eyes. Aidan could see what had attracted his brother. What he hadn't seen, or known, was how close they had become. After Ryan's death he hadn't thought that Carly would ever come back to Treadwater. Now, she wanted answers from him.

She wore black motorcycle leathers and boots, her crash helmet sat on Kimberley's dining table. There'd be hell to pay if it got scratched. Carly had lowered the zipper on her jacket. He saw her white T-shirt beneath and the swellings of her breasts. It would have been an alluring sight but for the pistol firmly pointed in his direction. He considered faking unconsciousness so that she might leave him alone, but then he thought that she was just as likely to put a bullet in his head on her way out the door. That was before he was aware of the house being surrounded by the bizzies. Kimberley must have called the police. Maybe they could save him from this mad bitch. She'd had a discussion with one of the cops outside, shouting through an open window. She said she would only deal with that detective, DI Grogan. But they said that wasn't going to happen. In the end, she told them that either the bizzies let her go or she would kill him. She gave them half an hour to organise it. When she turned away from the window, he realised that she hadn't finished her interrogation.

'I've popped your buddies, Tyler and Craig, and one wee fucker was lucky last night that I didn't get him too. Can't think of the wee shite's name but I know he was in the house that night when Ryan was taken away. Tried to feel me up. So don't be thinking because you're Ryan's brother that I won't kill you. Somebody in the Vipers shot Ryan that night, and I want to know who.'

'Wasn't Vipers,' Aidan said, gasping with pain. 'Your lot from Belfast did it. They wanted Ryan dead because he was running his own deals and you were helping him. Why do you think he was called back to Liverpool?'

She jumped from her chair and kicked out at his wounded leg. He yelled for mercy.

'Stop your whingeing! I know about Fitter and my da. They wanted Ryan sorted, but my da wouldn't have let anyone hurt him. He knew we were together. He just wanted him reeled in, that's all. I got a telling off from him. Tyler tried to tell me that some blokes from Estonia were in on it. They were there that night. Is that true?'

Aidan was confused; not knowing which answer would appease her.

'Is that true, Aidan? Fuckin' answer me!' She pointed the gun at his other knee.

'No, no! Wasn't them. They'd nothing to do with it.'

Carly's face paled.

'Don't lie to me, Aidan. Tyler said they were there, baying for blood.'

Aidan shook his head, sniffing back tears and snot.

'It was Fitter gave us the shooter. Ask him yourself.'

'Who did it then? Tyler? Or Craig? Or were they too chicken to do the job themselves?'

Aidan didn't answer, the pain erupted in his leg. He wanted it all to end. First Ryan, then Tyler and Craig. He was surely next.

'Did they get one of their lackeys to do it? Some wee fella? Thought it was cool? You're going to tell me who it was, Aidan. Or do I have to shoot the whole fucking lot of you?'

'I don't know, Carly, honest. I wasn't there that night.'

'Bollocks. You're lying, you wee shite.'

She aimed the gun at his left knee and squeezed the trigger. It was a fatal mistake. Aidan screamed in pain as his knee disintegrated, but in seconds both the front and back doors of the house were rammed open and armed police surged inside.

Carly held the gun at Aidan's head, ready to fire again.

'It was me! *I* killed him! I had to. Your old man told Tyler I had to do it. It was my bro who'd fucked up, so I had to sort him.'

She was taking it in, processing this piece of truth, that her beloved Ryan had been killed by his own brother. On the orders of her father. She didn't get the chance to squeeze the trigger again. She didn't get a chance to raise her hands in surrender. She turned to face them, pointing her gun. It was obvious to the armed officer that she would use her weapon. Three shots. Two in the body and Carly slumped to the floor; the third bullet entered her body through her forehead.

CHAPTER 81

I'd been fucking careless. Me, the meticulous planner, had messed up. Should have kept them tied up the whole time. Tied up and fucking out of their heads on roofies. But I just couldn't wait to have them. I thought by getting my end away with Aisling first, it would leave me time to do all that I wanted and dreamed of and fantasised about doing with Tara. Then FUBAR – Fucked Up Beyond All Recognition. I stuck a knife in Aisling to shut her up, to get her off me.

I knew I couldn't stay in harbour and wait for the storm to pass. Things were turning nasty. I tried to focus on my real purpose for snatching Tara. I had to rid myself of the one person who had sussed me out. The one person who knew what I'd been up to, for years. Tara had guessed at the number of women I'd taken, and she wasn't far wrong. But she didn't have real proof, only her suppositions had led her to suspect me. But that was already too much for me. I had to get rid of her before she ruined my life completely. Wish I'd never laid eyes on the clever wee bitch.

With Aisling bleeding away and Tara still out of it, I planned how to get myself out of a bad situation. First, I motored Mother Freedom into a rough sea. When I got far enough out from land, I would have my final reward from Tara. I would leave a little something of myself inside her and then dump her in the sea, along with her mate. Then I would make for Ireland. The best alibi I could think of was to concoct a story of me fishing off the County Down coast and having to make for a port to avoid the storm.

The sea was as rough as I had ever experienced. It was all I could do to keep Mother Freedom's bow pointing into the swell. Couple of times I thought she would roll over. I prayed the wind would soon drop, giving me time to do my best for Tara. I was still off Anglesey, the shore only a quarter of a mile away, when everything went tits up.

I heard something below. A series of noises, the first was a whistle. I slowed the engine and hoped I could leave the wheel for a few seconds to check it out. One of the girls was moving about.

I opened the hatch to the galley and stepped inside. I caught a glimpse of what was coming my way, but I had no chance. Suddenly, the pain on my face was unbearable. I was doused in boiling water as my head hit the kettle. For a second, I couldn't be certain it was Tara. I yelled and collapsed onto the bunk, my hands trying to wipe the scalding liquid from my face, my eyes and then my neck, as water trickled down my front and back. She poured the water over me until the kettle was empty. Then, she pushed past me and climbed outside. I went after her. I could only see with one eye. The left side of my head had borne the brunt of the impact with the hot kettle.

'You fucking bitch!'

I scrambled outside, my whole body shaking from the heat now sinking into my flesh. She was yelling her tits off, calling for help. Mother Freedom had swung about, her bow pointing towards land. Waves were crashing into her side, causing her to pitch one way then the other. I was sure we would roll over. Tara watched me stagger towards her. I wanted to rip the clothes right off her, ram myself inside her and be done with her. But she moved easily to avoid my lunging. I collapsed on the deck. I could feel my face pulsing, and with a hand I felt the blisters rising. Suddenly, the engine roared. She was fucking about with the controls. I could do nothing to stop her. I was in too much pain. Gradually, I found the strength to get to my feet. When I turned, I saw her watching me. But only I saw what was about to happen.

CHAPTER 82

There was a thud, followed by a prolonged scraping as the hull rode over those rocks lying just beneath the surface. Then Mother Freedom tilted sideways, and Tara was thrown off her feet. The engine whined as its power forced the hull onwards before the bow crumpled into a wall of black basalt. Slowly regaining her feet, she saw James Guy on all fours, moaning, disoriented by pain. Then he raised his head and stared her full in the face. She was shocked by the damage she'd wrought upon him, the boiling water having loosened and reddened his skin that now drooped below his chin in plump blisters.

But she saw the look in his one open eye and knew she was still not safe from him. The stern of the boat rose and fell with consecutive waves, but the bow remained grounded among the rocks.

In only her black tights and white blouse, soaked with Aisling's blood, she grappled her way over the side and dropped waist-deep in foaming water. She saw Guy watching as she let go of the boat. A malevolent wave threw her against the rocks and for a second, she floundered, trying to get a grip of something to prevent herself being washed away. She swallowed a mouthful of salt water, her stomach retching as she caught hold of dark brown seaweed. At first, it came away in her hands but there was so much for her to grasp that she held on as the water receded.

In the lull, she crawled over the weeds and made it to rocks that sat above the tide. When the next wave broke, only the spray caught her as she stood trying to figure out a route to safety. To her left and right there were rocks and seaweed as far as she could see. There were no sandy beaches, no paths or piers and not a living soul. Shivering, she realised that if she didn't get to help soon, the cold would claim her if James Guy didn't.

She could see no easy escape. Cliffs directly in front of her, she stumbled and picked her way over the flatter rocks searching for a break, a route to safety. Her feet had to feel ahead for a painless step, her tights already torn on jagged slabs. In her mind she had been walking for ages. She hoped she had put quite a distance between her and the boat and, more importantly, James Guy, but when she glanced behind, she'd made only twenty yards. Sniffing back tears, she struggled on, hoping that soon she would spy an easy way out. Might someone already be searching for her? Would she see a rescue boat, a helicopter, someone waving from the clifftop? Surely, around the headland a cottage, a road, a sandy beach awaited.

Rain lashed down but she was soaked already from the sea and the spray sent up by crashing waves, a torturous gauntlet to run. Her feet were numb and gave way beneath her, so she toppled over a low precipice and splashed into a rock pool. She could give in now. Lie in this chilled pool, let the water soak the remaining warmth from her body. At least Guy couldn't have her. But she had justice to serve on this man. Justice for every soul he'd taken, stolen from their families and discarded as garbage. She would make him pay. He must pay. She would make sure he paid for her beloved Aisling. Without that hope, that aim, why should she bother to survive?

Dragging herself from the pool, Tara stumbled on, daring once more to glance toward the boat. The vision sent another chill striking through her. He was coming. Unsteady on his feet but heading her way. He was gaining ground quickly. She was barefoot, while he, despite his injury, was wearing shoes of some kind. If there was no change in the terrain, soon he would be upon her.

She looked again at the cliffs rising above her. Could she climb her way out of here? Surely, there must be another way. She struggled on, whimpering in fear and shivering from cold. Suddenly, her last hope revealed itself. A narrow gully, a fault in the rock face of the cliff. Could she climb up there? She had to try. James Guy wasn't giving up.

Spurred on by the faint prospect of escape, she scrambled to the base of the cliff and gazed at her route to freedom. Water trickled down the gully. In places it looked quite benign, at others it appeared vertical. A place for the gulls – and she saw a few gliding high above her. She must try. Another look towards the boat and she saw James Guy now at the spot where she'd tumbled into the rock pool. She turned her back and began to climb.

Immediately, she felt the vulnerability of height. She could be ten thousand feet up on a mountain peak, or twelve feet up a cliff face. It didn't matter, she could fall easily. In places the rocks were slimy with moss, and she gripped helplessly at tufts of grass spurting from cracks in the cliff. At times she had purchase and could heave herself upwards. Then, something would give, and she slid back down, the rocks scraping her flesh and drawing blood. She couldn't yet see the top. She couldn't judge how far she'd climbed, but her pace had slowed, exhaustion and cold set to claim her. She looked downwards and cried out when she saw him take to the cliff.

'Playing hard to get, eh, Tara?'

She heard his call above the roaring wind that, for a second, pinned her to the rock face. She could no longer summon strength. She hung on, keeping hold of some long grass with both hands. She prayed.

It seemed only a few seconds before he was almost onto her. She cried with frustration. She was about to die. He gripped her left ankle, and she could do nothing but weep. He had her now.

She steeled herself to look him in the face, defiant to the last. But what she saw was a desperate man. A man who needed to kill her, to secure his own survival. She was the only one who knew what he'd done. His left eye had closed, his face ravaged by the boiling water, his hands reddened also from her attack. But he had a firm grasp of her ankle. He pulled hard, and she began to slip.

But she held on to the tough grass. She had purchase. With all her remaining strength, she kicked downwards with her right foot. She felt it making contact, but she couldn't be sure. Not until the responding cry and the sudden release of her ankle. She'd caught him in the throat. James Guy at first slipped downwards, then toppled into the air. When next she saw him, he lay sprawled on his back on the jagged rocks.

CHAPTER 83

She opened her eyes to see Kate sitting by her bed and holding her hand. She wanted to smile at her, but Kate wasn't smiling and instantly she realised why. For the two of them should be three. As it had always been. Kate,

Aisling and Tara. There should be heady laughter, glasses of chardonnay, wonderful clothes and outlandish hair colours. There should be plans forming for their next night out, for their next holiday, for news of their latest fella.

Empty. She already felt that way, despite waking only a few minutes ago. Comfortable in a hospital bed, her friend beside her, caressing her hand. Asking her how she was feeling. Yet apart from her warmth, her relative comfort and her steady breathing, Tara was dead. She had no feelings of a life within her. How could she? She was every bit as dead as Aisling, except she had this bizarre consciousness wherein she had to deal with shock and fear and sadness and utter despair.

She closed her eyes again.

A while later, it may have been days, she wasn't counting, and Murray was at her bedside. He'd hugged her close when he came into the room, so glad was he to see her safe and sound. If only. Then he tried acting all professional – as if she cared how he behaved anymore. She knew he wanted to ask all manner of questions, all the hows, whys and wherefores of her ordeal, but he did at least show some sensitivity. Then, he told her how he really felt about her, and she warmed slightly to his praise. She loved him in a way she could not and could never explain. He had been at her side throughout the past few years. He had saved her life several times. She knew he was trying to say that he cared for her. But what did it matter, between work colleagues? None of this comforting chat would bring Aisling back.

Tara hadn't even asked about James Guy. She had a faint recollection of being hauled up a cliff face in a stretcher, of multiple voices telling her she was OK, of the steady rumble of a helicopter hovering above her. Then sleep.

On what she believed to be his second visit, Murray had thought it prudent to up the chatter. He began talking about Wilson and his great work done at St Anne Street when they'd been searching for her. He'd traced her mobile as a signal pinged off masts all the way into Wales. He'd done the same with Guy's phone and discovered frequent registration with a mast in the Bangor-Penrhyn area. Immediately, they had local police check out the harbours and marinas in the vicinity. An air and sea search ensued until the wreck of Mother Freedom was spotted on the Anglesey coast.

Murray passed on regards from Tweedy and his message that he would pay her a visit later that same day. All this served only to bore and irritate her. Callously, she asked something she hoped would steer him away from her own recent experience.

'What about the Boswell case?'

He looked at her, as though trying to convince himself that she was really interested in receiving an answer to her question. When she said nothing further, he launched into an account of the incident on the Treadwater Estate, where nineteen-year-old Carly McHugh had died from a gunshot wound to the head, dispensed by Merseyside's finest. Tara found difficulty in showing any emotion. Her bruised and scratched face remained passive, although she did remind Murray that she'd wondered about Carly McHugh from the start.

'It seems she was besotted with Ryan Boswell and completely devastated by his murder. She went on the rampage. Did a lot of damage, shot two people dead. Aidan Boswell was screaming like a baby when he was rescued and confessed to the killing of his own brother.'

Murray paused, no doubt expecting an informed response from his DI, but nothing came. She looked exhausted by the subject, and he quickly rounded it off.

'DCI Weir was half right about a gang feud,' he said. 'The heavies from Belfast were pulling all the strings as far as the Vipers were concerned, but the whole episode has put paid to months of undercover work by his men and the PSNI in trying to dismantle the drug business between

Northern Ireland and the North of England. McHugh and Fitter have been arrested in Belfast, and it seems that Aidan Boswell will implicate the pair of them in the murders of his brother Ryan and the members of the Tallinn Crew. But Weir will have to explain why he let Carly McHugh go free – and she then killed Craig Lewis and two days later she shot Aidan Boswell.'

When Murray looked at her, Tara was fast asleep.

EPILOGUE

I told them everything. Everything I could remember. Didn't see the point in holding back. I knew the names of every one of my girls: their real names and the pet name I'd given them when I had first chosen them.

I don't think the cops were particularly grateful. They didn't thank me or anything. My solicitor said that it would help with my sentence, but he made it sound as though I'd been done for multiple episodes of shoplifting. Like I'd stolen from Marks and Spencer as well as Sainsbury's. What an arse. Besides, my sentence didn't much matter to me. Not with the way I am now.

Officially, I was convicted of the murders of Aisling Doherty and Linda Meredith. Seemed logical since they had both of their bodies. I disputed the murder charge for Aisling, which resulted in my having a trial. As far as I was concerned, I'd stabbed Aisling in self-defence. The jury didn't seem impressed by that.

I told them the approximate locations where I'd dumped the bodies of the others. Don't know if they will ever find all of them, but I suppose the families now know that their daughters had some kind of resting place. During my trial, my defence counsel wanted to wheel in a busload of psychologists to explain why I had ended up the way I am. That because my mother had abandoned me, I was somehow scarred for life, and it drove me to do what I did. They thought it might elicit a certain amount of sympathy from the jury. I didn't care much. What's the difference between one life sentence and twenty or even thirty-four life sentences? I wasn't going to see the light of day again, anyhow.

Tara, of course, appeared as a witness at my trial. She looked well. Tucked nicely into a plain dark trouser suit and heels but her hair was nice and shiny, and her wee cheeks glowed. She had the strength, even during the questioning about Aisling, to look me in the face. Takes a lot of guts, that does. Tara is made of strong stuff. I'll forever rue the day I first set eyes on her when I saw her on TV at that motorway services. Funny, that was the day I had Lady Victoria and Lucy the TV star lying in the back of my van. Those were the days.

I suppose I stirred up quite a bit of interest after my arrest. Lots of stories and theories appearing in the papers. The pictures of me weren't terribly flattering. Seemed to be a competition in the press over who could print the ugliest shot of me. Loads of speculation too, over the exact number of girls I'd killed. At one point it ranged from twenty to three hundred when journalists began looking into every case of a missing woman in the last fifteen years. And then I started getting letters from women who were apparently turned on by me and what I'd done. Some of the things they were willing to do for me would make your teeth curl. But things quietened down after my trial.

Quiet is right. You see, I don't say much these days. Tara did a good job on me. Her foot caught me in the throat, virtually ripped my vocal cords from their moorings, to use the nautical term. Broke my spine when I landed on the rocks. As they say, it's not the fall that does the damage, it's the sudden stop when you land.

So, after I was convicted and sentenced to life in prison, with the recommendation that it be a full life term, no chance of parole, I did receive one consolation for all my confessions. I didn't go to prison. I was deemed unfit, or I should say that there were no prisons in England deemed fit to house me. As a quadriplegic I require nursing care, so I was placed in a specialised unit attached to a swanky nursing home in Cheshire. Now, you might think that's a disgrace, a serial killer living in the lap of luxury at the taxpayer's expense, but how would *you* like to spend the rest of your days in a wheelchair, unable to speak, paralysed from the neck down, shitting in a bag and peeing in a nappy? I'd be better off at the bottom of the Irish Sea.

Kirsty came to see me. Just the once, after I'd been convicted. She didn't even come into the room where I was sitting. Looked at me through a window from the corridor. She was crying, dear love her. Doesn't know how lucky she is. If she hadn't taken a shine to me, I might well have given her one of my pet names and she'd have been done for.

I'm a da now, too. Kirsty brought our daughter on the same visit. She held her up to the window for me to see. Felt as if she was saying to me, *see what you missed, you evil bastard*. I hope wee Jenn – Kirsty named her after her mother – has a good life. That she stays safe.

They fitted me up with one of those electronic voice boxes, so I can communicate with the staff and any visitors I might get. Once Kirsty had been that one time, I wasn't expecting anyone else. The staff nicknamed me the Stephen Hawking of Chester, seeing as I speak using the movements of my eyelids. I don't sound like him, though. My voice box is more middle-class Englishman than Hawking's American astronaut tones. I sound more like the speaking clock. Makes me seem a jolly chap. The glass-half-full type and all that shit. Once I got used to it, I started to have a bit of fun with the nursing staff. In fact, just as I'm telling you all this stuff, in walks nurse Samantha. She's not that great-looking but she makes up for it in other ways. Put it this way, I never would have snatched the likes of her off the street and done the business.

Some of the staff, though, haven't taken kindly to me being here. One nurse, her name is Angela, is a cruel bitch. She's in her thirties, I'd guess, trim body, a girl about town, gagging for it, too. She brings me breakfast. Fucking porridge. I never asked for it, but she makes sure I eat every spoonful, especially when she's pissed in it first. Does it right in front of me. Couple of times she's brought used condoms with her and adds the contents to my strawberry yoghurt. One day, she used my useless hand to wipe her arse. I'm at her mercy. What can I say?

'How are we today, James?' says nurse Samantha.

There is a bit of a delay while I compose some witty reply.

'Fine.'

'Anything in that nappy of yours?' She lifts my blanket and pulls my shorts down a little way. Then she prises the nappy from my leg. There's no stench. 'All clean for now.' She examines my wizened penis and smiles. A conceited smile, her knowing what I used to be capable of and seeing how I am now.

She fusses about my room, checking my drinking water, taking my temperature with some jobby she sticks in my ear. Meanwhile, I'm trying to get something into my bloody voice box.

'Hey, nurse,' says the machine politely. 'Show me your tits.'

Samantha, she's about forty, heavily built with dark hair and a wide mouth, looks down her bobble of a nose at me and frowns. She's not smiling. Me, I'm fucking pissing myself.

'James, I've told you before, if you abuse that voice machine, I'll switch it off.'

Another delay while I attempt a reply.

'Sorry, nurse…' She searches for the switch on the console. 'No, please don't. Aw, f–'

If you enjoyed this book, please let others know by leaving a quick review on Amazon. Also, if you spot anything untoward in the paperback, get in touch. We strive for the best quality and appreciate reader feedback.

editor@thebookfolks.com

ALSO IN THIS SERIES

Visit www.thebookfolks.com for more details

OTHER TITLES OF INTEREST

Investigating a cold case about a missing person, DCI Gawn Girvin stumbles upon another unsolved crime. A murder. But that is just the start of her problems. The clues point to powerful people who will stop at nothing to protect themselves, and some look like they're dangerously close to home.

JOHN DEAN

THE
VENGEANCE
MAN

Vigilante justice meets mob rule in this murder mystery

When a youth is scared out of his wits by a man dressed all in black in the local church graveyard, the police don't think much of his tales about a bogeyman. But when a murder later takes place there, DCI John Blizzard will have to suspend disbelief and work out the identity of The Vengeance Man before he wreaks havoc in the neighbourhood.

All our books are FREE with Kindle Unlimited and available in paperback.

www.thebookfolks.com

Printed in Great Britain
by Amazon

13486329R00161

Battlegroun

GALLI
ANZAC THE LANDING

Soldiers from C Company, 9/AIF, aboard HMS *Beagle*.

Battleground Europe

GALLIPOLI

ANZAC
THE LANDING

Stephen Chambers

Series Editor
Nigel Cave

Pen & Sword
MILITARY

First published in Great Britain in 2008
and reprinted in this format in 2015 by
PEN & SWORD MILITARY
An imprint of
Pen & Sword Books Ltd
47 Church Street
Barnsley, South Yorkshire
S70 2AS

Copyright © Stephen Chambers, 2008, 2015

ISBN 978 1 84415 722 8

A CIP catalogue record for this book is
available from the British Library

Printed and bound in England
By CPI Group (UK) Ltd, Croydon, CR0 4YY

Pen & Sword Books Ltd incorporates the Imprints of Aviation, Atlas,
Family History, Fiction, Maritime, Military, Discovery, Politics, History,
Archaeology, Select, Wharncliffe Local History, Wharncliffe True Crime,
Military Classics, Wharncliffe Transport, Leo Cooper, The Praetorian Press,
Remember When, Seaforth Publishing and Frontline Publishing.

For a complete list of Pen & Sword titles please contact
PEN & SWORD BOOKS LIMITED
47 Church Street, Barnsley, South Yorkshire, S70 2AS, England
E-mail: enquiries@pen-and-sword.co.uk
Website: www.pen-and-sword.co.uk

CONTENTS

Series Editor's Introduction

Without a shadow of a doubt, the area of the Gallipoli landings is amongst the most beautiful and tranquil places that I have had the pleasure of visiting. To spend time there is to take a large step away from the contemporary world and to move into an almost timeless landscape, only periodically interrupted by the signs of modern civilization. When Steve and I spent ten days together on the Peninsula in 2001 this was starkly illustrated by the events taking place in New York on 11th September – it seemed another world away.

I still recall clearly the gathering of the livestock in the evening into corrals made up of thorn bushes, keeping them in and the predators out. Then there was the sight of the shepherd, walking across the wide-open, unenclosed fields of Suvla, with his flock scattered, their neck bells clanging and the dogs attempting to maintain order in a rather half-hearted fashion.

Yet it is a landscape marked by the tragic events of April 1915 to January 1916 – only eight months or so, but how much longer it seems to us and what an eternity it must definitely have felt to the men who fought in that extraordinary conflict.

The landings in late April 1915 have a particular resonance to two, then, new countries and have built up from there into an essential part of the histories of New Zealand and Australia. I had the pleasure this year (2007) of attending my first Anzac Day ceremony, in Rome, and a moving occasion it was too. Certainly there was no problem finding officiating clergy – it was probably the only ceremony world-wide where the clergy and sisters significantly outnumbered the lay participants!

The landings at Anzac (like those at Helles) witnessed extraordinary heroism by men of all sides. Obviously space has to be found for the whats and the whys on the grander scale, but so often it is a tale of effective command exercised at a low level and by individual and small group feats of courage and endurance that can leave us only wondering. The landscape – the scrub, the beaches and, towering over all, the heights, all serve to underline the challenges that those men faced. The cemeteries, leaving a message even in their names, give an indication of the human cost, underlined by the memorials at Lone Pine and Chunuk Bair (though the latter refers only to New Zealand casualties from August onwards).

If you can, do not hasten around this area – give it time, give two good days to the site of the Anzac Landings and the subsequent fighting. Make the most of Steve's excellent account. This place has so much to tell us; certainly of waste and loss of potential (it would be stupid to say otherwise) but also of some of the finest characteristics of humanity – endurance, responsibility, courage, humour in adversity and teamwork. I know of none who has not been moved by their time at Gallipoli.

Nigel Cave
Collegio Rosmini, Stresa

Introduction

The Allied objective in the Gallipoli Campaign was to force Germany's ally, Turkey and its Ottoman Empire, out of the war by capturing Constantinople (now Istanbul). This would open an ice-free sea supply route from the Aegean through the Dardanelles into the Black Sea to aid Russia. It was also hoped that pressure on Turkey would influence the neutral states of then Bulgaria, Romania and Greece to enter the war on the allied side.

After the failure of the naval actions that culminated on 18 March 1915, when British and French battleships attempted to force a path through the Dardanelles, a land campaign was planned. The purpose was to aid the Navy's attack by the capture of the Dardanelles' forts and minefields.

The amphibious landing on 25 April 1915 at Anzac Cove was only part of the Mediterranean Expeditionary Forces' invasion of the Gallipoli Peninsula. This landing on the Peninsula's Aegean coast, north of Gaba Tepe, was carried out by soldiers of the Australian and New Zealand Army Corps (ANZAC) and was its first significant military operation of the war. The French landed on Asia Minor at Kum Kale, whilst the main thrust was made at Cape Helles by the British.

Unfortunately, the plan for a swift land campaign fell into a long and bitter eight-month struggle after the inevitable stalemate of trench warfare had become established. The opposing armies suffered heavy casualties and had endured great hardships throughout this period that ultimately ended in defeat for the allies. During that period the Anzac battlefield changed little from the first days of the landing. The area captured was less than three-quarters of a square mile (two square kilometres), which became the home for over 20,000 men until the inevitable evacuation, in December 1915.

The landing at Anzac did not yield the optimistic results that the High Command had wished for, although this does not mean that the Anzac forces failed to try. Plagued with problems from the start, the covering force had landed on the wrong beach and found themselves in difficult topography which hampered movement. Having got hopelessly mixed up, any kind of a quick and organised thrust inland proved impossible. This was exacerbated by the premature changing of orders that led to the loss of any chance to secure the Sari Bair heights and Third Ridge. Unfortunately the drive and enthusiasm of the troops did not make up for their, and their officers' inexperience. Success was finally denied by the rapid reaction of the Ottoman army that put up a stubborn defence, stopping the Anzac advance. Under these difficult circumstances a landing was nevertheless made and a secure bridgehead was established. Unfortunately any chance of success was arguably lost that first day and future attempts to break out were countered at every stage by an underestimated Ottoman army that was fighting to safeguard its homeland.

Acknowledgements

Thanks are due to a number of individuals and organisations that have helped in the writing of this book. I am hugely indebted to Patrick Gariepy who has again been of great help with biographical details of Gallipoli casualties, Julian Pitt for permission to quote from his grandfather's diary and Bruce Denny for information on his grandfather, Major David Grant. I would also like to thank John Meyers for permission to quote from the Tiegs diary, State Library of South Australia for permission to quote from Jack Jensen's letter, Alexander Turnbull Library in New Zealand for permission to quote from the Malone and Bollinger diaries and the Mitchell Library of NSW for permission to use quotes from the Silas diary. I would also like to thank Chris Newbery and Matthew Little of the Royal Marines Museum for permission to use their archives and to quote from the diaries of Oppenheim and Pare, and John Peters for supplying photographs of the cemeteries as they were in the 1920s. And as always the staff at the National Archives, Australian War Memorial, Imperial War Museum and the Commonwealth War Graves Commission, all who have been of immense help. In Turkey, I would like to thank Erol Baycan and his wife for always providing great hospitality and a wonderful base to work from when in Gallipoli, and both Eric Goossens and William Sellers, both of whom are never-ending fountains of knowledge and beer. As always thanks is due to Nigel Cave, Series Editor, who has helped and inspired along the way. To all these people and any I have mistakenly forgotten to mention, please accept my sincere apologies and thanks.

This book would not have been possible to write without contemporary material: war diaries, divisional, regimental, battalion and unit histories and the excellent Official History of Australia in the Great War by C.E.W. Bean. Charles Bean was an official war correspondent who landed with the Anzacs on 25 April 1915. From first hand experience, the interviewing of veterans and examination of documents he managed to construct a meticulous record of what happened. I have referenced many personal accounts in the form of letters and diaries as well as a large assortment of maps and photographs, many having never been published before. The originators of these must all be thanked, because without this material there would be no book. Any copyright holders I have not been able to trace, please accept my sincere apologies, and feel free to contact me if you feel it necessary. I have sought to tell the story of Anzac during its first days of the landing using this wealth of information, but unfortunately, due to the limited space available, please be assured that the omission of any unit, key individual or event does in no way suggest that its part at Anzac had little or no significance.

Anzac Day

ANZAC Day, 25 April, marks the anniversary of the first major military action fought by Australian and New Zealand forces during the First World War. It became Australia's and New Zealand's most important national occasion from the time the first news of the Gallipoli landings had reached those at home; and remains so to the present day.

The failure of the Gallipoli Campaign did not mar the actions and sacrifice of the Anzacs, which bestowed an intangible but powerful legacy. The 'Anzac legend' that was created became an important part of the national identity of both antipodean nations, shaping the ways they viewed their past and future. Commemorated since 1916, when the First World War was still raging, the Anzacs developed a comradeship and pride that still endures to this day. Australians and New Zealanders recognise 25 April as an occasion of national commemoration when services are held at dawn, the time of the original landing, allowing both nations to reflect on the many different meanings of war.

Over ninety years on there are, sadly, no longer any living survivors of the campaign but the legacy continues. Anzac Day has survived, and each year many make the pilgrimage to Gallipoli, where crowds gather in their thousands. Gallipoli not only marks the arrival of Australia and New Zealand on the international stage, but it is also a landmark in the birth of modern Turkey.

The Australian and New Zealand troops have indeed proved themselves worthy sons of the Empire – George R.

Advice to travellers

Stop wayfarer! Unbeknownst to you this ground
You come and tread on, is where an epoch lies
Bend down and lend your ear, for this silent mound
Is the place where the heart of a nation sighs

By poet Necmettin Halil Onan

The best time to visit Gallipoli is between April and October. Outside this period the weather can get very wintry, cold and wet. In the spring, Gallipoli is covered by numerous wild flowers; smothered with a profusion of red poppies, white daisies and blue larkspurs. The fertile land is scattered with fields growing crops of wheat, sunflowers, melon and cotton; a very different picture to the one you may conjure up from reading books or browsing through photographs of the Gallipoli campaign. However, during the April landings this area was just as fertile before war savaged the land. During the height of summer, between June and August, the weather is baking hot and on most days the temperature goes well into the red. September and October are slightly cooler and thus good months to visit, the late summer leaving the ground sun-baked, hardened under foot, reminiscent of the 1915 period. During these months the scars of the old battlefield are still visible, as crops are harvested, and the grass sun-scorched and all but gone. All that remains are the hardy scrub and the scattering of pine trees. This is significant as on the high ground at Anzac, before battle had swept it away, this was the landscape that the men fought through during the first few days of April 1915. The unforgiving and mountainous landscape of Anzac is little changed, and today it is scattered with many cemeteries and memorials of the campaign. The biggest threat, sadly, is tourism, which has brought increasing numbers to the area, resulting in the building of car parks and roads that have altered many areas of the battlefield beyond repair. However the memory is kept alive as interest from Turk, Australian, New Zealander and Briton has not diminished over the years.

HMAT *Themistocles*, leaving Australia in December 1914, it helped take 1st Australian Division to war.

Equipment: When visiting the battlefields, preferably with at least one other person, take a good supply of bottled water, a packed lunch, a walking stick (also useful to fend off any farm dogs), sun cream, a wide-brimmed hat, long trousers, pen/notepad, penknife and a pair of sturdy boots with ankle support. If you are unfamiliar with the area and going off the beaten track, a map and compass is recommended. Put this altogether in a small rucksack with a first aid kit and this book and you should have a good recipe for an informative trip. A mobile phone can also be useful in emergencies (with the number of hotel, local emergency services and, if applicable, the car-hire or tour company). It is also a good idea to tell someone where you are planning to go for the day and what time you are planning to return. Most importantly, bring a camera with a good supply of film or digital storage.

Warning: Do not forget that the whole of the Gallipoli Peninsula is a national historical 'Peace Park', dedicated to the memory of those who died on both sides. Please respect this. A lot of the area is still farmland and private property. When walking please be aware of the crops and respect the privacy of the people who live here. If you do find a wartime relic, like a shell, grenade or bullet, please leave it alone. Photograph it by all means, but please do not touch it as these things are usually in a highly dangerous condition and can still cause death and injury. It is also strictly forbidden by the Turkish authorities to remove any artefact from the battlefield.

Under the terms of the Armistice with Turkey, the British Army re-entered the Peninsula at the end of 1918 and cleared the battlefields of the bodies still unburied. You will find that the Commonwealth War Graves Commission cemeteries at Gallipoli are different from those in Belgium or France. Because of the nature of the ground they have small tilted sandstone tablets for grave headstones. The Stone of Remembrance and white stone Cross of Sacrifice, a slightly different style than those found in Europe, can also be found in all the cemeteries. Row after row of headstones are interspersed with small plants and shrubs that adorn many of the beautifully kept cemeteries. Mature trees, including the odd Judas Tree (*Cercis siliquastrum*: the tree that Judas was believed to have hung himself from in his remorse at having betrayed Jesus), grow majestically, providing valuable shade on a hot sunny day.

Getting There
Arriving in Turkey by plane, there are two international airports that best serve you for getting to the Gallipoli region. These are Istanbul, where the Atatürk Havalimani Airport is situated about ten miles west

of the city, and Izmir, where the Adnan Menderes Airport is about five miles outside the city.

Istanbul (Constantinople) is a beautiful city, which is steeped in history and culture. If you have time to stay there, you can visit many historical sites dating back from Ottoman rule to the Romans and Ancient Greeks. General shopping and visiting the Grand Bazaar is also a must. Investing in a good city guide book is also recommended. Izmir (Smyrna) is not as picturesque, but its drive to Gallipoli is through some breathtaking landscape, and stops at the ancient city ruins of Pergamon (Bergama) and Troy (Truva) are worthwhile. Hiring a car is the best way to get to Gallipoli and, with costs roughly the same as in the UK, vehicles can be hired before you go. Make sure the car has air conditioning for the summer months; it is definitely worth paying the extra. Alternatively there is a regular bus/coach service that can take you to the region very cheaply, the journey takes about six hours, although once there you will need your own transport to get around. There are many specialist battlefield tour companies that run trips to Gallipoli. These can range widely in quality and price, some spend several days on the battlefield, others just a few hours.

The trip from either Istanbul or Izmir will take approximately five hours, totalling around 230 miles. Road conditions vary greatly, but the majority of the way is now on solid asphalt roads. Follow the signs to Çanakkale (Chanak) or Gelibolu (Turkish for Gallipoli), the town that gave its name to the Peninsula. Eceabat (had the Greek name of

Tents of 3 Australian Infantry Brigade at Mena Camp, Egypt.

Maidos in 1915) is the major town on the Peninsula that also acts as a central hub for a tour of Gallipoli, with Helles and Anzac/Suvla close by. The nearest, if not the only, petrol station on the southern part of the Peninsula is here, as is the car ferry (Feribot). There are two ferry sailings that go regularly from Çanakkale to the Peninsula. The larger goes to Eceabat, and the smaller one goes to Kilitbahir, both take vehicles and complete the crossing in about fifteen minutes.

Most of the hotels are not expensive and include breakfast and an evening meal. Eceabat and Çanakkale have a good selection of restaurants and cafes, eating out being very cheap. For the easiest access to Anzac it is best to stay in Eceabat. Çanakkale offers pretty much everything, although you will need to take the ferry every morning to cross the Narrows, and the drive will cut the time you could spend at Gallipoli by nearly an hour. Do not expect the luxuries that you may be accustomed to at other European hotels, rooms are often basic, although many do have air conditioning. This part of Turkey is now firmly on the tourist map, many of the visitors being Turks, who come to the region in ever increasing numbers.

Check out some of the following from the internet, or visit the Çanakkale Tourist Information Office near the Ferry terminal.

Çanakkale Hotels
Hotel Akol
Tel: + 90 (286) 217 9456
Website: www.hotelakol.com
Hotel Anzac
Tel: +90 (286) 217 7777
Website: www.anzachotel.com
Hotel Anafartalar
Tel: +90 (286) 217 4454
Website: www.hotelanafartalar.com
Hotel Truva
Tel: + 90 (286) 217 1024
Website: http://canakkale.turkeyhotelstours.com/buyuktruvahotel.asp

Eceabat Hotels
Hotel Kum
Tel: +90 (286) 814 1455
Website: www.hotelkum.com
TJ's Hotel Eceabat
Tel: +90 (286) 814 2458
Website: www.anzacgallipolitours.com

The Gallipoli Houses
Tel: + 90 (286) 814 2650
Website: www.gallipoli.com.tr

Seddülbahir Hotels
Pansiyon Helles Panorama
Tel: + 90 (286) 862 0035
Website: www.hellespanorama.com

Other Useful Addresses:
Çanakkale Tourist Information Office
Tel: + 90 (286) 217 1187
Commonwealth War Graves Commission (CWGC)
Tel: +44 (0) 1628 634 221
Website: www.cwgc.org
Imperial War Museum
Tel: +44 (0) 207 416 5000
Website: www.iwm.org.uk
Australian War Memorial
Tel: +61 (02) 6243 4211
Website: www.awm.gov.au
Gallipoli Association
Website: www.gallipoli-association.org

The Gallipoli Association's key objectives are to keep alive the memory of the Gallipoli Campaign of 1915/16, in order to ensure that the men who fought and died in the campaign are not forgotten, and to encourage and facilitate the study of the campaign so that lasting

benefit can be gained from its valuable lessons. An excellent journal called *The Gallipolian* is produced three times a year for members, and contains many articles and useful information. The Association also runs visits to the Gallipoli battlefield.

Stephen Chambers,
West Sussex, 2007

16

THOSE HEROES THAT SHED THEIR BLOOD
AND LOST THEIR LIVES...
YOU ARE NOW LYING IN THE SOIL OF A FRIENDLY COUNTRY.
THEREFORE REST IN PEACE.
THERE IS NO DIFFERENCE BETWEEN THE JOHNNIES
AND THE MEHMETS TO US, WHERE THEY LIE SIDE BY SIDE
HERE IN THIS COUNTRY OF OURS...
YOU, THE MOTHERS
WHO SENT THEIR SONS FROM FAR AWAY COUNTRIES,
WIPE AWAY YOUR TEARS.
YOUR SONS ARE NOW LYING IN OUR BOSOM
AND ARE IN PEACE
AFTER HAVING LOST THEIR LIVES IN THIS LAND THEY HAVE
BECOME OUR SONS AS WELL.

Kemal Atatürk, 1934

Mustafa Kemal Atatürk was born in 1881 in Salonika, Northern Greece, the son of an Ottoman bureaucrat. He graduated from the War Academy in 1905, and after experience during the Italo-Ottoman War 1911-12 and the Balkans War 1912-13, where he had attained the rank of lieutenant-colonel, he went on to become military attaché at Sofia from 1913-14. In 1915 Liman von Sanders appointed him commander of 19th Ottoman Division, and on 25 April 1915 he successfully defended the Anzac landing, quickly becoming a military hero. Following the end of the Great War and the subsequent Turkish War of Independence, Kemal went on to be the founder and first President of Turkey in 1923. He was accordingly awarded the distinction of Atatürk (Father of the Turks) by the Turkish parliament. He died, aged 57, in 1938, after fifteen years as president.

Mustafa Kemal, commander of 19th Ottoman Division.

17

The Gaba Tepe Plan

I have absolute faith in you, and believe few, if any finer, Brigades have been put to the test.

The task allotted to Lieutenant General Sir William Birdwood's Australian and New Zealand Army Corps (ANZAC) was to sever the Turkish north and south communications by effecting a landing north of Gaba Tepe. Once a bridgehead at 'Z' Beach was secured, the Anzacs would then advance towards Maidos, thereby cutting the Peninsula in two. Maidos was a central communication point that had a small harbour and a road that led down to the southern tip of the Peninsula. A threat to this town would prevent enemy reserves going south to Cape Helles where the main British landing would be, and also cut off retreating Turks from this area.

The Gaba Tepe (Kabatepe, meaning Coarse Hill) promontory was believed to be heavily defended, so the intended landing was to be placed just north of it, where resistance was understood to be lighter. Intelligence at the time reported only a few unconnected trenches and a series of gun emplacements, many appearing vacated. With a company in reserve near Gaba Tepe, the Turkish 2nd Battalion, 27 Regiment had deployed its remaining three companies to defend just over five miles of coastline, from the point where Aghyl Dere meets the sea just north of Ari Burnu to Semerly Tepe, just south of Gaba Tepe. The main concern to British command was the large deposition of troops that were known to be in the area, which was estimated to comprise two divisions, approximately 20,000 troops. These two

Lieutenant General Sir William Birdwood, GOC Australian and New Zealand Army Corps (ANZAC).

18

divisions were part of General Essad Pasha III Corps, consisting of the 19th Ottoman Division, based near Boghali and which formed General Otto Liman Von Sanders' Fifth Ottoman Army general reserve, and five battalions of the 9th Ottoman Division that were camped on the Kilid Bahr Plateau, south-west of Maidos (see Appendix I).

The landings were by no means viewed as straightforward. The Official History states that a serious difficulty connected with an opposed landing on the coast of a little-known country is the impossibility of effecting any adequate reconnaissance of the ground over which the first battle must be fought. Contrary to the belief that it was a 'little-known country', adequate reconnaissance was carried out. Intelligence gathered was a mixture of sea observation, aerial reconnaissance and a selection of reasonably accurate maps of the region, some of which were provided by

General Liman Von Sanders, GOC 5th Ottoman Army.

individuals who toured the area before the war. Enemy dispositions and defences were fairly accurately known, but this was not going to be the main obstacle. Once ashore, the Anzacs would be faced with the broken and precipitous hills of the Sari Bair (Yellow Ridge) range that extend north-east from the sea, about three-quarters of a mile north of Gaba Tepe. It consists of three long and tortuous ridges, which contain numerous gullies and depressions. The head of this range was crowned by three rounded hills of near identical height, Chunuk Bair, Hill Q and Koja Chemen Tepe (971 feet), which commanded views of the surrounding area, including the Narrows at Chanak. Under the shadow of Chunuk Bair are two smaller hills, Big 700 (690 feet) and Baby 700 (591 feet). From these hills three long, scrub covered ridges extend down to the sea. For the landing these objectives were referred to as the 'First', 'Second' and 'Third' ridges. These obstacles had to be taken before the army could cross the plain of Maidos, a wide depression that extends from Gaba Tepe to Kelia Liman, and reach the Narrows beyond, a distance of approximately twelve kilometres.

19

The place chosen for the landing was 1600 yards of sandy beach about a mile north of Gaba Tepe and immediately south of what became Anzac Cove. The landing was officially called 'Z' Beach, a follow on from the code names of S, V, W, X and Y Beaches, where the British were to land further south at Cape Helles. There were also to be two diversionary attacks, one by the Royal Naval Division at the Gulf of Saros to the north and the other by the French at Kum Kale on the Asiatic side of the Dardanelles to the south.

The proposed plan for the Anzac landing was fairly straight-forward, on paper anyway. A covering force consisting of one brigade (3 Australian Infantry Brigade) of the 1st Australian Division would land its 4000 men to secure a bridgehead, thus allowing the follow-up of two divisions. To do this they would push forward as quickly as possible to set up covering positions on Third Ridge. With the advance being on a broad front, if there was a hold-up in any part of the line, the flanking troops would help out the portion pinned down by threatening the enemy's flanks and rear. The left would position themselves on Big 700 (Battleship Hill) and Chunuk Bair whilst the right were to clear Gaba Tepe, destroying any guns they found. The reported guns on Second Ridge by 400 Plateau were also to be destroyed as quickly as possible, before the force would move to occupy Scrubby Knoll up on Third Ridge. The covering force's left flank was to be secured by the immediate landing of 2 Australian Infantry Brigade, which would arrive moments after the initial wave. Their objective was to extend the line northwards to the summit of Hill 971, about two kilometres distant, and out along North Beach to Fisherman's Hut. Next to land would be 1 Australian Infantry Brigade, which was to be held in reserve near the beach. If the landing was successful at this stage this reserve brigade, together with 4 Australian Infantry Brigade and the New Zealand Infantry Brigade from the New Zealand and Australian Division, would leapfrog through the newly captured positions, and from the south capture Mal Tepe, a rise of about ten kilometres from the landing. Here the Anzacs would threaten the northern flank of the Kilid Bahr Plateau, engage the Turkish reserves in the area and cut off those retreating from Helles. They would then wait for the main British advance to join them.

The original plan was for the landing of the first tow of wooden rowing boats to correspond with the setting of the moon. Birdwood, the General Officer Commanding ANZAC, was convinced that the best chance of success lay in a surprise night landing, so needed the covering force in its first positions by daybreak. A problem arose when

TURKISH DISPOSITIONS
BEFORE THE
LANDINGS

BULGARIA

T H R A C E

Keshan

Enos

CAVALRY BRIGADE.
Ibrija

5.

Sharkeui

GULF OF SAROS

Sakla Bay

SEA OF MARMARA

Bulair

Yeni Keui

7.

Ejelmer

GALLIPOLI

2 Bns GENDARMERIE

Suvla B.

DARDANELLES

19

Boghelo

Gaba Tepe

Maidos

Nagara Pt.

Kilid Bahr

Chanak

9

Krithia

C.Helles

Sedd el Bahr

Kum Kale

Yeni Shehr

RABBIT I.
MAVRO I.

3

Hissarlik
RUINS OF TROY

Besika Bay

II.

TENEDOS

Erene

CHANAK
GENDARME Bn

ÆGEAN SEA

NOTE.

Fifth Army H.Q.

Divisions . . . . 5. O 19.

Bulair Lines . . . . ⌐_⌐_⌐_

SCALE OF MILES.

5   0   5   10   15   20

21

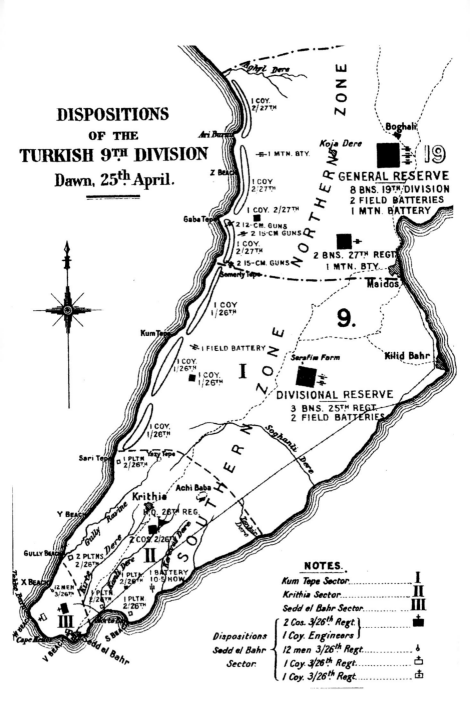

DISPOSITIONS
OF THE
TURKISH 9TH DIVISION
Dawn, 25th April.

Aghyl Dere

1 COY. 2/27TH

Ari Burnu

Koja Dere

NORTHERN ZONE

Boghali

19

GENERAL RESERVE
8 BNS. 19TH DIVISION
2 FIELD BATTERIES
1 MTN. BATTERY

1 MTN. BTY.

Z BEACH

1 COY. 2/27TH

1 COY. 2/27TH

Gaba Tepe

2 12-CM. GUNS
2 15-CM GUNS

1 COY. 2/27TH

2 15-CM. GUNS

Semerly Tepe

2 BNS. 27TH REGT.
1 MTN. BTY.

Maidos

9.

Kilid Bahr

1 COY. 1/26TH

Kum Tepe

1 FIELD BATTERY

Serafim Farm

DIVISIONAL RESERVE
3 BNS. 25TH REGT.
2 FIELD BATTERIES

1 COY. 1/26TH

1 COY. 1/26TH

I

1 COY. 1/26TH

Soghanli Dere

Sari Tepe

1 PLTN. 2/26TH

Yazy Tepe

Achi Baba

Krithia

H.Q. 26TH. REG.

SOUTHERN ZONE

Y BEACH

Gully Ravine

2 COS. 2/26TH

II

1 PLTN. 2/26TH

1 BATTERY 10·5 HOW.

GULLY BEACH

2 PLTNS. 2/26TH

1 PLTN. 2/26TH

X BEACH

12 MEN 3/26TH

III

1 PLTN. 2/26TH

Cape Helles

V BEACH

Sedd el Bahr

S BEACH

NOTES.

Kum Tepe Sector	I
Krithia Sector	II
Sedd el Bahr Sector	III

Dispositions
Sedd el Bahr
Sector
{
2 Cos. 3/26th Regt. 1 Coy. Engineers	∎
12 men 3/26th Regt.	♂
1 Coy. 3/26th Regt.	⚑
1 Coy. 3/26th Regt.	⚑

22

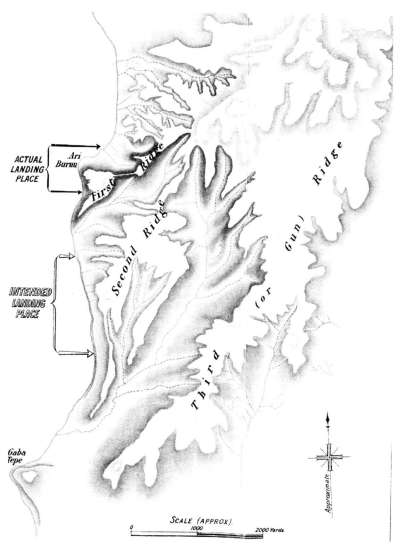

the landing had to be postponed from 23 April (St George's Day) due to bad weather. This had the effect of reducing the time from moonset to dawn by almost two hours, an important factor as the selected beach faced due west, which meant the moon was not due to set until 2.57 am on 25 April, giving the invasion force only one hour of complete darkness. Because of this, any ships approaching within five miles of the coastline could be seen by the enemy, and the first tows would be hitting the beach about 4.30 am, which would now be half an hour after the first light of dawn, thus losing any sense of surprise.

The covering force, commanded by Colonel Ewen Sinclair-

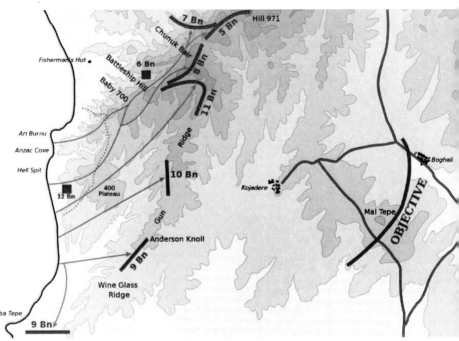

MacLagan, would be landed in three waves. The first wave, consisting of 1500 men, were to start two miles from the shore in three Formidable-class battleships; HMS *Queen*, HMS *Prince of Wales* and HMS *London*, to be distributed between twelve tows, each made up of a steam picket boat, a cutter (30 men), a lifeboat (28 men) and either a launch (98 men) or a pinnace (60 men).

The second and third waves, each of 1250 men, would land from seven destroyers immediately afterwards (HMS *Ribble*, HMS *Usk*, HMS *Chelmer*, HMS *Scourge*, HMS *Foxhound*, HMS *Colne* and HMS *Beagle*). The destroyers would wait near the island of Imbros and join the battleships, about two kilometres from the mainland, at 4.15 am. The destroyers would then sail to within 100 yards of the shore, each towing a number of lifeboats borrowed from various transport vessels. By this means, 2750 men would be ashore within a few minutes of each other. The returning tows would then be used to land the remaining 1250 troops

Colonel Ewen Sinclair-MacLagan, commander of 3 Australian Infantry Brigade.

of the third wave.

The remainder of the main body of 1st Australian Division would arrive in eight transports and were to approach the shore at 5.00 am. The battleship's twelve tows would meet the first four transports. The other four transports were to wait until the seven destroyers had disembarked the remainder of the covering force and then to take on the new troops so that they could be taken in closer to the shore. It was calculated that the whole 1st Australian Division would be ashore by 9.00 am. The remainder of the Corps, including vehicles, animals and supplies, would be landed as quickly as possible after that.

In a letter dated 21 April 1915, Sinclair-MacLagan wrote an inspirational address to his Brigade:

> I had hoped to have been able to see the battalions of my brigade personally and put these matters before you. Circumstances have prevented this, so I am asking your commanding officers to read you this letter. It is necessary that you should understand that we are about to carry out a most difficult operation, viz. 'Landing on an enemy coast in the face of opposition'. Such an operation requires complete harmony of working between the navy and the army and unhesitating compliance with all orders and instructions.
>
> You have all been selected by the divisional commander as the covering force, a high honour, which we must do our best to justify. We must be successful at any cost. Whatever footing we get on land must be held onto and improved by pushing on to our objective, the covering position which we must get to as rapidly as possible, and once obtained must be held at all costs and even to the last man. In an operation of this kind there is no going back. We shall be reinforced as the Navy can land troops. And meantime 'Forward' is the word, until on our position, when 'Hang on' is what we have to do, until sufficient troops and guns are landed to enable us to push on. We must be careful and not give the enemy a chance of any kind; no smoking or lights or noise from midnight onwards till after daylight. Take every chance of reorganising (under cover if possible).
>
> Attacks must be rapid, as ground will allow. You will have to drop your packs; but carry tools forward as far as you can, it may mean saving lives later in the day. Until broad daylight the bayonet is your weapon, and when you charge, do so in as good a line as possible; one or two good pieces of bayonet work now may stand us all in good stead later on. Every man must keep his

The transports would carry the remainder of the 1st Division towards the shore.

The band of 8/AIF aboard HMS *Agamemnon*, a week before the landing.

Sunday 18 April 1915 – The 8/AIF band entertains crew and troops aboard HMS *Agamemnon*.

eyes skinned and help his officers and non-commissioned officers to the utmost by reporting quickly things seen. Look out for your flanks. After taking a charger out shut the cartridge pocket. Once ashore don't be caught without a charger in the magazine. Look after each cartridge as if it was a ten-pound note. Good fire orders, directions, control and discipline will make the enemy respect your powers, and give us all an easier task in the long run. Wild firing only encourages the enemy.

Keep your food and water very carefully; we don't know when we shall get any more. Don't show yourselves over the skyline

27

and give your position away, if you can avoid it. We must expect to be shelled when in our positions, but remember that is part of this game of war, and we must "stick it", no matter what the fire. One thing I want you to remember all through this campaigning work is this, and it is most important: you may get orders to do something which appears in your position to be the wrong thing to do, and perhaps a mad enterprise. Do not cavil at it, but carry it out wholeheartedly and with absolute faith in your leaders, because we are after only a very small piece on the board. Some pieces have often to be sacrificed to win the game, and after all it is to win the game that we are here. You have a very good reputation you have built up for yourselves, and now you have a chance of making history for Australia and a name for the Brigade that will live in history. I have absolute faith in you, and believe few, if any, finer Brigades have been put to the test.
E G SINCLAIR-MACLAGAN
Colonel Commanding 3rd Infantry Brigade
21/4/15.

Indian Mountain Battery.

Chapter One

The Landing – 25th April 1915

... the damned fools have landed us a mile too far to the north

To be in close contact with Rear-Admiral Cecil Thursby (commander of the 2nd Naval Squadron), General Birdwood and his Headquarters moved from the transport *Minnewaska* to HMS *Queen* (flagship) on 23 April, whilst the 1st Australian Divisional Headquarters went aboard HMS *Prince of Wales*. During 24 April the 1500 men of the first wave boarded the battleships; 500 (two companies) of 9th Battalion, Australian Imperial Force (9/AIF) were on HMS *Queen*, 500 of 10th Battalion, Australian Imperial Force (10/AIF) were on HMS *Prince of Wales* and 500 of 11th Battalion, Australian Imperial Force (11/AIF) were on HMS *London*. A detachment of the 1/Field Company Australian Engineers was also included.

Leaving Mudros Harbour, on the Greek island of Lemnos, aboard HMS *London*, Private Joseph 'Fred' Fox, 11/AIF, a married 35-year-old commercial traveller from Perth, Western Australia, wrote of his experiences:

> There was tremendous enthusiasm, and about 3 p.m. the flagship took up her position, and away we went, amid a storm of cheering from both the French and English transports and warships. We were in wonderful spirits, and soon made friends with our naval comrades, who entertained us in the way that only Jack can do. We had a short service on the quarterdeck, in which the chaplain spoke most kindly to us, and then, left to our own devices, we had a look round the ship. Some of the time was spent in playing cards, and there was also a good impromptu concert. As night settled down, we made ourselves as comfortable as possible and composed ourselves to sleep. All lights were, of course, extinguished.[1]

During the afternoon of Saturday 24 April the three battleships, along with the 'covering' ships of HMS *Triumph*, HMS *Majestic* and HMS *Bacchante*, set course for the prearranged sea rendezvous five miles west of Gaba Tepe (Latitude 40 degrees, 13.0 minutes, North; Longitude 26 degrees, 10.0 minutes East). HMS *Triumph* was given the responsibility as marker ship for this point. Along with them was the second wave of about 2500 men, including the remaining companies of 9/AIF, 10/AIF and 11/AIF and the reserve battalion,

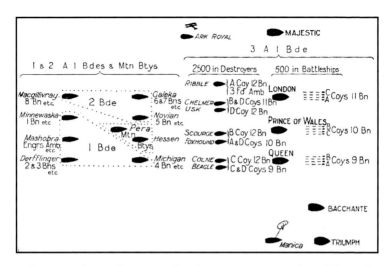

12/AIF. At the rendezvous point the men were transferred from the transports to the destroyers for their journey to shore.

Thursby's orders of 21 April, for HMS *Triumph*, stated:

> *It is absolutely essential for the success of the expedition that your ship should be accurately in this position. After anchoring you are to verify it by every possible means in your power. You should then also note the directions and strength of the current, and communicate both this and your position to me.*

The troops on the battleships were roused at 1.00 am on Sunday

HMS *London*, a Formidable-class battleship, that had two companies of 11/AIF aboard.

HMS *Queen*, with two companies of 9/AIF aboard.

morning and given a hot meal and drink while the tows were being got ready under the moonlit night. When ready, the troops began to be loaded via rope ladders on either side of the battleships, where they descended into their designated tows below. The weather was good, and apart from a shallow mist, the sky was clear and the sea was calm. Private Herbert Pare, Royal Marine Light Infantry (RMLI), aboard flagship HMS *Queen*, wrote:

> The moon is really too bright for landing at present, but it will have probably gone down before we are ready. About 1.30 a.m. we could see a single light straight ahead. (We are now steaming direct into the shore and can just make out the faint outline of the hills in the distance. The light is being shown on the Triumph, which is marking the landing place.) About 2 a.m. we stopped engines and began to get the boats out; this was done very creditably and hardly any noise was heard. Strict silence was the order of the day.[2]

Sunrise was due at 5.15 am, but the first streaks of dawn were at 4.05 am, which gave approximately an hour of complete darkness from the time the moon set.

> During the hour of inky darkness that preceded the dawn the faint night breeze died suddenly, and the surface of the Aegean

31

HMS *Prince Of Wales*, with two companies of 10/AIF aboard .

grew smooth and still as glass. In face of the coming drama, the
very elements appeared to hold their breath.[3]

Within half an hour the men were ready for mustering into companies.
This operation was carried out with great efficiency; no one spoke, and
even orders were given in whispers. The only sounds were the shuffling
of boots, the odd cough and the sound of the men climbing into the
tows.

Aboard HMS *Prince of Wales* was Private Alfred Richard Perry,
10/AIF, a married 32 year old miner from Broken Hill, New South
Wales:

*"Come on, lads, have a good hot supper – there's business
doing." So spoke No.10 Platoon Sergeant of the 10th Australian
Battalion to his men, lying about in all sorts of odd corners
aboard the battleship* Prince of Wales, *in the first hour of the
morning of April 25th, 1915. The ship, or her company, had
provided a hot stew of bully beef, and the lads set to and took
what was provided, alas, to many, their last real meal together.
They laugh and joke as though picnicking. Then a voice: "Fall
in!" comes ringing down the ladder way from the deck above.
The boys swing on their heavy equipment, grasp their rifles,*

32

silently make their way on deck and stand in grim, black masses.
All lights are out, and only harsh, low commands break the
silence. "This way No.9 - No.10 – C Company." Almost blindly
we grope our way to the ladder leading to the huge barge below,
which is already half full of silent, grim men, who seem to realize
that at last, after eight months of hard, solid training in
Australia, Egypt and Lemnos Island, they are now to be called
upon to carry out the object of it all.[4]

It took about forty minutes to load the boats with their heavily laden
cargo. Each soldier carried 200 rounds of .303-inch ammunition, three
days' rations of bully beef and biscuits, a filled water bottle, three
empty sandbags, a SMLE rifle and web equipment in full marching
order, all totalling around seventy pounds. Orders were given to
remove the pack, which contained the greatcoat, spare ammunition and
rations, immediately upon landing and go for the enemy with the
bayonet. No shooting was permitted until daylight. As ordered, general
service shovels and picks were to be carried as far forward as possible,
as these would be needed later to dig-in and secure the captured
positions (see Appendix II). Private Herbert Pare continued:

The soldiers were mustered very quietly on the upper deck
and then into the boats. The Triumph, *who had no soldiers on*
board, sent her boats to us. Altogether the ships each had two
steamboats, one launch, one pinnace, and two cutters, except us
who had double that number, having the Triumph's *boats as well*
as our own. When all troops were on board the boats a signal
was made from all ships by wireless (no lights were to be shown)
that they were ready to proceed. We all at once got under way in
line abreast with the boats in between each ship and steamed in
towards the shore. About two miles off the beach all ships were
stopped and the boats ordered to go full ahead and land the men.
They shot forwards at once and vanished in the darkness. The
moon had already dipped and the night was quite dark, making
it an ideal night for operations.

By 2.35 am all the tows were ready. Twenty minutes later the moon
sank behind Imbros which was the signal for the three battleships,
followed by their twelve tows, to approach the peninsula. Following
them were the newly arrived destroyers with the remainder of the
covering force.

Private Alfred Perry, 10/AIF, described his journey from HMS
Prince of Wales to the shore:

"Full up, sir," whispers the midshipman in the barge. "Cast

The destroyer HMS *Beagle*, embarking troops for their journey ashore.

off and drift astern," says the ship's officer in charge of the embarkation. Slowly we drift astern, until the boat stops with a jerk, and twang goes the hawser that couples the boats and barges together. Silently the boats are filled with men, and silently drop astern of the big ship, until, all being filled, the order is given to the small steamboats: "Full steam ahead." Away we go, racing and bounding, dipping and rolling, now in a straight line, now in a half-circle, on through the night.

The moon has just about sunk below the horizon. Looking back, we can see the battleships coming on slowly in our rear, ready to cover our attack. All at once our pinnace gives a great start forward, and away we go for land just discernible one hundred yards away on our left.

Private Fred Fox, 11/AIF described his journey from HMS *London*:

It was all very weird in the absolute silence, with a very, very pale moon shining. I had no idea how far we were from the shore, but we had steamed under the lee of the battleship for some time, when orders came from the captain to "carry on" on our own. Now was the critical time. I shall never forget that sight. There were three or four lines of us, with a space of perhaps 100 yards between, going stealthily and slowly towards – what?

About the same time, just before the moon had set, Lieutenant Faik, who was a company commander in 2 Battalion, 27 Regiment (9th Ottoman Division), had been looking out to sea from his position on Ari Burnu. Through his binoculars he saw a large number of ships. Two other duty patrols also reported to him the same sighting. It was not clear if they were stationary or moving, but he sent a report of the sighting to his battalion commander, Major Ismet Bey, who re-assured him that from information to hand, if there was to be a landing, it would be at Gaba Tepe.

I went to a new observation point and kept watching. This time I saw them as a great mass which, I decided, seemed to be moving straight towards us. In the customary manner, I went to the phone to inform divisional headquarters. That was about 2.30 a.m. I got through to the second in command, Lieutenant Nuri Efendi, and told him of it. He replied, "Hold the line. I will inform the Chief of Staff." He came back a little later and said, "How many of these ships are warships and how many transports?" I replied, "It is impossible to distinguish them in the dark but the quantity of ships is very large." With that the conversation closed. A little while later the moon sank below the

Men from Captain Milne's C Company, 9/AIF, aboard HMS *Beagle*.

horizon and the ships became invisible in the dark. The reserve platoon was alerted and ordered to stand by. I watched and waited.[5]

As the Australian boats neared the shore Lieutenant Ivor Margetts[6], a Hobart school teacher in 12/AIF, was later to recall:

I am quite sure few of us realised that at last we were actually bound for our baptism of fire, for it seemed as though we were just out on one of our night manoeuvres in Mudros harbour.

The suspense was daunting as, at any moment, the men expected a hail of gunfire to be coming towards them from the shore, instead of which there was just silence. The tense excitement in the boats carried them to shore where the Turks lay, waiting.

Colonel Sinclair-MacLagan planned for the Queenslanders (9/AIF) to land on the right, the South Australians (10/AIF) in the centre and the Western Australians (11/AIF) on the left. The defences at Gaba Tepe were to be cleared by A and B Companies of 9/AIF, whilst C and D Companies were to take up positions about a mile east of their landing place at Anderson Knoll on Third Ridge, or Gun Ridge as it later became known. On their left, 10/AIF, after capturing the guns on 400 Plateau, were also to proceed to Third Ridge and occupy Scrubby

Knoll. Chunuk Bair and the northern part of the line, including Baby 700 and Big 700 were to be seized by 11/AIF. The remaining battalion (12/AIF) of the covering force, mainly Tasmanians with a few men from South and West Australia, were to form the reserve. Also allotted were an Indian mountain artillery brigade, who were to land later on in the morning and support the covering force.

The men were motionless and silent, cramped together in the tows as they neared the shore. The night was cold and, with greatcoats stored in the packs, the men shivered as the boats chugged their way through

Men from 12/AIF aboard HMS *Beagle*.

the darkness. The little boats varied in length from just nine paces for the lifeboats to fourteen for the launches and what little space was left by the men was filled by two boxes of ammunition, twelve picks, eighteen shovels, a hundred sandbags, three jars of water and rations.

Keeping a lateral distance of 150 yards between them, the twelve steam pinnaces continued their journey at about six knots, which was estimated to take them about forty-five minutes. Lieutenant John Waterlow[7] RN, commanded No.1 Tow on the right (southern end), and was responsible for guiding the line in on the correct bearing. Commander Charles Dix RN, the senior naval officer in charge, was on the port side (northernmost tow) in No.12 and in charge of the flotilla. The steamboats had problems almost immediately keeping the ordered distance between themselves, as in the darkness it proved difficult for the boats to see each other. This in effect caused them to bunch closer together and, with erratic steering, some boats crossed the lines of others, an early contributor to the mixing of the battalions. The boat that Private Fred Fox, 11/AIF, was in started zigzagging despite several calls from another boat commander to,

> *"Be more careful". He appeared to take no notice; and his superior roared: "For heaven's sake, steer straight, or you will spoil the whole show!"*

About 4.00 am the silhouette of the shore could be made out, which faintly showed the Ari Burnu headland. At this moment Waterlow realised that the tows were being taken too far to the north, so he made several efforts to correct the course, but was ignored (see Appendix III). As they were now quickly nearing their approach on Ari Burnu, Waterlow had no other option other than to stay with the other boats. Breaking the silence, Dix was reported as saying: 'Tell the Colonel the damned fools have landed us a mile too far to the north.'[8] If this was not bad enough, the inky darkness was suddenly illuminated by a fountain of sparks that shot up three feet into the air from a funnel on one of the boats. This lasted for about thirty seconds and could be seen from all around. Had the element of surprise been lost? With darkness quickly fading, at 4.15 am the tows, each with a midshipman and five seamen to row the boats, were set adrift to row the last fifty yards to the shore. As the first boats approached Ari Burnu a bright signalling light was seen upon a knoll to the south (later named Queensland Point). The splash of oars continued until the silence was broken a few yards from the shore, when the first shots rang out. The Anzacs' baptism of fire had begun.

Lieutenant Faik, 2/27 Battalion, who needed to delay the landing as

Waiting to 'push off'. Men from C Company, 12/AIF leaving HMS *Beagle*.

long as possible in order for reserves to arrive, continued:

> *In a little while, the sound of gunfire broke out. I saw a machine gun firing from a small boat in front of Ariburnu. Some of the shots were passing over us. I immediately ordered the platoon to occupy the trenches on the high ridge which dominated Ariburnu and sent only two sections under Sergeant Ahmed to the trenches on the central ridge overlooking the*

Heavily laden men from 12/AIF having just 'pushed off'.

> *beach. At the same time, I wrote a report to the battalion*
> *commander stating that the enemy was about to begin landing*
> *and I was going to a position on the far side with a reserve*
> *platoon.*

Whilst doing night inspections north of Gaba Tepe, the regimental commanding officer, Lieutenant Colonel Şefik Aker Bey, was also aware that something might be astir. When he had returned to his headquarters he began to hear gunfire in the distance, which he understood might be from a potential landing. In this area, 2/27 Battalion were strung out about six kilometres along the coast, defending possible landing places from north of Kum Tepe to Fisherman's Hut. The battalion's four companies were dispersed with 6 Company holding the southern area at Gaba Tepe, 7 Company holding Brighton Beach, 8 Company were north of Ari Burnu, whilst 5 Company was held in reserve behind Gaba Tepe.

A 15-year-old Royal Navy Midshipman, Eric Bush, who was in charge of the tow from HMS *Bacchante*, describes in his book called *Gallipoli* the courage of a fellow midshipman:

> *Midshipman Eric Longley-Cook was in charge of the* Prince
> of Wales' *picket boat, No.5 tow ... 'Go fo'ard and get both*

bowmen up out of the fore peak and tell them to feel for the bottom with their boathooks,' he told his coxswain, Leading Seaman Albert Balsom, when the boats were nearing the shore. Balsom had served with Captain Scott in the Antarctic and was a fabulously strong, brave man. 'Why only one?' Longley-Cook asked a minute or two later. 'I couldn't get the other able seaman up, Sir. He's too frightened to move,' Balsom replied; and while they were speaking a rifle bullet entered the compartment and struck the A.B. in the spine, killing him instantly. A few minutes later, an Australian officer in one of the boats started to issue some orders, whereupon he was interrupted by Longley-Cook who, in a clear authoritative voice with a polished English accent (so I was told by an Australian who was there), said to the officer: 'I beg your pardon, Sir, I am in charge of this tow.' The officer subsided into silence immediately and the troops in his boat were heard to mutter, 'Good on yer, kid!'

Bush was the youngest man to be awarded the Distinguished Service Cross (DSC) for 'courage and endurance under shellfire' at Gallipoli and, going on to become a captain in the Royal Navy, he was awarded the Distinguished Service Order (DSO) with two bars in World War Two.

That last fifty yards to the beach was a real test for the men, who were in the hands of the Navy until they reached the shore. Private Albert Tiegs, 11/AIF, was to recount:

It seemed a terrible long way to the shore. About fifty yards from shore a bullet spat out, followed by a perfect fusillade of bullets, also several bursts of machine-gun fire. No one was hit in our boat. As the boat grounded I jumped over the side up to my waist in water and flopped down into cover about 20 yards from shore.[9]

Tiegs survived Gallipoli, was later commissioned in 28/AIF, but was killed in France in 1917. He is buried in Bailleul Road East Cemetery, St Laurent-Blangy near Arras.

The first boats to hit the beach, shortly before 4.30 am, were those of 9/AIF, who just got ashore before the firing had begun. Three tows on the left that carried 11/AIF landed 200 yards north of Ari Burnu and were in good order. The remaining nine tows arrived, mixed up and clustered together, around the head of Ari Burnu. When the first shots rang out there was an immediate rush for the remaining boats to get to the shore anywhere, regardless of position. Some boats grounded on the seabed a little way off the beach, immersing the exiting soldiers up

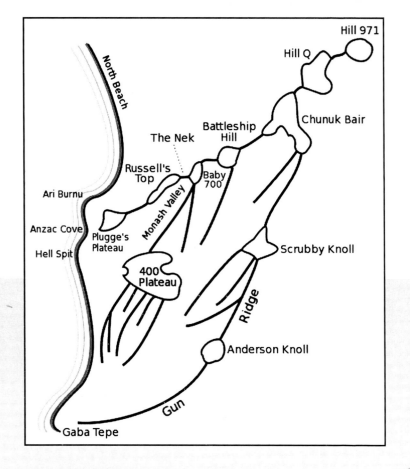

to their waists in water. In some places the stones on the bottom were round and slimy, causing men to slip and fall into the water. A few unlucky ones unknowingly plunged themselves into deep water and, held down by the weight of their equipment, were drowned. The boats were quickly emptied and the first echelon was safely ashore.

Private Perry, 10/AIF, describes in a Boy's Own fashion his experience getting ashore:

Then-crack-crack! ping-ping! zip-zip! Trenches full of rifles upon the shore and surrounding hills open on us, and machine guns, hidden in gullies or redoubts, increase the murderous hail. Oars are splintered, boats are perforated. A sharp moan, a low

... the damned fools have landed us a mile too far to the north. View of the Anzac Commemorative site and Sphinx from the sea. (Eric Goossens)

gurgling cry, tells of a comrade hit. Boats ground in four or five feet of water, owing to the human weight contained in them. We scramble out, struggle to the shore and, rushing across the beach, take cover under a low sandbank.

"Here, take off my pack, and I'll take off yours." We help one another to lift the heavy, water-soaked packs off. "Hurry up, there," says our sergeant. "Fix bayonets." Click! and the bayonets are fixed. "Forward!" And away we scramble up the hills in our front. Up, up we go, stumbling in holes and ruts. With a ringing cheer we charge the steep hill, pulling ourselves up by roots and branches of trees; at times digging our bayonets into the ground and pushing ourselves up to a foothold, until, topping the hill, we found the enemy had made themselves very scarce. What had caused them to fly from a position from which they should have driven us back into the sea every time?

A few scattered Turks, showing in the distance we instantly fired on. Some fell to rise no more; others fell wounded and, crawling into the low bushes, sniped our lads as they went past. There were snipers in plenty, cunningly hidden in the hearts of low green shrubs. They accounted for a lot of our boys in the first few days, but gradually were rooted out. Over the hill we dashed and down into what is now called "Shrapnel Gully" and up the other hillside until, on reaching the top, we found that some of

A contemporary Ottoman Red Crescent postcard depicting the Anzac landing.

the lads of the 3rd Brigade had commenced to dig in. We skirted round to the plateau at the head of the gully, and took up our line of defence.

As soon as it was light enough to see, the guns on Gaba Tepe, on our right, and two batteries away on our left opened up a murderous hail of shrapnel on our landing parties. The battleships and cruisers were continually covering the landing of troops, broadsides going into the batteries situated in tunnels in the distant hill-side. All this while the seamen from the different ships were gallantly rowing and managing the boats carrying the landing parties. Not one man that was left of the original brigade will hear a word against our gallant seamen. England may well be proud of them, and all true Australians are proud to call them comrades.

With the exception of a few trenches, the Turks had not fortified the Ari Burnu area, as it was thought unsuitable for a landing. The Australians were also expecting the low sandbanks of Gaba Tepe: not the sheer and scrub covered cliff faces and ravines that they were now confronted with. Both the Turks and Australians were taken by surprise. The Official History of the campaign explains that:

Even in the time of peace, the precipitous ridges and tortuous ravines which formed the first Australian and New Zealand battlefield are an arduous climb for an active and unarmed man, while the steep, scrub-covered gullies are so confusing that it is easy to lose one's way. To preserve the cohesion of an attack across such country, immediately after an opposed landing in the dark and without previous reconnaissance, would be an impossible task for the best-trained troops in the world.

Confronted by an unfamiliar landscape that offered the defenders all the advantages, and with Gaba Tepe out of sight, there was immediate confusion. Only a few units spent any time trying to reorganise, most set off intermixed in an effort to push inland as quickly as possible. It had been drilled into them the importance of pushing forward, so very quickly the keen and eager men, after dropping their packs, fixed bayonets and scrambled to the summit of the first ridge, later called Plugge's Plateau. The plateau was named after the British-born Lieutenant Colonel Arthur Plugge, commander of New Zealand's Auckland Battalion, who later established his headquarters there. The Turkish called this hill Hain Tepe, which translated means Cruel Hill. Towering 338 feet (a hundred metres) above the Ari Burnu knoll, it was precipitous in places and covered in coarse scrub and thorny holly-oak bushes, but caused no obstacle to the Australians, who scaled its heights in less than twenty minutes. Upon reaching the top they routed any remaining Turkish resistance. One of the first to be killed was 40-year-old Captain W. R. 'Dick' Annear, C Company, 11/AIF, who had climbed up from the beach with the first wave. Annear was lying on the parapet of an unoccupied enemy trench when Turkish fire from the direction of MacLagan's Ridge found its mark, hitting him in the head and killing him instantly. Annear, from Subiaco, Perth, Western Australia, is recorded as being the first Anzac officer to be killed at Gallipoli.

The handful of surviving Turks that had survived the bitter hand-to-hand fighting on Plugge's Plateau retired down a zigzag path on its southern side into the valley below. Others were seen running down MacLagan's Ridge and either took shelter in the thick scrub or were seeking an escape route up onto Second Ridge beyond. Before a brief halt could be called to reorganise, some Australians excitedly ran on in pursuit. The actions of these men were commendable, but those who pushed forward too quickly and too far became isolated from the main body of troops, and in forward positions were either mistaken for the enemy or overrun during the later Turkish counter-attacks.

Aspinall-Oglander in the Official History indicates that the Turks were not the only enemy:

> The delaying power of well-armed and well concealed marksmen, favoured by a perfect knowledge of the ground, is undoubtedly very great. Nevertheless there can be little doubt that the extreme difficulties of the country played an even greater part than the opposition of the enemy in frustrating the Australian plan.

From Plugge's summit the error of the landing was soon recognised; 400 Plateau, the first objective for the left flank, could be seen a thousand yards over to the right, not on the immediate left as expected. To the north the crest fell away to a steep drop-off where a narrow sharp ridge feature, thereafter known as the Razor Edge, ran below, preventing a direct advance across Russell's Top.[10] This barred the way onto Baby 700 and the objective of Hill 971 beyond. Projecting down from Russell's Top were a number of lesser known spurs; the most prominent was an eroded outcrop which was named the Sphinx. This had a striking resemblance to the ancient Egyptian Sphinx by which the Anzacs had camped in Egypt.

At about 5.00 am, half an hour after they had come ashore, two companies from 10/AIF were organised and sent down from Plugge's

A modern day view of Ari Burnu from the heights of Plugge's Plateau. The Turkish defenders fired down from this position into the Australians.

into Shrapnel Valley to climb the steep path up onto the objective of 400 Plateau. Most of 9/AIF were widely scattered, as many of them had earlier dashed after the retreating Turks. What remained went with Major Alfred Salisbury to 400 Plateau, whilst those from 11/AIF were reorganised by Major Edmund Drake-Brockman in Rest Gully. Others found their way into Rest Gully by climbing the precipitous Razor Edge, and were to join those already collecting there. Following as closely to the original plan as permissible, Drake-Brockman tried to organise what troops there were in the area, sending men of 9/AIF to the right (south), 10/AIF to the centre of the line (east) and men of the 11/AIF with him to the high ground to the left (north).

Observing the landing from the sea, Sir Ian Hamilton, who was aboard HMS *Queen Elizabeth*, wrote in his diary:

> The day was just breaking over the jagged hills; the sea was glassy smooth; the landing of the lads from the South was in full swing; the shrapnel was bursting over the water; the patter of musketry came creeping out to sea; we are in for it now; the machine guns muttered as though chattering teeth – up to our necks in it now. But would we be out of it? No; not one of us; not for five hundred years stuffed full of dullness and routine.

By 5.35 the rattle of small arms quieted down; we heard that about 4,000 fighting men had been landed; we could see boatloads making for the land; swarms trying to straighten themselves out along the shore; other groups digging and hacking down the brushwood. Even with our glasses they did not look much bigger than ants. Wave after wave of the little ants press up and disappear. We lose sight of them the moment they lie down.[11]

Also aboard HMS *Queen Elizabeth* was Captain Oppenheim, RMLI, who wrote:

The first party got ashore all right and it was apparently some time before the enemy discovered them. Musketry fire then became fairly brisk, also some howitzer fire at the troops' transports. The London *replied – somewhat inadequately – with 6-inch. About 6 a.m. the musketry fire had died down, and we received a signal from the shore that the landing was progressing favourably. We seem to have taken possession of a high ridge... Landing very successful in spite of making a mess of the actual spot...the landing will now be extended to the south so as to embrace the proper landing place.*[12]

At this time Plugge's had been secured and parties from 9/AIF and 10/AIF had captured the undefended 400 Plateau and begun to probe towards Third Ridge. Men of 11/AIF, soon to be joined by 12/AIF, had also begun to climb onto Russell's Top.

With a ringing cheer we charge the steep hill – a contemporary artist's impression of Australian soldiers storming the heights.

Out at sea the seven destroyers began to move at 4.00 am towards the shore; approaching within 500 metres, they released the remaining wave of the covering force. HMS *Ribble* was the furthest north with A Company 12/AIF and 3/Field Ambulance aboard and HMS *Beagle*, with C Company 9/AIF and a half company of 12/AIF, was the furthest south. In *Beagle's* position, just off Brighton Beach, which was within view of Gaba Tepe, the ship soon received the attention of Turkish rifle and machine-gun fire.

From the southern end of Anzac Cove, around Hell Spit, the remaining elements from the second wave were landed in good order. The remaining

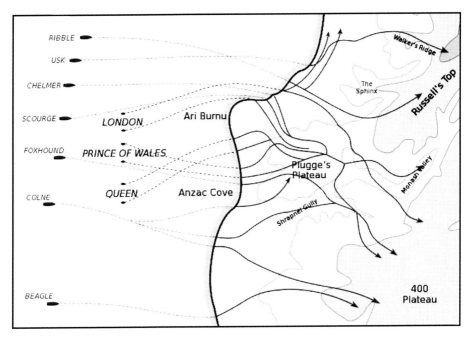

two companies of 9/AIF were under the commands of Captain I.
Jackson, landing from HMS *Colne* and Captain J. A. Milne from HMS
Beagle. Jackson's company beached just north of the entrance to
Shrapnel Valley and Milne's company landed about 500 yards further
south, on the northern end of Brighton Beach by McCay's Hill.[13] Both
parties penetrated inland, meeting on the top of McCay's Hill and
headed towards 400 Plateau via Brown's Dip. Even though these last
two companies of the Battalion were landed twenty minutes after the
first wave, because they were landed in good order further south, they
had an easier path than those who had to climb Plugge's. This resulted
in them making faster progress inland, which allowed them to get to
400 Plateau about the same time as the men from the earlier wave.
Both companies were instructed to head south towards the
fortifications of Gaba Tepe, where they had orders to silence the guns
and to capture a hump at the end of Third Ridge called Anderson
Knoll.[14] These objectives were never achieved; both officers were
wounded during the morning and their companies set up position on
the seaward ridge (Bolton's Ridge) thus affording initial protection to
the right flank.

400 Plateau was a wide, scrub covered, heart-shaped area of
relatively flat ground which had two lobes. The northern lobe became
known as Johnston's Jolly, after Lieutenant Colonel G.J. Johnston,
commander of 2 Australian Field Artillery Brigade. The southern lobe

was initially called Lonesome Pine after the song and also because a solitary stunted pine tree was growing there, but it was soon abbreviated to simply Lone Pine. Dividing both lobes was a gully that ran down into Legge Valley, called Owen's Gully. The Australian advance was so quick that they had soon overrun a Turkish mountain gun battery in The Cup, a hollow dip that ran off Owen's Gully. Small groups of men dashed down the inward ridge that became known as Pine Ridge and into Legge Valley and then towards Third Ridge, the final objective of the covering force. So far the landing was going relatively well, Turkish resistance had been minimal and Australian groups had captured both first and second ridges and the leading scouts were nearing their final objectives.

Further along the beach, north of Ari Burnu, the landing was a little less successful. The men of the first wave had gotten ashore but, due to heavy firing from the area of Fisherman's Hut and above, from both Walker's Ridge and Russell's Top, they found themselves pinned down on the beach. Men in the open boats had suffered many casualties, shot down before they had even reached the shore. Those who did reach the water's edge found little cover behind which to shelter from the murderous fire that was now pouring down on them. Amongst those killed in the boats was 3/Field Ambulance's first casualty, Private Donald Cadoux of C Section. Private Frank Gill, who was in the same boat, wrote: 'You have no doubt heard of poor old Don Cadoux's death. He, poor fellow, never even got out of the boat, he was shot clean through the heart.'[15] A small town in Western Australia was named after Donald Neville Cadoux who settled there in 1909 from Leicestershire, England. Cadoux, a stretcher-bearer in the same section as Jack Simpson, soon to become the legendary 'Man with the Donkey', was hit as his boat emptied near the shore, and presumably the boat with his body was then towed back to the transports where he later died aboard ship and was buried at sea. Cadoux is commemorated on the Lone Pine Memorial and also has a memorial plaque in King's Park, Perth. The men from C Section 3/Field Ambulance were the first medical unit ashore, and suffered heavily during the landing. As Jack Simpson jumped from the boat, the man in front was shot dead as well as the man following him. These were Privates Alfred Eccles and Frank Hudson.[16] Simpson made it to shelter: however several more men from the section were wounded. One of these men was Private Stephen Sheaf,[17] who was shot through the spine and died of his wounds nine days later. The survivors of this landing were not afforded the cover of Anzac Cove, although many were able to find some shelter in broken

Landing at Anzac. A still from the 1931 film *Tell England*.

ground a few yards from the beach. Intermixed and many without their leaders, they were in a state of confusion about what to do next.

The second echelon which landed only ten or twenty minutes later, found these men still pinned down under the precipitous cliffs by the Sphinx. Lieutenant Colonel Lancelot Clarke, commanding officer 12/AIF Battalion, took charge. He sent a platoon under Lieutenant Rupert Rafferty, 11/AIF, a former schoolmaster, to silence the machine-gun post at Fisherman's Hut, whilst he took the remaining men with him to the top of the ridge above. This was quite an ordeal as they ascended the steep crags of the northern end of Russell's Top near the Sphinx, an almost impossible task for a young soldier, let alone a 56-year-old colonel. The Turks continued to fire from the top, but were soon outflanked by the speed of the advance. Clarke and approximately sixty men reached the ridge of Russell's Top, cleared a Turkish trench near the Sphinx and started moving his men inland, following the direction of the retiring Turks towards Baby 700. Orders were given that any Turks encountered were to be despatched by the bayonet and,

51

as it was still quite dark, rifles were not to be loaded until daylight.

Between the Turks and Australians was a narrow open area or saddle that became known as The Nek, completely devoid of cover apart from some low scrub. Clarke was in the motion of writing a note to Sinclair-MacLagan when he was killed, the fatal shot coming from across the valley to the right, where Turks were sniping from amongst the scrub. Almost at the same time another shot rang out that killed his runner as he stood there waiting to take the note. Second-in-command, Major Charles Elliot, then went forward to where Clarke and the runner lay, and seconds later was also shot, the bullet wounding him in the shoulder and elbow. Elliot, who collapsed to the ground, shouted for the others to keep down and away from them. The fire soon died down as further parties under Captain Tulloch (11/AIF) and Captain Lalor (12/AIF) reached the ridge moments later, joining Clarke's men near The Nek.

Grave of Lieutenant Colonel Clarke, 12/AIF, killed by a sniper on Russell's Top.

From the beach Private Albert Tiegs, 11/AIF, one of Tulloch's men, described the scene:

> *Fire seemed to come from a ridge on our right and a trench on our left which ran right on to the beach, and the ridge on our left front. A perfect fusillade of bullets flew over us for about ten minutes, meantime our boys fixed bayonets as they landed and charged up the hill. I called for my mate and we ran forward and went up a deep gorge. The Turks retreated very quickly on our left flank, which was our position, and our boys went ahead so fast that we never caught them up. We attended several wounded, including the second in command[18] of 12th Battalion; the colonel of 12th was shot dead beside him.[19]*

Albert Tiegs landed with Captain Eric Tulloch, a Melbourne brewer, and the remainder of 11/AIF. They avoided the bottleneck on Plugge's, where most of the men were heading, by following the beach to the north and ascended onto Russell's Top via Walker's Ridge. The other party, led by Captain Peter Lalor, had reached Russell's Top by ascending the cliff face on the southern side of the Sphinx. When Tulloch reached the top, Clarke was already dead, so he took charge of Clarke's men, who were a mixed group from 11/AIF and 12/AIF. With no further Turkish resistance ahead he took about sixty men with him over Baby 700, leaving Lalor and his men to dig in at The Nek.

Colonel Sinclair-MacLagan had come ashore with the second wave of the covering force shortly before 5.00 am. He climbed the southern shoulder of Plugge's Plateau, thereafter becoming known as MacLagan's Ridge and, upon reaching the crest, found his brigade in almost total disarray, fragmented in small groups all over the area. Chaotic as it was, a landing on a hostile shore had been made, winning the element of surprise, and advanced parties had already penetrated almost a mile inland. The advantage was still with the Anzacs. The covering force were safely ashore and were heavily outnumbering the thinly spread men of the Turkish 2/27 Battalion. The Turks had to hold the Australians at all costs to allow time for their reserves to enter the battle. Arguably the most important time of the battle was now, and within a precious few hours it would be decided if the landing were to be a success or a failure.

Sinclair-MacLagan briefly established his Brigade HQ on Plugge's before moving it forward onto 400 Plateau. By 6.30 am scattered groups of Australians were in undisputed positions on Second Ridge, from the top of Monash Valley and down along the ridge, across the eastern slopes of 400 Plateau and Pine Ridge to the coast. The only resistance was sniping, which was not something Sinclair-MacLagan was too worried about. A few small unsupported parties had actually gone further and reached Third Ridge, the covering forces' final

View across Shrapnel Valley towards Queensland Point where Captain Jackson's company of 9/AIF crossed to reach 400 Plateau.

McCay's Hill

Hell Spit
(Queensland Point)

Shrapnel Valley
Cemetery

Island of
Imbros

MacLagan's
Ridge

HMS *Beagle*.

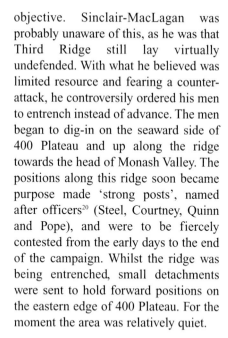

objective. Sinclair-MacLagan was probably unaware of this, as he was that Third Ridge still lay virtually undefended. With what he believed was limited resource and fearing a counter-attack, he controversily ordered his men to entrench instead of advance. The men began to dig-in on the seaward side of 400 Plateau and up along the ridge towards the head of Monash Valley. The positions along this ridge soon became purpose made 'strong posts', named after officers[20] (Steel, Courtney, Quinn and Pope), and were to be fiercely contested from the early days to the end of the campaign. Whilst the ridge was being entrenched, small detachments were sent to hold forward positions on the eastern edge of 400 Plateau. For the moment the area was relatively quiet.

Damage to the *Beagle*'s Maxim machine gun. ... *the Turks on Gaba Tepe at once sighted the* **Beagle,** *and opened upon her with every rifle and machine gun. The range was long but one machine gun had it accurately.*

54

On the left, along Russell's Top and The Nek, the situation was little better. Units were equally fragmented and the 'line' consisted of shallow foxholes which were manned by men who did not always know who or what was to the left, right or even in front or behind. The country was difficult territory. Pushing ahead, Captain Tulloch and his small party of men had reached the crest of Baby 700 and were advancing steadily across the lower landward slopes of Big 700 (soon to be called Battleship Hill) towards Chunuk Bair.

Reinforcements were needed to advance further, but few were coming forward. 12/AIF was supposed to be held as brigade reserve after the landing; however it had become hopelessly fragmented during disembarkation, which was not helped by the battalion's dispersal across all seven destroyers. Landing about 5.00 am on a wide front, under fire and with the confusion of being on the wrong beach, the scattered men quickly got caught up in the enthusiasm of the advance, leaving no reserve, apart from a company that Drake-Brockman had managed to keep back. The main body of the Division that comprised 1 Brigade and 2 Brigade had been delayed in their landing, which was originally intended to be at 5.30 am. This was caused by the late arrival of the steam pinnaces back from landing the initial waves. The last of these brigades did not get fully ashore until 1.00 pm.

As soon as the two leading battalions of 2 Brigade, 6/AIF and the remainder of 7/AIF that had not come ashore at Fisherman's Hut, had

A contemporary drawing depicting the landing on 25 April 1915.

Spectacular view from Plugge's Plateau of the Sphinx and the impassable Razor Edge.

landed, Sinclair-MacLagan ordered them to the right of the line instead of putting them, as per the original orders, to protect the left flank and to advance north. As soon as Colonel James McCay (2 Brigade commander) had landed, Sinclair-MacLagan convinced him that the original plan could not be carried out and that he must divert his entire Brigade to guard the right flank. He was fearful that this southern area was at immediate risk from a strong Turkish counter-attack from the direction of Gaba Tepe, and without his men the right would almost certainly break. McCay was recorded as saying 'it is a bit stiff to disobey orders first thing', but reluctantly accepted Sinclair-MacLagan's revised orders against the original plan. With this action Sinclair-MacLagan was not ignoring the importance of Baby 700 and the heights of the Sari Bair range, but understood this to be relatively safe at this time. He knew that Baby 700 was a natural junction of the second and third ridges and the gateway to Chunuk Bair and Hill 971. It also commanded views of Monash Gully, the only line of communication from the beach to Second Ridge.[21] However, with 2 Brigade now protecting the vulnerable right flank, this left him with no great strength to push on from the left and capture Hill 971. All that was available to him was Drake-Brockman's reserve company, which he duly sent to occupy the eastern slopes above Monash Gully. The northern flank would remain vulnerable to Turkish attack until the time that Sinclair-MacLagan could send adequate reserves there. His decisive move was made, and all that he could do now was to wait for 1 Brigade to land in adequate numbers in order to send them to the north.

Fisherman's Hut
The bullets zipped around us like bees

As the crackle of rifle fire came from the shoreline, which was the sound of 3 Brigade in action, it was now the turn of the men from 2 Brigade, in particular Lieutenant Colonel Harold 'Pompey' Elliott's 7/AIF, to land. Steaming closer to the shore, the *Galeka*, that carried 6/AIF and 7/AIF, reached its designated position punctually at 4.45 am. But there was no sign of the tows that were to take the battalions to the shore. The captain of the *Galeka*, Bernard Burt, continued a course to the shore, but still with no tows in sight.[22] By this stage the ship had started to attract shrapnel from Turkish artillery which put the ship and the men who were crowding her decks at risk. It was decided that there was no time to lose waiting for the tows to return, so the landing was commenced using the ship's rowing boats. Elliott was aware that his orders were to land to the left of 3 Brigade's covering force and to guard the flank in the area of Fisherman's Hut. He was slightly concerned, as there were no naval guides to show them the exact landing position, and no machine guns to protect the approach to the beach. Reluctantly he duly despatched three platoons of B Company 7/AIF, under the command of Major Alfred Jackson, into four of the ship's boats. As they neared the shore they could see the Red Cross flag from 3/Field Ambulance to the right and a low sandy knoll ahead, so they knew they were heading in the correct direction. Unknown to them they would be rowing directly towards the heavily defended position at the Fisherman's Hut, which had already been harassing 3 Brigade's landing further along the beach.

The platoon in defence of Fisherman's Hut, commanded by Second Lieutenant Ibrahim Hayreddin, had one machine gun, which withheld its fire until the four rowing boats were within 200 yards of the shore. In an interview with Bean, Captain Layh recalled:

> *As we drew near we could see that the water was being churned up by the bullets and that we were in for a hot time. The rowers pulled hard, and we entered the beaten zone at a good*

A view from Fisherman's Hut looking towards Russell's Top on the left, the flat crest of Plugge's Plateau to the right with Ari Burnu below.

Fisherman's Hut from the sea. (Eric Goossens)

pace. The bullets zipped around us like bees.

One by one the rowers were hit, although that did not stop the boats as others immediately seized up their oars. In one boat five out of the six oarsmen were shot. One of these was 20-year-old Private Alexander McArthur, a red-head from Ascot Vale, Victoria, who was mortally wounded, shot through his femoral artery. He continued trying to row, as a colleague attempted to staunch the flow of blood, when McArthur was reported to cry, 'I'm done!' before collapsing. In command of one boat were two Melbourne bank clerks; at the bow was 30-year-old Captain Herbert Layh, who cheered his men on through the fire, whilst in the stern, operating the tiller, was 20-year-old Lieutenant Albert Heighway. As the boat's keel scraped the shingle, Heighway was shot through the chest and immediately collapsed to the bottom of the boat. With the boat now beached, Layh jumped over the side and into the water, where he was immediately shot through the hip and seconds later through the leg. Those who could move or were not hit scrambled to the shore and took shelter behind grass-tufted sand hummocks which fringed that area of the beach. Out of the 140 men that left the *Galeka*, only thirty-five reached the beach unscathed or slightly wounded, the remainder lay in the boats or on the beach, dead or dying. By the time the survivors had rejoined the rest of the Battalion, only eighteen remained.

About the same time Lieutenant Rafferty, with his platoon from A Company, 12/AIF, ordered earlier by Clarke to silence the machine gun post, was approaching Fisherman's Hut. He had with him about forty men, who had already crossed 800 yards of open scrubby ground below Walker's Ridge. To his left a smaller party, under Lieutenant Frederick Strickland, 11/AIF, was working its way along North Beach in support of Rafferty. Rafferty soon found himself pinned down in a six foot deep dry river bed, in front of which was a field with a single olive tree. This gave him little cover as Turkish fire from high ground to his right began to hit his flank. At this time Rafferty noticed the four white boats of 7/AIF heading towards Fisherman's Hut so, escaping the fire in the exposed creek bed, and in hope of supporting the landing he ordered his men up out of the cover and ran across the open field to a sandy knoll ahead. A fusillade of bullets tore into the ranks as soon as they had got into the open, leaving only Rafferty, a sergeant and six others who managed to reach cover at the far end of the field. At that end of the field he was able to climb the lower slopes of what became known as No.1 Outpost, where he was in a position to overlook the Turkish positions above Fisherman's Hut. Rafferty observed that the boats had already landed, but saw little movement. Unable to attract the occupants' attention, he sent Private Arthur Stubbings, a 33-year-old miner from Hobart, forward to get in touch with them. He returned soon after with the news that all were dead or dying. There were a few survivors, who were with Captain Layh, hidden by the grassy tussocks on the foreshore, but Rafferty did not know about these men. Likewise, Layh's men believed that all of Rafferty's party had been killed. At about 5.30 am, after the firing had died down, Rafferty returned along the beach with his surviving men to continue their original mission of escorting the Indian Mountain Battery from the beach.

Second Lieutenant Ibrahim Hayreddin, afraid of being outflanked, by the Australians in the aea, evacuated his position above Fisherman's Hut and retired inland. This allowed Layh and the other survivors of 7/AIF finally to move up off the beach and to take a defensive position upon the now vacated Sandy Knoll. Layh remained in this position until just after 2.00 pm when large groups of Turks (2/57 Battalion) were seen approaching the area from the direction of Baby 700. Heading towards No.1 Outpost, they were already in the foothills above, thus threatening to cut off Layh's position. Compelled to withdraw, and under fire for most of the way, they returned along the beach to rejoin the remainder of his Battalion that had landed earlier at Anzac Cove. Only eighteen of the original force got back safely. Major Jackson, who was also still alive, had earlier managed to work his way along the beach in the direction of 3/Field Ambulance to arrange stretcher-bearers for the wounded. The stretcher-bearers tried to recover these men and the dead, but several of the volunteers who went to help were hit from renewed sniper fire from the foothills. There were

Fisherman's Hut today with the low sandy knoll behind.

about twenty men on the beach and more within the boats.

Lance Corporal Noel Ross, Canterbury Battalion, NZEF, who was the son of the Official New Zealand War Correspondent, Malcolm Ross, describes what he saw:

On our left, along the beach about half a mile, a boat, sunk in the surf, rocked uneasily. With the aid of a glass I could see its freight. Sitting upright were at least eight dead men, and on the beach another twenty. A sailor, distinguishable by his white cap, covert, lay in an attitude strangely lifelike, his chin resting on his hand, his face turned to our position. The next afternoon I casually turned my glasses on the pathetic group, and saw that the sailor was now lying on his back with his face to the sky. There was no mistake: he had been alive, and perhaps even now, after lying there nearly thirty-six hours, he was still alive. I was destined to get yet another thrill. In the centre of the heap on the beach there was some movement. And then I saw distinctly a khaki cap waving weakly, and presently a man detached himself from the group and hobbled slowly towards us along the beach. Immediately the snipers started afresh.

Four other men and myself made off along the beach to meet the sad figure, who by this time had collapsed. Ten yards out from our trench we drew fire, and the bullets whispered confidingly "Duck," as they entered the water or hit the stones by our feet, "Run like the devil". I personally cut out the first hundred yards in well under eleven seconds, and although my style might have been ragged it was good enough and got me to a small sandy knoll where I was able to talk to the man. There were four others still alive out there, he said, and "last night there were eight, but it was cold, and they'd no water or food and couldn't last it out."

We got him in slowly, and afterwards the others, but not until one of the warships had dealt with the snipers. Later we buried all the others. One of the men we brought in had been out there half in the water and half out, shot through both knees, but he was cheery and bright, and asked first about his brother in another company, and then explained where the Turks were sniping from.[24]

Most of the wounded were eventually got away over the next couple of days in two of the boats that remained floating, towed away by a trawler. Those that died were buried close-by in No.2 Outpost Cemetery.

1. Hammerton, Sir John, *The Great War, I Was There,* Vol.1, (1938), p.327.

2. Unpublished diary of Private Herbert Pare, RMLI. Royal Marines Museum (11/13/036)

3. Aspinall-Oglander, Brigadier General C.F., *History of the Great War, Military Operations Gallipoli,* Vol.1, (1929), p.173.

4. *The Men of Anzac, The Anzac Book,* (1916), p.1.

5. Quoted by Lieutenant Colonel Shefik Aker, 27/Turkish Regiment's commander, *Canakkale-Ariburnu Savaslari ve 27 Alay, Askeri Mecmua,* (1935).

6. Margetts survived the Gallipoli Campaign, but was killed at Pozières, Somme in July 1916.

7. Lieutenant John Waterlow DSO remained with the Anzac Beach Party until promoted to commander on 30 June. He was killed when HMS *Black Prince* was sunk at the Battle of Jutland on 31 May 1916.

8. Reveille, Journal of the Returned Soldiers League (March 1932).

9. Unpublished diary of Private Albert Tiegs, 11/AIF. (Private collection).

10. Russell's Top was named after Brigadier General Sir A.H. Russell, KCMG, Commanding Officer of the New Zealand Mounted Rifles Brigade.

11. Hamilton, Sir Ian, *Gallipoli Diary,* (1920), Vol.1, p128.

12. Unpublished diary of Captain Godfrey Oppenheim (later Orde), RMLI, Royal Marines Museum (11/13/034)

13. Named after Colonel J. McCay, who established his HQ here on the day of the landings.

14. Named after Major S.M. Anderson, Brigade-Major of 1/Australian Division Field Artillery.

15. From a letter written by Gill in June 1915, later reprinted by the YMCA in the PYM (Perth Young Men) Magazine. Frank Gill was later killed on 22 August 1915 when his dugout was hit by a shell. He is buried in Beach Cemetery (II.F.17).

16. Hudson and Eccles were originally buried side by side near the Clearing Hospital under Walker's Ridge, but the graves were lost after the evacuation. Along with Cadoux, they are now commemorated on the Lone Pine Memorial.

17. Private S.B. Sheaf, died of wounds on 4 May 1915 at the Lemnos Base Hospital. Today he is commemorated on the Chatby War Memorial, Egypt.

18. Major C.H. Elliot assumed second in command after Major Sydney Hawley was hit by a bullet in the spine and paralysed whilst exiting the boat.

19. Lieutenant Colonel Lancelot F. Clarke DSO, commanding officer 12/AIF, was killed in action, aged 57, 25/4/15. He is buried at Beach Cemetery.

20 Major T. Steel, 14/AIF, Lieutenant Colonel R. Courtney, 14/AIF, Major H. Quinn, 15/AIF and Lieutenant Colonel H. Pope, 16/AIF.

21. Monash Gully was named after Colonel (later General Sir John) Monash, at the time commanding officer of 4 Australian Infantry Brigade. Monash Gully was a continuation of Shrapnel Valley.

22. Master Lieutenant Commander Bernard Burt later commanded the Hospital Ship, *Glenart Castle,* and was killed when it was torpedoed by German submarine *UC56* off the Devon coast on 26 February 1918. Burt lived in Crowborough, Sussex.

23. Private Alexander James McArthur, 475, 7/AIF, died 25 April 1915 and is buried in No.2 Outpost Cemetery.

24. Ross, Noel, *Ross and His Work,* (1919), p.18.

Chapter Two

The Main Body Lands

It was a perfect day for the landing

By this stage the Turks had recovered slightly from the surprise of the landing and had begun to subject the Australians, who had so far dominated the battle, to ever increasing small-arms fire. Off the coast the destroyers had also come under fire from Turkish snipers hidden in the undergrowth. Turkish artillery was not reported to have started shrapnel fire until 5.10 am, which was almost an hour after the first Australians had landed. The battery that was probably responsible for this was captured on 400 Plateau about an hour later, but fire still continued from the direction of Gaba Tepe which never got silenced. The only suppression to the fire at this time was by the navy, in particular HMS *Bacchante*, which lay off Gaba Tepe and, at almost point blank range, bombarded the fortifications and the well hidden gun positions. However, as soon as the *Bacchante* ceased shelling and withdrew, the guns would open up again. The navy had minimal effect

HMS *Bacchante*, a Cressy-class armoured cruiser, that helped cover the Anzac landings on 25 April.

in countering the Turkish artillery, although they did manage to knock at least one gun out of action. Lieutenant Ralph Prisk, 6/AIF, who was on Pine Ridge, noted that '*Bacchante* blew one gun clean over'. This was probably one of the guns from the Turkish battery on Anderson's Knoll, which went on later to harass the men on 400 Plateau. Turkish artillery was virtually unmolested all day, so had free rein to fire at the ships off shore as well as the inland Anzac positions. No Anzac artillery had been landed at this stage, so the shrapnel and high explosive fire had to be endured.

It was a perfect day for the landing – calm and clear. A great number of transports were lying off Gaba Tepe, also the Triumph, Queen, Prince of Wales *and* Majestic. *The* Talbot *and* Minerva *were steaming close in firing, when we slowed down, astern of the* Bacchante. *The latter was lying close in, firing at the scrub and trenches above. Just as we arrived the* Manica *sent its balloon up. The landing was now in full swing, destroyers and trawlers, as well as picket boats towing the cutters, etc in. Shrapnel was bursting over the water and shore in little white puffs...our men could be discerned climbing the scrubby ravines under a sharp rifle, maxim and shrapnel fire, the former being continuously heard... the covering ships were shelling rapidly, but still the beach was covered in white shrapnel puffs.*[1]

Midshipman G.M.D. Maltby,
HMS Queen Elizabeth, 25 April 1915.

An anonymous account of the landing recorded in the 2/Field Ambulance War Diary describes the scene whilst waiting for transport to take the men ashore:

Gradually the sun rose behind the hills and shone out with the result that everything was clothed in beautiful colours and it seemed that we were once more tourists viewing some famed country. But again this thought was dispelled from our minds by renewed activity on the part of the warships.

Out at sea the Turkish shrapnel had started targeting the ships with increased accuracy, causing casualties amongst the naval personnel as well as the soldiers on the crowded decks.

We suffered our first casualty, Stoker P. O. M'Court [Stoker Petty Officer Bernard Wilfred McCourt, Royal Navy] *being killed while on deck, where he had been assisting to cast off the lighters. We had been under a very heavy shrapnel fire all day whenever we were within a mile of the beach, and even when close in numbers of shells and bullets were falling all around us.*

*We were exceedingly lucky in not having more casualties, as the
ship was repeatedly hit by shrapnel and rifle fire. Two shrapnel
cases and fuses were picked up on deck on this, the first day.*[2]

Unlike the first wave in the battleship tows, many of the destroyer men
came under fire throughout the whole of the journey ashore. The Turks
were shelling the approach, the beaches and gullies around. An extract
of a letter written on 28 August 1915 by Private John Jensen, 955
1/AIF Battalion, who was later awarded the DCM and MM, wrote:

*The third brigade landed first at four o'clock in the morning
& we landed at 6 o'clock. We were lucky getting ashore as
nobody was hit in the boat although shells were falling all
around us. A big shell dropped close to the boat & nearly upset
it when it exploded.*

*As soon as we got on to the beach a shell fell right into my
platoon & killed one & wounded six, three of whom died
afterwards from the wounds. The man at one side of me was hit
in the stomach & the man right in front was hit in the side of the
face, the bullet taking his eye right out. A few yards further
another shell dropped among us knocking over 9 or 10, the
officer included.*

*About two hours afterwards when they made a count, there
were only thirteen left out of fifty. The sergeant who counted
shook his head & said he didn't like it as thirteen was an unlucky
number. A few minutes afterwards he was killed himself.*[3]

With the covering force fully ashore, it was now the turn of the main
force to be ferried from the transports with the aid of the destroyers.
Aboard the transport *Clan Macgillivray* was Private John Gibson Pitt,

Two hours after the landing, 25 April 1915.

Landing at Anzac Cove – 6.30 am, 25 April 1915.

8/AIF, who recalls the landing from his diary entry of 25 April 1915:

7.15 am. Embarked in destroyer, one boatload of our battalion went before we did. Transferred wounded and dead from destroyer to Clan Mc. H.M.S. Triumph, Bacchante etc bombarding fort and gun positions as hard as they can. Boats were lashed to the side of the destroyer so that their bottoms just skimmed the water and the men were able to get in them while she was going. When she had got as close to the shore as the depth of the water would allow her, she slowed down and the

The sun rises over the Armada – SS *Novian* and SS *Galeka* (Anzac Book).

boats were released from her side, then a Pinnace towed us in as far as they could and we rowed the rest, having to jump in the water, knee deep to land. The 3rd Brigade were covering party and landed first. We formed up in platoons on the beach and forced our way through the thick and prickly scrub. There being another line in front of us, who had driven the Turks before them, we did not meet with a great deal of opposition, although we got the benefit of a good many bullets fired at the front line, and some shrapnel.[4]

Privates Frederick Symonds and his brother, Edgar, were on board the transport *Novian* with men from 5/AIF. Fred describes the landing:

Landed this morning. The country looks very difficult, and is full of Turks. Our first load got it very hot from the beach; many killed in the boats. I heard the sailors coming back after landing the first lot saying that they made a magnificent charge with only fixed bayonets - did not wait for orders, but jumped into the water before the boats were beached and got rid of their packs after they got the first trenches. There were thousands of Turks, and our first party consisted of only a couple of hundred men. The sailors said they never saw anything like the way our men went at them. I think the main body of Turks must be further inland. We were acting as supports to the advanced line, and landed about 8 o'clock. It took a long time to get all the firing line men ashore. We were under heavy shrapnel fire while landing; they had some guns on a peninsula about two miles away which covered the whole of our landing, and they gave us pie. The first sight that greeted us was some dead comrades and a host of wounded. We went up a gully to the right, and took our packs off just before getting to the steep climb. We had a long climb before getting near the ridge on the top of the gully, and it was then that we began to hear the bullets and shrapnel. One of our chaps had been hit on the leg further back where we took our packs off; that was the only casualty we had so far.[5]

After the incident at Fisherman's Hut, Anzac Cove became the main landing area for the whole Corps throughout the remainder of the morning and the next few days. This little cove was out of the sight of the Turks but, because they knew the Australians were concentrating their landings there, the little beach was never without shrapnel. The Turks shelled the front lines, supply routes, beaches and transports. During the morning the fire was also supported by the Ottoman battleship *Torgud Reis*, which was moored in the straits between

MacLaurin's 1 Brigade rowing ashore just before 10.00 am, 25 April.
(Anzac Book)

Maidos and Chanak. It had been firing over the peninsula unmolested into the shipping off Ari Burnu, until it was eventually observed by aerial reconnaissance. The ship was temporarily seen off by HMS *Triumph*, but later returned to continue its bombardment. *Torgud Reis* eventually withdrew completely in the late morning, probably after it received word that the Australian submarine *AE2* was in the area.

The whole scene looks very much like a picture in the illustrated papers – the hilly landscape, and little puffs of white smoke spurting up here and there marking the shrapnel bursts. At 9.30 a.m. a shell pitched just over us and struck a destroyer – I thought it time to leave off sightseeing for a bit then. Shortly afterwards two more shots of the same type arrived and dropped just between the Queen *and the transport. The order was given to weigh anchor, and proceed out a bit further from the shore;*

View of the landing taken during the early morning of 25 April. Shrapnel bursts are just visible over the newly captured positions.

Battleship Hill   Baby 700   Walker's Ridge   Sphinx   Plugge's Plateau   Anzac Cove

Bombarding the shore – tows in the foreground are returning for their next loads.

> *things were getting beyond a joke. The Turks must have had a good spotter concealed somewhere.*

Captain Oppenheim, RMLI, HMS *Queen Elizabeth* in his diary entry for 25 April 1915.

As mentioned already, there were delays to the plan for getting McCay's 2 Brigade and MacLaurin's 1 Brigade ashore. This was partly caused by the transports having to re-anchor away from the shelling

Shrapnel Valley   400 Plateau and also by the disregard of the orders for the evacuation of the wounded, when some of the designated landing boats as well as the specially allocated medical boats. Boats were thus delayed returning to the transports that then had to unload wounded before they could embark fresh troops. Both Brigades should have completed disembarkation by 9.00 am, but it was not until 1.00 pm that the last battalion (4/AIF) of 1st Australian Division had been landed.

Lieutenant Colonel Marks, who was the Regimental Medical Officer with 3/Australian Field Artillery Brigade, recounts being anchored off Hell Spit early in the morning, awaiting orders to land:

> At daybreak we were able to see the troops moving on the shore and particularly across open stretches, such as Shell Green, the landing having taken place before we arrived. After we had anchored for about 2 hours, two shells landed in the water in our direction. We all felt rather shaken at the time. The next thing we knew was a roaring in the air and a shell passed between the funnel and the after-mast. In all 13 shells landed round us, one shell landing just under the bows of a T.B.D. [Torpedo Boat Destroyer] lying near by and making the boat list. Everyone had the wind up. Our boat up-anchored and drew out beyond the shell-fire.[6]

Once the remaining two brigades had started arriving, they were guided into Shrapnel Valley and into the front line. Confusion reigned as groups, almost as soon as they arrived, were directed into different parts of the line to fill the gaps. Some did not wait for orders and, using their initiative, found their way into the lines; others got lost in the deep ravines, which not only caused delay but sometimes took them into different parts of the front.

As soon as Sinclair-MacLagan had the right flank seemingly secure with 2 Brigade, he then set about reinforcing the left flank, which he had originally thought to be secure. At about 10.45 am the Auckland Battalion and two companies of the Canterbury Battalion from the New Zealand Infantry Brigade (A&NZ Division) had landed from their transport, the *Lützow*. Major Thomas Dawson of the Auckland Battalion wrote, in contrast to earlier accounts, how little shelling and fire they were receiving:

> We were surprised how peaceful was our trip ashore. A little shelling. Some dropping rifle fire but only two casualties in our battalion. The landing was peaceful but distinctly wet, particularly for us small ones. It is surprising what a lot of water a ship's boat draws. The quietness of our narrow strip of beach

Landing at Anzac Cove, 25 April 1915.

was also surprising. A few Australians forming up; an Indian mountain battery and some wounded and dying men.

Lance-Corporal Noel Ross, Canterbury Battalion, described the scenes that met him:

As we approached the shore there came to our ears the continuous rattle of musketry, first scarcely perceptible, but at last growing to an ear-racking roll as of giant kettle-drums beaten without reason. Through glasses I could see one of our skirmishing lines advancing from the boats on the beach. It was

HMS *Scourge*, off Gaba Tepe, waiting to land the next wave of troops.

HMS *Scourge* and HMS *Prince of Wales*.

as though one watched a cinematograph screen. The white boats on the beach and some brown figures sadly still on the grey sand, the green grass, and a toiled field across which advanced lines of our attacking force formed the foreground. Steep hills, clay-faced and covered with dense scrub and dwarf ilex, over which the cotton-wool puffs of shrapnel appeared and disappeared, made the background.

8/AIF waiting to be directed into the line.

These troops were immediately ordered to reinforce the left flank on Baby 700, where a battle for its possession was now raging.

Noel Ross continues his account:

> *"Reinforcements at the double on the left," roared an officer through a megaphone, and then added as a shell burst overhead, "Keep in under the bank – shrapnel's unhealthy."*
>
> *Then came a toilsome, tiresome scramble over the high bluffs to the firing line. On the top of the first ridge [Plugge's Plateau] we came through a Turkish trench. In it were a dead Turk, bayoneted, a box of ammunition, and many flies. Stooping low we doubled to the brow, ever with the purring bullets overhead. Wounded on the way to the beach passed us cheerfully, saying, "It's hot as hell up there!" And it was. When we had crossed a gully and gained another ridge, half an hour's scrambling and sliding, we were scarcely 200 yards from the last, so steep is the ground.*[7]

The first company of the Auckland Battalion only reached Russell's Top just before 1.00 pm, which was over two hours after they had landed. Why did their journey, once ashore, take them so long? Initially Lieutenant Colonel Arthur Plugge, Commanding Officer Auckland Battalion, led his Battalion towards a steep ridge that appeared to lead on up to Russell's Top. As his Battalion was ascending the path to the top, he received an order from Brigadier General H.B. Walker, the New Zealand Infantry Brigade commander, to stop as the ridge [later to be

Compare left: the same view today.

Anzac Cove – note the horse boats that have just landed the mules and guns of 26 (Jacob's) Indian Mountain Battery. HMS *Bacchante* is in the background. (Anzac Book)

called Walker's Ridge] was thought to be too rugged, exposed and its narrow single file track would mean the men would join the battle in small and disorganised groups. Instead Walker, who was relying on his map, thought there was a direct route from Plugge's Plateau up onto Russell's Top, which in reality was the Razor Edge, a narrow and eroded ridge which falls steeply away on both sides. This last minute change caused delay and chaos; many of the men could not be recalled so continued their ascent onto Russell's Top, those that were diverted onto Plugge's were stuck without a path forward and were systematically exposed to enemy shrapnel and rifle fire. Seeking an exit, many went down into Shrapnel Valley, and then got lost and separated from their companies; many were even directed into the fighting elsewhere. Lance Corporal Noel Ross was one of those who got separated and ended up with the Australians. So, in trying to prevent disorganisation, the end result was just that, augmented by long delays in getting the badly needed reinforcements into position.

The treacherous terrain at Anzac was a problem that affected movement, observation and communication. Climbing the heights had been helped in places by the scrub being there to hold on to, but it also turned out to be a more sinister friend. This natural obstacle slowed any advance, blocked from view any neighbour and in some places it was so thick that men had to find alternative routes. The scrub was commonly chest height and had sharp and hardened thorns that pricked and tore at the men as they fought their way through it. It also concealed enemy snipers, who could easily pick off chosen targets amongst the advancing troops. Many of the snipers had got behind the lines and were not cleared until many days after the landing. There is a story about one of these snipers who had concealed himself behind the Sphinx and, when he was eventually killed, they found a generous

74

supply of food and water, enough to sustain him for many days.

Turkish fire had steadily increased since early morning and by midday the troops were under almost constant shrapnel fire, to which there was no reply. As the Official History says:

> To lie out in the thick scrub under this shrapnel fire, separated from and out of sight of their comrades, unsupported by friendly artillery, ignorant of the situation, and imagining that they were the sole survivors of their units, was a severe strain to young troops in their first day of battle.

No records exist as to the percentage, but casualties suffered by artillery fire must have been very high during the first few days, contributed to by the exposed positions and shallow trenches.

At this stage of the battle artillery fire could not be suppressed due to the unavailability of Australian field artillery and the ineffectiveness of naval fire. The heavyweight fire of the navy was of little use due to the flat trajectory of their guns, which made it difficult to target and hit positions inland. Additionally there were problems distinguishing friend from foe, which was not helped by the nature of the terrain and the confusion of troop movements. As observation improved, the navy's fire became more effective, although there were still problems locating the Turkish artillery batteries and distinguishing the enemy troops amongst the thick scrub. Sea planes from the Royal Naval Air Service helped with observation, but the Turks ceased fire whenever an aircraft was near, so spotting any camouflaged gun position proved extremely difficult.

Captain Oppenheim continues his account of the Anzac landing:

> The Majestic opened up about 1 p.m., but was stopped for some inexplicable reason by the Queen, because the soldiers reported '2000 short'. At 4 p.m. she opened fire again with aeroplane spotting and quickly knocked out a battery of three guns. This might have been done three hours earlier. All we can hope for now is to entrench ourselves on the crest of the hill for the night and wait for the other attacks to develop. The soldiers keep on urgently asking for their howitzer batteries to be landed: poor devils, they must be suffering fearful losses from the enemy's unchallenged batteries. All our tremendous strength in ships' guns is being wasted – we are lying idle. The battle continues with unceasing roar and rattle.

The Indian 26th (Jacob's) Mountain Battery began to land the first of its three small 10-pounder guns at 10.30 am, having been escorted as planned by Lieutenant Rafferty's remaining party of men on their

A contemporary photo postcard showing the landing of 4/AIF and 26 (Jacob's) Indian Mountain Battery. MacLaurin's 1 Brigade Staff are in the foreground.

return from Fisherman's Hut. Although severely hampered by the terrain, the artillery eventually got into an initial position behind the crest of 400 Plateau, and went into action at exactly 11.55 am. The Indian 21st (Kohat) Mountain Battery was supposed to land at 8.30 am but had to remain aboard its transport as no lighters had arrived to take them ashore. They did not start towards shore until 5.30 pm, landing thirty minutes later. Once they got onto the beach, they were then confronted by the same difficulties with the terrain and finding a suitable position as faced by Jacob's gun batteries. Captain Oppenheim mentions this in his diary by saying:

> *5.30 p.m. Mules have been landed, and it is to be hoped that the guns will soon follow, so as to be able to get into position during the night. Much will depend on tomorrow.*

With only a few low-calibre guns ashore, their effectiveness against the Turks was arguably of limited value, although as a morale booster they could not have been bettered. Jacob's Battery was only in action for a couple of hours at 400 Plateau when, at 2.25 pm heavy casualties caused by accurate Turkish counter-battery fire had forced its withdrawal. The remainder of the field artillery was still aboard the transports, and had no orders to land, even though it was desperately needed ashore. Three 18-pounder guns were eventually landed about 3.30 pm, but these were turned away almost immediately by Major General Bridges. A follow-up order was sent from General Birdwood to Rear-Admiral Thursby to stop sending field artillery ashore. The reluctance of command to land the artillery was said to be due to the lack of good gun positions and methods of getting the guns to the few positions that were available. The decision was probably also influenced by the precarious and seemingly deteriorating situation ashore and the fear of losing the guns.

Lieutenant Colonel Marks, Regimental Medical Officer (RMO), 3/Australian Field Artillery Brigade, who was supposed to have landed at 7.00 am, was invited ashore with his commanding officer, who went to find out what the delay was:

> About 11.00 a.m., Colonel Rosenthal, the O.C., decided he would land in a rowing boat, and reported to Headquarters to find out what was doing. I asked him for instructions regarding myself and he said I had better come with him, along with my Medical Orderly and 3 A.M.C. [Army Medical Corps] men. We had lunch immediately and got into a rowing boat with a volunteer crew about 12 noon. I took with me my No.1 Field Pannier, Surgical Haversack, Medical Companion, Water Bottles, 2 Field Fracture Bags and several stretchers. We each carried a haversack and what personal gear would go in it, a rug or blanket, ground sheet and blanket. Our iron rations were the only provision for, I think, two days. On approaching the beach, somewhere about Hell Spit, shrapnel burst in front of us on the beach – this being our first acquaintance with fire. On grounding, we carried our equipment under the cover of the cliff,

Drawing of the landing. (Ellis Silas)

Engineers from No.2 Field Company landing at about 6.30 am 25 April 1915.

slightly protected from Gaba Tepe, from which the shrapnel was coming. There were no casualties on landing except that, when returning to the Cardiganshire, *shrapnel burst over it and one man was wounded, the shrapnel bullet passing in at his neck and landing at his mediastinum. This boy died later at Malta and was the first casualty in the 3rd Artillery Brigade.*

Lieutenant Colonel Charles Rosenthal was frustrated with Major General Bridges' seeming unwillingness to land the guns, although one 18-pounder gun from 4 Battery did get ashore and came into action that day. It had to be manhandled into position at Hell Spit, and opened fire at 6.00 pm, putting 62 rounds into the battery at Gaba Tepe. Whatever the effect on silencing the Turks, the guns had a great effect on morale. Eventually guns were placed on Plugge's Plateau, Shrapnel Gully and Bolton's Ridge, so they now had something with which to answer the Turks. As soon as visibility was lost at dusk (which was 6.48 pm) the Turks ceased their artillery fire, giving a temporary respite to the Anzacs.

Also still at sea aboard their transports was Colonel John Monash's 4 Australian Infantry Brigade and the remaining half of the New Zealand Infantry Brigade (Otago and Wellington Battalions). Their immediate landing was requested. Aboard the transport *Haidar Pasha*

78

was Private Ellis Silas, who was a signaller in 16/AIF.

At 5.30 pm as the Battalion was getting ready to disembark, he wrote:

> We have been told of the impossible task before us, of probable annihilation; yet we are eager to get to it; we joke with each other about getting cold feet, but deep down in our hearts we know when we get to it we will not be found wanting. The Assembly is sounded – I have never seen it answered with such alacrity – there is a loud cheer as we gather together in the hold. There, for the last time in this world, many of us stood shoulder to shoulder. As I looked down the ranks of my comrades, I wondered much which of us were marked for the Land Beyond. We were well in the zone of fire, and every second I was expecting a shell to come bursting through the side of the ship, to answer my question.
>
> We are on the battlefield, well under fire of the enemy – it is difficult to realise that every burst of flame, every spurt of water, means death or worse. I don't think I can carry my kit – I can scarcely stand with the weight of it. We are descending on to the destroyer "Ribble", which is alongside us. Noise of the guns simply frightful. Colour of the sea beautiful. We are packed very tightly on the destroyer. The sailors are very kind to us, I think they know what we are going to face – can see boat-loads of wounded being towed from the shore – shrapnel just burst over our heads, thank God no damage – getting nearer the shore.

The Last Assembly by Ellis Silas. This depicts the mustering of 16/AIF aboard the transport. (Ellis Silas)

Turks pelting us like anything. It was a relief to get ashore; we are packed so tightly in the boats and moreover so heavily laden with our kit that, had a shot hit the boat, we should have no chance of saving ourselves – it was awful the feeling of utter helplessness. Meanwhile the Turks pelted us hot and fast. In jumping ashore I fell over, my kit was so heavy; I couldn't get up without help – fortunately the water was shallow at this point, otherwise ...[8]

Following the original timetable was proving difficult for the navy, shown by almost a four-hour period between 12.30 pm and 4.00 pm when no infantry were landed. The wounded were still using the boats allocated for landing troops, and the return journey was longer as Turkish artillery fire had forced the shipping to withdraw further out to sea to avoid being hit. The remaining Australian and New Zealand brigades were desperately needed ashore, but they remained helplessly aboard their transports waiting for the order to disembark. When they eventually did land it was too late to save some of the advantages of the morning's fighting, namely the retention of Baby 700 and the advanced areas in front of Second Ridge.

1. Unpublished - Diary of Midshipman G.M.D. Maltby, HMS *Queen Elizabeth*.
2. Diary of HMS *Queen Elizabeth* January to May 1915, (1919), p.43.
3. Letter written by John (Jack) Jenson to his aunt dated 28 August 1915. (SLSA: D7720[L]).
4. Unpublished diary of Private John Gibson Pitt, 8/AIF. (Private collection).
5. Unpublished diary of Private Frederick Symonds, 5/AIF. (Private collection).
6. Interview with Colonel Marks 1914-15. (NA:WO 95/4342).
7. Ross, Noel, *Ross and His Work*, (1919), p.19.
8. Ellis Silas, *Crusading at Anzac, AD 1915*, (1916) and *Diary of an Anzac* – held by the Mitchell Library, State Library of NSW (ML MSS.1840).

16/AIF Leaving HMS *Ribble*. (Ellis Silas)

Chapter Three

400 Plateau

See, e-,ee . . . bang . . . swish!

Despite the initial confusion of the landing, the covering force attempted to carry out their original planned orders and, crossing 400 Plateau, some small parties headed for the final objective of Third Ridge. One of these was led by Queenslander Lieutenant Eric Plant, 9/AIF, who advanced south across Pine Ridge, down into Legge Valley and up onto Third Ridge. By about 6.30 am he had reached a position about 200-300 metres south of Anderson Knoll (*Kavak Tepe*) but soon noticed a large formation of Turkish infantry rapidly approaching the ridge. As Plant's small party was heavily outnumbered, he had no alternative other than to withdraw back to Pine Ridge. A little later Lieutenant Ralph Prisk, 6/AIF, led a platoon with a few stragglers from 9/AIF down from Bolton's Ridge and across the easterly spurs of 400 Plateau into Legge Valley, in an effort to reach Third Ridge. Prisk also noticed a large number of Turks on Third Ridge, so he too withdrew his men to a defensive position on Pine Ridge. From there he eventually had to pull back again, not due to the enemy, but because of friendly fire from Australians to the rear who thought his small party were Turks!

The deepest penetration that morning was made by two 10/AIF battalion scouts, Privates Arthur Blackburn, an Adelaide-born solicitor, and Lance-Corporal Philip Robin, a bank accountant, who were sent forward to reconnoitre Third Ridge.[1] They reached and passed beyond the crest of Scrubby Knoll, circling what was later to become Mustafa Kemal's headquarters that day. Finding no Turks in the vicinity, they moved southwards along the far slope of the ridge where they soon spotted Turks in a valley to the east. Both men withdrew back to their unit on Johnston's Jolly and reported their sighting. Blackburn and Robin also noted another party of Australians on a lower spur of the ridge when they were returning; these belonged to Lieutenant Noel Loutit.

Lieutenant Loutit, an engineer from Adelaide, had advanced quickly from the beach with his men from 10/AIF, getting to the northern lobe of 400 Plateau very early on. From Johnston's Jolly he could see a Turkish mountain gun battery over on Lone Pine that was in the process of limbering up. Loutit ordered his men to open fire but,

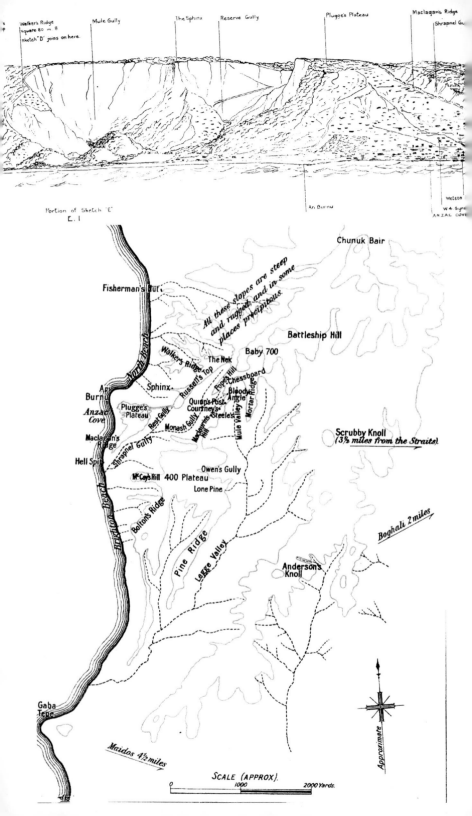

Walkers Ridge
square 80 m. B
sketch "D" joins on here.

Mule Gully

The Sphinx

Reserve Gully

Plugge's Plateau

Maclagan's Ridge

Shrapnel Gu

Ari Burnu

Watson

W 4 Sign
ANZAC COVE

Portion of Sketch "E"
E. I

Chunuk Bair

Fisherman's Hut

All these slopes are steep
and rugged and in some
places precipitous.

Battleship Hill

Walker's Ridge

The Nek

Baby 700

North Beach

Russell's Top

Pope's Hill

Chessboard

Sphinx

Bloody
Angle

Ari
Burnu

Quinn's Post
Courtney's

Mortar Ridge

Anzac
Cove

Plugge's
Plateau

Rest Gully

Steeles

Maclagan's Hill

Monash Gully

Mule Valley

Scrubby Knoll
(3½ miles from the Straits).

Maclagan's
Ridge

Shrapnel Gully

Hell Spit

Owen's Gully

M°Cay's Hill 400 Plateau

Lone Pine

Boghali 2 miles

Bolton's Ridge

Pine Ridge

Legge Valley

Anderson's
Knoll

Gaba
Tepe

Approximate

Maidos 4½ miles

SCALE (APPROX).
0   1000   2000 Yards.

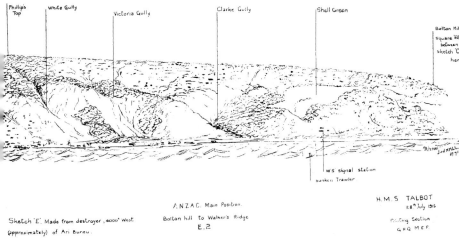

as he did so the battery very quickly disappeared into Owen's Gully. In pursuit Loutit also moved down into the gully and unknowingly by-passed the battery. He did find a tented camp with oil lamps still burning, but no Turks. The time was just after 6.00 am and, with no sign of the battery, he quickly pressed his men on into Legge Valley, making for Third Ridge. The battery was actually hidden off one of the branches of Owen's Gully at the head of a depression called The Cup. Moments later men from 9/AIF, who landed earlier as part of the second wave, reached the battery's position and killed most of the crew, capturing three mountain guns, though the fourth had already escaped with its crew across Legge Valley.

With no opposition, Loutit, who was then joined by Lieutenant James Haig also of 10/AIF, and just over thirty men from 9/AIF and 10/AIF, crossed the flat and grassy plain of Legge Valley and ascended onto Adana Spur, one of the lower ridges that led up to Scrubby Knoll. At the top he observed a large party of Turks further along Third Ridge, making their way towards them. These may have been same ones that Blackburn and Robin and also Plant and Prisk had seen earlier. If they were not the remnants of 2/27 Battalion, they were probably the advanced parties of 1/27 and 3/27 Battalions that were approaching the area at this time. Loutit took a couple of men up to Scrubby Knoll in order to get a better view, but almost immediately came under fire, so returned to the others he had left below with Haig. Loutit sent a runner back for reinforcements and a party of about thirty men returned under the command of Captain John Ryder, 9/AIF. No other support crossed the valley that morning, although numerous groups of Australians were sighted digging in on 400 Plateau. Loutit had quickly established an extended line with Ryder's men along the spur, but was soon faced with increased Turkish resistance. After mounting casualties, the early

83

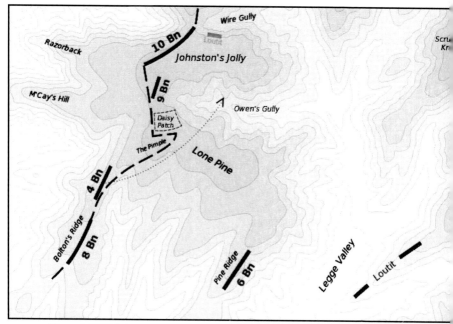

Map of 400 Plateau.

withdrawal of Ryder and in fear of being cut off, Loutit was forced to retire. Having held his position on Third Ridge for over three hours, at about 10.00 am, Loutit's party was forced back across Legge Valley, hotly pursued by the Turks; of the men that started out with Loutit and Haig, only eleven returned.

Well before this stage Sinclair-MacLagan had already decided to change the plan and made the decision, for which he has been heavily criticised, to consolidate the position on Second Ridge instead of pushing on to hold Third Ridge. Calling a halt at about 7.00 am, Sinclair-MacLagan decided to wait until sufficient strength in the form of 2 Brigade had arrived before pushing on to the ridge ahead, which at that time still lay undefended. This decision was undoubtedly influenced by pre-landing intelligence reports that indicated a large body of enemy troops close to the area. When Bridges, the divisional commander, reached 400 Plateau at about 8.00 am, he commented that there appeared nothing to prevent the advance continuing, but then remained cautious and did nothing, leaving MacLagan to continue his entrenchment of Second Ridge and await the Turkish counter-attack. Small parties from 9/AIF and 10/AIF, who had begun to collect together on 400 Plateau, were ordered to dig in. They probably thought that this was only a momentary delay before continuing the advance.

Not everyone received those orders, including those in forward positions. Some of the men continued with the original orders, like Loutit, to push on to Third Ridge. Many were never heard of again.

Lieutenant-Colonel William Malone, Wellington Battalion, NZEF, who was to land later on that day, commented:

> *The Australians had carried the heights surrounding the Bay but instead of being content with that and then digging in hard and fast had scally-wagged for miles into the interior, some three or four miles, got scattered and so became a prey to the Turks who had been surprised in the first place and had (it is said) only some 500 defending troops at our landing place. Their troops encamped at Bijuk Anafarta and Koja Dere were brought against the scattered Australians and slaughtered them.[2]*

Earlier Lieutenant Colonel Şefik Aker Bey had quickly sent mounted patrols from the 9th Ottoman Division to the area of the firing and then contacted Colonel Halil Sami Bey, the divisional commander, to inform him of the situation. Halil Sami was cautious and ordered Aker Bey to wait for more information before deploying the rest of his regiment. This caused a slight delay, but soon he had received enough information of the landing to deploy the remaining two battalions of 27 Regiment, along with an artillery battery and machine gun company that were camped nearby at Maidos. Just before 8.00 am the two battalions of 27 Regiment and a machine gun company reached the southern end of Third Ridge near Anderson's Knoll and began to deploy along its length up towards Scrubby Knoll. Reinforcing the survivors of Ismet's 2/27 Battalion, which had been fighting since 4.30 am, they quickly prepared to make the first counter-attack of the day. As predicted, this was to fall on Sinclair-MacLagan's right flank.

Major Cemil Bey's 1/27 Battalion was ordered to attack the landward slopes of 400 Plateau whilst Major Halis Bey's 3/27 Battalion crossed the lower slopes of Incebayir Ridge to attack Mortar Ridge (*Edirne* Ridge). The remnants of 2/27 Battalion that had done so well in delaying the Anzac advance were held back on the left flank. Initially there was no artillery support for the infantry's attack as Şefik Aker's mountain battery was late arriving, only being deployed at 10.30 am. Once it did get into position it started bombarding 400 Plateau with high explosives and shrapnel. The battle for Second Ridge had begun.

When 2 Brigade started to arrive, Sinclair-MacLagan made the decision to advance 9/AIF from the middle of the firing line on 400 Plateau, in order to meet the developing Turkish counter-attack. The opportunity to advance to Third Ridge soon diminished as large numbers of Turks were seen advancing towards the Australian positions from that direction. 9/AIF, which was almost complete up until now, was advanced in sections. Almost immediately they got into the open they were cut down by Turkish machine-gun fire from the direction of Third Ridge. Those that were not killed immediately scattered, seeking cover amongst the waist-high scrub as bullets swept the plateau above. Quickly realising his mistake, Sinclair-MacLagan attempted to rescind the order, but by this time the Battalion was fully dispersed across a wide area of the plateau. As a coherent unit, 9/AIF ceased to exist that day. As soon as men from Colonel James McCay's 2 Brigade, which had landed in fairly good order, reached Sinclair-MacLagan, they were ordered forward into the gap that 9/AIF had left.

McCay established his headquarters on a westerly spur of 400 Plateau that became known as McCay's Hill. His Brigade was positioned across 400 Plateau with most of 5/AIF on Johnston's Jolly, large portions of 6/AIF on Pine Ridge, who helped protect the right flank of the division, whilst 8/AIF was deployed along Bolton's Ridge. 7/AIF, minus the company that had landed at Fisherman's Hut, plugged the gap on the plateau that had developed between the remnants of 9/AIF and 10/AIF.

The day's fighting on 400 Plateau was confused. The thick scrub meant that men lying prone were invisible, which made it difficult to maintain contact with adjacent units. When standing up to move, the men were visible to the enemy, thereby summoning a hail of small-arms fire and shrapnel.

Colonel James Whiteside McCay, commander of 2 Brigade.

Lacking any coherent organisation, small groups of men would advance, either following the original orders to reach Third Ridge or Sinclair-MacLagan's new orders to reinforce the newly established firing line. Many of the men went forward in search of the 'firing line', but this was in vain as no line had been established across the plateau. What existed were small groups of men that had become detached, lost, pinned-down and further reduced by casualties. Many of the actions that day went unrecorded as scores of these small and isolated groups were wiped out, lost forever in the small gullies and thick scrub-covered spurs of the plateau.

Private Alfred Richard Perry, 10/AIF, recalls the situation on the plateau:

See, e-,ee ...bang ...swish! The front firing line was now being baptised by its first shrapnel. Zir-zir ... zip-zip, machine guns, situated on each front, flank and centre, opened on our line. Thousands of bullets began to fly round and over us, sometimes barely missing. Now and then one heard a low gurgling moan and, turning, one saw near at hand some chum, who only a few seconds before had been laughing and joking, now lying gasping, with his life blood soaking down into the red clay and sand. "Five rounds rapid at the scrub in front," comes the command of our subaltern. Then an order down the line: "Fix bayonets!" Fatal order - was it not, perhaps, some officer of the enemy who shouted it? (for they say such things were done). Out

A warm corner of the firing line. Soldiers in shallow rifle pits along Second Ridge.

The remains of Australian trenches near 400 Plateau today.

flash a thousand bayonets, scintillating in the sunlight like a thousand mirrors, signalling our position to the batteries away on our left and front. We put in another five rounds rapid at the scrub in front. Then, bang-swish! bang-swish! bang swish! and over our line, and front, and rear, such a hellish fire of lyddite and shrapnel that one wonders how anyone could live amidst such a bail of death-dealing lead and shell. "Ah, got me!" says one lad on my left, and he shakes his arms. A bullet had passed through the biceps of his left arm, missed his chest by an inch, passed through the right forearm, and finally struck the lad between him and me a bruising blow on the wrist. The man next to him - a man from the 9th Battalion - started to bind up his wounds, as he was bleeding freely. All the time shrapnel was hailing down on us.

By 1.00 pm a rough line had been established across the plateau but it was dangerously thin and in many places not continuous. Turks from 1/27 Battalion were already on the inland slopes of the plateau, and were infiltrating forward, sniping at any movement they could see. Both 2 Brigade and most of 3 Brigade had been swallowed up into the line already, and 1 Brigade was quickly becoming committed to the fight. The only reserve unit left was 4/AIF, which Major General Bridges was holding back until the situation was critical. He eventually had to commit them into the line just before 5.00 pm.

Private Fred Symonds, 5/AIF, was part of the reinforcements being thrown into the line earlier on. The Battalion had been waiting only ten minutes below the crest of 400 Plateau when the order to advance was given:

> *After we had been there for about 10 minutes we got word that we were wanted in the firing line, so they sent Mr Levy [Lieutenant Leopold Levy] with No. 15 platoon. Shortly after we got word that Captain Saker [Major Richard Saker, killed 26/4/15] was badly wounded, and must have more supports, so No.14, our platoon, got the order to advance to the firing line. We no sooner got over the ridge than we were met by a hail of bullets and shrapnel. We covered the ground in short, sharp rushes, taking cover in all depressions. The enemy had the range of all the cover that was worth taking, and kept a constant fire of shrapnel over it. In one place the shells were bursting right on top of us, and coming almost as quick as one could count them. It was then that our men started to fall out. I got hit in the shoulder with a piece of shell just before we reached the firing line, and was told to go back with a man who was badly wounded just behind us, so I left my kit and rifle there and got hold of this chap, who, poor fellow, was hit in about eight places, and would have been killed had he stayed there much longer. I had a terrible job to get him down to the station. The first difficulty was to get him away from the fire zone. We had to go slowly, and I expected we would both be riddled but, by some good fortune, we got over the ridge without a mishap.*

At about 4.00 pm the Australians had to evacuate their position in The Cup as it became increasingly exposed to enemy fire as the Turks crept ever nearer. The area had been continually shelled and now machine-gun fire from Third Ridge and lower parts of Owen's Gully were being directed into it. As soon as they pulled back, Turks from 27 Regiment re-occupied the position and recovered the three mountain guns they had previously lost in the morning. The Turkish attack was now pushing hard against Johnston's Jolly, with many of the forward areas now lost or under heavy attack. The central part of Lone Pine by The Cup had been recaptured by the Turks and the southern spurs of this lobe were being infiltrated by snipers who had got behind the

Trenches along the top of Bolton's Ridge. Entrenched during the first day, the lines changed little throughout the campaign.

Australian positions on Pine Ridge. Further north, along Second Ridge and the 'Posts', the Turks were already pushing the Anzacs back, they had broken their defence on Mortar Ridge and Baby 700 was about to fall.

On Bolton's Ridge, south of Lone Pine, 8/AIF had established a strong position by 10.00 am which protected the right flank. Colonel McCay who gave the order to dig in and hold the ridge, simply exclaimed: 'That will be our right flank.' Private John Pitt, 8/AIF, noted in his diary entry for 25 April 1915:

When we got to the first ridge inland, we were ordered by Lieut-Colonel Gartside[3] to strengthen the line already established there and dig in as he considered that all our fellows out in front would have to retire there before night, as they had met with considerable forces of the enemy and were losing heavily. Tom Keddie[4] and I dug in next to one another and then turned our attention on a very troublesome sniper on our left front, he moved about and we could not get a good shot at him as he was so hard to see in the thick scrub. He eventually got Tom K in the calf of the leg, the bullet must have passed over me. I was dug in deeper than he was. Bandaged him up and took him to the rear, he gave me his automatic. Our fellows in front were

90

compelled to retire during the afternoon after losing very heavily, especially in officers. Entrenched as hard as we could at night, firing all night. Shrapnel did us the most damage, and we had no artillery on land, and the warships were of course at a disadvantage, although they did splendid work. The Turks made repeated attacks during the night but were always repulsed.

Major Henry Gordon Bennett, second in command of 6/AIF, was amongst those 'fellows in front'. Earlier he had led about 300 of his men forward from Bolton's Ridge up onto Sniper's Ridge and then forward to Pine Ridge, but was then wounded and had to return. Small pockets of men were all along this ridge in advanced and fairly strong positions overlooking Legge Valley. A platoon under Lieutenant Levy, 5/AIF, as mentioned by Fred Symonds, had advanced across the exposed plateau and, with a group from 6/AIF, had found and taken cover in an abandoned Turkish trench and artillery position. Located at the northern end of Pine Ridge where it joins Lone Pine, it was found to be reinforced with pine logs and covered in clay. Two companies of 8/AIF, one led by Major John Sergeant, were in the process of reinforcing Bennett's 6/AIF when a shell landed amongst them, mortally wounding John Sergeant. The two companies continued and were able to establish a rough line to the north of Bennett. These

The view from Bolton's Ridge looking across the scrub-covered spurs down towards the objective of Gaba Tepe.

Mate O' Mine. The grave of Major John Sergeant.

advanced parties held on for most of the day, until they were eventually forced to retire in the late afternoon.

Around 5.30 pm the men on Pine Ridge came under a heavy and sustained attack from 1/27 Battalion, which by nightfall had succeeded in outflanking their position. The remaining body of men was quickly encircled and, fighting a last stand action, many were killed to a man. Those killed included Bennett's younger brother, Sergeant Godfrey Bennett, who is today commemorated on the Lone Pine Memorial. Their bodies, identifiable by their coloured battalion patches, were discovered in 1919 when their remains were found in small groups all along Pine Ridge. One group of five lay upon a small mound in a semi-circle which they had defended, whilst many others were found in the gullies to the rear of the ridge, probably the wounded

The forward position on Pine Ridge, as held by 6/AIF before they were overrun.

92

who had crawled there. Charles Bean later wrote that 'they needed no epitaph. It was enough that they lay on Pine Ridge'. A few men from 6/AIF did manage to escape before being surrounded, where they went on to join the next line of defence on Bolton's Ridge.

After Pine Ridge was recaptured by 1/27 Battalion, the Turks continued to filter forward across the lower spurs of Lone Pine to threaten those on Bolton's Ridge. Reinforcing 27 Regiment was the long awaited arrival of 77 (Arab) Regiment, which began arriving just after dusk. They had been despatched by Kemal earlier in the morning, but made slow progress, partly due to having a longer march and also due to a false signal reporting another landing near Kum Tepe, whence the regiment was temporarily diverted to. Once it was known that no landing was taking place there, they were ordered to support 27 Regiment's attack on 400 Plateau. As both 27 and 57 Regiments were exhausted and extended over a wide area, Lieutenant Colonel Saib Bey, commanding 77 Regiment, was instructed by Kemal to enter the battle between the two.

Confusion and mayhem was to follow, which was not helped by the early shelling of the regiment when the navy spotted them moving over Third Ridge. As they crossed Legge Valley, some of the men began firing wildly in all directions, effectively firing into their own men. To the north was 57 Regiment and to the south was 27 Regiment, who were both unaware that 77 Regiment had come into the line between them, so each thought that the other had started firing. As soon as 77 Regiment got to the lower slopes of 400 Plateau and begun to be targets of Australian fire, many panicked and dispersed amongst the surrounding scrub and gullies. In their scattered positions to the rear of the line they continued to fire, inflicting casualties on both 27 and 57 Regiments. The Arabs were soon withdrawn, but not before they had pulled back men from 27 Regiment that were in forward positions on 400 Plateau. This temporarily left the majority of Lone Pine and Johnston's Jolly deserted of Turkish troops. It is not known if this was fully apparent to the Australians, but in their weakened state there is arguably little they could have done to exploit the situation. Kemal later withdrew 77 Regiment from the line completely and sent them to hold the quieter area south at Gaba Tepe. Major Mehmet Munir Bey's 72 (Arab) Regiment, however, were to prove more reliable, and supported 57 Regiment when it went into action south of Baby 700 during the early evening. The whole of 19th Division at this stage had been committed to the battle along with 27 Regiment (9th Division) which now came under the direct command of Kemal.

Adams Brothers

Two brothers from Mildura in Victoria also became casualties during the first day of the landing; Privates Frederick James Adams and Edgar Robert Colbeck Adams. Fred was born in Yorkshire, England and with his family immigrated to Australia when he was two. His young brother, Edgar, was born at Mildura. Fred became a fruit grower, and his brother was about to enter the field of surveying and engineering when the war broke out. Joining 8/AIF in 1914, they were soon on their way to Egypt for training.

Private Fred Adams, 868, was killed on 25 April 1915 and was buried in Artillery Road West Cemetery (later re-interned in Shell Green Cemetery). He was 25 years old. In Ron Austin's battalion history *Cobbers in Khaki*, veteran Bill Groves of C Company remembers Fred: *The shooting started and we got caught in the crossfire...* [the battalion was then given orders to dig in] *I was on the shovel and a fellow named Fred Adams was on the pick. He got shot through the forehead and he died instantly.*

Private Frederick James Adams, 8/AIF. (AWM H05906)

Private Edgar Adams, 1127, his 18-yea-old younger brother, was believed to be captured on 25 April 1915 and died whilst a Turkish prisoner of war. The circumstances surrounding his death are unknown, and it was not until November 1915 that anyone knew he was a prisoner. Originally posted missing after the landing, his fate became known when a member of 9/AIF found a

Private Edgar Robert Colbeck Adams, 8/AIF. (AWM H14064)

bottle on 1 November washed up on Montaza Beach near Alexandria in Egypt. The bottle contained a message that read: *Am prisoner about 2 miles from where we landed between the dried lake and the other – E.R.C. Adams 8 AIF.*

If Adams was held as a prisoner he did not appear on any of the PoW lists provided by the authorities, although we know today that casualty lists had many inaccuracies. Edgar is commemorated on the Lone Pine Memorial and his date of death is put on or about 25 April 1915.

Fellow Victorian, Private Fred Symonds, 5/AIF, noted in his diary entry on 20 May 1915:

Heard the other day that Fred and Rolun [sic] Adams, of Mildura, whom I know well, were killed and missing respectively since the first Sunday, so looks like both dead. Terribly hard for their parents, as they are the only two boys in the family. I feel upset over it, as they were such decent chaps.[5]

From about 8.00 pm the men defending Bolton's Ridge reported hearing whistle blowing and bugle calls in the gullies ahead, but it was not until 10.00 pm that the Turks attacked. Under cover of darkness, waves of Turks came running over the Wheatfield yelling 'Allah, Allah, Allah.' The machine guns and rifle fire from 8/AIF and 4/AIF, defending the area, destroyed the attack before they reached their trenches. Some Turks got within fifty yards of the line, but were dispersed by a bayonet charge. The survivors melted away and, apart from a half-hearted attack later on during the night, the area fell quiet. From the sea up to Bolton's Ridge, across Lone Pine and Johnston's Jolly there was now a rough line established, in front of which the ground lay open, covered by the dead and dying.

1. Later commissioned, Blackburn went on to win the Victoria Cross at Pozières, France. Lance Corporal Philip De Quetteville Robin was killed 28 April 1915. Commemorated on Lone Pine Memorial.
2. Unpubished diary of Lt Col William Malone, Wellington Battalion (Alexander Tunbull Library: MSX-2552).
3. Lieutenant Colonel Robert Gartside, VD, killed in action 8 May 1915. Buried Redoubt Cemetery, Helles.
4. Private Tom Keddie, 856, 8/AIF, a state school teacher at Byaduk, Victoria. Evacuated from Gallipoli, he recovered from his gunshot wound, but was later medically discharged with neurasthenia (shell-shock).
5. Five other sets of brothers were known to be killed on 25 April 1915: Sergeant E.R. Larkin and Private M.J. Larkin (1/AIF), Private M. Foley and Private P. Foley (6/AIF), Private A.W. Veitch and Private D. Veitch (7/AIF), Private C. Reid (7/AIF) and Second Lieutenant M.L. Reid (11/AIF), Private F.H. B. Adcock and Private F.B. Adcock (11/AIF).

Chapter Four

Baby 700

I am with you boys to the finish

In the early morning, Captain Eric Tulloch, 11/AIF,[1] leading a small party of men, about sixty in number, from Russell's Top, across the Nek and working his way around the inland slopes of Baby 700, had made steady progress. He had been driving the thin line of defenders from 2/27 Battalion back inland and, pushing on at all costs, he had soon reached the inland slopes of Big 700 (Battleship Hill). This hill was the prearranged rendezvous point for 11/AIF and, looking around, they were the first to arrive. Ahead lay Chunuk Bair and about a mile behind that was Hill 971, the highest peak of the Sari Bair range. It is recorded that Tulloch and his men were so intent on making for the ridges that lay ahead that few of them noticed the triangle of shining water, the Narrows, that lay off to the east. Tulloch was soon faced with a problem: up ahead was a deep ravine, above which a small group of Turks had gathered to defend the position. Unable to advance any further, Tulloch temporarily halted his men and took cover in the scrub to await reinforcements.

Captain Eric Tulloch, 11/AIF, who managed to advance to Battleship Hill.

Lieutenant Colonel Mustafa Kemal, commander of 19th Ottoman Division, was at his headquarters in Boghali early on that morning when he heard firing from the direction of Ari Burnu. He received a report about 6.30 am from Colonel Halil Sami Bey, commander of 9th Ottoman Division, giving the news of a landing. Upon hearing that the enemy had reached the heights above Ari Burnu, Kemal immediately ordered two-thirds of his division (57 and 77 Regiments, including a mountain battery) towards the fighting, leaving 72 Regiment in reserve. 57 Regiment, recruited from the province of Edirne near the Turkish Bulgarian/Greek border, was thought to be the most reliable regiment in his division. The other two, 72 (Arab) Regiment and 77 (Arab) Regiment, mainly comprised Syrian Arabs, many quite old and most unable to speak Turkish, and believed to be less trustworthy. Kemal was originally instructed by General Liman von Sanders to send only a single battalion as he believed the landing at Gaba Tepe was only a feint, and the main blow would fall at Bulair, where he retained two divisions for its defence. As the Australians were reported making for the heights of Chunuk Bair and Koja Chemen Tepe (Hill 971), this was enough to convince Kemal that this was not a feint. Kemal personally led the three battalions of 57 Regiment, which was already on parade as part of a planned morning exercise, towards the heights. Kemal realised that he needed to get there before the Australians as this highground was key to the area; a race, unknown to the Australians, was on.

Mustafa Kemal reached the summit of Chunuk Bair just after 10.00 am, which was almost two hours after Sefik Aker's 27 Regiment had engaged the Australians on the battlefield in the south. The delay was due to a tougher march over a rough, road-less terrain, which was covered in scrub and intersected by a maze of gullies and spurs, with only the odd goat track for ease of movement. When he arrived with the forward elements of 57 Regiment, he could clearly see the invasion force in the bay below. Continuing on with his ADC and two other senior officers towards Baby 700, he soon met a small and exhausted group of soldiers from 2/27 Battalion who were in retreat. Kemal stopped them in their tracks and asked why they were withdrawing. They replied that they were out of ammunition and that the enemy were advancing and pointed to a group of enemy skirmishers (probably Tulloch's men) that had advanced past Baby 700. Immediately, Kemal made them fix their bayonets and ordered them to lie down on the ground. As they lay down the Australians halted and also lay down, thus gaining Kemal the valuable time he needed to deploy his troops.

Major Zeki Bey, 1/57 Battalion commanding officer, took his men forward over the inland side of Baby 700 from the southerly direction of Mortar Ridge, whilst Captain Ata Bey manoeuvred his 2/57 Battalion over the seaward side of Battleship Hill to attack Baby 700 from its northern slopes. Kemal kept Captain Hairi Bey's 3/57 Battalion in reserve. It was about 10.30 am when Tulloch noticed more Turks coming from the direction of Chunuk Bair and also parties making their way around the seaward side of Battleship Hill and towards Mortar Ridge to his right. Large numbers of Turks were observed collecting together in the dead ground ahead and, with both flanks now threatened, Tulloch decided to withdraw back from his advanced position on Incebayir Ridge. The strength and sudden speed of the Turkish counter attack had taken the Australians by surprise, as until then they had had a virtually unchallenged path to the heights of the Sari Bair Range.

With the Australians in forward positions now falling back upon Baby 700, a new battle was about to begin. The importance of Baby 700 was recognised by both the Australians and Turks. This hill needed to be retained by the Australians for them to continue the push towards Hill 971: if the hill was lost, this strategic position would seriously threaten continuation of the advance. The hill would change hands several times during the course of the battle; eventually falling to the Turks after Kemal's relentless attack and overwhelming numbers proved decisive in crushing the Anzac defence. It was here that Kemal issued his famous order:

I don't order you to attack, I order you to die. In the time it takes us to die, other troops and commanders can come and take our places.

With 57 Regiment deployed, Kemal then moved further south and set up his field headquarters on Third Ridge at a place

Mustafa Kemal.

called Scrubby Knoll, later known to the Turks as Kemal Yere (Kemal's Hill). Australian scouts from 10/AIF had only been in this position a couple of hours before. Just north of the Knoll, Kemal brought his mountain battery into action against the Australian positions on Baby 700 and those around the head of Monash Valley.

When Tulloch advanced his party just before 7.00 am he had left Captain Peter Lalor, 12/AIF, digging a semi-circular defensive line just short of The Nek, thus protecting Russell's Top from counter-attack. The area had become fairly quiet except for the occasional long range shot. Bean described the lull in the fighting:

The sun had risen on a glorious spring morning, and only scattered, distant shots now broke the silence on most of the battlefield. Men felt that the greatest difficulties were past.

At about 8.30 am, having received no word on Tulloch's progress and hearing firing ahead, Lalor decided to go onto Baby 700 to see for himself the situation ahead. With him went Major Sydney Beresford Robertson, commanding B Company 9/AIF, who had brought a small

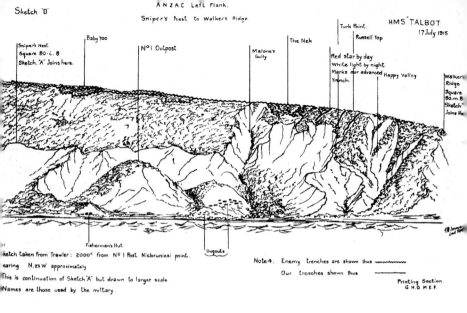

Turk Point.

Russell Top

The Nek

Baby 700

N°1 Outpost

Malone's Gully

Sniper's Nest
Square 80·i. 8
Sketch "A" Joins here.

Red star by day
White light by night
Marks our advanced Happy Valley
Trench.

Walker's
Ridge
Square
80.m.B
Sketch"
Joins He

Fisherman's Hut

Dugouts

Sketch taken from Trawler : 2000° from N° 1 Post. Nicbruniesi point.

earing N.23W approximately

This is continuation of Sketch 'A' but drawn to larger scale

Names are those used by the military.

Note 4. Enemy trenches are shown thus ~~~~~~~~~
Our trenches shown thus _____

Printing Section.
G.H.Q. M.E.F.

party of men with him. Robertson, a pre-war lawyer's clerk from Ipswich, Queensland, had become separated from most of his company when his boat had drifted further north than the others and beached itself somewhere near the Sphinx. Robertson took his men to the seaward side of Baby 700 and established a firing line above a deep gully that ran west of Baby 700, later called Malone's Gully. Lalor had his men set up their position on the inland slope of the hill just below the crest, overlooking Second Ridge. Lieutenant Ivor Margetts, one of Lalor's men, took up the central position with his platoon, on the far side of the crest. Once over the summit, Margetts had a clear view of Big 700, but there was no sign of any other advanced party, including that of Tulloch, who would have been hidden from view by its inland spurs. Bullets quickly started to fall on Margetts' position, forcing him and his men to lie down amongst the scrub. He soon noticed that Turks were advancing over the seaward shoulder of Big 700 and then disappearing behind one of the spurs that led from Baby 700.

Opposite Robertson's position, at the head of Malone's Gully, was a Turkish trench from which two communication trenches ran back behind one of the scrub-covered spurs. The Australians had briefly captured this trench in the morning but were quickly driven out by enfilade machine-gun fire. Two further attempts in the afternoon to capture the trench also failed, again due to enfilade fire from the flank. Tulloch, who was far advanced on the right, had already pulled back in fear that the Turks who were coming round the seaward slopes would outflank his position. When the party pulled back from the Turkish trench on the seaward side, the left looked very exposed and this unfortunately led to the whole of the flank retiring. Margetts, seeing Robertson's retirement, then ordered his men back over the crest of Baby 700 and set up a position about 150 yards behind the summit. Behind Margetts, Lalor was still in position on the lower slopes towards his right. This unfortunate action, which was due more to lack of communication and awareness of the situation than enemy attack, left the slopes of Baby 700 open for the Turks to filter forward.

By 11.00 am 1/57 Battalion had followed the Australian withdrawal and, with little fighting, they had forced the Australians back from both Battleship Hill and Baby 700. The Turks had got as far as The Nek before they were finally halted by the concentrated firepower of the Australians. This fighting was being observed by Sinclair-MacLagan from his headquarters on MacLaurin's Hill, who immediately sent a message to Major General Bridges saying Russell's Top was 'seriously threatened'. It was not until this time that 1 Brigade had started to land in sufficient numbers that they were available to aid the troops on the left flank. With the right flank along Second Ridge now secure, Bridges ordered a company from 1/AIF and two from 2/AIF towards The Nek and Baby 700.

The first of the reinforcements to reach the area was D Company, 1/AIF under Major Blair Inskip Swannell, who reached the position by climbing up from Rest Gully and onto Russell's Top. With Swannell was Major F.J. Kindon, second in command of 1/AIF, and together they reached the lower slopes of Baby 700, where they met the remnants of Robertson's and Lalor's men. Swannell, an old international rugby footballer with a reputation for playing rough, had a premonition that he was going to be killed, promising Kindon the bottle of whisky he was carrying in his pack, and remarking: 'I shan't come through today.' Just after 11.00 am, with the added weight of Kindon's fresh troops, Swannell led his company, together with the survivors of 11/AIF and 12/AIF, in a charge to retake the hill. This took the Turks by surprise and for the second time that day the Australians were over the crest of Baby 700. Margetts took up position in the middle, flanked by Swannell on the right and a newly arrived company from 2/AIF reinforcing the left. The Turks poured rifle, machine-gun and shrapnel fire into the new Australian line and, as there was no trench to take cover in, all they could do was to lie prone and, keeping as still as possible, return fire. Casualties soon mounted; Robertson, who was already thrice wounded, was killed whilst rising from the cover of the

101

A British Lion – Major Blair Inskip Swannell.

scrub. Before he died he said, 'Carry on, Rigby', and then moments later Rigby [Lieutenant W.J. Rigby, 9/AIF] was killed. Swannell met his death in a similar fashion; whilst kneeling to show his men how to take better aim, he was shot dead. C.E.W. Bean mentions Private Reginald Donkin, 1/AIF, as having 'two bullets in his left leg; a third pierced the top of his hat and cut his hair; one ripped his left sleeve; three hit his ammunition pouches and exploded the bullets; another struck his entrenching tool'. Donkin was killed later in August. These types of wound and close shaves were not uncommon in other accounts of the battle and goes to show how intense the fighting was and how exposed the men were to the fusillade of small-arms and shrapnel fire.

Over on the left flank, the men who were holding out on the seaward slope on the far side of Malone's Gully were fighting a bitter struggle with the Turks. Ata's 2/57 Battalion had deployed down the seaward spurs of the heights towards Fisherman's Hut and, along with elements of Zeki's 1/57 Battalion, subjected the Australians to murderous fire. Even with added support from Lalor's men at The Nek, the ferocity of the Turkish attack eventually forced the Australian left flank back across the gully. For the second time this flank had to retire from their position; still clinging to the position forward of the crest was Margetts' group of men, but they were quickly dwindling. Bean remarked that: 'The strain on the men lying out upon the forward slope was becoming almost unbearable.' On the right Kindon was holding out but was also in a position that was quickly becoming untenable. Reinforcements were again in desperate need, but so far no more were forthcoming.

As soon as the Auckland and Canterbury Battalions from the New Zealand Brigade had landed, Bridges sent them immediately to bolster the Anzac left. The New Zealand Brigade was under the temporary command of Brigadier General H.B. Walker, who replaced Colonel Francis Johnston who had become ill just prior to the landing. After the initial delay in getting ashore and then being redirected onto Plugge's Plateau, at about 1.30 pm 16th (Waikato) Company of the Auckland Battalion was the first to begin reinforcing Kindon's thinning line of

Australians, which by this stage had dwindled to half a dozen unwounded men. The New Zealanders then extended the line down the landward slope of the hill, where a large gap had formed between Kindon and those further down on the upper shoulder of Mortar Ridge.

About 3.00 pm the Turks started shelling the Australian positions around The Nek and the heads of Malone's Gully on the left and Monash Valley to the right. At the same time the fire upon Kindon and the New Zealanders that were protecting the right flank of Baby 700 grew. Kindon later said:

We were faced with a machine gun on the flank and shrapnel in front and rifle fire. We were up against a trench and couldn't shoot much. We could simply lie there, and they couldn't come on while we were lying there.

The Turks were trying to break through on the right, towards Monash Valley, but their first frontal attack was soon broken by the steady rifle fire of the Aucklanders. The Turks continued to probe Kindon's right and, with casualties quickly mounting and no reinforcements, he reluctantly had to relinquish the position. He pulled back the remnants of the line about seventy yards to the rear of their original position, where Major David Grant's 2nd (South Canterbury) Company of the Canterbury Battalion and two New Zealand machine guns had set up.

Further up the line, Margetts had left the crest several times to go back for reinforcements and ammunition, mustering what he could. The situation on Baby 700 had become critical and casualties were mounting; most of the men that went forward onto the hill to reinforce the firing line disappeared into the fighting, many never being seen again. The exhausted Margetts was eventually ordered by Lalor to stay in the support position and to send up support and stretcher-bearers, whilst Lalor took forward what men he had to reinforce 2/AIF on the left of the hill. Holding Baby 700 was dependent on the successful defence of the flanks; if they could not hold back the Turks there, the hill would be lost.

By 3.15 pm Lalor had advanced the line across the head of Malone's Gully again and onto the spur on the far side. There was a fair amount of Turkish rifle fire being directed onto Lalor's position that appeared to be coming from the lower slopes that ran down to the beach. By this time 2/57 Battalion had retaken Fisherman's Hut and were in positions around No.1 Outpost and up along the high ground towards Malone's Gully. In an effort to find out exactly where this was coming from, Lalor stood up and said: 'Now then, 12th Battalion', and was immediately shot dead. Lalor had left behind his famous family sword, which was reputedly used during the Eureka Rebellion, at The Nek before he went forward. It was later picked up by Lance-Corporal 'Harry' Freame, 1/AIF, but was then lost during the heat of the battle. It is understood that Private Clive De Mole, 11/AIF, then found, but later lost it near the beach. Where the sword is today, nobody knows.

Major David Grant, Canterbury Battalion, killed on Baby 700.

Back on Plugge's Plateau frustration was being felt by the New Zealand battalion commanders, Lieutenant Colonel Arthur Plugge (Auckland Battalion) and Lieutenant Colonel Douglas MacBean Stewart (Canterbury Battalion). They had not been able to make contact with their forward companies for most of the afternoon. To find out what was going on, Stewart gathered as many men as he could from the plateau and, with two companies of his Battalion, he climbed up Walker's Ridge and advanced towards The Nek. He arrived just after Lalor was killed and re-established the defensive line across The Nek. To his left, ahead of Malone's Gully, were the remnants of Lalor's men and a few others from 2/AIF who were extended along the summit and seaward slopes of Baby 700. On Stewart's right along the inland slope was the composite line made up of Kindon's men, now commanded by Major Grant. The line was made up of men from the Auckland Battalion and Australians from 1/AIF, 2/AIF, 11/AIF and 12/AIF. Stewart had the Canterbury Battalion deployed with two companies on the left and two on the right.

The situation was still deteriorating for the Anzacs as the Turks continued to attack their weakening positions. Much of the fighting that had begun as exchanges of rifle and machine-gun fire soon developed into fierce hand-to-hand mêlées as bayonet charges from both sides tried to take the advantage. By 4.00 pm the Turks changed their tactics and began to lay down heavy shrapnel fire on the hill and surrounding areas. Noticing that some of the men on the left were being hard-pressed by a Turkish counter-attack, Lieutenant Colonel Stewart went back and brought up 200 Australians, 'encouraging them in every way, and fearlessly exposing himself'. Whilst leading these men he was hit in the head by shrapnel, killing him instantly. Private A. Pauline of B Company, Canterbury Battalion, mentioned in a letter home the manner of Stewart's death:

Yes, poor Colonel MacBean Stewart died a noble death. He was directing the boys' fire with his walking stick when he was

suddenly hit in the head, death being instantaneous. He only had
about three hours' life on the battlefield.[2]

Douglas Stewart, a father of three from Christchurch, New Zealand, is commemorated on the Lone Pine Memorial.

With insufficient machine guns and no artillery support, lack of adequate reinforcements and their flanks in the air, the Anzac position was near breaking point. At about 4.30 pm all three battalions of Colonel Hüseyin Avni Bey's 57 Regiment, with support from the blue uniformed Broussa Gendarmerie Field Battalion, made a combined attack on the weakened Anzac line. Lieutenant Alfred John Shout, 1/AIF, noted their blue uniforms and recorded that:

during the afternoon the Turks began to come on – blue
coated fellows. Before then the Turks we saw lying in the slope
were all khaki.

For about thirty minutes the line held, but the weight of the attack soon overwhelmed the small band of Anzacs that were holding out on the hill. They were forced back over the crest of Baby 700 for the last time. Captain Oppenheim, observing the battle from sea, wrote:

4.30 p.m. the Landing is not going very well here now.
Apparently our men advanced a bit too far on the other side of
the hill and about 3 p.m. came in for a regular storm of shrapnel
from all sides ... As a result, having no guns themselves at the
time, the enemy's howitzers were able to fire undisturbed, doing
tremendous execution. After the shrapnel mentioned above our
men had to retire, and could be seen running back over the crest
of the hill, carrying their wounded with them.

Many of the survivors retreated back across The Nek, or ran into the safety of Malone's Gully and Monash Valley, whilst others mistakenly fled into Turkish held Mule Valley and were either killed or captured. One of several Anzacs captured during the first day was Bugler Frederick Ashton, 11/AIF. Ashton, from 13 Platoon, D Company, was caught when trying to obtain a stretcher for a wounded man. He found himself cut off on Baby 700, so tried to make his way back through Monash Valley, but mistakenly ended up in Mule Valley instead, where he was captured by a small party of Turks. He spent the rest of the war as a prisoner until repatriated from Constantinople on 16 November 1918. One of those who was not so lucky was Private Thomas Hayes Burgess, 12/705, Auckland Battalion. Burgess lay wounded on Baby 700 for three days where he was clubbed or bayoneted by every Turk that passed. He was eventually taken away by Turkish stretcher-bearers and ended up in Tash Kushla Hospital where he died five months later on 25 September 1915. Burgess is buried in the CWGC Haidar Pasha Cemetery in Istanbul, where many other PoWs from the campaign are also buried.

The Turkish 57 Regiment had sustained about fifty percent casualties by this stage and, although they had succeeded in recapturing Battleship Hill and now Baby 700, the momentum of their earlier advance had slowed. Approaching The Nek, their attack met stiff resistance from a thinly held line of about 50 Anzac survivors, under a New Zealand sergeant, with three machine guns. They were holding the horseshoe-shaped trench and rifle pits that Lalor had originally dug during the morning. Close behind them, in support, were the remnants of Stewart's Canterbury Battalion and, unknown to both parties, were men from B and C Companies, 2/AIF, under Lieutenant Colonel George Braund. They had been ordered up from reserve about 1.30 pm, and had ascended the steep goat track of Walker's Ridge, to dig in and hold the ground where the ridge meets Russell's Top.

One of the officers who had survived the fighting on Baby 700 was Lieutenant Alfred Shout, 1/AIF, who was awarded the Military Cross and a Mention in Despatches for his efforts during the battle. New Zealand born and a Boer War veteran, Shout was later posthumously awarded the Victoria Cross for bravery at Lone Pine in August 1915. Shout had gathered approximately 200 stragglers of different battalions in the beach area, and led them back into the line. Wounded several times, he helped hold back the Turkish attack on Russell's Top. Even when wounded again by a bullet that rendered his arm useless, he refused to leave the battlefield, telling his men: 'I am with you boys to the finish.'

Captain C.K. Millar, 2/AIF later remarked of Shout:

> Here was a man – a born leader, with wonderful control. I first saw him when we lay behind a ridge with bullets cutting the leaves and twigs of the bushes just above our heads. Hell! I was scared; almost every second man was dead, and hope was lost! I prayed as I had been taught as a kid. If somebody had said run for the beach I would have been an easy winner. Along the ridge came an officer, just strolling, carrying a stick and a revolver – it was Shout! A brave leader who sensed the position, he rushed us over the skyline into a better possie; gave fire orders, and passed on, unhurt. This was my first experience of individual courage – the stuff we call 'guts' – and I've never forgotten Shout.[3]

Further inland, on the opposite side of the valley, the other survivors from the Baby 700 fighting were holding fresh positions on Pope's Hill, Dead Man's Ridge, Bloody Angle and Quinn's Post. The collapse of Baby 700 had a domino effect on those holding Mortar Ridge, one of its southern spurs. Those in position on Bloody Angle and Quinn's Post could see the Australians on the ridge in front, but could not respond to their calls for ammunition and reinforcements as the Turks had this area also under fire, and any movement from cover was beaten back by rifle and machine-gun fire. Captain Charles Leer, a Sydney schoolteacher, with half a company from 3/AIF, was one of those in front on the lower part of Mortar Ridge. Between Leer and Kindon, on the upper part of this ridge, was Captain Harold Jacobs, 1/AIF. From these positions they were providing valuable flank protection for those further up on Baby 700. As soon as Leer's party reached the ridge he observed large parties of Turks coming towards him from the direction of Scrubby Knoll. As Baby 700 fell, the high ground of Mortar Ridge that was held by Jacobs also fell, pushing him back to Dead Man's Ridge. Leer, who received a posthumous Mention in Despatches, and about sixty men continued to hold out, but they soon succumbed to the ferocity of the Turkish attack. When the left flank fell back the Turks were able to get around Leer's northern flank, which signalled the end for the few remaining defenders. Under fierce attack since 2.30 pm and the scene of some of the most violent

Captain Peter Lalor, killed on Baby 700.

fighting that first day, small parties of men held out until about 5.00 pm, without reinforcements and with ammunition supplies nearly exhausted, before they were forced to withdraw. Leer was killed and is today commemorated on the Lone Pine Memorial.

Behind Mortar Ridge Major Thomas Dawson, second-in-command of the Auckland Battalion, had been digging in at the top end of Shrapnel Valley, at the apex where Second Ridge meets Russell's Top. He commanded a mixed bunch of Australian and New Zealanders in a series of unconnected rifle pits, behind which was a sheer drop back into Monash Valley. This position was marked on the maps as I.3 sq 224, and was soon to pass into legend as Quinn's Post. In between Dawson and Braund's party on Walker's Ridge was an undefended gap that Major General Bridges was anxious to fill before the Turks could exploit it. To do this he had to wait for reinforcements to arrive.

At about 6.00 pm 16/AIF was ashore with its commanding officer, Lieutenant Colonel Harold Pope. To fill this gap he led his Southern and Western Australians along with two platoons of the Auckland Battalion to the head of Monash Valley, to a prominent spur that was soon known as Pope's Hill. Private Reginald Lushington, C Company, 16/AIF, described the arrival of his unit:

> *We were greeted with thankfulness by the remains of the 12th Battalion, who were resting under the shelter of the cliffs. "Who are you?" they asked. "16th," we replied. "Good on you, the 16th; give it to the blighters, there's only 60 of us left."*[4]

Other small parties who were still out in front, like those under Captain Jacobs, then fell back onto Pope's Hill and helped set up the new defensive position.

Silas, also in 16/AIF, noted:

> *It is commencing to get dark – we are now climbing the heights. I am given a pick to carry – half way up I had to drop it, it was far too much for me. The lads on the top of the hill are glad to see us for they have been having an anxious time holding their position on the Ridge – "Pope's Hill"– they had scarcely time to throw up more than a little earth to take cover behind. The noise is now Hell. Now some of the chaps are getting it – groans and screams everywhere, calls for ammunition and stretcher-bearers, though how the latter are going to carry stretchers along such precipitous and sandy slopes beats me. Now commencing to take some of the dead out of the trenches; this is horrible; I wonder how long I can stand it.*

Colonel Pope had got his men into position on the hill but had little information as to the situation around him. He was led to believe that Indian

Lieutenant Colonel Harold Pope, 16/AIF.

108

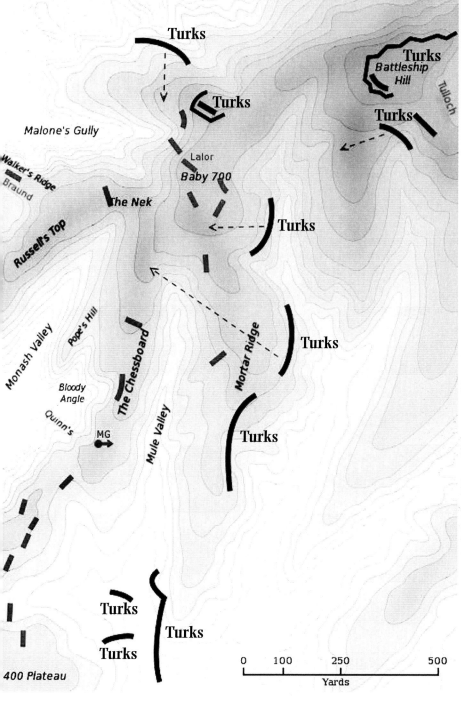

Baby 700 – Afternoon 25 April 1915.

troops were positioned to his left, so sent Lieutenant W.E. Elston with Private Lushington, who could speak Tamil and Pathan, forward towards the area. It was dark and Pope could hear Elston and Lushington talking to someone ahead. The battalion adjutant, Captain R.T.A. McDonald, went forward to investigate, shortly followed by Pope himself. Suddenly Pope, seeing several armed men with rifles and bayonets, realised that they were Turks, and dived into a gully, escaping amidst a flurry of rifle shots. McDonald, Elston and Lushington were not so lucky and were taken prisoner. There are several accounts during the first day of Turks being mistaken for Indian troops and ruses being played by the Turks to lure the Anzacs out of cover. Some succeeded; others were met by rifle fire. When it was confirmed by divisional headquarters that no Indian troops were in the Anzac sector, Sinclair-MacLagan ordered that anyone in front of the firing line was to be shot.

By dusk Kemal had brought forward 3/57 Battalion and ordered

Dead Man's Ridge   Quinn's Post   Monash Gully   Johnston's Jolly

them to concentrate their attack on the small group of men to Pope's left, who were holding the horseshoe trench on Russell's Top. The Anzacs in this shallow trench managed to defend the position well, although many were wounded, and against all the odds they held the line and awaited reinforcements. As it got dark the Turks had managed to get around on either flank, as well as behind them, which made the position untenable. The Canterbury support line, believing that those ahead had already been overrun, had withdrawn during the night. This left no option to the small and gallant band holding the horseshoe other than to withdraw. In contact with the Turks all the way, they retired to the end of Russell's Top and set up a new defensive position in the old Turkish trench that Lieutenant Colonel Clarke had cleared during the morning.

Captain Oppenheim wrote:

7.20 p.m. We have now for nearly two hours been carrying out a fairly heavy bombardment on the reverse slopes of the ridge,

Lone Pine Pope's Hill

showing that our men have been driven back to the crest line. I presume they want to shake the enemy before nightfall so as to reduce his chances of counter-attacking.

The lack of organisation of ships' fire is distressing. At 7.40 p.m. the soldiers requested us urgently to fire at a trench in a certain "square". The Queen *apparently ignored the signal. Had observers been sent ashore to spot fall of shot we could have smashed up any number of enemy guns.*

A small party of Turks, from Captain Hairi Bey's 3/57 Battalion, had broken through the thinly held line at The Nek and had infiltrated along the inland side of Russell's Top. There, above Monash Valley, they could fire into the rear of the men on Pope's Hill and across the other side of the valley to positions

111

on Second Ridge. The seaward side was still protected by Braund's men who were lying out in the scrub by Walker's Ridge, defending any Turkish probes. The Turkish penetration on Russell's Top temporarily split the left and right flanks of the Anzac firing line and, if exploited, could have been a decisive blow to the Anzacs. However the Turks had insufficient numbers so had to withdraw before dawn. With their backs against the wall, the line of surviving Anzac riflemen, supported by machine guns and naval artillery support, had saved the left flank from virtual annihilation.

1. Eric William Tulloch survived Gallipoli and the remainder of the war, only to be murdered by a burglar at a guest house in East Melbourne in May 1926.
2. Letter was published in the *Wanganui Herald*, 16/9/15.
3. Millar, Captain C.K. MC, 'Control Over Fear: The Secret Of Leadership'. Reveille Vol.9, No.8 (1936).
4. Lushington, R.F., *A Prisoner With The Turks 1915-1918*, (1923), p.4.

Chapter Five

The Night

… you have got through the difficult business; now you only have to dig, dig, dig, until you are safe.

In all the confusion, by mid-morning the landing had appeared to go well. The troops had advanced from the beach and through the surrounding hills and had started to reach Third Ridge and the high ground around Baby 700. By midday the situation had changed quickly. Turkish reserves in some force had contained the advance and the forward Anzac positions were soon becoming threatened. Shelled almost continuously by Turkish artillery without any effective reply, the Anzac line was steadily being weakened and demoralised. Dispersed, tired and confused groups of men, often without officers, were holding on as best they could, hoping that sufficient reinforcements would allow them to continue their advance. Stragglers as well as the wounded were drifting back from the front, many being found wandering through or taking shelter in the gullies, or making their way to the already congested beach. The non-wounded were soon organised into carrying parties to take ammunition and water to the front, whilst the wounded were cared for as best possible. Morale was taking a downturn.

These factors negated the fact that the Anzacs still outnumbered the Turks almost two-to-one, a fact unknown to command at this time. There were approximately 15,000 Anzacs ashore compared to about 8,000 Turkish troops, but both sides were exhausted. With the Anzacs pinned into a small beachhead, less than two kilometres in length and under a kilometre from the shore, all they could do now was to wait for the British advance from Helles.

> *There was no rest, no lull, while the rotting dead lay all around us, never a pause in the whole of that long day that started at the crack of dawn. How we longed for nightfall! How we prayed for this ghastly day to end! How we yearned for the sight of the first dark shadow.*[1]

It was beginning to get chilly; and then a steady drizzling rain began to add more misery to the death and pain already suffered.

Close by Russell's Top, 16/AIF were still holding Pope's Hill. Signaller Silas wrote:

> *It had been raining a little, I found it almost impossible to*

keep my foothold, I kept slipping down all the way along.
Colonel Pope seemed very worried and tired; have just heard
from our Signal Lieutenant Wilton that Sergeant Major Emmett
badly wounded in abdomen. Turks playing funny bugle calls all
night long and yelling out, always in English. Bursts of fire from
our men – officers doing all they can to stop it as we are getting
short of ammunition.

Sergeant Major Verner Allen Emmett died of his wounds a couple of
days later and was buried at sea. Lieutenant Signal Officer Eric
Arundel Wilton survived Gallipoli. Throughout the night the Turks
continued to put pressure on the Anzac positions, and many in isolated
positions became victims to the onslaught.

Darkness came at long last, but there was no cessation of that
fire. The Turks came streaming out of the night, gigantic waves
of them, mad, brainless charges which cost them thousands of
lives. We held fast. Stalkers and snipers crept through the scrub
of what was now No Man's Land, fired upon the men who had got
adrift, gone too far ahead when we started to dig; shot, stabbed,
slashed unmercifully at the wounded lying out there … all night
we dug and fired, dug and fired – till we fell asleep in our holes.[2]

The situation was dire for the Anzacs, and there were doubts amongst
the high command that they could stand the strain of another day.
There were an estimated 5000 casualties (500 dead, 2500 wounded and
2000 missing). Those that held the line were in poor condition, and
reinforcements were few, or still out at sea, as was most of the artillery.
Medical facilities were atrocious, with too few personnel and transport
to cope adequately with the number of wounded. The Turks, who had
been quick to counter-attack, were estimated to be in force and were
punishing the Anzac lines with their artillery. They were also on the
high ground and now, with the Anzacs encircled, the door for any
further advance had been shut. The two Anzac divisional commanders,
Major General W.T. Bridges and Major General Sir A. Godley,
reviewed the situation. With the threat of a major counter-attack in the
morning and partially motivated by optimistic Staff reports that the
landing at Helles was a success, they were of the opinion that
evacuation was the best course of action. If they were to get off Anzac
the decision had to be made immediately. Birdwood landed later that
night and met with them. At first he was shocked by the idea of
abandoning Anzac, but when the full situation was explained to him,
he considered this course of action. A message was hastily written for
Sir Ian Hamilton:

Both my Divisional Generals and Brigadiers have represented to me that they fear their men are thoroughly demoralised by shrapnel fire, to which they have been subjected all day after exhaustion and gallant work in the morning. Numbers have dribbled back from the firing line and cannot be collected in this difficult country. Even the New Zealand Brigade, which has only recently engaged, lost heavily and is to some extent demoralised. If troops are subjected to shell fire again tomorrow morning there is likely to be a fiasco, as I have no fresh troops with which to replace those in firing line. I know my representation is most serious, but if we are to re-embark it must be at once.

There is some controversy how this message got to Hamilton, who was still aboard the flagship HMS *Queen Elizabeth*. The un-addressed message was written by Godley, signed by Birdwood and delivered initially to Rear-Admiral Thursby on HMS *Queen*. Thursby was opposed to the idea when he read the note. If the evacuation was to proceed, he estimated it would take two days to complete because of lack of transport. Be that as it may, he issued a precautionary order for the transports to stand-by for re-embarkation.

Captain Oppenheim recalled:

Rather curious – about 10 p.m. a piquet boat came round and told us "all available boats to go in at once to take off wounded". Then about midnight a boat came round and said transports were to close in and all boats to get ready to re-embark troops.

Sir Ian Hamilton.

When the message arrived at HMS *Queen Elizabeth*, which was on its way up from Cape Helles, Hamilton was asleep. He was woken and went to talk with the senior staff aboard the ship – de Robeck, Thursby, Braithwaite, Keyes, Cuncliffe-Owen and Carruthers. All except Thursby and Keyes were for the evacuation, fearing Anzac was on the verge of collapse. The latter, although realising that the situation appeared bad, feared that re-embarking two divisions whilst in contact with the enemy, even if they had the boats available, which they did not, would also be a disaster. Hamilton listened to these views but was solidly against evacuation. He had started to pen a reply when news arrived that the Australian submarine HMAS *AE2*, under the command of Lieutenant Commander Henry Stoker, had broken through the Dardanelles defences, sunk an enemy ship off Çanakkale and was now

in the Sea of Marmara. This news could not have come at a better time, thus adding weight to Hamilton's reply to Birdwood:

Your news is indeed serious. But there is nothing for it but to dig yourselves right in and stick it out. It would take at least two days to re-embark you, as Admiral Thursby will explain to you. Meanwhile, the Australian submarine has got up through the Narrows and has torpedoed a gunboat at Chunuk. Hunter-Weston, despite his heavy losses, will be advancing tomorrow, which should divert pressure from you. Make a personal appeal to your men and Godley's to make a supreme effort to hold their ground.

Ian Hamilton

P.S. you have got through the difficult business; now you only have to dig, dig, dig, until you are safe.

Aspinall-Oglander in his official history of the campaign wrote that:

The effect of this resolute and definite order, quickly taken ashore by Admiral Thursby, was electrical. All the vague doubts which had spread round the beach were settled. From that moment there was no further talk of evacuation at Anzac, and all ranks were soon filled with the same determination as the men in the front line, none of whom had had any idea that a retirement was under discussion.

Lieutenant Colonel William George Malone, commander of the Wellington Battalion, stated:

I know there were some questions amongst the generals of our having to re-embark. Personally I could see nothing to require it.

Australian submarine *AE2*.

117

The day ended with uncertainty of what tomorrow would bring. The rapid arrival of the Turkish reinforcements had stemmed the Anzac advance and they had recaptured Battleship Hill, Baby 700, Mortar Ridge, Pine Ridge and parts of Russell's Top and Lone Pine. Pushed back to the seaward edges of Second Ridge, the Anzacs continued to enlarge their shallow scrapes in the ground, hoping that they would afford them some protection from Turkish counter-attack or until the advance was renewed. On the other side of the line the Turks were also getting into position, using the cover of darkness to entrench. A temporary stalemate had been established, and what dawn would bring no one knew.

1. Craven, 'Digger' and Blackledge W.J., *Peninsula of Death*, (1936), p.32.
2. Ibid, p.32.
3. *AE2* went on to harass Turkish shipping in the Sea of Marmara until 30 April 1915, when she was damaged by a Turkish torpedo boat and had to be scuttled to avoid capture. The crew were taken prisoner.

Chapter Six

A New Day Dawns – 26 April 1915

I suppose I'll get my lead pill next

Dawn came on 26 April with no Turkish counter-attack. The overnight rain had ceased and, as the sky cleared, the sun rose and lit up the debris of battle below. Digging was still going on as positions were strengthened; elsewhere dugouts behind the front lines were taking form all over the scrub-covered slopes. With Anzac still in a state of complete disorganisation, with little opportunity to break out, all they could temporarily do was to hold the tiny bridgehead and wait for Sir Ian Hamilton's advance from the south. The Turks had suffered casualties almost as heavy as the Anzacs on the first day and were equally exhausted; both sides had fought themselves to a standstill. They had also, like the Anzacs, been committed piecemeal into the battle on the first day, and had equally missed opportunities to break the Anzac line. The day began with both sides licking their wounds, entrenching and filling the gaps in the line.

The first shelling of the day was begun by the navy and the few guns of the field artillery that had been landed. HMS *Queen Elizabeth* was offshore, and at 5.30 am started bombarding the Turkish gun positions with her 15-inch shrapnel shells.

> *Her shrapnel is a knockout. The explosion of the monstrous shell darkens the rising sun; the bullets cover an acre; the enemy seems stunned for a while after each discharge. One after the other she took on the Turkish guns along Sari Bair and swept the skyline with them.*[1]

Battleship HMS *Queen Elizabeth*, Sir Ian Hamilton's mobile HQ. The ship also provided valuable artillery support to those ashore.

During the night fresh troops from Colonel Monash's 4 Brigade had completed their transfer ashore and had reinforced the front line along Second Ridge. The Anzac position, that was so precarious only a few hours before, was now secure.

Lieutenant Colonel Malone, who had landed with the first two companies of the Wellington Battalion, wrote in his diary:

> Generals Birdwood and Godley ... were very disappointed when they found my Battalion (less half a Company) were still at sea. The Naval people for some unknown reason knocked off disembarkation. I got the General to wireless to the ships to carry on and about midnight the remaining one and a half Companies in Itonus got ashore and were sent to hold the ridge just above the beach. Malone was not pleased, as the Battalion tools were still aboard another transport; however he had soon got together a detail of men to go along the beach and collect all the tools they could. They got quite a number and then I sent them up to the ridge to enable the men to dig.

One of the men following on with the remaining half of Malone's battalion was 26-year-old former bank clerk, Corporal George Wallace Bollinger, 10/1024, Wellington Battalion.[2] He landed on Gallipoli during the night with the remaining part of the Battalion, and was immediately sent to reinforce the left flank upon Walker's Ridge:

> Monday 26th April 3.15 am. "Packs on" was roared out. Torpedo destroyers are alongside to take us ashore. 9.40 am. On shore in the thick of it. The first casualty in our company was in my section. Just before dawn we were on the destroyers waiting for surf boats to take us ashore. Stray bullets were landing around us and suddenly Private Tohill, who was standing just in front of me, dropped with a bullet through his shoulder.[3] Immediately after, Private Swayne was shot in the forehead. It was a relief to get ashore. The Australians were frightfully cut about effecting a landing yesterday. They say there are at least 6000 casualties. They did heroic work and the whole world will know of it. We are in a gully immediately behind the firing line and will be called in to relieve at any moment. The din and roar and whistle of the missiles is awful. As we sit here the ambulances are passing with wounded on the stretchers. 5.00 pm. We climbed heights to take our place in reserve, to the firing line. We are right in the fire zone and saw some awful sights.

Lieutenant Colonel Malone, who was later killed at Gallipoli, was critical of the way his men were committed to the battle, and wrote:

As the New Zealanders landed they were rushed up to the heights, mixed up higgledy-piggledy amongst themselves and with Australians with the result, in the case of my men anyhow (in my opinion), in serious avoidable loss.[4]

Birdwood placed Godley's NZ&A Division on the left flank to protect the bridgehead from the beach, up along Walker's Ridge, Russell's Top, across Pope's Hill and through Quinn's and Courtney's Posts. The right flank was protected by Bridges' 1st Australian Division, which continued the line from 400 Plateau and down Bolton's Ridge to the sea.

To the immediate right of Bollinger and the others up on Russell's Top was Ellis Silas, 16/AIF, who was still fighting on Pope's Hill. He started a diary entry for 26 April:

Pope's Hill – daybreak – down in the Valley, in the midst of this frightful hell of screaming shrapnel and heavy ordnance, the birds are chirping in the clear morning air and buzzing about from leaf to leaf, placidly going about its work, is a large bee – to think of what might be makes me weep, for fighting is continuing in all its fury. Our signallers have been nearly all wiped out – I suppose I'll get my lead pill next. It has now been a ceaseless cry of, "stretcher bearers on the left" – they seem to be having an awful time up there – one poor fellow has just jumped out of his dugout frightfully wounded in the arm; I bound it best I could, then had to dash off with another message. All along the route, scrambling along the side of the exposed incline, my comrades offered me a dugout for me to take cover as the

Anzac Cove, a few days after the landing.

Men from Pope's 16/AIF in Western Australia. A little over six months later they would be fighting at Gallipoli.

snipers are getting our chaps every minute, but as the messages are important I must take my chance. All along the route I keep coming across bodies of the poor chaps who have been less fortunate than I.

Still fighting furiously – now all signallers have been wiped out of A and B Companies except myself. Just had a shell each side of my dug-out – I felt in a real panic as it is a most horrible sensation. Our ships have missed the range and sent eleven shells into us in a minute; I do not think anyone has been hit – the Turks' trenches are so near ours that it is marvellous how accurately the ships find the range.

Silas, who survived his ordeal of the first few days on Gallipoli, was eventually evacuated on 17 May 1915 with neurasthenia, otherwise known as shell-shock. He left on the hospital ship *Galeka* and, after spending some time in an Egyptian hospital, was sent to England to convalesce, eventually being discharged from the army in August 1916 as medically unfit. Trained as an artist before the war, he continued this trade, finally settling back in England, his country of birth, in 1925, and dying in London in 1972.

Oppenheim continues his diary, describing the morning's bombardment on 26 April and wounded coming aboard. Talking to a New Zealand major who was wounded on Baby 700, he gave the following account:

He was on the left, where they were outnumbered by about four to one. The enemy fired at certain areas, although neither we nor they could see each other. They had the advantage of previous preparation and knew the exact ranges of certain areas we should have to pass over. We must have lost large numbers of wounded prisoners. One of the worst things is to hear the cries and groans and screams, such as, "for God's sake take me back" – the men of course have a horror of falling alive into the enemy's hands – and very rightfully too. It is feared that few of the wounded taken prisoner will ever be seen again, poor devils. A lot of the units on our left were simply decimated. The wounded lying on the ground would be hit several times…Our right flank got too far inland i.e. to the East, and so was unsupported and practically got the flank turned. It is difficult to hold the Australians back. Lack of proper communication and consequent lack of co-operation was to a certain extent responsible for a good deal of trouble.

10 a.m. Received a signal from 3rd Infantry Brigade stating that they were very grateful for our fire. Unless we can make good today by means of our gun fire, it seems now that we may have to give up the operation for the time being – if not for good. We could have done with three times the number of men we actually had.

11.45 a.m. For some time we could plainly see Turks coming over the hill on our left. We told the Queen *but very little firing has been done. The* Majestic *fired a number of rounds near the waterline – what on earth for I don't know. The* Queen Elizabeth *early this morning fired some 15-inch with aeroplane spotting* [RNAS Seaplanes from the HMS *Ark Royal*], *at enemy howitzers, which effectually silenced them. Except for that we have seen no aeroplanes today. The balloon keeps well to the rear and has now come down. It cannot have performed much useful service. We had to cease firing at 10.20 a.m. as we were informed we were shelling our own troops. This was shortly after the message thanking us for our fire, so possibly we have advanced a little.*

As Silas has already mentioned, the lines were very close in places, and even with good spotting from the land it was difficult to distinguish the Turks from the Anzacs, as both wore similar khaki uniforms. Steaming up from Cape Helles on board HMS *Queen Elizabeth*, Midshipman Maltby continued his diary. Part of this ship's success in shelling the

Turks was due to the innovation of zeroing in on the bursts of the friendly field artillery, which had better observation than the navy:

> We steamed to Gaba Tepe, the balloon being sent up, as usual, in addition to a seaplane. A very heavy shrapnel fire was being carried on over the entire hill; also brisk rifle fire, as usual. Bacchante, etc firing continually. "Cornwallis" class anchored in line to northward; also firing. Transports at anchor…it is very hard to make out the position of our troops and the great difficulty throughout the whole operation is to be able to distinguish our own men, the Turks having a khaki rig as well. But to our great gratification we noticed that the Australians had got six guns to work on the upper ridges. Nevertheless, the enemy's shrapnel began to search them out shortly after we fired 15-inch at the batteries over the hill with satisfactory results. The Australians heliographing: "O.K. O.K. – give them another dose!"

Everyone expected the artillery to be ashore by 26 April, and even though Colonel J.J.T. Hobbs, 1st Australian Divisional artillery commander, sent an urgent message to land the guns so they could be in position for dawn, none arrived until midday on the Monday. As on the previous day, something had gone wrong with the artillery planning that was not made any easier by clashes between Major General Bridges and the artillery commanders. There were a lot of contradictory orders throughout the first day concerning the landing and re-embarkation of the artillery. As the situation deteriorated during the late afternoon of 25 April, Bridges ordered the field artillery to be re-embarked, which duly happened at 7.30 pm. Then at 9.30 pm orders were issued to land two batteries at 2.00 am on the Monday. When these guns were landed, they were ordered to be re-embarked again and were towed back out to sea. At 7.00 am they were towed back to the beach again, but positions were not found for them until 6.30 pm on 26 April. When the guns were nearly in position they were ordered back to the beach once again for re-embarkation. The War Diary states that: 'This was a big undertaking as the floats had grounded with the receding tide.' At 8.30 pm the guns, as ordered, were towed back out to sea and then reloaded back on the transports. Bridges was an artilleryman at heart and, similar to the navy's fear of losing ships, he probably feared losing the guns. To Bridges the support of the infantry was always going to be secondary to risking the safety of the guns.

The infantry were in desperate need of this artillery support to supplement the naval fire. All expected the field artillery to have been

Pope's 16/AIF. The photo dates from 26 April 1915 when the battalion was entrenched on Pope's Hill.

The powerful guns of the Royal Navy support the infantry ashore.

brought into position during the night, but most guns were still at sea. Private John Pitt, 8/AIF, noted in his diary:

Monday April 26th – Artillery expected ashore today, warships still bombarding. Barney Allan shot through mouth. Wounded men everywhere, SBs and doctors scarce. 12 am. Casualties estimated at 4,000, 75% 8th Battalion officers out of action, 60% dead, very sad. A.M.C. out all night and did splendid work. Rejoined company on battalion's left flank, made dug outs till 4pm, then went in trenches to help cover advance to be made on our left. They advanced and were repulsed time after time, shrapnel fire awful. Slight advance at last. The warships helped us considerably. Splendid shooting today. In trenches all night, several minor attacks. No sleep.

Private Fred Symonds, 5/AIF, who had become detached from his unit, went into the line with his fellow Victorians from 14/AIF:

26th – I got up to the firing line before dawn. Had to get in with the 14th Battalion, could not find our crowd; feel terribly exhausted, and don't know how our men can hold the line, it is so weak and broken, but they are wonderful. Food is out of the question; may have to go a week on 24 hours' rations and water. Our firing position here is on the top of a steep incline, almost perpendicular, and if one gets hit he has a chance of rolling down to the gully, a distance of about 200 feet or so. We are in a pretty warm quarter; the fighting is very fierce. The trouble is we can't see much of the enemy on account of the dense scrub. I notice the warships are giving us more help to-day. The Queen Elizabeth *is sending some 15-inch shells into the Turks. They make a terrible mess of things. If they land anywhere near us they shake the whole hill. Some more men came up this afternoon; we need more still ... Went back to the firing line at dusk in case of danger. There are a great number of Turks, but they seem to be frightened to attack us in a body. They keep sniping, and creep up through the bushes. There are a lot of snipers in behind our lines picking off men from behind, but it's impossible to find them, and they must be dressing in uniforms taken from our dead men. We had a lot of casualties to-day; feel terribly weary; don't know what keeps us going, excitement, I suppose. Have seen some terrible sights; we must all be savages.*

Major Richard Saker was one of those in the centre of the fighting on 400 Plateau during the first day. By 4.30 pm his men had been forced

127

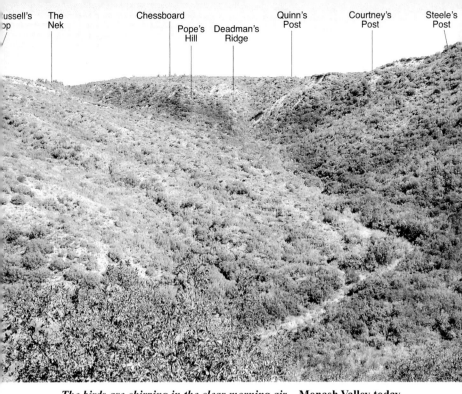

ussell's
op

The
Nek

Chessboard

Pope's
Hill

Deadman's
Ridge

Quinn's
Post

Courtney's
Post

Steele's
Post

The birds are chirping in the clear morning air – **Monash Valley today.**

back, despite gallant efforts, from their exposed positions on the plateau to take up the defensive line near The Pimple. Just after noon on 26 April, Major General Bridges inspected the line and ordered it to be straightened. Without clear orders, Saker advanced his men from their protective trenches towards the open ground of the Daisy Patch. Before he had gone fifty metres he was killed,

> *Meeting his death while organising the firing line ... Wounded on the previous day, this gallant soldier, with an imperturbability and courage peculiarly his own, carried on with a fine disregard for his own safety, and steadied the reeling, broken line.*[5]

Thinking that a general advance was on, 4/AIF then raised themselves from their newly-dug trenches and advanced forward. Leading this reckless and unnecessary movement was their CO, Lieutenant Colonel Onslow Thompson and his second in command Major Charles MacNaghten. Some of the Battalion, on the extreme right by 8/AIF, did not hear the verbal command to advance and remained in the trenches. Thompson's battalion quickly overran Lone Pine, driving the Turks before them, but as soon as they neared the open area of the Daisy Patch a hail of shrapnel was rained down upon them. The survivors found shelter where they could, many sought cover in The Cup and the old Turkish gun emplacements that had been overrun the previous morning. Thompson set up his HQ in Owen's Gully, where an Australian officer was found who had been wounded there on 25 April. Most of 4/AIF, however, crossed Owen's Gully and took up a position on Johnston's Jolly. Unsupported, the Battalion were in No Man's Land with open flanks to their right, advancing at right-angles to their line in a northerly direction. In the confusion it was soon realised that the advance was a wasteful mistake, none of the officers were in receipt of any orders and with mounting casualties, Thompson was forced to withdraw his now shattered Battalion. During this retirement Thompson was killed and MacNaghten badly wounded, shot in the chest and throat. The Battalion War Diary states:

> *4.30 p.m. got word for general advance, evidently in error. Turks cleared from line of trenches in front, after which no orders and movements could be obtained. Advance moving to left approx 1 mile. Shrapnel opened on us. We were compelled to retire. Advance recommenced but very mostly repulsed. A mixed party approximately 200 men became isolated under Lieut Col Onslow Thompson. At 7.00 p.m. they were compelled to retire under heavy fire. Lieut Col Onslow Thompson was shot dead during retirement. Battalion eventually reoccupied its original position. Casualties estimated at approx. 150.*[6]

Ironically Major General Bridges and Colonel McCay were totally unaware that this advance had taken place until afterwards, when they learned of Thompson's tragic death. The confusion of battle, or fog of

Landing the guns of the long awaited artillery.

The battlefield grave of Thompson, originally placed into the trench side.

Grave of Lieutenant Colonel A.J.O. Thompson, commander of 4/AIF, killed leading his battalion on 26 April.

LIEUTENANT COLONEL
A.J.O. THOMPSON VD.
4TH BN. AUSTRALIAN INF.
26 APRIL 1915

war, cruelly took its toll that day, on a Battalion that up until that point had remained virtually intact. During the night the isolated parties of 4/AIF, along with others from 7/AIF, 10/AIF and 12/AIF, that were in advanced positions on Johnston's Jolly and areas of Lone Pine, were recalled. This left most of the ground on 400 Plateau open to the enemy.

The Turks did not make any full scale attack on 26 April as their reinforcements were not forthcoming. The seriously depleted 9th Ottoman Division was holding back the British advance at Helles, whilst 19th Ottoman Division was hard pushed at Anzac, and 5th and 7th Ottoman Divisions were still with Liman von Sanders in the north. It was here that the Royal Naval Division had delivered their feint at the strategically important Gulf of Saros (Xeros) near the town of Bulair. It could have been disastrous for Anzac if Hamilton had not planned this diversion, which fooled von Sanders into keeping two divisions there for two days. This was partly due to the exploits of one man, New Zealand born Lieutenant Commander Bernard Freyberg, Hood Battalion, RND. Whilst the diversionary group of destroyers and transports waited off the coast, a small boat took Freyberg within two miles of the shore from where he swam to the beach, towing a waterproof canvas bag containing three oil flares and five calcium lights, a knife, signalling light and a revolver. After a seventy-five minute swim in the bitterly cold Aegean, he reached the shore and lit flares as per the plan. On the return swim he was lucky to be picked up as the night was pitch black and, after several hours in the cold sea, he was badly cramped and almost dead from cold and exhaustion. For his gallant efforts Freyberg was awarded the DSO.

Bernard Cyril Freyberg was born in Richmond, London, on 21 March 1889, the youngest son of James, a surveyor, and his second wife, Julia *née* Hamilton. When he was two he came with his family to Wellington in New Zealand, received his early schooling from his mother, before attending Wellington College. Although not academically inclined, he made his mark as a sportsman, becoming the New Zealand 100 yards junior swimming champion in 1905 and 1910. He also played competitive water polo and was a keen yachtsman. Nicknamed 'Tiny' as a child, he quickly grew and soon stood over six feet tall with a strong physique.

Upon leaving school, Freyberg qualified as a dentist in 1911 and a year later received a commission in the New Zealand Territorials. Switching career, he briefly became a stoker aboard a ship to Australia and then in March 1914 left New Zealand for the USA. It was believed he headed to Mexico during the uprising and fought with Pancho Villa, but in later life he denied he had ever been there. Upon hearing of the outbreak of war in Europe in August 1914, he immediately set off for England

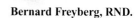

Bernard Freyberg, RND.

where he quickly secured a commission in Churchill's newly formed Royal Naval Division, where he was given command of a company in Hood Battalion. He took part in the brief and unsuccessful attempt to defend Antwerp in October 1914, before returning to England from where the RND was sent to Egypt. During the night of 24 April 1915 he volunteered to swim ashore to light flares at Bulair (Bolayir) to divert the Turks' attention from the main landings. He escaped this daring mission unscathed and his successful exploit earned him his first DSO. Returning to his Battalion on Cape Helles he

131

was later wounded, evacuated but returned to become commander of the Hood Battalion. In July 1915 he was severely wounded again, eventually leaving the Peninsula for good in January 1916 when Gallipoli was finally evacuated.

After the Gallipoli campaign Freyberg was sent to France. On 13 November 1916, when he was in command of Hood Battalion on the Somme, he won the Victoria Cross. When the war ended, Freyberg was a temporary brigadier general with the 29th Division. He had won the VC, the DSO and bar, the CMG, was mentioned six times in despatches and had been wounded nine times.

After the war Freyberg held various military posts and also dabbled in politics. He retired from the Army in 1934, but was recalled in September 1939 to become General Officer Commanding the Salisbury Plains Area. In November 1939 the New Zealand Government invited him to command the New Zealand Division in the Middle East. For a short time in 1941 he was Allied Commander-in-Chief in Crete and was responsible for evacuating the troops there. He led the New Zealand Division through the Greek, African, and Italian campaigns, winning a third bar to his DSO in Italy in 1945.

In June 1946 Freyberg became Governor General of New Zealand and, in 1951, was elevated to the peerage, taking the title Baron Freyberg 'of Wellington, New Zealand and of Munstead, Surrey'. From 1953 until his death he was Deputy Constable and Lieutenant Governor of Windsor Castle, where he died on 4 July 1963, when one of his war wounds ruptured. He is buried in the churchyard of St Martha on the Hill, Guildford, Surrey.

---

1. Hamilton, Sir Ian, *Gallipoli Diary* Vol.1, (1920), p.145.
2. Bollinger, later commissioned as an officer, died of his wounds on the Western Front on 10 June 1917. He is buried in Bailleul Military Cemetery. His brother Herman, another Gallipoli veteran, died of his wounds in March 1918. George and Herman had eight cousins who also died on the Western Front but fighting for the other side. Unpublished diary of Corporal Bollinger (Alexander Turnbull Library: MS-2350)
3. Private Albert Joseph Tohill, 10/1012 was wounded again later in the campaign and died in an Egyptian hospital on 19 August 1915. Buried in the Alexandra (Chatby) Military Cemetery and Memorial. Private Swayne appears to have survived.
4. Killed in action on 8 August 1915 at Chunuk Bair, aged 56.
5. Keown, A.W., *Forward with the Fifth* (1921), p.43.
6. War Diary of 4/AIF (NA:WO 95/4353).

Chapter Seven

The Wounded

It was frightful work

Upon landing, the covering force's regimental stretcher-bearers became dispersed with their battalion and due to the ensuing fragmentation of troops many of them were out of contact with their Regimental Medical Officers (RMOs). Those RMOs who managed to collect together some bearers quickly went about setting up Regimental Aid Posts (RAPs) near the fighting. When 2 Brigade landed the situation was not much better. One of the few RMOs to be able to work successfully with his own unit was with 8/AIF, who were entrenched on Bolton's Ridge. The RMOs in 1 Brigade did however manage to keep their bearers together and went on to select suitable spots for the RAPs. These bearers could work with an effective system of reliefs, allowing forward collecting posts near the heads of the gully to dress the casualties and then bring them down from the firing line to secondary collecting posts further down the valley who would then take the wounded the remainder of the way to the beach. Once the RMOs were established, they could direct the walking wounded and also get the bearers or slightly wounded to help the serious cases.

The regimental bearers worked with those from the field ambulances in what became common ground, but they were far from being systematic and organised, leading to delays in getting the wounded away. 3/Field Ambulance landed first with its brigade at 4.30 am, followed by 2/Field Ambulance at about 6.30 am and 1/Field Ambulance at 9.30 am. Lightly equipped with stretchers, medical companions, surgical haversacks and medical water bottles, the field ambulance and regimental stretcher-bearers were kept busy all day and night tending the wounded on the beach and those in the newly captured positions further inland.

The War Diary of 2/Field Ambulance describes the medical experiences of Captain Roy William Chambers:

> *The main line of evacuation for our bearers was down what afterwards was called Shrapnel Valley, and well was it named. Touch with the R.M.Os was maintained fairly well but they became somewhat scattered and we found we were evacuating cases from the 1st Brigade and particularly the 1st Bn. from Capt. Thompson's R.A.P., which was in Monash Gully. Towards*

Australian wounded on MacLagan's Ridge.

the afternoon the supply of stretchers had given out and there was no reserve to draw from. We had brought no reserve with us and the small stock that the C.C.S. had was soon exhausted. Eventually some stretchers were reclaimed from the wounded that were lying on the beach, leaving the casualties to lie on the sand until they could be evacuated.[1]

Private Fred Symonds, 5/AIF, was one of those stretcher-bearers:

The stretcher-bearers are absolutely unable to cope with the casualties; some of the wounded have been lying out for 24 hours, and may be here for another 24 hours by the look of things. If they would only get some more men up here a few of us could help the wounded till dark, which would be a great help. Went on stretcher-bearing this afternoon; a cry came up for spare men to volunteer, as a whole line of men had been enfiladed by an enemy machine gun, and were lying under fire. It was frightful work getting the poor fellows down those hills; it took five men in some cases to get one wounded man out, and a lot of the bearers are being shot; we have lost 10 out of 40 already.

The stretcher-bearers had an almost impossible task during the first days of the landing, often facing enemy fire and under the constant risk of shrapnel; they not only had problems retrieving the casualties, but then they had to get them by stretcher or by hand through the treacherous scrub-filled gullies and steep ravines back to the aid posts and beach. Colonel Fred Waite in the book *The New Zealanders at Gallipoli* described the invaluable and brave work carried out by these men:

The stretcher-bearers were magnificent. From the order, "Stretcher squads fall in" at the moment of landing, these men slaved on the ridges and in those valleys of torment. A man without a load can dash from cover to cover, but the stretcher-bearers, with their limp and white-faced burdens, must walk steadily on, ignoring sniper and hostile gunner. From the front line it took about two and a half hours to get a patient to the hospital on the beach. Hour after hour the work went on, until after twenty hours' stretcher-bearing these unheeded heroes fell in their tracks from sheer exhaustion. Volunteers took up the work, but after a few hours' rest, the gallant souls were out again — medical officers, stretcher-bearers and hospital orderlies literally working themselves to death in an endeavour to mitigate the awful anguish of the wounded men of Anzac. "I shall never

Stretcher-Bearers, the unsung heroes of Anzac. (Ellis Silas)

forget that night," said a sergeant of the N.Z.M.C., "a twelve-stone weight on the stretcher, a dark night, a little drizzling rain, groping our way down a steep incline through prickly scrub, our wounded man crying with pain and begging for a drink every few yards, incessant rifle fire, and bullets whizzing all round us." Except those who lay so very quietly up in the scrub or on the shell-swept beach, no one rested that night. The firing line was gradually becoming a little defined as the tired soldiers on both sides became exhausted.

The casualties who could walk made their own way to the beach; Private Fred Symonds, 5/AIF, describes what he saw when he was approaching the line on 400 Plateau:

When we got to the ridge we retired there, and could see wounded men coming down helping each other over the steep ground, which was very nearly perpendicular in places. Some had stretchers, but it was almost impossible to use them. How the poor fellows got back to the dressing station I don't know; it must have cost some of them hours of agony.

Most of the wounded managed to get themselves towards the aid posts, whilst those who were badly wounded had to rely on luck so that they would be found amongst the dense scrub. Colonel A.G. Butler wrote:

On the hillsides of the range it was difficult during daylight even to communicate with the fire line. It was impossible in most parts to bring up stretchers or to crawl back; the only way of leaving the line was to run, crawl, roll, or be dragged to the edge of the slope and thence slide down the cliffs.[2]

Unfortunately, with the retirement in the afternoon from some of the more forward positions, a lot of the wounded had to be left. During the night there were successful attempts to recover some of these men, but many were unrecoverable. There are few reports of wounded from the first day of fighting being made prisoner of war by the Turks, although they did capture several Anzacs during the day's fighting. Bean mentions only four Australians captured on the first day and it is known that at least one New Zealander was also taken prisoner. Numbers of prisoners for the first day were almost certainly higher and there has been mention of captured soldiers accidentally killed during the Royal Navy's bombardment of Maidos on 29 April, when a hospital that housed wounded was destroyed.

Private Alfred Richard Perry, 10/AIF, described how he was wounded on 400 Plateau when trying to aid one of the battalion officers:

"Oh-h!" comes from directly behind me, and, looking around, I see poor little Lieutenant B- [Lieutenant Albert John Byrne], *of C Company, has been badly wounded. From both hips to his ankles blood is oozing through pants and puttees, and he painfully drags himself to the rear. With every pull he moans cruelly. I raise him to his feet, and at a very slow pace start to help him to shelter. But, alas! I have only got him about fifty yards from the firing line when again, bang-swish! and we were both peppered by shrapnel and shell. My rifle-butt was broken off to the trigger-guard, and I received a smashing blow that laid my cheek on my shoulder. The last I remembered was poor Lieutenant B-groaning again as we both sank to the ground.*

Another account about Byrne comes from Private Walter Pavey, also of C Company. Pavey, originally from Crawley in West Sussex, was working as an assistant to a surveyor in Port Augusta, South Australia, before joining up in September 1914. Pavey wrote:

About 4 pm there was a slight lull in the firing. Then I heard a pitiful cry of 'Water! Water!' I asked the Captain next to me at the time, 'Who is it?' He said, 'Lieutenant Byrne, (my platoon commander) will you go and give him a drink?' He was lying out in the open, so I had to crawl to him. I reached him in safety and quenched his thirst. There was a clump of thick bushes on the left

Lieutenant A.J. Byrne, 10/AIF.

The original wooden cross over Byrne's grave in Beach Cemetery.

Byrne's grave in Beach Cemetery today.

of us, about 20 yards away, and if we could reach it he might be left in comparative safety. As he was shot in both legs and in the left side, I had no alternative but to carry him. I raised him as gently as I could and got under him; then staggered to my feet, and had gone half way when 'thud', and down I went on top of my unfortunate officer. I felt a stinging in my thigh, and it was not until I endeavoured to get up and have another try that I realised I had got a bullet and could not use my leg. After laying still for a few minutes (during which the lieutenant gave another cry, indicating that he had received another bullet) I decided that to stay there was certain death, and started to crawl to the bushes, as I could do no more for Byrne.[3]

A 24-year-old public school educated officer from Broken Hill, NSW, Lieutenant A.J. Byrne was a popular officer in C Company, 10/AIF. He had been in the local militia for seven years before the outbreak of the war and was a fine shot, winning gold and silver medals in rifle shooting. He finally succumbed to his wounds on the afternoon of 25 April and was buried the next day in Beach Cemetery. Regaining consciousness, Perry was luckier:

When I came to I found myself in Shrapnel Gully, with an A.M.C. man holding me down. I was still clasping my half-rifle. Dozens of men and officers, both Australians and New Zealanders (who had landed a little later in the day), were coming down wounded, some slightly, some badly, with arms in slings or shot through the leg, and using their rifles for crutches. Shrapnel Gully was still under

138

MacLagan's Ridge and Anzac Beach on 26 April. Note the hospital tents.

shrapnel and snipers' fire. Two or three platoon mates and myself slowly moved down to the beach, where we found the Australian Army Service Corps busily engaged landing stores and water amid shrapnel fire from Gaba Tepe. As soon as a load of stores was landed, the wounded were carried aboard the empty barges and taken to hospital ships and troopships standing out offshore.

By mid morning a Casualty Clearing Station had been set up on the beach under the shelter of MacLagan's Ridge and during the late afternoon a dressing station was established at the northern end of the beach by the NZ&A Division. This helped with the concentration and classification of the wounded for evacuation, however many of the slightly wounded had already gone straight to the beach which was becoming congested. The wounded were collecting in their droves, which left precious little room for newly arriving men, animals, supplies and munitions. Lieutenant Colonel Malone, who had just landed, remarked: 'There didn't seem to be much organisation on the shore, in fact it was disorganisation. We evidently haven't got a Kitchener about.' The standard classification of the lightly and seriously wounded was normally done by affixing a white and red paper ticket to the casualty, however with such large numbers this became quite impossible, 'It was like trying to classify a crowded hall with others pouring in', one doctor remarked. The allocated medical tow was not made available for evacuating the wounded until the whole of 1st Australian Division had landed and even then was of limited capacity. Before that, and contrary to orders, some climbed into the boats that were returning to the transports to continue the landing, thus causing delays in getting the New Zealand Infantry Brigade and Australian 4 Brigade ashore, which had a knock-on effect, contributing to the loss of Baby 700 and any hope in reaching the objectives on the left flank.

Hit in the shoulder by a shell splinter, Fred Symonds, 5/AIF, left 400 Plateau with another wounded man:

> It took me four hours to get him to the dressing station, and as soon as I had my shoulder dressed, which by good luck was not seriously hurt, I got to work with a party taking ammunition to the firing line, first unloading it from a barge under a continual fire of shrapnel, then taking it up to the firing line – a terribly heavy task. Needless to say, I was greatly worried about Edgar all this time. I never expected to see him again; it seemed impossible for men to live for long under the fire our chaps were exposed to unless they got well dug in. About midnight two of us were struggling up the hill with a box of ammunition, nearly

Beach packed with wounded awaiting evacuation.

*fainting with exhaustion, for we had not eaten a bite since 3
o'clock the previous morning, and we were both wondering what
had befallen our brothers, for, strange to say, he had a brother in
the firing line somewhere, too. When we reached the firing line
the first man to come out was my mate's brother, and while we
were talking someone came out of the trench and asked if Fred
Symonds was there, and to my joy, the second-comer was Edgar.
It seemed strange that two of us should meet our brothers at the
same time and place, when everyone had been mixed up so
completely. After we came back we had a rest for an hour before
going up to support the line. The beach is an awful sight; our
men must be getting terribly butchered. All the fleet boats are
waiting near the beach expecting a retreat to the boats, but
judging from the spirit of our men there will be very few retiring.
The beach is lined from end to end with wounded.*

By 2.00 pm some 500 wounded men were on the beach by the clearing
station, lying there under almost constant shrapnel fire. By 3.00 pm a
pier had been constructed and made available for the re-embarkation
of the wounded.   By 5.00 pm the beach was still congested with
wounded, manifested by the mounting casualties and failure to
advance. No one expected such overwhelming numbers of wounded
would need to be evacuated on the first day, thus the limited boats
available made this process slow. By 5.30 pm however, returning tows
were made available for the wounded which speeded up the process
greatly. But by nightfall the backlog of wounded was growing and their
re-embarkation had fallen behind:

> *At 6.00 p.m. the disembarkation of guns and stores was
> discontinued, and we were sent inshore to await the arrival of
> wounded...we spent the remainder of the night towing them out
> to the ships. On one trip alone three hundred men were brought
> off in lighters.[4]*

The naval beach-master said:

> *... about 9 p.m. I became thoroughly alarmed at the state of
> affairs. The Beach at this time was a never-to-be-forgotten sight;
> the number of wounded lying about practically stopped all work
> on the Beach. It was decided that at all costs efforts must be
> made to relieve the congestion, and orders were given that all
> tows, after emptying their contents, would transfer wounded to
> the ships.*

The pier was used until about 11.00 pm when evacuation of the
wounded was temporarily ceased pending the possibility of a general

evacuation, but was soon resumed after Hamilton's order to 'dig, dig, dig'. By 3.00 am the beach was eventually cleared, after the evacuation of nearly 1800 casualties.

One of the stretcher-bearers was Private S.H. Tomes, New Zealand Field Ambulance, who in his diary entry for 25 April 1915 briefly describes the situation:

> *Left ship for shore on H.M.S.D.* Foxhound, *arrived on beach 6.30 p.m. Very busy attending to wounded, terrible number wounded by shrapnel. Everything very quiet at 11 pm, tried to have a sleep at 12pm.*

26 April saw little respite for the stretcher-bearers, Tomes continuing:

> *Slept from 12 till 5 am. Raining slightly. Very cold. We suffered very heavy casualties, all three hospital ships were loaded full and had to use some of the transports. There was some very good work done by both NZ & A men. Wounded very cheerful. Bombarding freely this morning, firing going on all through the night, very busy carrying wounded men all day till 10.30 lay down to sleep for the night.*[5]

The conspicuous white and green painted Hospital Ship *Gascon*, emblazoned with a red cross, arrived off North Beach at 7.00 am on 25 April. This was the only hospital ship allocated to Anzac, and had capacity for about 500 serious cases. To ease the situation, troopships were temporarily designated as auxiliary hospital ships and were also in position off the coast in their designated positions but, having no markings, they were subject to Turkish shelling and so had to withdraw at about 10.00 am to positions about three miles out. This not only caused the problem of lengthening the journey from the shore, but in an unknown position and with no markings, especially after it became dark and orders were given to darken all lights, it became impossible to find these ships. Luckily, before dark, Private Alfred Perry managed to get aboard one of these transports:

> *After going to ten different boats, we came at last to the troopship* Seang Choon, *which had the 14th Australian Battalion aboard. They were to disembark the next morning, but owing to so many of us being wounded, they had to land straightaway. And so, after twelve hours' hard fighting, I was aboard a troopship again – wounded. But I would not have missed it for all the money in the world.*

One of the problems was that in the planning, provision had only been made for the evacuation of the seriously wounded, not the lighter cases. So when the purposely provided tows and also the empty returning

A Field Hospital on Anzac Beach.

boats were available, wounded, regardless of classification, seemed to
have been evacuated. The plan was that the hospital ship *Gascon* would
take the serious cases, whilst the lighter wounded would be distributed
amongst the designated transports, namely the *Clan Macgillivray*,
Seang Choon and *Hindoo*. Having already disembarked the Auckland
Battalion, the *Lützow* was now designated a hospital ship for 200
serious, and 1000 lightly wounded men. However, this ship only had
two medical staff, Major Young, a veterinary doctor, and Private
Ormond Edward Burton, an NZMC orderly who went on later to write
the war history of the Auckland Regiment. They had to cope alone for
almost three days until they were eventually helped by a naval surgeon,
three doctors and a couple of NZMC officers. The *Lützow* only sailed
for Alexandria late in the afternoon on 27 April and still had 160 horses
on board.

The flow of wounded continued throughout the day, especially after
the relaxation of the order for using tows after 1st Australian Division
had been landed. The conditions aboard the ships were dreadful, a

The wounded being lifted aboard a hospital ship.

result of poor preparation and inadequate facilities on board the transports. By early evening the limited number of spaces aboard these ships had reached overflow point. By about 7.00 pm the *Clan Macgillivray* was full, the *Seang Choon* had taken on 500 wounded and had to refuse more as Lieutenant Colonel Courtney's 14/AIF was still aboard awaiting landing. At 9.00 pm the *Gascon* left for Lemnos with 548 cases, many being slight wounds, thus leaving no ships to take on the remaining wounded. The *Hindoo*, which had two much needed stationary hospitals onboard, had gone 'missing' and was later 'found' lying idle off Helles, only arriving at Anzac on 29 April. The boats from the shore were still coming, only to find that they were now being turned away. Many spent hours going from ship to ship trying to get the wounded taken onboard. Captain Oppenheim, RMLI, wrote in his diary on 26 April 1915:

> *The arrangements for disposal of wounded are very bad. They have been carting them all round the harbour at times trying to find out where to take them. Also the doctors in the squadron have not been organised, so that numbers of doctors are on board their ships doing nothing while many hundreds of men are in need of urgent attention.*
>
> *The accommodation for wounded and provision of medical officers is hopelessly inadequate. Wounded are still being brought off from the beach by hundreds. At last they are sending medical officers from the warships to the transports – although even that extra aid will be insufficient.*

On 26 April additional hospital transports, or 'Black Ships' as they were termed, with ambulance personnel and naval surgeons, were selected for taking on wounded, although these were quickly filled as the fighting continued. Then, even though the Black Ships were full and had inadequate facilities for any long term treatment, they were ordered to remain off Anzac for 48 hours. This was in the original plan in case the landing failed and they had to re-embark the troops. It only added to the suffering of the wounded who, even though safe from the perils onshore, had the danger of wounds festering and gangrene setting in. Many who required immediate surgery died and those which did not had to endure the thousand kilometre journey by sea to the British hospital in Alexandria. By the end of the first day some 1800 Australian and New Zealand wounded were evacuated, a staggering feat when one takes into account that the navy had already landed over 15,000 men, 300 mules and an amazing quantity of munitions and stores, all despite the poor planning and execution.

Transport HMT *Lützow*: after landing the New Zealanders of the Auckland and Canterbury battalions, it became a hospital ship.

No one exactly knows what the Anzac casualties were on 25 April 1915, but estimates have varied from 2500 to nearly 6000.[6] Bean estimates that there were 8570 casualties for the first six days, acknowledging that the majority were on the initial day of the landing. The best estimate of killed and wounded for the first day is probably 5000, with 1200 killed and 3800 wounded. The casualties suffered were remarkably high; out of the 15,000 troops put ashore that day, a third became casualties before the dawn of the following day. To put this into context the Anzac casualties are twice the amount suffered by the British on the Helles beaches. It is however difficult to be accurate, as individual war diaries rarely had any casualty figures until weeks later, due to the majority of the men being classed as 'missing'. The priority was holding the Anzac perimeter, not counting the dead. Back home the newspapers were full of news of the glorious landings and bravery of the Anzacs and even a month after the landing had still only reported 350 deaths. Accurate figures for Ottoman casualties are even harder to come by, but estimates put the figure at well over 4000. For example both 57 and 27 Regiments had sustained fifty percent casualties on the first day, which equates alone to 3000 men, and that doesn't include the casualties sustained later in the day by 77 and 72 Regiments that remain unrecorded. Kemal said later that 57 Regiment was completely wiped out on the 25 April.

Numerous graves at Anzac today are still marked with date ranges, for example 25/29 April 1915, as the true date of death is unknown. The story of the Adcock boys is an example of the confusion on the first day; the fate of the two brothers was not confirmed until a whole year later.

146

OUR HEROES OF THE DARDANELLES.

LANDING OF THE SUPPORTING PARTY AFTER THE COAST HAD BEEN GAINED.

Our Heroes Of The Dardanelles (*Sydney Mail*, 12 May 1915)

The Adcock Brothers

Frank Adcock

My truth is a sword

Fred Adcock

John and Charlotte Adcock had two sons, Frank Henry Burton, the eldest and his younger brother Frederick Brenchley. Originally from Melton Mowbray in Leicestershire, the family had settled in Perth, Western Australia. Frank worked as a labourer in Fremantle, whilst his brother Fred took to the sea as a sailor. The boys enlisted at the outbreak of war in August 1914, joining the newly formed 11/AIF, the first battalion to be recruited in Western Australia. After only two weeks of preliminary training at Black Boy Hill, they left Fremantle on H.M.A.T (A11) *Ascanius* on 2 November 1914. The *Ascanius* formed part of the convoy of thirty-eight troopships carrying approximately 35,000 Australian and New Zealand troops destined to join the Mediterranean Expeditionary Force in Egypt, arriving there in early December 1914. The Battalion was camped at Mena, ten miles from Cairo, at the foot of the Great Pyramids, where they continued their training until 1 March 1915 when they embarked aboard H.M.T (A23) *Suffolk*, its destination unknown to the troops. Three days later the *Suffolk* arrived in Mudros Harbour, Lemnos, about sixty miles from the Gallipoli Peninsula. Training and preparations for the landing began. Frank and Fred were assigned to No.8 Platoon, B Company and landed, as part of the covering force, at Anzac during the early morning of 25 April 1915. This historic day was to be their last; both were to lose their lives.

It was not until 22 June 1915 that their mother received an official telegram reporting that both sons were wounded, but not seriously and, at that time, no more information was available. As further news had not followed, Charlotte contacted the authorities in late September asking anxiously for information with regard to her sons, in particular to the nature of their wounds and the hospital in which they were being treated. Once this request was received the authorities cabled Egypt for news on their condition and their whereabouts. In a July edition of the *Western Mail*, the newspaper published photos of the wounded; amongst these were two separate photographs of Frank and Fred with simply 'wounded in action' by them.

The correspondence then became contradictory and confusing; were the boys wounded and missing on 25 April or did they survive the battle, as other reports stated, but were later wounded two months after the landing? A supporting report of the boys being wounded later mentioned that they were drafted to the front only in June and employed in special services in connection with landing troops. This news was passed on verbally by a soldier who said one of them was wounded in the leg and the other in the arm. A further letter followed in November 1915 stating that both sons had in fact been reported wounded on 25 April and that an investigation into their condition and whereabouts was continuing. This must have been very distressing for the mother who was anxiously trying to get in touch with her sons.

In December 1915 new information was sent from Cairo, reported by Private William Shields, who: ...knew two brothers called Adcock in his company but he did not know their numbers, nor their Christian names. They were both in the original landing and both survived it, and were both all right about three weeks later, though one had been wounded in the hand and lost some fingers and the other (the elder) had been shot through the lungs. The elder was in No.15 General Hospital at Alexandria with the informant in May last.

In March 1916 further details were reported by Sergeant Percy Dunham, who stated that: ...two men named Adcock in the 11th Btn were in hospital recently in England. He says they were both in his platoon on the Peninsula and he inquired about them from Corporal Kirton, of B Co 11th Btn, who recently returned from England, and the latter stated that he saw them both at Manchester hospital in England when he was there. Following this promising news the hospital records of 170 hospitals that comprised No.2 Western General were searched, but no trace of anyone named Adcock of the Australian Forces was found. In April 1916 a Court of Enquiry, held in France, finally pronounced both Frank and Fred as officially killed in action on 25 April 1915.

In June 1916 Mrs. Adcock was still enquiring about her sons' whereabouts, as there was still doubt that they were dead. Even though she was told that they were both killed during the landings, other reports contradicted this. Their mother was not going to rest until she was sure of the fate of her sons, which took another turn when a card was received from Egypt bearing a post date of Alexandria 22 May 1915. This was sent to her by her son Frank, originally written and dated 1 May 1915, that said: 'Fred and I have been cruising about in an old whaler for the past month. We have had a glorious time. Occasionally we would take a walk over the hills.' Is this written date correct, or was it in fact 1 March 1915 when they were embarking for Egypt, and posted later when they had already left?

In July 1916 Private Baxter Westbrook, B Company, reported seeing both men listed as missing in the *Western Mail* newspaper of 2 June 1915. Westbrook was in the same platoon as the boys, landing together on the Peninsula. The last he saw of them was that first day and since then had heard nothing. The following August a Private Percy Clarke, 11/AIF, wrote from a hospital in Croydon, England stating that: 'On Monday April 26th at Anzac beach I saw one of the Adcock brothers being carried on to a hospital ship, wounded. I cannot tell which one it was. I was running past the stretcher and called out to him. I was afterwards told [by Private Charles Braidwood, B Company] that he died.' Could this have been Fred?

Today Frank Henry Burton Adcock, aged 25, rests in a marked grave, Row D.24 in Baby 700 Cemetery, a mile north-east of Anzac Cove. His younger brother, Frederick Brenchley Adcock, aged 22, is commemorated on panel 33 on the Lone Pine Memorial. Looking at the facts such as they are, both sons were probably wounded and then reported missing on 25 April 1915. Frank's body was found after the war and buried on Baby 700, the northernmost point of the first day's advance, where he was wounded and later killed. Fred was probably wounded alongside his brother and taken back down to the beach where he was evacuated, but later died aboard ship and was buried at sea. Frank's grave epitaph is: 'My Truth Is A Sword'.

1. War Diary of 2/Field Ambulance (NA:WO 95/4340).
2. Butler, Colonel A.G., DSO, VD, *The Australian Army Medical Service in the War of 1914-1918* Volume 1, (1938).
3. Lock, Cecil B.L. *The Fighting 10th. A South Australian Centenary Souvenir of the 10th Battalion, AIF 1914-1919*, (1936).
4. Diary of HMS *Queen Elizabeth* January to May 1915, (1919), p.43.
5. Unpublished war diary of Private S. H. Tomes, NZMC. (Private collection).
6. Williams, P., *The Battle of Anzac Ridge*, (2006), p.146.

Chapter Eight

Stalemate – 27 April 1915

...they came on in masses, shoulder to shoulder

26 April 1915

The GOC Australia and New Zealand Army Corps wishes to place on record his appreciation of the gallantry and dash with which the 3rd Australian Brigade carried out the difficult operation entrusted to it of landing in face of opposition on an enemy beach. In spite of the enemy being ready, and of heavy casualties inflicted at short range, the Brigade pressed on carrying successive positions in face of enemy fire, and completing a hazardous operation in a manner reflecting the highest credit on the commanders and on the troops engaged. During their advance the Brigade captured three Krupp guns. The GOC Army Corps is sure that all will be gratified to hear that the Australian submarine has succeeded in passing the Narrows of the Dardanelles and sinking a Turkish warship there.
W.R. BIRDWOOD GOC ANZ Army Corps.

On Tuesday 27 April the Turks made a full scale counter-attack against the Anzac perimeter in what could be seen as the climax to the battle of the landings. By Monday night the survivors were completely exhausted, but they were still holding on to the same precarious line of shallow trenches that they had held since the evening of 25 April. They had not slept for days, in reality probably not since the night of 23 April.

Private Fred Symonds, 5/AIF, was still on stretcher-bearer duty on 27 April:

Went on stretcher-bearing again today, as I had not a very good position in the firing line. Came across some of the 5th Battalion fellows; they are gradually picking one another up; will join them as soon as work eases off here. There are a lot of snipers behind our lines. We caught several today, but there must be lots more. Want food badly; half a biscuit and water, if you are lucky, for a meal, and a little salt meat once a day. They are gradually getting reinforcements up, and our firing line is getting stronger, but the men are getting weaker.

Private John Jensen, 1/AIF Battalion, wrote of the days that followed the landing:

151

During all those three days I lay in one little hole & never closed my eyes night or day or ate a bite of food. When my own water bottle was empty I crawled out to the dead & took the water off them. My rifle was in my hand all the time & sometimes it was that hot with the shooting that I couldn't touch any of the

Ottoman troops waiting to go into the attack.

*iron part. All those three days which I will never forget I was not
touched once although I had two dead men fall into my hole. One
chap brought up some ammunition to me & just as he was giving
it to me a bullet hit him & he fell in on top of me. He just said,
"I'm gone" & died.*

Turkish reinforcements had started to arrive and by the morning of 27

April Mustafa Kemal was ready to launch an all-out attack on the Anzac line. The 19th Ottoman Division was reinforced by 33 Regiment, ferried across the Narrows from the Asiatic side, and 64 Regiment from the north, along with two field artillery batteries. These were all the men that von Sanders could make available to Kemal as he also needed to counter the British advance at Helles. Kemal's 72 (Arab) Regiment was relatively untouched by the recent actions, so alongside the worn battalions of 57 and 27 Regiments he launched an attack.

With the attention of driving the Anzacs into the sea, Kemal issued an order:

> *There is no going back a single step. It is our duty to save our country, and we must acquit ourselves honourably and nobly. I must remind all of you that to seek rest and comfort now is to deprive the nation of its rest and comfort forever. I have no doubts of your courage. I know that until the enemy is hurled back into the sea not one of you will show signs of weakness.*[1]

Kemal's plan was to attack the entire Anzac perimeter, in a coordinated all-out attack, using 57, 64 and a battalion of 72 Regiment in the north

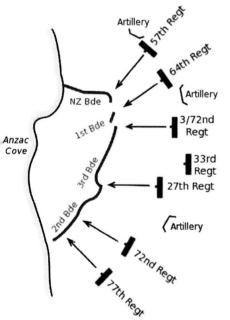

against Russell's Top and the head of Monash Valley, and 27, 77 and the remaining two battalions of 72 Regiment against the line from 400 Plateau and down Bolton's Ridge. 33 Regiment was to be held in reserve in the area of Scrubby Knoll. The attack did not go according to plan. 64 and 33 Regiments were slow in getting to the front, so the main attack had to be delayed. 33 Regiment only arrived at 6.30 pm, and did not get into action until about 8.00 pm.

During the morning Turkish artillery opened up on the Anzac positions, concentrating their fire on the frontline trenches and beach area. The heaviest part of the attack was to fall on the Anzacs' extreme left, at Russell's Top and Monash Valley, where Kemal knew it was at its weakest. This was the apex of the Anzac position, and the Turks knew that if they could break the line there it would be the beginning of the end for the Anzacs. Commanding Russell's Top was Lieutenant Colonel Braund, who had been defending the area since the first day with 2/AIF and a few New Zealanders. The Turks almost succeeded in breaking the line here, but the situation was saved when further New Zealand reinforcements arrived at one of the most critical moments of the battle.

Corporal George Wallace Bollinger, Wellington Battalion, went on to record in his diary the happenings of Tuesday 27 April:

At daylight this morning a terrific artillery duel raged. The Turks put hundreds of shells onto our landing place. At 10.00 a.m. we were marched north along the beach, and as we got under the heights we met crowds of wounded coming down. Oh how callous one gets. Word rushed down from above for Hawkes Bay and Wellington-West Coast Companies to reinforce at the double, as our fellows were getting massacred. We fixed bayonets on reaching the top and got into it. The country is terribly hilly and covered with scrub from four to five feet high. On we rushed against a rain of bullets and our men began to drop over, before they fired a shot. We started to get mixed up and were everywhere amongst the Australians. Our men were dropping in hundreds.

The attack Bollinger was referring to was personally led by Braund in an effort to force back the Turks who had infiltrated themselves onto Russell's Top. At 1.30 pm, with bayonets fixed, Braund led forward his much weakened Battalion, along with two companies of Wellington reinforcements who were under the command of Major Herbert Hart. The Turks fled before them, allowing this small group of men to get into an advanced position overlooking The Nek and the head of Malone's Gully. Lieutenant Colonel Malone describes these first two New Zealand companies of the Wellington Battalion as: '…some 450 of the best soldier men in the world. They were being sent to chaos and slaughter, nay murder.' What was apparent to Braund was the dire need to keep possession of Russell's Top, the left flank had to hold no matter what the cost. During the night the Turks had managed to creep onto the ridge and had to be removed so that Braund could properly secure this flank.

Malone wrote:

I then brought up the remaining one and half companies to about half way, which the Australian Brigadier told me to hold in Reserve. On doing this, more yells for reinforcements. I took on myself to stop the yelling and say no more reinforcements should

155

Lieutenant Colonel W.G. Malone, commander of Wellington Battalion, who was killed later in the campaign.

go up in that irresponsible way. I went up myself to find out the position. A long climb along and up a ridge [Walker's Ridge]. I struck a sort of natural fort along it, entrenched and occupied by about forty Australians and two machine guns, one major, a fat chap. I asked him what he was doing there sending down yells for reinforcements. He said he was passing the yells on. I asked him why he did not go himself and take his men with him. He said he had orders to stay. I went on, passing a score of Australian men wounded, lying all along the track. Finally I got to a Colonel Braund, who said he was in command of the show. I asked for some explanation of the position and why he had left his own men down the ridge and called for reinforcements from the New Zealanders. He did not know and knew nothing. Had no defensive position, no plan, nothing but a murderous notion that the only thing to do was to plunge troops out of the neck of the ridge into the jungle beyond. The Turks, of whom very few were seen by any of my officers, were lying down, shooting down all the bits of track that led from the ridge outwards; having range marks fixed, and dropping our men wholesale. Majors Young and Cunningham [Major W.H. Cunningham and Major R. Young, Wellington Battalion] grasped the situation soon and told who they could to dig in. This was begun, but Colonel Braund came along and ordered the Platoon Commanders to go on and plunge into the jungle further and further. On their protesting he claimed, as Senior Officer, their obedience to his orders, and so, on and on they went and got slaughtered ... I made Colonel Braund send back and take all the Australians forward and to shift his Headquarters forward. I then went back to Brigade Headquarters to report and was told to bring up my remaining one and a half Companies to the fort.

Braund held this advanced position for an hour before he was forced to withdraw due to mounting casualties. As Braund's men started withdrawing, some of them on the extreme left suddenly broke into a stampede, shouting in a panic that the Turks are coming in their thousands. What they witnessed was the main Turkish attack by 57 Regiment. Only visible to the Anzacs from the extreme left and the sea below, it was reported that six waves of men were steadily advancing down Big 700 towards them. Malone continued:

> *After getting them up* [the remaining one and a half companies] *I started to go forward again up the track to get a grip of things but was met by a lot of Australians tearing down the track yelling 'Fix bayonets, the Turks are coming.' I whipped back to the fort and put two machine guns on the front slope with a line of best shots of the Ruahine and sorted the other men out in readiness to hold back the Turks. I really believed we were in for a solid thing and told the men we would have to stick it out at all costs. I then went forward and found that the panic, for such it was, had been stopped, thanks mainly to Major Hart, who had been sent on by me ahead of the Reserve to get a hand of things ... He, like the good chap he is, steadied the men ...*

The attack by 57 Regiment was in progress and, although masked to the Anzacs by Baby 700, it was in full view of the navy. HMS *Queen Elizabeth* was able to put six of her 15-inch shells amongst the advancing Turks, having the effect of breaking the attack. Bean wrote:

> *As the dust of each explosion cleared, the Turks could be seen running round, dazed, like ants on a disturbed nest. For a few minutes scarcely anything of the hill was visible except a low-lying curtain of green smoke.*[2]

With the help of the navy, the attack against The Nek and Russell's Top had been crushed even before it had reached the Anzac positions. From then on Big 700 became known as Battleship Hill because of the naval shelling on that day. The fighting continued, but now the Turks were only dribbling forward in smaller numbers, many of them resorting to sniping rather than frontal attacks.

Malone wrote:

> *By now wounded men by the score were being brought back and laid along the track, all sorts of wounds. The stretcher-bearers couldn't cope with the number and soon there were no stretchers. I got an immediate demand from Colonel Braund for more reinforcements but sent him a firm refusal. He then said as I would not send him up more reinforcements he would have to*

retire to his first position. I told him he never ought to have left it ...Colonel Braund then came to see me and, on my asking why he had been doing as he had, said that the truth was he feared that if he didn't go on, his men would run away. I said that was no reason to sacrifice my men.

I went and reported to General Walker and asked that the whole of the Australians be withdrawn as soon as possible. He came back with me to the position. We struck lots of Australians who hadn't moved. I ordered them up and drove them ahead, pelting the leading ones on the track when they stopped with stones and putting my toe into the rear ones.

By this time wounded men were being brought back in scores (my Battalion's casualties out of two and a half Companies, say 450 men, were about 45 killed and 150 wounded in about first hour of action) and left on the track, no stretchers being available. They were all very brave. No cries or even groans. One man kept saying "Oh Daddy", "Oh Daddy" in a low voice. Many greeted me cheerfully "Well Colonel I've got it." Many smiled. My men are wonderful. The world never saw better men or braver, I am sure. After the frightful murderous slaughter bungled by Colonel Braund of the Australians they hurry on, fired at from all quarters, yet unable in the jungle to see many of their enemy [and] *dug themselves in.*

Lieutenant Colonel G.F. Braund, commander of 2/AIF.

Grave of Lieutenant Colonel Braund.

Braund was a strong leader and was unjustly criticised by Malone, who even went as far as considering asking for his court-martial. Braund had bravely held this isolated but vital position for three days and three nights with his men who were exhausted in the face of fierce attack and weakened by heavy casualties. Whatever his methods, he had held on until 28 April with no rest until he and what was left of 2/AIF were eventually withdrawn, replaced by Malone's men. 2/AIF had suffered the loss of 16 officers and 434 men. On 4 May Braund, whilst taking a shortcut through the scrub, was shot dead. Being slightly deaf, he had failed to respond to a sentry's challenge. He is buried in Beach Cemetery.

Malone continued:

> *I went up with Hart and we divided up the ground held – sent up picks and shovels and the night was passed by all hands dig dig digging. Turks firing from a distance all the night with shrapnel, machine guns and rifle. Hart, poor chap, directing operations, got shot in the leg. Flesh wound only I am glad to say. He will be back in about a fortnight. He was shot by a Turk within a few yards. The Turks threw hand grenades at us through the night.*

At about 9.00 pm and under the cover of darkness, the Turks renewed the attack on Russell's Top. For the first time in the campaign the Turks used hand grenades to try to break the Anzac line, but an hour later the attack had again been driven off. Throughout the remainder of the night the Turks continued to make probing attacks against the line, but by the first streaks of dawn these had faded away.

Out of direct contact with Braund's and Walker's men on Russell's Top, 16/AIF were still holding Pope's Hill. Signaller Ellis Silas, 16/AIF, wrote of 27 April:

> *Morning. Facing our extreme left, on the ridge opposite where there is a single fir tree the New Zealanders* [Otago Battalion] *are advancing – they are nearer the enemy than they suppose – they may get cut off – from our positions we can see the enemy and their danger. From Captain Margolin – 'Get a signal through to them, Silas.' I get up to do so, and receive immediate attention from the Turkish snipers; some of the boys told me to take a less prominent position – if I do the New Zealanders will not be able to see my signal – it is hardly necessary to state the course I had to take.*

Captain Eliazar Lazar Margolin was a Russian born Jew who left Palestine to emigrate to Australia in 1902. Known by his troops as 'Margy', he commanded B Company, 16/AIF. He was later awarded the DSO and survived Gallipoli and France where he was wounded several times. He was promoted lieutenant colonel and went on to command 14/AIF for a period before accepting command of a Jewish battalion of the Royal Fusiliers, going on to fight the Turks in Palestine.

Silas got his message through and, weary from lack of sleep and exhaustion, he soon collapsed. Signallers as well as stretcher-bearers were highly respected by the men as they were often dangerously exposed to enemy fire with nothing more than a signal flag or a stretcher for protection. Silas wrote:

> *The stretcher-bearers have been doing splendid work, poor chaps, along this precipitous ridge where it is difficult to gain a foothold and under incessant fire from snipers, for at this the Turks spared nobody, they shot at anything that moved.*

This area also came under a Turkish counter-attack; from the direction of the Chessboard and over Dead Man's Ridge approximately 300 Arab troops of 3/72 Battalion charged Pope's Hill and Quinn's Post. Bean wrote that: 'They were in ragged uniform. One officer led them with his sword flashing, and others, revolver in hand, were encouraging their men.' The defensive position of Pope's and Quinn's halted this onrush of the Turks dead in their tracks. An anonymous New Zealand sapper recalled that day when the Turks charged:

> *Led by their splendid officers, they came on in masses, shoulder to shoulder, and did all that in them lay to rush our trenches. They were met by a storm of bullets that would have staggered anything born of woman...they recoiled before that leaden blast that piled their dead and wounded up in ghastly heaps and ridges like broken-down walls. They charged, charged right through that hurricane of machine-gun and rifle fire – charged right up to our parapets...They had lost tremendously; the ground along our front looked like a heavy crop of wheat after the binder had been through it.*

Silas wrote:

> *Fighting still continuing with unabated vigour – will this*

15-inch and 6-inch guns of HMS *Queen Elizabeth*.

frightful noise never cease? I wonder what this valley will be like when there is no longer noise of fighting, no longer the hurried thread of combining forces – when the raw earth of the trenches is o'erspread with verdant grass. Perhaps here and there equipment of War will be lying with fresh spring sprouts of grass threading through interstices – underneath the sad little mounds resting sons of a great nation – in the clear sky overhead, instead of the bursting shrapnel, little fleecy clouds – the scream of shrapnel, the Hell noise of the firing, giving place to an unbroken stillness save for the chirping of a bird or the soft bussing of the bee!

Private Arthur Ernest Bolger, 14/AIF, who was killed and buried at Quinn's Post, 27 April 1915.

The strong defence of Russell's Top, Pope's and Quinn's, aided by the guns of the Royal Navy, had checked the Turkish attack in the north, but it had been at a high cost to the Anzacs.

Yards and yards of trench were at times empty of all save dead and wounded men, and in some cases the Turks effected a footing in them; they were always driven out again. Our fellows were simply magnificent; budge they would not...to make room for the living we had to throw the bodies out over the back.

Because the thin trench line at Quinn's was right on the lip of the crest, the bodies used to roll down to the foot of the hill.

When reinforcements were making their way in single file up this track they had to scramble in and out, through and over, dead men lying tossed about anyhow, while all the way right down to the valley the wounded were lying 'heads and tails' awaiting transport to the beach. It wasn't the most encouraging sight in the world for the fellows coming straight off the transports.

Kemal now concentrated an attack from the direction of Mule Valley towards the middle of the Australian line at Courtney's Post, MacLaurin's Hill and Johnston's Jolly. The 72 (Arab) Regiment with the reserve 33 Regiment were organised to attack simultaneously, but for some reason 72 Regiment did not enter the battle, which left 33 Regiment, with its three battalions, to attack alone. The open ground

Contemporary drawing of the Turkish counter-attack.

they crossed was to prove murderous to the advancing waves, who were cut down by rifle fire directed from advanced 'battle outposts'. These were manned by a mixture of men from 3/AIF and 11/AIF who had been out in front of the main Anzac line since 25 April. Supporting them along the main entrenched line was the newly arrived 14/AIF,

under Lieutenant Colonel Richard Courtney. His Battalion's machine guns helped protect the advanced posts from being overrun and together they were able to destroy the Turkish attack.

Private John Jensen, 1/AIF, wrote of the Turkish attack:

On the Tuesday night we could see the Turks in front of us in a terrible big force. So we had orders to retire back on to the second line as soon as it got dark. This we did & crawled away about a hundred yards when we heard the Turks coming. They kept shouting Allah & jumped over the trenches & into the ridge where we had been. We stopped then & fired a few more shots & they lay down & started firing where they saw the flashes of the rifle. We kept on going back & stopping & firing a few shots & then going back again. After a while they got a machine gun going & kept on sweeping all over us with it but the shots were going too high. Just as we were getting near our second line, which was a good trench, they started to shell us & the man next to me got hit in the back. The corporal who was the other side of me got hold of one arm & I got the other & we started to half-drag & carry him into the trench. When we were quite close to it another shell burst & a piece hit me in the right thigh. I fell straight down & seemed to lose all power of my leg for a while. I thought it was broke. The corporal, who was a big man over seventeen stone, caught hold of my hand & dragged me & the other chap into the trench. I found out then that my leg was only bruised & a few days after I could walk as well as ever although I was still black for a month.

We were the last ones to leave the ridge & we were very sorry to have to do it after holding it so long. I did not get a chance to put any bayonet into any of the Turks but the corporal who was next to me bayoneted two who had nearly got into his dugout.

Colonel Henry MacLaurin, commander of 1 Brigade, killed by a sniper on 27 April.

In command of this area was Colonel Henry MacLaurin, of 1 Brigade. MacLaurin, as ordered by Bridges, had already relieved the tired Sinclair-MacLagan during the afternoon of 26 April and took control of the posts along Second Ridge. His command was to be cut short as MacLaurin and his Brigade Major were both killed on 27 April. The fatal shots appeared to have come from snipers who had infiltrated themselves into positions on the northern end of Russell's Top, where they had a clear line of fire across the rear Anzac line along Second Ridge. Nowhere on Anzac was safe.

Further south of the line, on 400 Plateau, the counter-attack began at 11.00 am, but was stopped about an hour later by 4/AIF and 6/AIF. The advancing

164

waves dissipated into the valleys between the two lobes of Johnston's Jolly and Lone Pine, where they remained until night. Under cover of darkness the Turks renewed their attack, the heaviest part of which was across the open space of the Wheatfield, where the rush got to within twenty-five yards of the Australian trenches. During the attack 7 Australian Battery had its guns close to the front line, one of which was opposite the Wheatfield where the Turks came head on. By the time the attacked petered out, 677 rounds had been expended by the battery, crushing the attack.

Private John Pitt, 8/AIF, who was entrenched on Bolton's Ridge, described his day:

> *In trench all day, plenty of shooting, some marvellous escapes. Went to beach for water at dusk with Jim Price, we were just coming away carrying a tin full of water between us when he was mortally wounded. Sergeant Smith accidentally shot himself in the foot. Heard fighting all night, Jack Hutchinson shot dead 3 yards away from me, Didsbury wounded. Reinforcements expected tomorrow morning, God speed them, our casualties are very heavy.*[3]

The original wooden cross above MacLaurin's grave in 1915 (Anzac Book).

The grave of MacLaurin today in 4th Battalion Parade Ground Cemetery.

The Turkish counter-attack on 27 April had been a complete failure. Those that got close to the Anzac positions were driven off at high cost. The naval fire had been devastating and from then on the Turks always tried to avoid attacking in daylight where the ground was exposed to naval fire. The attack was planned to be simultaneous, along the whole front, but became a disjointed affair, caused mainly by poor communication and the broken ground over which the troops had to advance. With delays getting the troops to the front, Kemal, in a

165

piecemeal fashion, threw what battalions he had available at the Anzac perimeter. These attacks varied from half-hearted probes at some points of the line, to badly synchronised frontal assaults, all being beaten back with heavy loss. At the time Anzac command did not even realise that Mustafa Kemal was trying to launch a major coordinated attack. Stalemate had now set in; the Turks had failed to break the Anzac defences, as the latter too, had failed to break out.

The Staff since Sunday 25 April had been trying to reorganise 3 Brigade and the front line, however continued fighting proved this impossible. An initial effort was made during the Sunday night, when about 200 men of each battalion were reorganised on the beach. Once this was done they had to be put back into the line; 9/AIF and 10/AIF to 400 Plateau, 11/AIF to Steele's Post and 12/AIF to MacLaurin's Hill. The Anzac front was now organised so that in the north General Walker (who had relieved Braund) held Walker's Ridge and Russell's Top with his New Zealanders, and Colonel Monash's 4 Brigade held the centre from Pope's Hill to Courtney's Post. With the NZ&A Division now together in the north, 1st Australian Division held the remainder of the line, with MacLaurin's 1 Brigade and 3 Brigade holding 400 Plateau, whilst Colonel McCay's 2 Brigade held the southern part of the line down Bolton's Ridge to the sea. There was little rest for the weary Anzacs during the first few days and it was not until 28 April that they were partly relieved with the landing of a Naval Brigade from the Royal Naval Division. By then, the Anzac legend had been born.

The build-up of supplies in Anzac Cove, three days after the landing.

Before ANZAC, April 25, 1915

The splash of the salt waves awash phosphorescent,
The outlines of hills grim and mystic and grey,
The hush of the dawn ere the night curtain vanish,
And morn brings the light of this fame-laden day.

The wave-bitten stretch of the grey sandy beaches,
The beaches of Anzac the foreshores of death,
The blood of a thousand of braves soon to bleach them,
The foretaste of hell in the shell's fiery breath.

Dark looming hills whether death lurks behind them,
Or whether life waits me with garlands of fame;
How can I banish the scenes of remembrance,
The dear tender thoughts of a much-cherished name?

Duty and danger call me from the darkness,
The hour of my baptism fiery draws nigh;
I wonder and dream whether destiny waits me
With kisses of welcome or one brief good-bye.

Memory sings softly and croons of Australia,
Songs of my home in the Southern seas set.
Home and remembrance, the land of my fathers,
Scenes loved and lost to me can I forget?

Flame of the wattle, the fire of the forest,
The scent of the woodbine and songs of the birds,
Incense of blossom from trees all a-flower,
The tinkle of bells from the wandering herds.

Carols of magpies when dawn is a-quiver,
The outlines of trees gaunt and ring-barked and dead,
Flash of the waratah blooming in glory,
The click of the parakeet's flight overhead.

Glimpse of the waterfowl feeding and playing
Over the face of the sleeping lagoon,
Glint of the beams opalescent and gleaming,
Silver shafts hurled from the young crescent moon.

One little home in the midst of the fallow,
The grass springing green to the wooing of spring,
The green of the Lucerne, the fruit trees in blossom,
My home way down under how memories cling.

Ah, whether I perish or whether I follow
The scenes of the chapter of blood to the last,
My soul will dwell eager for time without ending
On dearly loved days that are banished and past.

And now I made ready for death or his master,
This thought as the moments in flight hurry by,
If I live 'tis my privilege all for my country,
For Australia to live, for Australia to die.

By Gunner Frank E. Westbrook, 4th Battery, 2 Brigade, Australian Field Artillery (*Anzac & After*, Duckworth and Co., London, August 1916).

1. Rhodes, James Robert, *Gallipoli*, (1984), p.166.
2. Bean, C.E.W., *Official History of Australia in the Great War – The Story of Anzac*, (1921), p.511.
3. Private James Owen Price, 631, 8/AIF died of wounds 27/4/15. Buried Beach Cemetery. Private John Hutchinson, 238, 8/AIF killed 27/4/15. Buried Shell Green Cemetery. Private James Didsbury, 1298, 8/AIF received a gunshot wound to the chest, went on to fight on the Western Front, where he was wounded again and, upon discharge in 1919, fought in Russia. Sergeant Harold Smith, 934, 8/AIF, on the casualty form is described as 'wounded in action'. The bullet damage to his left foot eventually led to a medical discharge in December 1915. Ironically, he was Best Shot in the Victoria Rangers 1902-03.

Chapter Nine

Tours of the Battlefield

These by the Dardanelles laid down their shining youth
In Battle won fair renown for their native land,
So that their enemy groaned carrying war's harvest from the field
But for themselves they founded a deathless monument of valour.
(Translated from an Athens memorial to soldiers who fell in the Dardanelles
in 440 B.C.)

The two main tours are designed to cover the Anzac area that is relevant
to the first few days of the battle, 25 – 27 April 1915. They can be covered
by car or similar vehicle in a single day along with the optional tours if time
permits. You could equally do these tours entirely on foot if you have more
time, each tour will probably take a full day.

Anzac is within the Gallipoli (Gelibolu) Historical National Park, which
today encompasses the Gallipoli battlefield from Suvla in the north down
to the tip of the Peninsula at Cape Helles. At Kelia Liman on the northern
outskirts of Eceabat (called Maidos in 1915) is the **National Park Main
Information Centre**, opened in 2005. This building has many modern
facilities, including a library, cinema, conference centre, internet
resources, souvenir shop, exhibitions and refreshments.

At the time of the landing there were two battalions of 27 Regiment in
reserve at Maidos, from where they were sent to reinforce the rest of the
regiment at Ari Burnu. The small town had approximately 4000 occupants

Gaba Tepe Museum and Memorial.

in 1915, but was steadily reduced to ashes after naval shelling and aerial bombing during the campaign.

From the main information centre it is approximately eight kilometres to Gaba Tepe (*Kabetape*). When you arrive, do visit the **Gaba Tepe Information Centre and Museum**. The museum contains an interesting collection of battlefield artefacts, uniforms, photographs and maps of the campaign. In the grounds is Wounded Soldiers statue, depicting two Ottoman soldiers, one holding up the Turkish flag, the other a rifle and bayonet twined with an olive branch. In the same area are some stunning wall friezes, a symbolic Ottoman cemetery and a bronze Ross Bastiaan Plaque, one of several on the Gallipoli battlefield. Erected for the 75th anniversary of the Gallipoli Campaign, the plaques give a brief summary of the importance of the immediate area. From the grounds there are some good observation points where you can view the Sari Bair Ridge, the Lone Pine Memorial on the seaward lobe of 400 Plateau and the high ground of Baby 700, Battleship Hill and the memorials at Chunuk Bair. The Information Centre is built on the lower seaward slopes of Third Ridge, just up from Gaba Tepe. This ridge was one of the objectives of the covering force, but was only reached by a few Australian scouts before they were forced to withdraw. During the remainder of the campaign the Turks used the area to position artillery batteries; hence it was soon named Gun Ridge and was similarly known to the Turks as *Topçuluk Sirt* (Artillery Ridge).

Bronze frieze depicting the Australian attack.

Tour One – The Lower Beach Road

Approximate time by car:	2 hours
On foot:	5 hours
Optional Walks:	Plugge's Plateau (extra 1 hour)
	Shell Green (extra 1 hour)

Leave the Information Centre and follow the road signs in a northerly direction towards Anzac Cove. As you drive along note the Gaba Tepe Sub-Information Centre and recreational area. The valley that opens up to the right is Legge Valley, named after Lieutenant General J.G. Legge, and known to the Turks as *Karayürük Dere*. It was crossed by scouts from the covering force on the day of the landing, but never entered again for the remainder of the campaign. The road to the right rises out of the valley onto Pine Ridge (Tour Two), but for now continue on the lower road that skirts the coastline. To the left is Brighton Beach, reputedly named after a Melbourne beachside suburb, which was originally designated as Z Beach, the intended landing place. This long and exposed beach stretches for almost two kilometres between Gaba Tepe and Hell Spit. Looking inland from this area you can see that the country facing a landing here is less rugged than the force actually encountered at North Beach and Anzac Cove. Even though the casualties suffered by 3/Australian Infantry Brigade that day were high, historians argue that casualties would have been greater had they landed at Brighton Beach because the defences there were stronger. The beach here would have been unprotected from the Ottoman guns at Gaba Tepe and a little further back at a position called the Olive Grove. Later on in the campaign the northern part of this beach was in Australian hands and became a natural overflow from Anzac Cove, where stores were kept and men swam in the sea, despite the sporadic shelling.

You are now entering the Anzac Battlefield Commemorative Area, which is controlled by the Commonwealth War Graves Commission (CWGC) according to the terms of the Treaty of Lausanne, 1923. Describing the Anzac cemeteries in his book *Gallipoli Today* (1926), T.J. Pemberton wrote:

> They are sacred now because of their associations, but the soil is still more sacred because of what it keeps forever. Once congested pits of death and destruction, these narrow plots of earth have been shaped by the hand of man into ordered gardens to commemorate the heroes of the past, and to keep their dust inviolate. But all about these sacred acres Nature, in its wildest mood, has done its best to obliterate the traces of human conflict.

To your right you will be approaching Bolton's Ridge, which stretches up from Brighton Beach to the heights of Lone Pine. Bolton's Ridge, known to the Turks as *Kel Tepe* (Bald Hill), was named after Lieutenant Colonel William Bolton, who commanded 8/AIF and established the line here on the first day of the landing. This ridge marks the southernmost limit of the

171

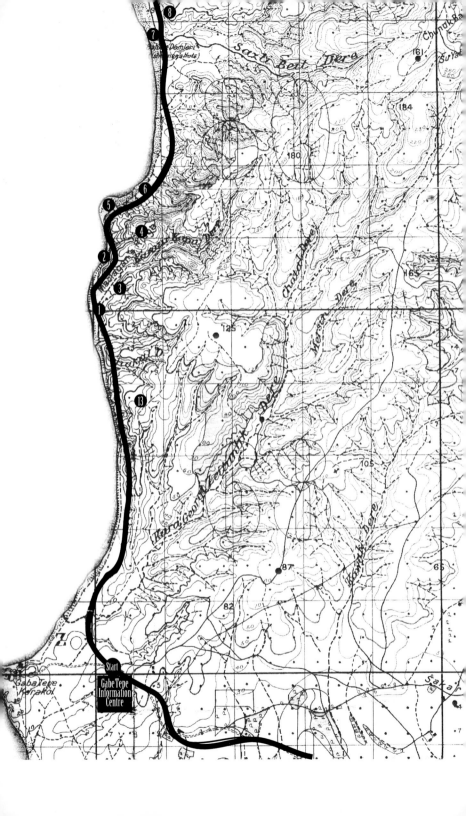

Anzac line and was later garrisoned by 2/Australian Light Horse Brigade in June 1915.

Further along the road to the right is a rough track that is signposted to CWGC Lone Pine Cemetery and Shell Green Cemetery. Stop and park. This track follows the path of the original Artillery Road, built soon after the landing to enable guns to be hauled up from the beach to the ridges above. On the sheltered side of the ridge and along the road were numerous dugouts and rest areas where units could shelter when out of the trenches. As the name suggests, there were also a number of Australian field artillery batteries positioned in this area, although probably attracting as many shells as they gave. Originally the road only reached as far as Shell Green Cemetery, but was widened and extended up to Lone Pine for the August offensive. The track is perfectly walkable throughout the year, although a little rough in

Artillery Road today.

places, so do not drive unless you have a 4WD vehicle. The trail leads up steeply to Shell Green Cemetery, which is approximately 510 metres distant; from there it reaches up to Lone Pine Cemetery, another kilometre on. You can also reach Shell Green Cemetery from Lone Pine. See the **Shell Green Walk (13)** in tour two. Return to the road.

Continue along the coastal road, passing Dawkins' Point, which today is marked by a post-war concrete bunker. The promontory here was named Hell Spit, but was known as *Küçuk Ariburnu* (Little Bee Point) to the Turks. In some memoirs and on maps it is also known as Queensland Point as boats from HMS *Beagle* landed men from C Company 9/AIF (Queensland) here on 25 April. This small knoll, about 100 feet high, is on the lower end of MacLagan's Ridge where it falls into the sea at Brighton Beach. Just after the sign to the CWGC Beach Cemetery, park your vehicle in the purpose made parking area for visiting the surrounding area. Walk to Beach Cemetery, noting the Ross Bastiaan Marker (No.2) and the Turkish Monolith on the rise behind the cemetery. The monolith has an inscription that reads:

A platoon of the 8th Company, 27th Infantry Regiment, faced the first wave of 1500 men of the Anzac Corps, who landed on the Ariburnu shore at dawn on 25 April 1915, and this resistance resulted in heavy casualties for the Anzacs, who were forced to shelter under the steep foothills of the beach.

Beach Cemetery (1) was begun on the day of the landing and continued to be used throughout the whole campaign. It contains 285 graves of Australian soldiers, fifty (including sailors and Marines) from the UK, twenty-one from New Zealand, three from Ceylon and twenty-one whose bodies are unidentified. There are also Special Memorials that record ten Australians and one New Zealander who are believed to be buried here. Of the burials, there are many from the landings. These include *(I.B.13)* Lieutenant Colonel Lancelot Fox Clarke, DSO, 12/AIF, aged 57, who was killed 25 April 1915 on Russell's Top, near The Nek. Another early casualty is *(I.A.39)* Major Sydney Beresford Robertson, 9/AIF, aged 29, who was killed on Baby 700. Wounded three times already, Robertson was shot dead whilst trying to raise his head above the scrub in order to look forward. Interestingly, the CWGC has his death on the grave marker as 25/28 April 1915, although from evidence he was almost certainly killed on 25 April. Note the grave of *(I.B.29)* Captain Sydney Raymond Hall, aged 31, who was the HQ Signals Officer with 10/AIF. He had been signalling throughout the day before being killed towards dusk on 25 April, when he was hit by shrapnel. A fellow officer in 10/AIF was *(I.K.13)* Lieutenant Albert John Byrne, aged 24 who, despite efforts to get him to safety, died on the afternoon of 25 April from multiple wounds.

Other interesting burials related to the landings include *(I.H.3)* Lieutenant William Henry Dawkins, Australian Engineers, aged 22, who was killed later in May whilst covering a water pipe. He was instrumental in finding water directly after the landings and gave his name to Dawkins Point. The cemetery also contains the grave of *(I.A.40)* Lieutenant Colonel George Braund, Commanding Officer 2/AIF, who held Russell's Top against the fierce Ottoman counter-attacks on 27 April. Braund was slightly deaf and was accidentally killed by a sentry when he ignored the challenge. Among other graves is 'the bloke with the eye-glass', *(II.G.5)* Commander Edward Cater, Assistant Beach Master, Royal Navy. Cater commanded a small beach party, detailed from HMS *Queen Elizabeth*, that was responsible for directing incoming boats and supervising beach parties at Anzac. He won the respect of all for his cool disregard of Ottoman shell fire whilst he assisted others on the beach. He was well

known to the Anzacs and stood out because of the large monocle he wore. The story goes that some Australians approached him one day with their identity discs in their eye. Cater looked at them, threw up his monocle into the air, caught it in his eye and said, 'Do that, you blighters!' He was killed by a shell on 7 August 1915.

One of the most legendary Anzac figures buried here is an Englishman from South Shields, *(I.F. 1)* Private John Simpson Kirkpatrick, C Section 3/Field Ambulance, who was killed aged 22 on 19 May. He is famed for being the 'Man with the Donkey'. Serving under the name of Private 'Jack' Simpson, he landed early on 25 April with his unit and began to work the beaches and inland slopes bringing in wounded men. The following day he found a lone donkey, which he used from then on to move the wounded. It is thought he used two different donkeys that went under several names, including 'Murphy', 'Duffy', 'Abdul' and 'Queen Elizabeth', all depending on what mood he was in. As with many soldiers, he became fatalistic and paid little attention to the shelling and sniping along his route from the ridge to the beach. On the morning of 19 May he was killed by machine-gun fire from the direction of Steele's Post.

On a clear day, looking from Beach Cemetery directly out to sea, you will see the Turkish island of Gökçeada or Imroz, the island where Hamilton set up his headquarters in June 1915. The island, which was originally Greek, was captured from the Turks during the Balkans Wars of 1912–13. In February 1915, the Greek government offered Imroz[1] to the British as a base for their assault on Gallipoli. In 1923 the island was ceded to Turkey under the terms of the Treaty of Lausanne, which brought a final post-war settlement to the area. During the campaign Imroz (also spelt Imbros) acted as a rest and recreation area for the troops on Gallipoli, where it housed a multitude of tented camps, casualty clearing stations, field bakeries, airfields and supply depots. Nestled behind this island to the north-west is the Greek island of Samothrace. It was on Samothrace that the statue of Nike, the Greek Goddess of Victory, was discovered and which today can be seen in the Louvre Museum in Paris.

Leave the cemetery by its northerly end, following the coastal footpath which will take you to **Anzac Cove (2)**, an easy five-minute walk. The Turkish words for Anzac Cove are *Anzak Koyu*, which became its official Turkish name in 1985. During 1915 the small and sheltered beach was 25 metres wide and 650 metres long. Although still recognisable, recent soil erosion, the construction of the road and its recent widening has sadly altered this historic site forever.

There is an evocative description about Anzac Cove, written in 1918 by soldier-poet Lance Sergeant Leon Maxwell Gellert, 10/AIF, who landed here on 25 April 1915. Gellert was evacuated from Gallipoli with dysentery in July 1915, shipped to Malta, where he contracted typhoid and then sent to England to convalesce. He was diagnosed as having epilepsy and discharged as medically unfit in 1916. He died in

Stacked high with stores. A general view of Anzac Cove after the landing.

The same area today.

Adelaide in 1977.

Anzac Cove

There's a lonely stretch of hillocks:
There's a beach asleep and drear:
There's a battered broken fort beside the sea.
There are sunken trampled graves:
And a little rotting pier:
And winding paths that wind unceasingly.
There's a torn and silent valley:
There's a tiny rivulet
With some blood upon the stones beside its mouth.
There are lines of buried bones:
There's an unpaid waiting debt:
There's a sound of gentle sobbing in the South.

**Poet, Lance
Sergeant Leon
Gellert, 10/AIF.**

From Anzac Cove return along the main road and stop by the small track on the inland side of the road that is signposted to 'CWGC Shrapnel Valley Cemetery – Plugge's Plateau Cemetery'. Walk down the short path into Shrapnel Valley and the cemetery.

Note the Ross Bastiaan Marker (No.3) by the entrance and the signs to Plugge's Plateau Cemetery to the left of the cemetery. **Shrapnel Valley Cemetery (3)** (also known as Shrapnel Gully Cemetery) contains 527 soldiers from Australia, fifty-six from New Zealand, twenty-eight from the UK, seventy-two unidentified graves and twenty-three Special Memorials. There are twenty-four burials here that date from the landings. The cemetery is the largest of the original cemeteries at Anzac (Lone Pine Cemetery contains more burials today but was created after the war). It was made soon after the landing and was enlarged slightly after the Armistice when nearby

The entrance to Shrapnel Valley with MacLagan's Ridge towering above.

isolated graves were concentrated together. Generally the layout of the cemetery today is the same as it was in 1915. After the evacuation the wooden crosses in the cemetery were used for firewood by the Turks and the cemetery almost vanished from view. However, in 1916 the Ottoman War Office remade Shrapnel Valley Cemetery when they heard that Pope Benedict XV had sent an envoy to check on the cemeteries. Even though it had the appearance of being well-tended, the newly created rock bordered burial mounds had little correlation with the original graves beneath. In 1919 the Graves Registration Unit used original cemetery plans, made just prior to the evacuation, to locate the 1915 graves and restored the cemetery to its original layout.

Shrapnel Valley, which was sometimes called Shrapnel Gully or even Long Valley, got its name in the early days after the landing. The Turks, who named the valley *Korku Dere* (Valley of Fear), realised that this had become the main highway for the Anzacs from the beach to the front, so the area was always under a constant rain of shrapnel. Confronted with this constant danger, the men quickly became 'fatalists' and thought that a particular shell or bullet had a man's name and number on it, so until it arrived it was best to ignore them and carry on as normal. This is the valley through which Jack Simpson (buried in Beach Cemetery) and his donkey brought wounded from the front. The upper part of this valley was called Monash Gully after Colonel (later Lieutenant General) John Monash who then commanded 4 Australian Infantry Brigade.

Return to your vehicle and continue to Ari Burnu, Turkish for 'Bee Point'. It was here that most of the first wave of the covering force landed at approximately 4.30 am on 25 April 1915. Park and visit the **Ari Burnu**

Shrapnel Valley Cemetery in the 1920s.

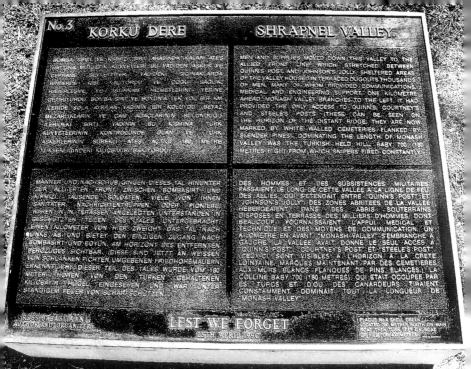

Shrapnel Valley Ross Bastiaan Plaque.

CWGC Shrapnel Valley Cemetery today.

Optional visit – Plugge's Plateau (4)

Time: Allow up to one hour

Follow the sign and path on the seaward side of the cemetery up to Plugge's Plateau. When you have reached the sign marked '570m', you have done the easy bit; the walk gets a lot harder as the path winds its way steeply to the top. Walk carefully, as the track can be quite rough at certain times of the year, and be aware of the steep sides along the walk, especially when upon the plateau, as there are some sheer drop-offs at the cliff's edge. This strenuous twenty-minute walk will take you along MacLagan's Ridge and then to the top of Plugge's Plateau and the CWGC cemetery, which is about a hundred metres above Anzac Cove.

This hill was named *Hain Tepe* (Treacherous Hill) by the Turks and Plugge's Plateau by the Anzacs after Lieutenant Colonel Arthur Plugge. He commanded the Auckland Battalion, NZEF during the landings and had set up his HQ there during the first day. Once up on the plateau you are rewarded by some spectacular views of the surrounding battlefield and all over the plateau are remains of trenches, walled sangars and gun-pits, although many have eroded away or have become covered by dense, prickly scrub. The views are truly superb (see panoramic photo on p.182-183); on the right, Bolton's Ridge rises up from the sea to meet Lone Pine, where its memorial is just visible behind the line of pine trees. Then from MacLaurin's Hill on the left and along the 'posts', to Monash Gully, which is hidden out of view by Russell's Top, and the spectacular views of the Sphinx and the Razor Edge close by. To the left of the Razor Edge is Reserve Gully where Clarke, Lalor and Margetts climbed up onto Russell's Top, and to its right is Rest Gully where other small groups of men ascended onto 400 Plateau. On the seaward side are almost aerial views of the initial landing beaches at Ari Burnu, North Beach and further along the coast to Fisherman's Hut. This is a great platform for orienting oneself with the battlefield, a view that the covering force would have had on that early morning as they cleared the Ottoman defenders from the top, before finding themselves confronted by the deep valleys and the amphitheatre of torturous ridges all around. It was on the top of this hill that Captain William Richard Annear, 11/AIF, was killed, the first Australian officer killed on Gallipoli [commemorated on Lone Pine Memorial]. Towards the evening of 25 April two Australian artillery pieces were hauled up onto Plugge's before being joined by Major Syke's 2/New Zealand Field Battery.

Plugge's Plateau Cemetery is the smallest cemetery at Anzac, containing the graves of twelve Australian soldiers, eight New Zealand and one that is unidentified. Of these graves, twelve were killed on 25 April 1915. One grave contains (B.8) Private Frank Batt, 477, 10/AIF, who was killed in action, aged 36 on that first day. He was the son of John and Harriett Batt of Camborne, Cornwall. Many of the soldiers serving in the Australian and New Zealand forces were in fact of British origin, as this and other graves show.

Return by the same path to Shrapnel Valley Cemetery.

Anzac Cove from the sea. Note Ari Burnu Cemetery in the foreground.

Cemetery (5), noting the Ross Bastiaan Marker (No.1). The cemetery contains the graves of 151 Australian soldiers, thirty-five New Zealanders, twenty-seven (including sailors and RND) from the UK, one from the Maltese Labour Corps, thirty-seven unidentified and five Special Memorials. Eighty-two are Australian Light Horse graves, most from the

CWGC Ari Burnu Cemetery today. This is where the first boats landed at 4.30 am on 25 April 1915.

Panoramic view from Plugge's Plateau of the Anzac battlefield today.

ill-fated attack at The Nek on 7 August. There are four identified graves for April 1915. Also note the Turkish Monolith, which was unveiled on Anzac Day 1985 and bears the words of Kemal Atatürk's 1934 address to the Allied pilgrims:

> *Those heroes that shed their blood and lost their lives*
> *You are now lying in the soil of a friendly country.*
> *Therefore rest in peace*
> *There is no difference between the Johnnies and the Mehmets to us*
> *Where they lie side by side*
> *Here in this country of ours.*
> *You, the mothers,*
> *Who sent their sons from far-away countries*
> *Wipe away your tears.*
> *Your sons are now lying in our bosom*
> *And are in peace.*
> *After having lost their lives on this land*
> *They become our sons as well.*

Drive on for another 250 metres to the **Anzac Commemorative Site (6)**. Until 2000, Ari Burnu Cemetery was the site of the Anzac Day Dawn Service, which is now held on North Beach. Along the ANZAC wall are ten information panels that depict various stages of the campaign, designed to tell the story of Gallipoli. There is a fitting quote from C.E.W. Bean there that says: 'Anzac stood, and still stands, for reckless valour in a good cause, for comradeship, and endurance that will never own defeat.' Look at the remarkable landscape above, dominated by the Sphinx. This view, although in the dim light of dawn, confronted the men leaving the boats that early morning. This site is situated where three boats containing men from 11/AIF landed, and although they suffered several casualties from Ottoman fire up above on Walker's Ridge, they managed to get ashore and storm the rises.

Leave the Anzac Commemorative Site and continue along the North Beach road, passing Canterbury Cemetery (made after the Armistice). The range behind is Walker's Ridge, that leads up to Russell's Top. This became one of the main supply routes to the positions above. Sadly this

Johnston's Jolly | 4th Btn Parade Ground | Lone Pine | Bolton's Ridge | Gat Tep

400 Plateau | Shrapnel Valley

route is now impassable due to almost a century of erosion. Continue pass the CWGC base and cottage, which is in front of the area known as No.1 Outpost. Continue for about 400 metres until you reach **Fisherman's Hut (7)**, marked today as it was in 1915 by a small stone hut. The dwelling is sited where the original Fisherman's Hut was positioned during the campaign, and even today it is owned by the same family who originally lived there in 1915. A second hut, that was originally situated on the inland side of the sandy knoll, called Shepherd's Hut, sadly no longer exists. It was on this beach that men from 7/AIF met such fierce resistance that morning from the Ottoman machine guns which Lieutenant Rafferty, 12/AIF, tried to silence. These guns were in an entrenched position on the sandy knoll above the hut. The men were sitting ducks in the boats and only forty out of 140 made it to the beach.

A little further on is **No.2 Outpost Cemetery (8)**, in front of the position that was called No.2 Outpost. This cemetery contains the known graves of thirty-two soldiers from New Zealand, seven from Australia, three from the UK and sixty-two who could not be identified. There are special memorials to sixty-six soldiers who are known to be buried in this cemetery. Of the graves there are twenty-eight identified as soldiers from 7/AIF who were killed or died of wounds during the landing at this point. One of these is (Sp. Mem. 27) Private Alexander James McArthur, 7/AIF, who was killed rowing one of the boats to the shore on 25 April 1915. Many of these have their date of death as 25 April – 2 May 1915, as it was not until early May that a proper roll call could be made. The New Zealanders set up a post here in late April, and the rise was sometimes referred to as Nelson Hill after Nelson Company, Canterbury Infantry Battalion, NZEF.

End of Tour One.

A fishing boat is peacefully beached where the men from 7/AIF faced such deadly fire.

Tour Two – The Upper Ridge Road

Approximate time by car:	3 hours
On foot:	7 hours
Optional Walks:	Shell Green (extra 1 hour)
	4th Btn Parade Ground (extra 35 mins)
	Chunuk Bair (extra 1 hour)

This tour begins at the Gaba Tepe Information Centre and Museum; when you get to the Sub-Information Centre, take the upper road. This road was built by the Turks soon after the evacuation and rises from the bottom of Legge Valley, up onto Pine Ridge and then onto Lone Pine and Second Ridge.

Just over a kilometre along the road you will come to a symbolic Turkish statue called *Mehmetcige Derin Saygi* which translates, to the **Monument of Deepest Respect for Mehmetçik (9)**. This is supposed to represent an event that took place near this point on 25 April when a Turkish soldier carried a wounded Australian officer back to the allied lines. According to the plaque this was reputed to have been witnessed by Lieutenant R.G. Casey, ADC to Colonel White, 1st Australian Division; however no evidence exists to prove that this actually happened. The statue is situated on the southern spur of Pine Ridge, which during the time of the landing was populated by twelve foot tall pine trees. The ridge was held by various units on 25 April, including those of 6/AIF led by Prisk and Bennett. Lieutenant R.C. Prisk, with a few men from 9/AIF, had initially protected the extreme right flank during that morning until they withdrew. Later in the morning Major H.G. Bennett had re-established the position on this ridge but by dusk the positions had been overrun. Ahead are the grassy plains of Legge Valley that rise up onto Third Ridge (Gun Ridge). This position was very exposed, and attracted not only Ottoman fire but also 'friendly' fire from Australians who thought Prisk's party were

Wounded Soldier Statue.

Turks. Eventually they had to abandon the position and any further attempts to advance to Third Ridge, withdrawing back to Bolton's Ridge. After the war, skeletons covered in ragged uniforms were identified by the red and violet sleeve patch as men from 6/AIF, lying in threes and fours down the length of Pine Ridge. After the afternoon of 25 April this ridge was never reached again and remained in Ottoman hands for the remainder of the campaign, so the bodies found here were almost certainly from the first day of the landing.

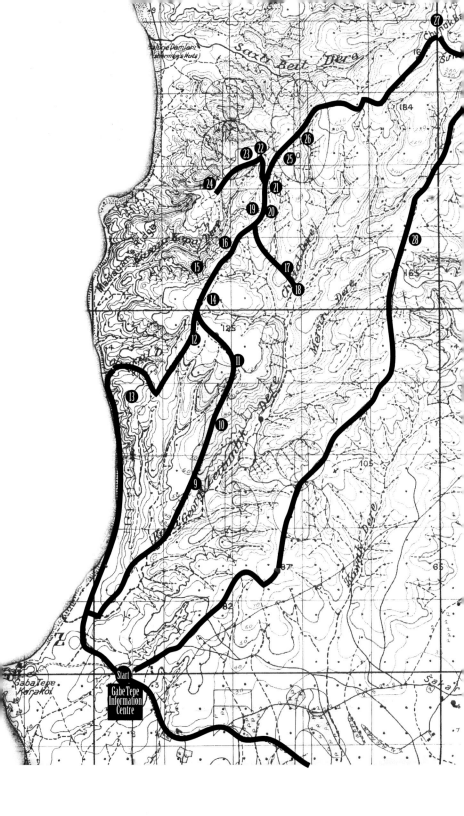

Karayörük Deresi (Black Nomad Streamlet) Cemetery.

Further along Pine Ridge road is **Karayörük Deresi (Black Nomad Streamlet) Cemetery (10)**, which is signposted to the right. The cemetery can be reached by a flight of steps that descends into Legge Valley. Reconstructed in 2006 over the site of the original Ottoman battlefield cemetery, it contains the burials of 1152 soldiers, including men from 72 and 77 (Arab) Regiments.

Continue along Pine Ridge road until you reach the **Kanlisirt Turkish Monolith (11)**, which rests on the Turkish slope of Lone Pine. The Turkish name for Lone Pine was *Kanli Sirt* (Bloody Ridge), a name it got later during the heavy fighting in May 1915. The monolith inscription refers to the Ottoman defence of Lone Pine during the August offensive. Continue along the road, note the gully on the right-hand side that is called 'The Cup'. It was here that the Australians overran the Ottoman mountain gun battery on the morning of 25 April, but after fierce Turkish counter-attacks in the late afternoon the position

Kanlisirt Turkish Monolith.

had to be relinquished, along with the guns. Continue on until you reach the **Lone Pine Memorial and Cemetery (12)**. Note the Ross Bastiaan Marker (No.5). Lone Pine is the southern spur or lobe of 400 Plateau, which derived its name from the song 'The Trail of the Lonesome Pine' and the single pine tree that stood on this plateau during the early days of the campaign. The area was reached by elements of 9/AIF early on 25 April. Subsequent heavy fighting took place during the next few days as Turks and Australians jostled for its capture. This was a strategic position as it overlooks Gaba Tepe to the south and the gullies leading up to it from the coast. By May it was in Ottoman hands who then set about turning the area into a fortified strongpoint, with trench positions reinforced by pine logs. It was held until its eventual recapture by the Australians in August 1915; seven VCs were won in this action. The remains of Turkish trenches still exist today on the southern side of the cemetery.

Lone Pine Cemetery, originally small and containing only forty-six graves, was enlarged after the Armistice by relocating many of the scattered battlefield graves in the area, plus those removed from Brown's Dip North and also the Brown's Dip South Cemeteries, originally located near the head of Victoria Gully. Today the cemetery contains 1167 graves, of which 651 are those of Australian soldiers, two New Zealand, fifteen sailors, soldiers or Marines from the UK and 499 men who could not be identified. There are special memorial tablets in the cemetery that commemorate the names of 182 Australian soldiers and one from the UK who are believed to be buried in this cemetery. There are seventy-three identified graves of men killed during the first few days of the landings.

Amongst those buried there are *(I.F.7)* Major Erle Finlayson Fethers, the commanding officer of A Company, 5/AIF. He was a 28-year-old former bank accountant from Melbourne, Victoria and was shot and killed by a sniper on 25 April whilst moving through the thick scrub on Johnston's Jolly. Similar thick scrub still covers the area today. A fellow Battalion officer in the adjoining grave is that of Liverpool born (I.F.8) Major Richard Saker, 5/AIF, who served pre-war in the Connaught Rangers. His brother Frank was killed as a captain in that Regiment at Ypres in 1914. At 6 foot 4 inches he was one of the tallest men in the Battalion, and was killed leading an advance on Lone Pine, over the Daisy Patch on 26 April.

Within the grounds of the cemetery is the **Lone Pine Memorial** that commemorates 4936 Australian and New Zealand[2] servicemen who died in the Anzac area whose graves are not known, or were buried at sea. Within the memorial is a small chapel that is occasionally opened.

There are many names on the memorial that relate to the landings, which include *(Mem.30)* Lieutenant William Rigby, 9/AIF, a 23-year-old insurance clerk from Brisbane, Queensland who was killed on 25 April on Baby 700. *(Mem.33)* Lieutenant Mordant Reid 11/AIF, a 33-year-old electrical engineer/manager from Coolgardie, Western Australia, who was killed on 25 April on Battleship Hill and has no known grave. *(Mem.19)* Captain Charles Leer, 3/AIF, a 43-year-old schoolteacher and Boer War veteran who was killed on Mortar Ridge on 25 April when his position was overrun by Turks. *(Mem.33)* Private Fred Adcock, brother of Frank, who died from his wounds and was later buried at sea. Another first day lander is New Zealand born *(Mem.12)* Captain Shout VC, MC, 1/AIF. A veteran of the Boer War, and a carpenter and joiner by trade from Sydney, he was heavily involved in the fighting on Baby 700 and was wounded just after the landings, where he was awarded the Military Cross for gallantry, and went on to win the Victoria Cross at Lone Pine on 9 August 1915. It was in this action that he was mortally wounded by a bomb that prematurely exploded in his hand. He died on a hospital ship

CWGC Lone Pine Memorial and Cemetery.

and was buried at sea. Also buried at sea was *(Mem.69)* Private Don Cadoux, 3/Field Ambulance, who was the first man killed in his unit whilst landing from his section's boat. On the same panel are his comrades Frank Hudson and Alfred Eccles, also killed during the landing. *(Mem.73)* Lieutenant Colonel Douglas Everard Stewart, commanding officer of the Canterbury Battalion is also on the memorial, who pre-war was a shipping agent/accountant from Christchurch, New Zealand. He was killed in action between The Nek and Baby 700, on 25 April, in an action that cost the lives of many New Zealanders from the Canterbury and Auckland Battalions. On the memorial is also the name of a Maltese soldier, *(Mem.33)* Private Charles Emanuel Bonavia, 11/AIF. Maltese born, Charles was the son of Emanuel, a registrar at the Malta Law Courts. He lived in Valletta and studied at the University of Malta, before emigrating to Perth, Australia in August 1911 where he was employed as assistant surveyor with the Lands Department before enlisting in 1914. He was initially reported missing on 25 April 1915, but later presumed killed. His service record states that: 'He was very much loved, and considered very clever by his regiment.' Malta played a significant role in the Gallipoli campaign, providing labourers who later served under Maltese officers, a naval base and also many hospitals and convalescent depots that looked after many thousand of casualties from the Gallipoli campaign.

There are some great views from Lone Pine: from the south-west Bolton's Ridge drops down to the sea near Gaba Tepe; to the south, in the far distance, is the hump of Achi-Baba and the toe of the Peninsula where the British and French lines were. In front is Third Ridge, which a few of the Anzac scouts reached on the first day, but after that it remained in Ottoman hands. Looking north-east, the Second and Third Ridge merge at Battleship Hill and behind that is Chunuk Bair. Looking along the road that today marks the old front line is Johnston's Jolly Cemetery and a little further along are Steele's, Courtney's and Quinn's Posts.

Leaving Lone Pine, the flat area where you rejoin the road, just before you meet the head of Owen's Gully, was a 100 metre square area that was known as the Daisy Patch. In April 1915 this area, then covered in red poppies, saw some heavy fighting, including the disastrous advance of 4/AIF on 26 April. To the left of the road you will find Australian trenches in various states of preservation and which are well worth a visit. Continue along the road for approximately 300 metres, passing a dip on the right which is known as Owen's Gully, named after Lieutenant Colonel R.H. Owen, who commanded 3/AIF. At **Johnston's Jolly Cemetery (14)**, park your vehicle and walk on. A little further along the road you will come to Johnston's Jolly, the northern lobe of 400 Plateau, called by the Turks *Kirmizi Sirt* (Crimson Ridge). The Australians named it after Lieutenant Colonel George Johnston, 2/Australian Field Artillery Brigade commander,

Optional Visit – Shell Green Walk (13)
Time: Allow up to one hour

The Shell Green CWGC Cemetery is approximately one kilometre down a rough track from Lone Pine. The track follows the original route of Artillery Road, which was built during the campaign and is now usually in a bad condition. Therefore it is best to walk, although in dry weather it is possible to drive down. Shell Green, originally a sloping cotton field on the seaward side of Bolton's Ridge, was captured by 8/AIF on 25 April 1915 and passed by as the Battalion advanced on up to the ridge in front. Being so close to the front line, the area was subject to frequent Ottoman shelling. At the time of evacuation the flat open area in front of the cemetery was used for a cricket match held on 17 December to deceive the Turks into thinking all was well. The cemetery was used from May to December 1915. Originally two separate cemeteries, they were brought together after the Armistice along with various isolated battlefield burials and graves that were moved from Artillery Road, Artillery Road East, Wright's Gully and The Eighth Battery Cemeteries. There is a

Kelia Liman plot comprising post-war graves removed from the Kelia Liman Cemetery in 1927, which was originally situated near Maidos (Eceabat). There are a total of 409 burials, of which eleven are unidentified. Of those identified, twenty-two are listed as being killed during April. Note the Ross Bastiaan Marker (No.4).

Buried here is the uncle of Alan Moorehead, the author of the classic book *Gallipoli*. (Artillery Rd. Plot.19) Private Frank Moorehead, 8/AIF, aged 24, was killed between 25-28 April and was originally buried in Artillery Road Cemetery. His body was interred here after the Armistice. Another early burial is that of Boer War veteran (Artillery Rd. Plot.6) Major John Edwin Sergeant, aged 45, who commanded B Company, 8/AIF. Wounded through the hand earlier in the day, he was killed 25 April by a shell whilst leading his company forward from Bolton's Ridge. He was later mentioned in despatches. His epitaph reads 'Mate o' Mine'.

Return to Lone Pine via Artillery Road.

Australian trench lines that remain near Johnston's Jolly.

who placed his field guns opposite this position in order to 'jolly up the Turks'. The position was taken on 25 April, but was lost the following day. The cemetery was made after the Armistice when those previously buried on the battlefield were brought in and re-buried. Today there are 181 graves, fourteen of which are unidentified. There are no early April burials in this cemetery. By the side of the cemetery is the preserved entrance to an original tunnel. This whole area was honeycombed with tunnels later on in the campaign; many still exist just a few feet down, so be careful when walking this ground. The scrub covering the plateau today is similar to the dense undergrowth that faced the Anzacs in April 1915, so it is worth spending a few minutes walking the area to get an understanding of what it would have been like. On the other side of the road across from Johnston's Jolly Cemetery is the sign for the **4th Battalion Parade Ground Cemetery.(15)** Note the Ross Bastiaan Marker (No.6).

Continue driving along the road and after a few hundred metres you will come to **Courtney's and Steele's Post Cemetery (16)**. Both positions were initially occupied on 25 April 1915 by men of 11/AIF, and were never relinquished until the evacuation. Courtney's Post was named after Lieutenant Colonel Richard Courtney, commander of 14/AIF, who arrived with his Battalion here on 27 April. Steel's Post (officially named Steele's) was named after Major Thomas Steel, 14/AIF. Both posts were steep

Optional Visit - 4th Battalion Parade Ground Walk (15)
Time: Allow up to 35 minutes

From the sign, follow the 200 metre stepped, steep path down to the **4th Battalion Parade Ground Cemetery.** A little way down from the top, as the path veers to the left, are the remains of a dugout on the right. DO

The path that leads down to CWGC 4th Battalion Parade Ground Cemetery.

NOT enter – it is extremely dangerous, not only because it is a ninety-year old dugout in danger of collapsing, but also because of poisonous snakes that inhabit the area. This whole ridge was peppered with dugouts and tunnels during the campaign; this is one example that has survived the ravages of time.

The cemetery was started by 4/AIF at the end of April and used until the beginning of June 1915, where the Battalion buried thirty-four of its dead, and six from other units. It is built on the southern slope of Braund's Hill (named after Lieutenant Colonel Braund, who was accidentally shot by a sentry near here on 4 May), off a pathway called Bridge's Road that went from Wire Gully down through Shrapnel Valley and along to Anzac Cove. After the Armistice the cemetery was enlarged by the concentration of seventy-six graves from two smaller cemeteries that were close by (3rd Battalion Parade Ground and 22nd Battalion Parade Ground) as well as some isolated battlefield graves. Two of the graves moved from the 3rd Battalion Parade Ground were from soldiers who fell in April: these were *(D.1)* Lance Corporal Arthur Hallam, a native of Ashton-on-Mersey in Cheshire, who was killed on 25 April and *(D.2)* Private William Henry, a native of Sydney, who was killed two days later. Two high ranking officers are also buried here:

Colonel Henry MacLaurin, *(A.10)* was the commanding officer of 1 Australian Infantry Brigade. Born in Sydney, NSW, he was a qualified legal barrister. He was shot by a sniper on MacLaurin's Hill on 27 April 1915. The fatal shot came from Russell's Top behind the Australian position here, and was fired just ten minutes after Major Irvine, MacLaurin's Brigade Major, was killed just a few yards away at Steele's Post. This was unknown to MacLaurin, although Major Brown, 3/AIF, was not alone in telling him of the danger and that he would be sniped at: 'It's my business to be sniped at,' he said. The following moment, standing in his shirtsleeves, he was shot dead. He was buried near where he fell on the hill that bears his name. The grave was moved into the cemetery after the war.

Lieutenant Colonel Astley Onslow Thompson, VD *(A.11)*, was the commanding officer of 4/AIF, killed on 26 April, aged 50, on 400 Plateau. Originally from Pontypridd in Glamorganshire, Wales, he was director of several companies in Menangle, NSW. His body was later recovered when men found it whilst digging a forward sap. He was buried by Salvation Army Padre William McKenzie, who later recalled:

> *It was a relief to find the body of our colonel ... after it had lain out for a full fortnight. We buried it after dark, as it lay in an exposed position. I had to kneel and keep head and body in a crouching posture while reading the service. Hundreds of bullets swept over us while this was going on.*[3]

CWGC Courtney's & Steele's Post Cemetery.

niches, literally a slender foothold on to the ridge, which were defended throughout the campaign. The opposing front lines were separated by a No Man's Land the width of the road now running between them. It was here that Lance Corporal Albert Jacka, 14/AIF, was awarded Australia's first Victoria Cross of the war for his heroism in repelling an Ottoman bombing party on 19 May 1915 which had broke into Courtney's. The cemetery, built after 1919, contains 167 burials, seven graves are identified but all the others are unknown. There are fifty-four Special Memorials to men believed to be buried here, and twenty-four burials that date from April 1915, with most from Courtney's Battalion. Note the Ross Bastiaan Marker (No.6) by the entrance.

> Thus as we rode northwards along this road the trenches were never, except where a gully broke them, more than about fifty yards away on either hand ... It gave a strange thrill to ride along this space in front of Steele's, Courtney's and Quinn's where three years before men could not even crawl at night. The bones and tattered uniforms of men were scattered everywhere...[4]

Leave the cemetery and continue along the road until you come to the sign to the grave of **Lieutenant Colonel Hüseyin Avni Bey (17)**, on the right of the road. The grave is reachable on foot near the end of a kilometre long track that descends into Mule Valley. Avni Bey was the commander of 57 Regiment until he was killed in August 1915. There is a plaque by the grave that commemorates soldiers from his regiment, many of whom died during the first few days of the fighting. Leave the grave and continue along the track until you reach **Çataldere (Fork stream) Cemetery and Monument (18)**. The modern day cemetery, near the site of the original Ottoman cemetery, commemorates 2835 soldiers from various regiments including 27 and 57 Regiments that lie here. Return to the road.

Continue along the road, stopping at **Quinn's Post Cemetery (19)**. Note the Ross Bastiaan Marker (No.7). This post was established on 25 April by Major Thomas Dawson, NZEF, with an NZ machine-gun crew and a mixed force from the Auckland and Canterbury Battalions along with a few Australians. They dug-in and held this critical part of the line, which was only the size of a tennis court, against numerous Ottoman attacks. It was officially named Quinn's Post later in May, after Major Hugh Quinn, 15/AIF, of Charters Towers, Queensland. Quinn was killed at this post on 29 May 1915 and is buried in Shrapnel Valley Cemetery. The Turks later called this area *Bomba Sirt* (Bomb Ridge) because of the concentration of bomb attacks that took place. From the back of the cemetery there are fantastic views back down to the sea along Monash and Shrapnel Valleys, the main supply routes to this part of the line. By standing here you can understand what a key position Quinn's Post was. If the Turks could break the Anzac line here, they would enfilade the surrounding defences and would have dominating views of the Anzac supports in the valley below. Its loss would have been devastating, if not fatal, to the Anzac bridgehead. To the north-east of it is a gully that became known as The Bloody Angle where ferocious fighting continued for a week after the landing. Also, Dead Man's Ridge, which Captain H. Jacobs, 1/AIF, held throughout 25 April and to its left is Pope's Hill, the steep razor-backed hill that runs in front of Russell's Top and The Nek. This position was first occupied by Lieutenant Colonel H. Pope's 16/AIF on the first day. Pope had a narrow escape here when he fell for an enemy ruse and was almost taken prisoner.

The cemetery was made after the Armistice by concentrating 225 unidentified isolated graves and moving seventy-three other graves from Pope's Hill Cemetery, which was originally located at the foot of Pope's Hill. A further six graves were found later and also moved into this cemetery. 179 of the burials are identified. There are seven identified burials for 25 April, five for 26 April and twenty-four for 27 April, the latter reflecting the heavy casualties suffered in this area during the Ottoman counter-attack of that day. Burials include *(D.4)* Private Joseph Cornwall, Auckland Battalion, who was from Paraparaumu, New Zealand and was killed on 25 April and *(B.5)* Private Harold Pring, 11/AIF, who served under the name Clarke. He was a native of Bristol, England and was also killed on 25 April 1915. *(Sp. Mem. 33)* Private Arthur Ernest Bolger, 14/AIF, from Richmond, Victoria was killed on 27 April at Quinn's Post. His epitaph reads: 'He Gave God's Greatest Gift To Man, His Life.' He is one of thirty that were killed and buried the same day by the Battalion chaplain, Reverend Andrew Gillison, who himself was later killed in action. Only that morning they had come ashore and marched up Shrapnel Valley to Quinn's Post. An unfortunate incident happened as the company climbing the hillside was caught in the open by an Ottoman machine gun, a bitter introduction for the Battalion to Gallipoli.

On the opposite side of the road is the grave of **Yüzbaşi (Captain) Mehmet (20)**, who is believed to have been a company commander from 57 Regiment. Little is currently known about this officer, who was killed sometime during the campaign. Leave the grave and continue along the road until you reach the car park on the right of the road. Leave your

CWGC Quinn's Post Cemetery with 57 Regiment Memorial behind.

Turkish Soldier Memorial.

vehicle and visit **57th Regiment Memorial and Cemetery (57 Alay Sehitligi ve Aniti) (21)**. This regiment, under the command of Lieutenant Colonel Hüseyin Avni Bey, stemmed the Anzac advance in this area on 25 April, and contained all further attacks. The memorial park, opened in 1993, is built on the area known as the Chessboard, named because of the concentration of criss-crossed trenches that were there. The area was held by the Australians on the first day, but had to be relinquished when Baby 700 fell.

National park sign to The Nek and the Turkish memorial.

A couple of days later, during the Ottoman counter attack on 27 April, the Arab 3/72 Battalion charged across this area in an effort to break through the lines at Quinn's and Pope's. The park contains a symbolic martyrs cemetery, memorial plaques, a relief depicting the 25 April counter attack and an outdoor Mosque with fountain. Note the bronze sculpture of Turkish veteran Hüseyin Kaçmaz with his grand-daughter. He was reputed to be the last surviving Turkish veteran of the campaign, dying in 1994 at the age of 110.

Nearby is also a large Turkish Soldier Memorial that represents the successful blocking of the Anzac advance in this area. Behind this memorial are the slopes of Baby 700 (*Kiliç Bayir*, meaning Sword Slope), where one of the most crucial actions on 25 April 1915 was fought, and it was here that the courage and capability shown by the Turks arguably sealed the fate of the Anzacs. From the distant Chunuk Bair *(Conkbayiri)* Mustafa Kemal stood and observed the battle on 25 April. His decisive action in deploying 57 Regiment halted the Anzac advance to Chunuk Bair as, earlier in the day to the south, 27 Regiment halted any chance of advance there. Ultimately these first day positions where to change little for the remainder of the campaign.

Next to 57 Regiment Memorial and Cemetery is a flight of steps that descends to **Kesik Dere (Cut Stream) Cemetery**. This newly constructed cemetery, built in 2006, lists the names of 1115 soldiers of 19th Ottoman Division (mainly to 27 and 57 Regiment) who fell in the area. The original burial ground was on the opposite bank of the Kesik Dere.

Return to your vehicle and continue on until the road forks at the head of Monash Gully; take the left hand turn, which is signposted to *Mehmet Çavus Sehitligi*, CWGC The Nek Cemetery and Walker's Ridge Cemetery. This will take you onto Russell's Top, captured by the Anzacs

The original Sergeant Mehmet memorial at The Nek in 1927.
Inset: The same memorial today.

CWGC Walker's Ridge Cemetery.

Major David Grant was a popular officer in the Canterbury Battalion, he was keen and thorough and very highly respected by his men. Grant was mortally wounded during the afternoon of 25 April 1915 in a skirmish against an Ottoman machine-gun post. His body was not recovered until 24 May, when an armistice allowed the Turks and Anzacs eight hours to bury their dead that had been lying out in No Man's Land. His body was found in Malone's Gully and was buried in Walker's Ridge Cemetery.

A letter was sent to his widow, dated 27 May 1915, from Chaplain John A. Luxford, which brought her a little information on David's death and discovery. It reads:

> *Dear Madam, Officers of the Canterbury Battalion will have written you concerning the death of your brave husband on the battlefield. I was present as Chaplain when, during the armistice, his body was found. The intense interest and sympathy of all present was very marked. I read the service and affectionate mourners helped to bury the body. Of course you know an armistice had been declared for purpose of burying the bodies of both sides lying on this historic plateau. About 100 of the enemy and 45 of our own were discovered. Your brave husband had evidently been wounded and was being helped by a sergeant when both received their fatal wounds. A cross of white stones were placed on the grave and the Major's name was carved in a large stone placed at the head of the grave. We pray for you and trust you may feel the saviour's presence near to sustain. Another tie bonds us to the Eternal home where death is unknown.*

The second-in-command of the Canterbury Battalion, Major Albert E. Loach, was next to write, on 18 August 1915. Loach begins by giving his apologies as the letter he originally wrote on 28 April to Mrs Grant had been mistakenly returned to him. Loach was commanding the Battalion now, replacing Lieutenant Colonel D.E. Stewart, who was also killed the same day as David. He writes:

> *I cannot give you the exact circumstances of his death, but I know this much, that he died fighting bravely. When leaving the Beach for the plateau above, he saw me standing a little way off and saluted me. I took this at the time as a kind of "Good-bye old chap." Not long afterwards, I received a written message asking me if I could let him have his other two platoons, as when he arrived at the position he found himself with only two, and he thought I might have kept the other two back. Such was not the case, however, for he led his company up to the firing line, but, unfortunately, the two last platoons became detached somewhere on the position, and that is how he lost touch with them. I did not see him again and, at 4 o'clock that afternoon, I heard that he was badly wounded and beyond all hope, and was left behind when the men began to retire, but as this is in hearsay, I am just giving it you for what it is worth. I hope some of his men who were with him have written giving you an account of his last moments. The first day of the landing was an awful mix-up. It was impossible to find one's own troops, and it was not until the third day, that we began to get our battalion together again. Well, dear Mrs. Grant, I have got nothing further to add other than your husband died a glorious death for a glorious cause.*

Another letter, dated 26 September 1915, from Lieutenant Raymond A.R. Lawry, Canterbury Battalion, gives some more detail about his death and burial:

> *On the eventful morning of 25th April, I accompanied the Major as far as the crest of the second line of hills, and then in accordance with his orders took my platoon on ahead to reinforce the left flank of the*

Australian line where the Turks were attacking very strongly. I was there all that day and did not see the Major again until that unforgettable day – May 24th – Armistice Day, where I found his body during the burial operations between the two lines of trenches. Alongside was Sergeant W. A. Hamilton, whose waterproof sheet was thrown over the Major's face. I judged that both had been severely wounded and unable to get back, and had later been killed by subsequent fire probably the same day.

The two heroes were buried in the same grave, and more time than usual was given to the burial service conducted by Rev. J. A. Luxford of the N.Z. Chaplains' Dept (Methodist). Captain Brown, Lieut. Head and I, the only remaining officers of the old company, were present, while a number of men of the company, thinking of days now past, ceased their digging operations and, drawing near to the grave, stood in reverent attitude while solemn words of commitment and hope were recited.

A number of us built up a mound of earth over the double grave on which was placed a large white cross, made up of pieces of white rock firmly pressed into the soil. At the head of the grave was placed a very rough wooden cross (temporary) on which were printed the words:

HERE LIE
MAJOR D. GRANT AND
SERGEANT W. A. HAMILTON 2nd.
(S.C.) REGIMENT N.Z KILLED IN
ACTION 25th APRIL 1915.

At the foot of the grave was placed a large smooth stone on which Lieut. Wilson (who was also present) carefully carved the names of the two who slept in that far away grave.

You will be glad to know that the rumours of Turkish mutilation of the dead (with which Major Grant's name was so often coupled) were that day found to be false. No indication of anything of the sort was noticed.

In my base box at Alexandria I have a photographic film showing the site of Major Grant's grave on the top of Walker's Ridge, now known as Russell's Top. It shows Cape Nibrunesi and Suvla Bay etc. in the distance, and the curving beach below. If fortunes of war ever allow I will have a print run off and sent to you.

I would like to say how greatly I admired Major Grant not only as a military leader, but as a man, a man clean in thought and action, and one who exercised a splendid influence over all with whom he associated. And though very few remain now of those who trained under him on the sands of Egypt, yet those who survive will ever hold him in fond remembrance.

on the first day of the landings. Stop and visit **Çavus (Sergeant) Mehmet's Memorial (22)**. The memorial was erected soon after the evacuation and commemorates Sergeant Mehmet, 64 Regiment, and twenty-five of his men who courageously fought here in 1915. 64 Regiment attacked here during the night of 27 April, helping to drive the Anzacs from this end of Russell's Top. Incidentally, the memorial is built on the area where Captain Peter Lalor, 12/AIF and his men dug the horseshoe trench during the first day.

Walk to **The Nek Cemetery (23)**, which is a little further along. Note also the Ross Bastiaan Marker (No.8) and the recreated trenches that lie to the right of the track. The Nek, famed for the Australian Light Horse attack depicted in the 1981 film *Gallipoli*, was captured by the Australians on 25 April when they overran this area in the early morning before advancing up on to Baby 700 behind. The whole Russell's Top area was known to the Turks as *Cesarit Tepe* (Hill of Valour), which is where Braund fought his three-day battle to hold back the Turks' determined efforts to capture the ridge. The Nek Cemetery was made after the Armistice in what was No Man's Land and today contains 326 burials, 316 being unidentified. There is one known landings grave here, to one of Lalor's Tasmanians, *(A.13)* Private Alexander Campbell, 12/AIF, who was killed, aged 19, on 25 April 1915.

Leave The Nek Cemetery and continue on foot along the track until you reach **Walker's Ridge Cemetery (24)**. As with The Nek cemetery, there are some spectacular views all along this ridge. To the north, below and to your right, are the valleys and spurs leading up to Koja Temen Tepe and Chunuk Bair. In the distance are the Suvla Plains, encircled by the high ground that leads up to Kireçtepe and Tekke Tepe. The curving sweep of Ocean Beach leads up to Nibrunesi Point from where Suvla Bay opens into the Salt Lake, now permanently flooded. Walker's Ridge was the name given to the spur that stretches from the coast near Fisherman's Hut, south-eastwards to the middle of Russell's Top where you are now standing. On 25 April 1915, it was here that Brigadier General (later Major General) Sir H.B. Walker, then commanding the New Zealand Infantry Brigade, situated his command post. The cemetery was made during the campaign and originally consisted of two plots separated by eighteen metres of ground, through which ran a trench. This trench was started by Colonel Braund's mixed group of Australians and New Zealanders on 25 April and held throughout the campaign. The cemetery contains the known burials of forty New Zealand soldiers, twelve Australian soldiers, one Royal Marine and twelve unidentified graves. In addition, eighteen soldiers from Australia and eight from New Zealand are commemorated by special tablets.

The several early burials include *(Sp. Mem. 10)* Major David Grant of the Canterbury Battalion, NZEF, who died during the afternoon of 25 April. Aged 41, he was from Timaru in New Zealand. Grant in his pre-war career was a member of the large butchering firm of Grant and Seaton of Timaru. At the outbreak of war he was promoted to the rank of major, was keen and thorough, and very highly respected by his men. According to the *Auckland Weekly News*, he was mortally wounded during a skirmish on Baby 700 when he led a group to ambush a machine-gun post. His body was recovered near The Nek during the May 1915 Armistice. Interestingly, the CWGC records show he died 25–29 April, 1915. There is a memorial to Grant's granddaughter, 23-year-old Rosalind Webb, in the Nurses' Memorial Chapel in Christchurch, New Zealand and there is also a mention of her on her parents' grave in Woodbury Cemetery, South Canterbury. Rosalind was on a pilgrimage to Gallipoli in 1965 to visit her grandfather's grave when she was killed in a car accident near Lâpseki. She was believed to be the first member of the family to try to visit the grave at Walker's Ridge; sadly, after fifty years and travelling that vast distance from New Zealand, she died only a few kilometres away from her grandfather. Today she rests in the British Consular Cemetery in Çanakkale. Fellow traveller and nurse Jean Walker, aged 23, was also killed in the same car crash on that fatal day of 11 November 1965 and is buried alongside her. The Consular Cemetery is often locked, but you can arrange a visit by contacting the CWGC Çanakkale office.

Also from Major Grant's unit and buried in Walker's Ridge Cemetery is fellow New Zealander *(Sp. Mem. 27)* Lance Sergeant William Alexander Hamilton, who was killed in action the same day. His body was found alongside Major Grant during the Armistice and they were subsequently buried together. *(Sp. Mem. 11)* Private Robert Hargreaves, Auckland Regiment, who was a prominent footballer in his home town, also died on

CWGC Baby 700 Cemetery with Chunuk Bair behind.

that first day as did fellow Aucklander *(Sp. Mem. 23)* Private Charles Talbot. Talbot was a British born subject who used to work in the famed *J. C. Williamson Opera Company*, one of the largest theatrical firms in the world. Both the Canterbury and Auckland Battalions were in action that first day on Baby 700. Another native of England, but living in Queensland, was *(Sp. Mem. 19)* Lieutenant John Powe Roberts, 9/AIF, who is listed as being killed between 25/28 April 1915, but he is now known to have met his death in the old Ottoman gun position in The Cup, near Lone Pine, on 26 April. Also killed on 26 April and mentioned in the Wellington Battalion's War Diary is *(Sp. Mem. 19)* Lance Corporal Wilfred George Looney, who

The view in 1927 of Ari Burnu. Opposite inset: a similar view today.

met his death when he left the protection of a trench and, under heavy fire, proceeded to bandage up a wounded man.

Leave Walker's Ridge Cemetery and continue down the track to the end of the ridge. Be extremely careful here as there is a sheer drop into the ravine below. There are some excellent views (for the non-faint hearted) of Mule Gully below, Ari Burnu and the surrounding battlefield and coastline.

Return to your vehicle and head up the main road to Baby 700. A short distance on the right-hand side is a signpost for **Baby 700 Cemetery (25).** Baby 700, which is actually 590 feet high, connects Russell's Top to Big 700, later known as Battleship Hill. During the first rush the Australians reached the inland eastern slopes of Baby 700 and heavy fighting continued through the day that saw both sides pushing to and fro on and over the summit. The counter-attack at 4.30 pm finally threw back the Anzac line and thereafter the hill remained in Ottoman hands.

Park, and walk along the footpath to the cemetery. This cemetery is built near the area that Major F.J. Kindon, 1/AIF, held on 25 April. In 1919 many Anzac graves that had been made by the Turks during the campaign were found in this area. In one position thirty graves were found, some with uniform fragments and equipment identifying them as 1/AIF, 2/AIF and 12/AIF. In a different position a dozen graves were discovered, many of these bodies bearing the badges of the 16th (Waikato) Company of the Auckland Battalion and another with a badge of a New Zealand major. There was only one New Zealand major who died that day who was not accounted for, Major Frederick Stuckey, 6th (Hauraki) Company, Auckland Battalion. He is today listed on the Lone Pine Memorial. A little further along, over the top of the hill, further remains were found, which were probably part of Margetts' line. On the seaward spur of Baby 700 still more remains were found, lying thickly in the scrub, unknown men from first day actions that went unrecorded. All these bodies were from the fighting on the first day as these positions were never reached again. The majority of the burials in Baby 700 Cemetery represent the units who captured and fought to retain Baby 700 on 25 April. These include 11/AIF and 12/AIF, who were the first to seize the hill, and the reinforcements that comprised 1/AIF, 2/AIF and also the New Zealand Auckland and Canterbury Battalions, who held the line later on that day. It is possible to see the Narrows on a clear day, a sight preciously glimpsed by only a few on that first day.

The cemetery today contains the burials of 493 men, 449 of these being unidentified. There are several first day casualties buried here, including *(Sp. Mem. 10)* Major Blair Inskip Swannell, 1/AIF, who before the war was a British international rugby footballer before he emigrated to Australia, where he became a coach and referee for the game. Swannell remarked the night before the landing that he would: 'play this game as he had played rugby – with his whole heart.' He was considered to be a tough and courageous Forward, who played hard on and off the field. His prized possession was a pair of once white breeches, which he refused to wash, that he wore in every match. He was shot and killed when he kneeled to show his men how to take better aim. There is a memorial plaque to him in the church at Weston Underwood, Buckinghamshire. Another renowned officer was 30-year-old *(Sp. Mem. 4)* Captain Joseph Peter Lalor, 12/AIF. He was a grandson of Peter Lalor, who had led the Eureka Stockade revolt in Victoria in 1854. Leading the life of an adventurer, he made his way to London where he worked as a dockworker. During his colourful early life he also served as a boy in the Royal Navy before deserting; was with the French Foreign Legion in Algeria; and also reputedly had fought in a South American revolution. Returning to Australia in 1908 he joined the Australian army, being appointed to the permanent forces in 1912. He carried his family sword when he went into action on 25 April and was killed leading a charge in the afternoon, on the seaward spur of Baby 700. Whatever happened to his sword, believed to have been used at the Eureka Rebellion, we may never know. His epitaph reads *Dulce Et Decorum Est Pro Patria Mori*

The Mesudiye gun in the 1920s.

Optional Visit –
Chunuk Bair (Conkbayiri) (27)
Time: Allow up to one hour

Although never captured by the Anzacs during the landings, the position did briefly fall into their hands during the August 1915 offensive. The race to the high ground on 25 April was won by Mustafa Kemal, who reached the position just before Captain Tulloch.

The five stone monolith **Turkish Soldiers' Memorial** is called *Mehmetçik Park Aniti* in Turkish, representing a hand turned up to God. Of the inscriptions on the monoliths, two refer to the landings.

The first translates as:

After learning of the enemy landing at Ariburnu on 25 April 1915, Staff Officer Lieutenant Colonel Mustafa Kemal (Atatürk), Commander of the 19th Infantry Division, on his own initiative, dispatched the 57th Regiment to this sector. At this time, a small number of soldiers, whose ammunition was finished, were guarding the shore. They made a bayonet charge and gained enough time successfully to prevent the enemy reaching Conkbayiri.

The second memorial states:

On the morning of 25 April 1915, Mustafa Kemal (Atatürk) gave his order to the 57th Regiment, just before the regiment's attack on the enemy nearing Conk Slope: "I do not order you to attack. I order you to die. In the time which passes until we die, other troops can take our places and other commanders can master the situation." This order angered the Mehmetçiks, who continuously and undauntedly attacked the enemy under thick and impressive fire of the naval artillery and threw the enemy back to Cesarit Tepe [Russell's Top].

The remaining three panels tell the Turkish story of the August fighting.

Continue to the T-junction and turn left towards Chunuk Bair. On the left is the **Tomb of an Unknown Turkish Soldier**, the remains of whom were discovered in 1985. An impressive bronze statue to **Kemal Atatürk** is also in the grounds and is reputedly in the place where a piece of shrapnel hit him in the chest on 10 August, breaking the pocket watch which, quite likely, saved his life. Within the area is also the **New Zealand National Memorial** to their countrymen who fought on these slopes in August 1915, and a **New Zealand Memorial Wall** for those missing from the fighting here, situated opposite the **Chunuk Bair CWGC Cemetery**. In the park are newly constructed trenches that are reinforced with log supports, a memorial obelisk to 1st Lieutenant Nazif Cakmak, who was killed leading a bayonet charge on 8 August 1915, and a Ross Bastiaan Marker (No.9).

Return the way you came and follow the signs to *Kemalyeri*.

Lord Thou Knowest Best, [How Sweet is it To Die For One's Country]. Fred Adcock's brother, *(D.24)* Private Frank Henry Burton Adcock, 11/AIF, is also buried in this cemetery. Their Battalion was one of the first to gain a footing on the hill and held it throughout the day, until overwhelming pressure forced the Anzac line back. Another 11/AIF burial is that of *(D.18)* Private David John Simcock, a popular and successful Perth fruit seller, calling himself 'the little boy with the Pink Top' due to his bright red hair. He went from barrow boy to establishing a shop in Barrack Street, Perth, which still stands today, and another in Fremantle. Joining up to do his duty, he enlisted with the AIF and went to Egypt with the Battalion. A popular character in the Battalion, he is even mentioned in Bean's Official History who describes him:

> *A strange, ungainly, splay-footed soldier. His main anxiety – sedulously encouraged by his mates – had been how he should face barbed wire, and he had solved the problem by putting tin guards beneath his putties. His sergeant had ordered him to remain on the Beach as a sentry over the men's packs, but he refused, and came on with the rest. In the fighting on Sunday night – in an endeavour, it is said, to bring a wounded man into cover – Private Pinktop was killed.*
>
> *When his body was found it reputedly had guards made from biscuit tins beneath his puttees.*

Follow the dirt track that leads from the NW corner of the cemetery for approximately five minutes. This will take you over the crest of Baby 700 to the **Mesudiye Gun (26)** (There is also a sign to the *Mesudiye Topu* from the main road). The gun, which was placed here after the armistice, was salvaged from the wreck of the Turkish battleship *Mesudiye*, which was sunk off Çanakkale on 13 December 1914 by Submarine *B.11*. The submarine was commanded by Lieutenant Norman Holbrook, who was the first submariner to be awarded the VC. The gun rests on the inland slope of Baby 700, which is on the position that Major Kindon, 1/AIF, held for part of the first day.

Return to your vehicle, continue up the road which will take you over the crest of Baby 700. Ahead is Big 700, named **Battleship Hill** on 27 April 1915 after the concentration of naval shells that fell on the position. The hill is actually 690 feet above sea level and was known to the Turks as *Düztepe* (Straight Hill). The summit of Battleship Hill was the designated rendezvous point for 11/AIF on 25 April. Its inland slope was actually reached by a party led by Captain Eric Tulloch, 11/AIF, during the early morning of the first day. He set up a position on the right or eastern shoulder of the hill (*Incebayir* Ridge), approximately 75 metres from the present day road, with about sixty men, staying there until he could hold it no longer. Charles Bean interviewed Tulloch after the war. He recounted seeing an Ottoman officer calmly handing out messages, under a single stunted tree just under a kilometre away on the slope of Chunuk Bair. We will never know for sure who this officer was, however it has been suggested that Mustafa Kemal who, leaving his troops behind the summit of Chunuk Bair, had gone forward on foot to this area in order

Pine Ridge | Lone Pine | Johnston's Jolly | MacLaurin's Hill | Courtney's & Steele's Post | Quinn's Pos

400 Plateau

Mortar Ridge   Chessboard   Baby 700   Battleship Hill   Chunuk Bair

May 1915 Truce: an early attempt to clear the battlefield.

Harvest of Bones.

Collection of Bones & Skulls
on Gallipoli Battlefields.

to evaluate the situation. This was around the same time that Tulloch was in position. Before Tulloch withdrew he fired one shot at the officer, but missed.

Continue over the crest of Battleship Hill and upon the approach to Chunuk Bair take the road to the right that is signposted *Kemalyeri* (Scrubby Knoll). This will take you onto Third Ridge. After appoximately three kilometes you will reach **Scrubby Knoll (28)**, called *Kemalyeri* (Kemal's Place) by the Turks. The knoll is approximately 557 feet in height and is the northern highpoint of Third Ridge. This position was reached by two Australian scouts from 10/AIF, Private Arthur Blackburn and Lance Corporal Philip Robin, who reconnoitred the area during the morning of 25 April 1915. The lower ridge that runs from the knoll and into Legge Valley is called the Adana Spur; it was this ridge that Lieutenant Noel Loutit, 10/AIF, managed to reach on the first day. The HQ of Mustafa Kemal was located here in April, as was an Ottoman artillery battery. It is marked today by the Turkish Memorial monolith, inscribed with Kemal's 3 May 1915 Order of the Day:

> *All soldiers fighting here with me must realise that to carry out completely the honourable duty entrusted to us, there must not be one step towards the rear. Let me remind you all that your desire to rest does not merely mean that you are being deprived of your rest but may lead to the whole nation being so deprived until eternity.*

This order was given to the exhausted Turks after the week of intense fighting during which they had suffered terrible losses. Unable to break into the Anzac perimeter, Kemal realised now that they must stop any Anzac breakout by digging in to defend their country.

From the knoll are clear views of the Dardanelles to the east and excellent views, from the Ottoman perspective, of the Anzac perimeter to the west. Looking north from whence you came is the high ground of the Sari Bair Ridge with Chunuk Bair and Hill 971. Follow the slopes to the west down the double mounds of Battleship Hill and Baby 700, the latter marked by its CWGC cemetery, and then the slopes of Mortar Ridge descend the nearside of Mule Valley. Just visible is the Turkish 57th Regiment Memorial, which rests on the Chessboard, whilst its car park covers what was once the Turkish side of Quinn's Post. Further down Second Ridge are the positions of Courtney's and Steele's Posts, their CWGC cemetery which rests by MacLaurin's Hill. The ridge then sweeps across Wire Gully and onto the northern lobe of 400 Plateau, marked by a clump of trees which are behind Johnston's Jolly Cemetery. Then, divided by Owen's Gully, The Cup leads up on to the plateau's southern lobe which is clearly identified by Lone Pine Memorial and Cemetery. A little further down is the monolith of the Turkish Memorial which is built on Pine Ridge, before the high ground descends into Legge Valley and out towards the coast at Gaba Tepe.

Re-join the road and continue down Third Ridge, returning to the Gaba Tepe Information Centre that will soon appear towards the bottom of the ridge.

The Graves of Gallipoli

The herdman wandering by the lonely rills
Marks where they lie on the scarred mountain's flanks,
Remembering that wild morning when the hills
Shook to the roar of guns, and those wild ranks
Surged upward from the sea.
None tends them. Flowers will come again in spring,
And the torn hills and those poor mounds be green.
Some bird that sings in English woods may sing
To English lads beneath – the wind will keep
Its ancient lullaby.
Some flower that blooms beside the southern foam
May blossom where our dead Australians lie,
And comfort them with whispers of their home;
And they will dream, beneath the alien sky,
Of the Pacific Sea.
"Thrice happy they who fell beneath the walls,
Under their father's eyes," the Trojan said,
"Not we who die in exile where who falls
Must lie in foreign earth." Alas! our dead
Lie buried far away.
Yet where the brave lies who fell in fight
For his dear country, there his country is.
And we will mourn them proudly as of right –
For meaner deaths be weeping and loud cries:
They died pro patria!
Oh, sweet and seemly so to die, indeed,
In the high flush of youth and strength and pride.
These are our martyrs, and their blood the seed
Of nobler futures. 'Twas for us they died.
Keep we their memory green.
This be their epitaph. "Traveller, south or west,
Go, say at home we heard the trumpet call,
And answered. Now beside the sea we rest.
Our end was happy if our country thrives:
Much was demanded. Lo! our store was small –
That which we had we gave – it was our lives."

Anzac Book, 1916

Appendix I

<u>Order of Battle – Anzac 25-27 April 1915</u>

<u>Mediterranean Expeditionary Force</u>
Commander in Chief: General Sir Ian Hamilton
Note: The MEF comprised five Divisions, the other three were involved in landing operations at Cape Helles, Kum Kale and the Gulf of Saros.

<u>Australian & New Zealand Army Corps</u>
G.O.C. Lieutenant General Sir W.R. Birdwood KCSI, BGGS

<u>1st Australian Division</u>
Major General W.T. Bridges CMG

<u>1 Brigade (New South Wales)</u> – *Colonel H.N. MacLaurin BM*
      1/AIF (New South Wales) – Lt Col. L. Dobbin
      2/AIF (New South Wales) – Lt Col. G.F. Braund VD
      3/AIF (New South Wales) – Lt Col. R.H. Owen
      4/AIF (New South Wales) – Lt Col. A.J.O. Thompson
<u>2 Brigade (Victoria)</u> – *Colonel J.W. McCay VD, BM*
      5/AIF (Victoria) – Lt Col. D.S. Wanliss
      6/AIF (Victoria) – Lt Col. W.R. McNicoll
      7/AIF (Victoria) – Lt Col. H.E. "Pompey" Elliott DCM
      8/AIF (Victoria) – Lt Col. W. Bolton VD
<u>3 Brigade (Covering Force)</u> – *Colonel E. Sinclair-MacLagan DSO, BM*
      9/AIF (Queensland) – Lt Col. H.W. Lee VD
      10/AIF (South Australia) – Lt Col. S.P. Weir VD
      11/AIF (Western Australia) – Lt Col. J.L. Johnson
      12/AIF (SA, WA & Tasmania) – Lt Col. L.F. Clarke DSO, VD

<u>Artillery</u> – *Colonel J.J.T. Hobbs VD*

  2 Field Artillery Brigade (Victoria) – Lt Col. G.J. Johnston
  3 Field Artillery Brigade (Queensland) – Lt Col. C. Rosenthal
  Attached: 7 Indian Mountain Artillery Brigade
  Note: 1 Field Artillery Brigade (NSW) not landed at Anzac

<u>Engineers</u> (1, 2 & 3 Field Company) – Major G.C.E. Elliot

<u>Signal Coy</u> – Major H.L. Hackworth DSO

<u>Medical</u> – Col. W.D.C. Williams CMG

  1 Australian Field Ambulance (NSW) – Lt Col. B.J. Newmarch VD
  2 Australian Field Ambulance (Victoria) – Lt Col. A.H. Sturdee VD
  3 Australian Field Ambulances (Outer States) – Lt Col. A. Sutton

Australian and New Zealand Division
Major General Sir A. Godley KCMG, CB
Note: For this operation the Division comprised only two Brigades

4 Brigade – *Colonel J. Monash VD, BM*
    13/AIF (New South Wales) – Lt Col. G.J. Burnage VD
    14/AIF (Victoria) – Lt Col. R.E. Courtney VD
    15/AIF (Queensland & Tasmania) – Lt Col. J.H. Cannan
    16/AIF (S & W Australian) – Lt-Col H. Pope

NZ Brigade – *Brigadier General H.B. Walker*
    Auckland Battalion – Lt Col. A. Plugge
    Canterbury Battalion – Lt Col. D.M. Stewart
    Otago Battalion – Lt Col. A. Moore
    Wellington Battalion – Lt Col. W.G. Malone

Artillery - Three batteries: (No.1 and No.2 Field Artillery Batteries and the NZ Howitzer Battery)

Engineers (NZ Field Company)

Medical (4 Australian Field Ambulance & NZ Field Ambulance)

Order of Battle – Turkish

Fifth Ottoman Army
Commander in Chief: General Otto Liman von Sanders

Note: Comprised two Corps, a Cavalry Brigade and six Divisions. Only the following were active at Anzac during 25-27 April 1915. This breakdown does not include artillery, engineers, medical and other ancillary units.

III Corps
G.O.C. Brigadier General Essad Pasha

9th Division
Colonel Halil Sami Bey

Note: 25th and 26th Regiments were engaged at Cape Helles

27th Regiment – *Lieutenant Colonel Sefik Aker Bey*
    1/27 Battalion - Major Cemil Bey
    2/27 Battalion - Major Ismet Bey
    3/27 Battalion - Major Halis Bey
Attached: Broussa Gendarmerie Field Battalion

19th Division
Lieutenant Colonel Mustafa Kemal Bey

57th Regiment – *Colonel Hüseyin Avni Bey*
    1/57 Battalion - Major Zeki Bey
    2/57 Battalion - Captain Ata Bey
    3/57 Battalion - Captain Hairi Bey

72nd Regiment – *Major Mehmet Munir Bey*
77th Regiment – *Lieutenant Colonel Saib Bey*
33rd Regiment – *Lieutenant Colonel Sevki Bey*
64th Regiment – *Lieutenant Colonel Servet Bey*

Note: 33 and 64 Regiments attached for 27 April counter-attack.

Appendix II

Special Instructions

1. RIFLES ARE NOT TO BE LOADED, nor are magazines to be charged until troops have landed.

2. RESERVE AMMUNITION for M.Guns is to be carried by the 10 pioneers from Bn. Hdqrs. Reserve ammunition for Companies, when landed, is to be carried under Battalion arrangements.

3. ENTRENCHING TOOLS are to be carried by reserve Coys. of Bns. as far forward towards second objectives as possible. If discarded they should be left together under a guard of not more than two men. Bde. Reserve Tools are to be carried by a Coy. of the 12th Bn.

4. WATER - BOTTLES and water-bags are to be filled overnight.

5. NO RIFLE FIRE is to be employed until broad daylight. The bayonet only is to be used.

6. The greatest care is to be taken to CONSERVE water and ammunition.

7. The strictest maintenance of discipline as for night operations is essential to the success of the whole undertaking.

8. The inshore advance towards the main objective is to be conducted as RAPIDLY as possible.

9. Owing to thick scrub, it is inadvisable to send single men on messages or detached duties.

10. Each steamboat will be armed with a Maxim gun in the bows. The Naval Officers in charge of steamboats have orders not to open fire unless EXPRESSLY ordered by the SENIOR MILITARY OFFICER of the tow, who will be with the leading boat. Such fire is NOT to be opened unless imperative to effect a landing.

11. NO BUGLE CALLS are to be sounded after leaving LEMNOS.

12. NO bugles are to be sounded DURING THE CHARGE.

A.M. Ross, Captain,
Staff Captain for Brigade Major, 3rd Infantry Brigade

Appendix III

A misplaced landing?

We've landed on the wrong beach

The riddle of why the landing was misplaced is still disputed amongst military historians today. From eminent early authors like Bean, Moorehead and Rhodes-James to some of the modern writers like Broadbent, Carlyon, Winter, Steel and Hart; all have contributed their views. Did an Ottoman soldier swim out during the night to move a marker buoy? Was there a last minute change of plan and subsequent cover up by those commanders who were trying to absolve themselves of blame? Did the navy misjudge the currents in the area? If so, no supporting evidence has come to light. Other theories are substantiated so today we have a greater understanding of what occurred that morning.

Landing on the wrong beach was actually caused by a combination of factors, each contributing to the covering force being put ashore over a mile too far to the north. Firstly there was the initial positioning of HMS *Triumph*. During this period the navy used a combination of magnetic compass and dead-reckoning, both which were prone to error. Any error was then exacerbated by the darkness of the night. There was a current, but as the navy knew this part of the Aegean very well, it would have certainly been known and negligible enough to have caused the landing much trouble.

Maps and their inaccuracy were another factor to take into account. Both military maps and naval charts are now known to have been inaccurate, and when compared with modern versions, the poor charting is quite apparent. As the coastlines were inaccurately marked on the charts of Imbros and Gaba Tepe, positioning of the fleet could be said to rely more on luck than mathematical calculation. To make matters worse, the early naval maps had been converted from those used by the army, which used a different grid reference and originally had no longitude and latitude markings. Even though these factors may not have had a significant impact, they must not be ignored as a potential contributing factor to the navigational errors that occurred.

A night landing was always going to be a calculated risk, but it was thought that having the element of surprise would outweigh the risks involved. As the coast was shrouded in darkness and sea mist, it proved impossible to navigate by visual landmarks. The tows had therefore to keep closer together than originally planned. They were supposed to be 150 yards apart but they had to bunch together with only 50 yards between them. This in turn reduced the expected length of the landing from 1600 yards to less than 600 yards. As the tows got closer to the shore there was a mild panic as landmarks became visible, highlighting the erroneous positioning. But instead of correcting the course to steer towards Gaba Tepe, one of the tows took the covering force towards the north. This tow, commanded by Midshipman John Savill Metcalf, quickly changed its course, taking the tows fortunately to a less exposed spot of Ari Burnu.

Evidence of this was made in a statement sixty years later by Metcalf who stated:

> *I realised we were heading very close to the north side of Gaba Tepe which, because of its height, is very conspicuous. Knowing that there were Turkish troops there, and we would get an enfilading fire all along the starboard side as well as from ahead, I was confident we must be heading for a wrong place. There was no one to consult and I felt the lives of the men I was towing were my responsibility. Without any delay I altered course two points to port to get away from Gaba Tepe. After a quarter of an hour, finding that the tows were to the port of me and had conformed, I again altered course a point and a half to port.*

The other tows stayed with Metcalf who guided them to Ari Burnu. So the answer to the riddle of why the landing was misplaced is clearly answered with Metcalf's statement. The actions of this young midshipman had arguably saved many casualties, but it did throw the initial landing into disorder. Many of the following waves did in fact land further south on the northern parts of Brighton Beach, the designated landing beach, although many followed suit with Metcalf and steered towards the shelter of Anzac Cove.

There seems little doubt that the Navy landed the troops in a different place from where the army expected, however it was still within the area specified in the original plan. There was almost three miles of coastline, which ran from Fisherman's Hut to Gaba Tepe, that was allocated to the operation in order to account for any factors that may contribute to navigation errors. Braithwaite's written instruction to Birdwood, dated 13 April 1915, refers to a landing: 'on the beach between Gaba Tepe and Fisherman's Hut'. Birdwood's orders dated 17 April simply states that the corps is: 'to land north of Gaba Tepe and occupy the heights covering the beach'. Bridge's orders to his division say: 'the division will land between Gaba Tepe and Fisherman's Hut'.

The Navy's orders dated 19 April had boats from HMS *Queen* landing about one mile north of Gaba Tepe, and those of HMS *Prince of Wales* landing four cables (approximately 800 yards) north of Queen and those from HMS *London* landing another four cables north of *Prince of Wales*, which would put *London*, the northern most battleship, just off the shore at Hell Spit and Anzac Cove. Where the troops ended up landing was therefore only 500 yards to the north of where they had intended to land.

Regardless of where they had preferred to be landed, Ari Burnu and Anzac Cove was a better position, where the covering force faced lighter opposition and was still well placed to capture the Sari Bair heights and Third Ridge. It positioned 11/AIF about 750 yards closer to its objective of Battleship Hill, 10/AIF was no further away from their objective of Third Ridge, although 9/AIF were the worst off as they were unfortunately placed about 2000 yards away from their objective of Gaba Tepe. If the landing was placed at Gaba Tepe casualties could have been arguably much higher. As we have seen when 7/AIF landed in front of the heavily defended Fisherman's Hut, they were decimated by the machine gun there. When the second wave of 9/AIF landed on Brighton Beach, south of Hell Spit, they were targeted, albeit at long range, from the Gaba Tepe machine guns, so the following boats went on to land within the safer confines of Anzac Cove. Any troops approaching the beach near Gaba Tepe would have been exposed to the machine guns and artillery in the area even before they landed, and then there was danger of delaying subsequent waves until Gaba Tepe was taken. Anzac Cove quickly became the natural place to land troops. This fate of fortune was recognised by Birdwood amongst others who said that the landing at Anzac Cove was: an act of providence for which (they) were profoundly grateful.

217

Bibliography and Recommended Further Reading

Adam-Smith, P., *The Anzacs*, (Sphere, 1981).

Austin, R., *Cobbers in Khaki*, (Slouch Hat Publications, 1997).

Bartlett, E. Ashmead, *Despatches from the Dardanelles*, (George Newnes Ltd, 1915).

Bean, C. E. W., *Official History of Australia in the War of 1914-18 Vol.1: The Story of Anzac*, (Angus & Robertson Ltd, 1936).

Bean, C. E. W., *Gallipoli Mission*, (Australian War Memorial, 1952).

Bush, E., *Gallipoli*, (Allen & Unwin, 1975).

Cameron, D. W., *25 April 1915*, (Allen & Unwin, 2007).

Carlyon, L., *Gallipoli*, (Pan Macmillan, 2001).

Chasseaud, P. & Doyle, P., *Grasping Gallipoli: Terrain, Maps and Failure at the Dardanelles* (Spellmount, 2005).

Corbett, J., *Naval Operations, Official History of the Great War*, (IWM 1929).

Erickson, E. J., *Ordered to Die: The Ottoman Army in the First World War*, (Greenwood Press, 2001).

Fewster, K. & Basarin, V. & H., *Gallipoli – The Turkish Story*, (Allen & Unwin, 2003).

Frame, T., *The Shores of Gallipoli: Naval Aspects of the Anzac Campaign*, (Hales & Ironmonger, 2000).

Göneü, G, & Aldogan, S, *Gallipoli Battlefield Guide,* (MB Books 2006)

Hamilton, I., *Gallipoli Diary,* (Edward Arnold, 1920).

Hickey, M., *Gallipoli*, (Murray, 1995).

Holts, T. & V., *Major & Mrs Holt's Battlefield Guide: Gallipoli*, (Leo Cooper, 2000).

James, R. Rhodes, *Gallipoli*, (Pan Books Ltd, 1984).

Mackenzie, C., *Gallipoli Memories*, (Cassell and Company Ltd, 1929).

Moorehead, A., *Gallipoli*, (Hamilton, 1956).

North, J., *Gallipoli: The Fading Vision*, (Faber and Faber Ltd, 1936).

Oglander, A.-C. F., *History of the Great War: Military Operations Gallipoli*, (Heinemann Ltd, 1929-32).

Pemberton, T. J., *Gallipoli To-Day*, (Ernest Benn Ltd, 1926).

Pugsley, C., *Gallipoli: The New Zealand Story*, (Hodder & Stoughton, 1984).

Schuler, P., *Australia in Arms,* (Unwin Ltd, 1916).

Steel, N, *Battleground Europe: Gallipoli*, (Leo Cooper, 1999).

Steel, N. & Hart, P., *Defeat at Gallipoli*, (Macmillan, 1994).

Taylor, P., & P., *Gallipoli: A Battlefield Guide*, (Press Pty Ltd., 1989).

Travers, T., *Gallipoli 1915*, (Tempus, 2003).

Walker, R. W., *To What End Did They Die? Officers Died at Gallipoli*, (Walker Publishing, 1985).

Williams, P., *The Battle of Anzac Ridge,* (Australian Military History Pub., 2006).

Winter, D., *25 April 1915: The Inevitable Tragedy*, (Queensland Press, 1994).

INDEX